Yaqui Gold

Best wishes
Clint Walker

Other books by Kirby Jonas

The Dansing Star (1997)
Death of an Eagle (1998)
Legend of the Tumbleweed (1999)
Lady Winchester (2000)
The Devil's Blood (2002)

Books on audio tape

read by James Drury, The Virginian
(Available through the author or at *www.booksinmotion.com*)

The Dansing Star
Death of an Eagle
Legend of the Tumbleweed
Lady Winchester

Yaqui Gold

Clint Walker and Kirby Jonas

Cover art by K. Jonas

Howling Wolf Publishing
Pocatello, Idaho

A Note from Kirby Jonas

Dreams can come true—and they do. In 1998 I met my lifelong hero, James Drury—"The Virginian." Did I say dreams come true? Well, heck, that doesn't begin to describe this story. I wouldn't have dared dream this big. What I thought was a simple meeting and a shaking of hands— all I really dared dream for—became a deep friendship and love between me and Jim Drury, something I would never trade.

Friendship turned to a business partnership, of sorts, and I ended up with the magnificent reality of four of my novels on audio tape, read by the wonderful James Drury. Hardly a week goes by when some stranger from somewhere doesn't write or call to tell me how much those audios have meant to them on some long cross country drive.

But it goes on: Jim sent the audio books to his friend Clint Walker, another hero of mine since childhood and after whom I had modeled the character in my second novel. Clint liked my writing style so much that in our second phone conversation he asked me if I had any interest in partnering up with him to put an idea of his own into book form. Well, I can only say I couldn't spit out "yes" fast enough! And the icing on the cake? It was not some lame idea, but a tremendous seed for a novel, a seed which grew into the book you now hold in your hands: *Yaqui Gold.* Two years in the making, this story is the product of many hours of phone conversation, several face to face visits with Clint in California, dozens more hours of research on Yaquis and Mexico and non-stop dreaming by Clint and me.

Lest I forget to mention it, the book may not have been possible, or at least would not have come out with its pace and charm, without the inspiration of Sam Elliot, Tom Selleck, Woody Strode and Charles Bronson—"The Yaqui." *Yaqui Gold* is as inseparable now from these four characters as any marriage made in heaven. Boys, I take my hat off to you with profound gratitude. Woody and Charlie, I wish you could have stayed around to see it.

Kirby Jonas
July 2003
Pocatello, Idaho

To James Drury, forever riding on Shilo range.
And to Charles Bronson, never forgotten.

—K.J.

To Cory.

—C.W.

Kirby Jonas

Clint Walker

Chapter One

The big yellow bull was looking for someone to kill. But it was the crazy one-eyed cow that got the job done.

Mesquite and cactus choked the Texas plain, and in Sam Coffey's nostrils the only smells were leather, dust, horse sweat and stale coffee scalded into his mustache. Through this wall of thorns the vaqueros called the *brasada*, Sam struggled to see ten yards in any direction. The narrow-faced puncher wore leather gauntlets and *chaparejos*. Hanging down in front of his stirrups were leather coverings known as *tapaderos*, which kept thorns out of his boot toes and swept brush away so it wouldn't dislodge his feet. But even these precautions and his stiff gray hat couldn't keep the brasada from getting its claws in Sam Coffey.

His shirt was torn in four places, his right arm stinging from the spines of one clump of prickly pear as tall as Gringo, his buckskin gelding. Sam had been forced to make what seemed to be a reasonable choice between the giant prickly pear and a blackjack oak. From one large scratch beneath his right eye, blood had run down and dried up in his overbearing salt and pepper mustache, and dark brown lines of scab marked his numerous facial wounds from earlier in the day.

The brasada was home to whitetail deer untouched by human eyes, in company with the barrel-torsoed hog-like beasts they called javelinas, bobcats, cougars and an occasional jaguar. Sam had also seen rattlesnakes as big around as a man's leg and longer than his horse. From fifty feet away their warning rattles could be heard.

More than half an hour back, this same brasada had swallowed Sam's partner, Tom Vanse. But Tom could handle himself. Then there was Trina, the sixteen-year-old daughter of rancher Chet Sward. Sweet, innocent Trina. She had begged to go with them that morning, and because Tom Vanse, who ramrodded the ranch, was going to be there, and Sward trusted Vanse completely, he had granted the girl's wish. Tom's safety did not worry Sam. But Trina Sward's did. Stubborn girl. She just couldn't stand to be away from them for a day. It was a habit that could get her hurt.

Somewhere amid the fly-ridden brush and cactus Sam heard a cow bawl, soon answered by a calf. He shifted his whipcord-lean six-foot-two inch frame in the saddle, straining to hear other sounds of animals on the move. The two calls had come from some distance apart—not a good thing. These were feral longhorns, every bit as wild as the deer that ghosted through this brush and more dangerous than a bear on the prod. They were as fast as the deer, too, and strong enough to penetrate a wall of stone if their offspring were threatened. Although black bear sows were famed for being protective of their young, Sam had seen more than one desert its cubs in the face of great danger; he couldn't say the same of longhorns.

He waited for further bellowing. A trickle of sweat ran down behind his ear. Gringo's neck muscles quivered, a tremor running all the way down to his tail, tickling Sam's legs. The horse was perhaps as excited by the hunt as he was aggravated by the incessant flies zipping in to bump him, take a lick of sweat, and bounce away in dizzying circles.

Sam Coffey remembered the huge yellow bull from other moonlit nights trying to rope him. Always he escaped into the brasada with a number of cows and calves, but today it had been with two cowboys hot on his tail.

One night Sam had come so close to getting a rope on the bull that when his loop caught his left horn it jerked his head to the side. The loop slipped off, and luckily for Sam the bull continued his headlong flight into the brush. That nighttime ride had left the then fifteen-year-old Trina breathless. She had been so excited about the prospect of getting that bull down on the ground, trussed up where she could see him up close, and the three of them laughed and joked about how the feisty girl would probably be the one to finally rope and tie the bull. She was something, Trina Sward. In the three years Sam and Tom had worked the ranch they had come to love her like a sister.

But neither Trina nor any of the others had gotten hold of the bull, and this time Chet Sward had sworn death to the beast, so they were loath to concede defeat. The previous day, Sward had discovered another of his imported Herefords dead near a water hole. Since that time, he had made it clear: bloated in the brasada was how he wanted that bull. He had killed two of his imports now—two too many. Now Sam, Tom, Trina and five other cowboys, one a wizened Mexican named Reale, who looked to Sam like he must have been around when the first wild cattle came in, were separated in the brasada.

Again the cow bawled, then the calf. Except for the fluttering of his fly-harried skin, Gringo remained still. Sweat ran from the shade of Sam's hat brim and into his eyes, and he swiped at it and swore. Where was Tom? Trina? How about Reale and the others? Even in this brasada, as thick as beaver fur, he should have heard something of them. Instead—the buzzing of flies; Gringo breathing and making saddle leather creak; the occasional bawls of the cow and calf; grasshoppers clacking their wings; his own heartbeat in his ears; then once in a while the distant, raucous call of a jay.

Gringo urinated, the stench bitterly overpowering in the heat. Sam's spurs jingled against the horse's ribs, and they started through the brush toward the sound of the calf. Every time it bawled it came from the same locale, and by the strained sound of its voice Sam could tell someone had a string on it. Most likely it was Tom.

Threatened by a wall of brush and thorn, Gringo sought an opening. But he was a *caballo de la brasada,* in old Reale's terms—a horse of the brush country. Where he found no passage, he made his own. Gringo eased past the interwoven branches of a mesquite tree, limb and thorn grasping for loose clothing, mane or tail. With a quick scan for dangerous branches, Sam closed his eyes and ducked his head as the horse fought through. A prickly pear swept them, but the horse was careful to stay as far from it as he could, so its thorns and even the mesquite tickled teasingly at Sam's shirt but tore no new holes and drew no blood.

Again, the calf called, thirty yards to their right, and by the cow's nearby reply she had nearly reached her baby. Sam hustled up the horse with a squeeze of his knees, certain now that someone had the calf necked to a tree.

Sam glimpsed a clearing and jogged toward it. He and the cow reached it at the same time, but so intent was the cow on the other side of the clearing she didn't notice Sam. She was a lanky, muddy white thing, blue-black through the shoulders and ink-splattered on back and face. In place of her right eye were an ugly crease and a lump of ragged gray scar. Both scaly horns curved forward in wicked perfection, made to fend off wolves, bears ... and *anything* unfortunate enough to come between her and her babies.

This time that was Trina Sward.

The blond sixteen-year-old knelt with clenched teeth across the neck and shoulders of a five-week-old brindle calf. Face anxious, she shot a glance into the brush at her right.

Sam Coffey cursed and drew his pistol. He swore again, this time in relief, when he caught a glance of Tom sequestered back in the shadowy brush. He sat a big dark bay gelding, a loop shaken out in his forty-foot reata. The clearing and the brush smelled of cow, not just this one, but of the many that had used this place as a hideout through the years. Sign was abundant: broken branches, dried and fresh droppings, prickly pear pads trodden to pulp on the ground.

Between his legs Sam felt Gringo's muscles bunch as he holstered his pistol and took up his grass rope, shaking out a loop two feet bigger around than the cow's horns. The cow horse quivered, anxious to bolt across the clearing. Then the cow gave out a ferocious bellow—and charged Trina Sward.

Gringo launched through the air, and if Sam hadn't been ready he would have been lying in the dirt. Attention riveted on the cow, and loop whirring overhead, Sam gripped Gringo with his knees as the savvy horse bore down to intersect the course of the one-eyed cow.

Across the clearing Tom's horse bolted in, and Sam smiled grimly; Tom Vanse and his reata were in the fray now, and never a throw Tom missed.

Bawling, kicking and twitching its stumpy, green-splattered tail, the frenzied calf twisted its head back and forth, trying to break free of Trina's weight. Its mother was halfway across the clearing when Sam's loop settled over her head. He was a tie-fast man, his rope already bound to the saddle horn. He sank all his weight into the left stirrup a blink of an eye before the ink-splattered beast hit rope's end. In Texas, they said of the tie-fast man, "When you rope a cow, you've got her ... or she has you." The cow hit with the energy of a freight train, her ribby seven hundred pounds nearly toppling man and horse. *She has me, all right!* Sam thought. But then the horse dug in, and the cow went to wheeling, bawling and kicking around the clearing, her head toward Sam. No slat-sided old cow was going to beat the team of Sam Coffey and Gringo!

Tom Vanse's reata spun circles over his head, but every time he got set to toss, the cow, with seeming miraculous instincts and timing, threw her tail one way or the other and foiled his chances. Tom would hold his toss and wheel his bay to make another approach. But this heeler was Tom Vanse! Sam wasn't worried.

At least not until he heard the bull bellow.

In all his years cowboying, Sam Coffey had never seen a longhorn escape only to come back for more. He had choused mossbacks for years, had thrown loops at some enraged old monsters with wrinkles at the base of their horns and scars on their hides as thick as flies. And never, in all those years, had one of them returned to take its medicine … or its revenge.

But there like a demon specter loomed the yellow bull, blood streaming from his nostrils … and gleaming in his eye. What was left of cowhand Richard Sander's four-strand reata encircled his neck, five or ten feet of it dragging the ground behind him like an errant whipsnake.

The bull's eyes were drawn across the clearing at the furiously bawling calf. Trina had been enjoying the roping spectacle, but now she froze, her gaze riveted on the bull.

The bull shook his head, splattering the brush with blood, and clots of dried mud hurled away amid a cloud of dust. He pawed the ground and let out a horrific roar. It was the first moment Tom Vanse gave any sign he knew the bull was there.

And then the behemoth smashed into the clearing, his bloodshot eyes intent upon the only unmounted two-legged creature in sight … Trina.

Chapter Two

As the bull galloped for Trina Sward, two thoughts bombarded Sam Coffey. He should yell for Trina to let go of the calf, to run. He should charge the yellow bull and try to knock him off his feet. But he didn't do either, and Sam was still tied to the cow!

He had no hope of retrieving his rope from the furiously fighting beast until someone took her hind legs from under her. But the bull was already halfway across the clearing—halfway to Trina.

The calf was bawling murder, the frantic cow trying to choke herself down to reach her baby. Sam, swearing to convert to a dally man before he confronted another cow, cursed and shucked his Red River knife. He severed the rope from his saddle horn with one determined slash.

Sam wheeled Gringo and gigged him with his spurs, but there was no need, for the horse had foreseen his next opponent: the bull closing on Trina. Game as any bear hound, Gringo lunged and battered the bull's hip with his chest. He had aimed for the shoulder, but the beast was moving too fast.

The bull veered sideways, his back feet tangling with each other. His hindquarters buckled, and for an instant Sam thought he would go down. There was no time to sheath the Red River, so he let it go and grasped the butt of his gun.

Sam would never know how the bull recovered so quickly. His pistol lifted free, but he only had time to crack off one shot before the longhorn spun. Sam saw dust lift off the shoulder where bullet slapped scarred hide. The reata around the big mossyhorn's neck flipped, slapping his side like a whip, and the bull's fury consumed him.

With blood streaming from his nostrils into his mouth, he lunged at Sam and Gringo.

Tom tried to react to the new predicament, but the piebald cow was headed for his horse, head low and black horn tips shining. He started to rein the bay away, but the cow's head slammed into Tom's foot, both wicked horns sinking into the horse's side. Upward she ripped, surprisingly strong for a crusty old scrap of leather. Her thrust gutted Tom's poor cowhorse, which screamed in pain and threw itself sideways. Tom had only begun to kick his feet free of the stirrups as the animal went over.

Confused by the downed bay's flailing hooves, the cow sought an opening to Tom, whose leg was pinned beneath the horse. One of the horse's hooves struck her in a shoulder as he fought to regain his feet. This made the cow back up and curl her tail higher above her back. Then she bunched her legs with the obvious intent of jumping over—or on top of—the horse. But a bawl from her calf made her pause.

By instinct or by evil design, the bull meant to eviscerate Sam's horse the way the cow had done Tom's. But savvy Gringo lunged upward with impeccable timing as the bull reached them. To keep from being unseated, Sam grabbed for the saddle horn, and his pistol went flying.

Jumping would have been a perfect move, but Gringo came back down on top of the bull!

The bull, insane with rage, flexed his massive legs and shoved to full height, giving Sam the highest seat he had ever taken atop a horse. To keep from losing his reins, he had tied them together when they first ran into the brush, but somehow in jumping up Gringo tossed them over his head. Now Sam's only hold was the saddle horn, and he gripped it shamelessly—a rank greenhorn shaking hands with grandma.

Hearing her calf bawl, the cow whirled away from the downed man and horse, for no power on earth overrides the drive of a cow to protect her calf. The calf came to its feet at last, just as its mama turned. As her baby ran toward her, tail raised, all the cow seemed able to focus on was the two-legged creature who had tortured her baby for so long: Trina Sward.

Eyes nearly as wide open as her mouth, Trina stared at the cow. When the cow shoved off, the girl turned and bolted for the nearest tree. The tree was ten yards from Trina … the cow was only five.

The cow's head hit the girl with such force it should have knocked her twenty feet into the brush. But one of those wicked horns pierced her under the ribs, and when the cow flung up her head the girl catapulted over the horns, landing with a puff of dust on the cow's ink-stained shoulders.

With a hump of her back and a kick off the ground, the cow spun Trina up into the air, and she struck the hoof-churned ground with a thud, landing in a seated position. She let out a little whimper, an almost instinctive sound of pure shock—the first utterance she had made through the entire ordeal. The cow wheeled, tail in the air, and kicked the girl with both feet in the chest, knocking her five feet backward. There Trina lay still.

Tom's bay horse had lunged to its feet and scrambled for the brush, trailing innards. This left Tom defenseless on his hands and knees, pawing the dust in search of his pistol.

Underneath Gringo and Sam, the bull made one more skyward leap, this time throwing Gringo backwards off him. Before the horse could move, the bull spun and struck him in the hip with one horn. It sank in, and blood gushed as it pulled loose.

Gringo grunted, and his eyes rolled, showing white. When the bull came at him again he made another buck skyward. Again Sam found himself up high in the air, the bull beneath them both. But this time Gringo rolled left, blood painting the back of the bull.

And while Gringo rolled left, Sam Coffey rolled right.

The cow saw Tom Vanse scrabbling in the dirt for his pistol at the same time Tom saw her. He rolled and tried to make his feet, but his left leg buckled, and he fell face down. Rolling onto his back, he saw the cow bearing down on him. As she lowered her head to hook him, he kicked up hard with both feet. His sharp heels caught her in the forehead, and by mere chance his booted right heel slipped and the rowel of his spur found its way into her one good eye. The cow bawled and backed away, blood rolling down her cheek. Shaking her head, she spun and trotted off into the brush after her calf.

Sam landed on the bull's head as Gringo rolled sideways off his rump. The monster flexed his neck and tossed Sam, and he landed hard, the air jolted from him. But there was no time for the luxury of inhaling.

The horse had knocked the bull's rear end out from under him in rolling off, but now, as the bull re-gathered his legs, Sam pushed himself backward with his heels, trying to make space between him and the longhorn. Something jabbed painfully into his elbow. Wrenching around, he spied his knife and clutched it, looking back to see the bull nearly on him. He rolled to one side. The bull tried to hook him as he passed but managed only to slash another gaping hole in his shirt.

Sam swiveled as the horns came back at him, and he dove. A broad hoof dug into his back, but strangely he felt no pain, just the tremendous pressure. The bull's horns had missed him once more, but he rolled and looked up, and all he could see was a belly blocking the sky. Without conscious thought, he drove the knife upward through the tawny hide, and the bull roared like a buffalo. As he jumped over Sam one of his hind hooves struck him in the right shoulder, sending him backward. Sam tried to raise the knife again, but his limp arm wouldn't come up.

The bull whirled, blood streaming out his nose and from his belly. He raised his head and looked at Sam with one eye, making sure he had him well pegged, there on the ground. With a maddened roll of his eyes he let out a roar.

Then the bull lowered his head and scaly, wrinkled horns … to kill Sam Coffey.

Chapter Three

A man lives to build something, to make some kind of name. And when he lies dying he hopes what he built will make his legacy survive. All Sam Coffey could think suddenly was that his life had accomplished nothing. He had worked at a couple of dozen different jobs, winding up at last, at fifty-some years old, on this dried up Texas ranch. And now he was going to die by the very thing that had earned him his living for more than ten years of his life.

The bull came at Sam as a gush of hot wind sprayed already clotting blood out his nostrils into the churned up dust. A sound registered faint on Sam's brain, a sound he could not place. But the bull veered strangely to one side, then shook his head violently, throwing blood all over the ground and on Sam, who now cowered at his very feet.

With an earth-shaking *whoomph!* the bull fell onto his side, kicking his legs spasmodically. A tiny trickle of blood drained from a hole that had not been in his forehead before, and Sam managed to scoot back far enough from the bull to see his entire body shudder in final surrender. The clearing was filled with the stench of fresh manure, blood and choking dust.

Sam just stared at the dead bull. He knew Tom was there with him. He knew Vanse's horse was dead or soon would be, and he was afraid of what had become of Trina. But the quiet, almost feminine voice behind him, with its strong south-of-the-border accent was one he had not expected.

"Supposed to kill that bull," said old Reale the vaquero. "You take enough time to eat him."

The words struck a chord in Sam, and insanely he started to laugh. He dropped his head back into the dust and lay there laughing himself stupid. Finally, he rolled over and came to his knees when he realized his laugh was the only noise in the clearing besides Gringo's labored breathing.

The sight his eyes first fell upon was the one he most wanted not to see: Tom Vanse crouched not far away, the limp body of Trina cradled in his arms. Tom, all of six-foot-four in his socks and broad across the shoulders and back, made Trina look tiny. In life, she had been nearly five-foot-three, and sturdy of build. But there in her friend's arms she looked smaller, like a limp rag doll. Tom came to his feet and turned to stare at Sam, beseeching him. Sam was just rising, mindlessly dusting off his chaps as he stared at the body of the girl who had given them and so many of the other ranch hands so much joy.

Throughout the struggle with the bull and the cow, Sam had not had the proverbial experience of his life passing before his eyes. But now a good part of it did—the years he had spent with Trina.

They had met Trina as a perky thirteen-year-old, a girl whose incredible zest for life showed in every move, a carefree girl who let her long blond hair fly in the breeze, and sometimes, like today, even wore pants, much against her father's will and the conscience of the Victorian times. She was a lover of everything pretty, especially horses and calves with long, curly eyelashes. Not a spring had passed when she hadn't ended up nursing at least one bird or rabbit or even a baby fox until it could be set free to find its own way. No cowhand's moment of depression ever went unnoticed, nor untreated by Trina's sense of humor, sensitivity and love. Not one man on the K Bar Diamond Ranch had gone untouched by Trina's genuine care and devotion. Many a grown man would weep when the sad news made it back to the home place.

Tom walked toward Sam, then stopped. His shocked eyes dropped to the girl in his arms, unable even to cry. He turned and walked to the far edge of the clearing, jerked to a stop at some thought, then returned to where he had picked up the girl. He stood motionless until a flood of tears washed down his cheeks, then laid Trina down in the crushed grass where her blood still glistened.

Making no attempt to hide his tears, he stood and trudged from the clearing and disappeared into the brasada.

Sam stared at old Reale as the vaquero fumbled a smoke together with his wizened, sun-blackened fingers. He scratched a match across his pants, and when it flared to life he touched it to the cigarette, squinting as the acrid blue cloud wisped past his narrow eyes. He was a tough old man with years of toil and sorrow behind him. Even so, his eyes swam with tears, and he could not look at the girl.

Sam wiped at his big mustache, shaking his head and opening and closing his eyes exaggeratedly to clear his vision. He was just starting to feel the extent of his scrapes and bruises. He looked at the little Mexican, but Reale didn't return his glance, didn't even offer him a pull on his smoke as he gazed off into the brush.

Through his grief, concern for Gringo rushed to Sam, and he looked around to find him at the edge of the trees, his bad hip gushing blood. Thankful for the chance to allay his other emotions, Sam shucked his wool vest and went to the horse. The only thing he could think of doing was to plug the hole, for it looked too fierce to stop with mere pressure.

"Reale, get over here," he growled. The Mexican came over, and instinctively knowing what Sam needed, he took the horse's reins at the bit and crooned to him.

Sam started stuffing his vest into the gaping hole in gringo's hip. The horse fought him, as any animal would, but perhaps the shock had numbed him, for Sam was able to push most of his vest into the wound, leaving only a tail which he could grasp later to remove it. He turned to Reale. "I gotta get. This'll have to be doctored up in town."

Reale nodded. "You go, Sam. Me, I will take Tom Vanse with me. And the little girl." The old man's voice broke almost imperceptibly as he said the word "girl." His face was cut with wrinkles, but those between his eyes and across his brow seemed deeper than they had that morning, and his chin had a strange quiver to it. "That one, she was a good niña," he said, trying to smile. "I am going to miss her."

Sam frowned sadly and glanced in the direction Tom had gone, clenching his jaws. It was almost more than he could do to hold back his emotions. The vaquero waved him on. "Vaya! You have a long road to ride."

Sam Coffey and Tom Vanse could not stay on at the K Bar Diamond. Rancher Chet Sward didn't want them to go, and he made that plain. He even offered them both a five dollar a month raise, for good hands—in this case also good friends—were hard to find. But there was a ghost haunting the brasada that would never vanish. It was a ghost Tom Vanse couldn't bear. He had loved Trina Sward too dearly to have to work the ranch where she had died. Where, in his eyes, he had killed her.

To Sam Coffey's way of thinking, bad luck had followed him all his life, and he figured this was the cause of Trina's death. If he had told her to let the calf go, if his aim had been better and he had dropped the bull on the first shot so that he could deal with the cow … a dozen *ifs* haunted his conscience. Even if Tom hadn't wanted to leave the ranch, Sam would have left alone.

But Sam and Tom had been partners for years. Between the two lay an unspoken understanding that only death could separate them. Each carried another, older tragedy deep in his soul, two tragedies that bonded them together stronger than blood. They remained at the ranch for several weeks, long enough for Gringo's wound to heal over sufficiently, thanks to some expert care by the local doctor, who dabbled in animal care as well. Then they rode away from Texas.

Five weeks after Trina's death, around a fire on the New Mexico border, the partners took off their boots and compared the holes in their socks. They had agreed that to him with the fewest holes fell the honor of cooking supper and cleaning the dishes. Tom got done counting and looked up at Sam. "How many?"

Raising an eyebrow, Sam replied, "I ain't tellin' you first. Think I'm a fool?"

"Write it in the dust, then we'll compare," said Tom, dimples creasing his cheeks.

Sam scratched his number, and Tom did the same. The older man caught his partner peeking over his hand. "Cut it out! All right, let's see."

They raised their hands together, revealing their numbers at the same time. "Six!" Tom crowed, looking at the number Sam had written. "You're the sourdough tonight; I have *seven!*"

"That ain't a six, you fool! That's a nine! I was writin' it for me—you're lookin' at it upside down."

"Damn!" Tom shot out. "I lose."

"The hell you do," said Sam. "I'm the one has to eat your cookin'. *I* lose!"

Tom laughed, then hung his socks over his saddle horn. "How about another bet then?"

Sam scowled. "What now?"

"Get out that little frog sticker of yours. See that Hercules beetle crawlin' over there? Whoever comes closest to hittin' it gets out of cookin'."

"Hercules beetle? Where'd you ever hear that?"

"You act like I don't know anything! You oughtta pay more attention. Remember that bug scientist that came through workin' on a paper all about bugs? He told me that's what it was."

"Yeah, whatever you say. So what do I have to gain?" Sam asked suspiciously. "I already won the sock bet."

"Not only do I cook, but you choose what we're havin'."

"Sorta like sayin' 'choose your poison,'" Sam said with a grin. "All right. Poor bug. But at least he only has to die once. We both know *you* ain't gonna hit 'im! You go first."

Tom pulled out his jackknife and opened the blade. The huge gray beetle had stopped walking, which should have made it easier for Tom. But even though he studied his target for five seconds, when he threw the knife it was a good three inches away, and the blade didn't even stick in the dirt. The haft hit the caliche and went bouncing off into a bush.

Sam chuckled. "Things never change much." He reared back and let his knife go, sticking the insect squarely. "Poor bug died just to prove your bet. And I reckon we're havin' biscuits for supper."

Mumbling something under his breath, Tom went over to the pack they had laid out on the ground and rummaged through it to extract the fixings for bacon and his own special brand of biscuits. Sprinkled with sugar and baked to a stiff turn, they would serve not only as supper but as trail grub the next day, since they were firm enough to be carried in a cotton sack hung from the saddle horn.

He came back and plopped down across from Sam, digging into the flour sack as he said, "And I didn't make that up about the Hercules beetle." Looking up at Sam, he saw that he had not heard a word. Sam sat at the fire, staring at his bare, thorny feet, lost in his thoughts.

"What's on your mind?" Tom asked. Judging Sam's mood, his voice had taken on a softer tone, and the Hercules beetle became a dead issue.

Sam looked up. "Nothin'. Just thinkin' I got ugly feet."

One side of Tom's mouth ticked up in an attempted smile. But he knew well what was on Sam's mind. "Trina again, huh? You gotta let her go, pard," Tom said gently. "We both came close to gettin' killed tryin' to save her. There wasn't nothin' else you could do."

Sam was grateful to his friend for trying to soothe his feelings. The thought was nice, but it didn't help much. He finally looked up, deliberately moving on in the conversation. "I think we oughtta head north. Try the panhandle, maybe."

"Not on your life, Sam! We're headin' down to Nadia, and that's that. Ain't nothin' to me, I reckon, but you need to get back to your woman. You still love her; I can see it in your eyes."

"You can't see nothin' in my eyes. They're full of dirt." Sam scowled good-naturedly. "Besides, Nadia's probably married off by now. I ain't wrote her in more'n a year."

"You believe that then you're a fool. I saw the look in her eyes when we rode off. If you didn't write her for *ten* years she'd still wait."

Sam grunted. He pulled a plug of tobacco out of his shirt pocket and sliced off a big chunk, stuffing it inside his cheek. His mind ran over all the miles to Nadia Boultikhine. Her husband, Nikifor, had been gone now for five years. If his bones weren't decorating some wash or the underside of a wooden cross on some lonely prairie, he didn't love her and their son enough to come home. He had sent her enough of a stake a year or so after he disappeared for her to put a down payment on the boarding house she was running, but after a few more years without hearing from him again she had come to consider herself a widow. In a place as big and as wild and lonely as the West there was no one who would have questioned it. Anything could have come of her man.

Nadia Boultikhine was a Russian. In '74 she and Nikifor had come to Kansas with their families, helping settle the town of Peabody. They had brought with them the Turkey red wheat the town became famous for. But Nadia was no more a farmer than Nikifor, and when he wanted to drift to greener pastures she tagged along. The only problem was he kept on drifting—without her. One morning he rode away, leaving her and their son Nikolai in Tubac and heading south into Mexico to look for some fabled buried treasure. Everyone who paid attention had heard the stories of Mexican gold and silver. The lost Toyopa mine, El Naranjal, the famous silver ledge—others without name. The legends were well known, and probably each had some base in fact. But Mexico was as vast and trackless as the sky. The chance that anyone would ever locate any of those old diggings ... well, it was probably one in a million. The chance of dying, however, was not so very slim, not with the dangers that waited for a man in old Mexico. Still, the lure of treasure drew many a man on. If he was knowledgeable, hardworking ... and lucky ... he could be set for life.

"How old's the boy now?" Tom asked. "What's his name, Nick?"

Sam answered the last question with an upward tilt of his chin. "Nikolai. I figure ... he'd have to be eight by now. Maybe nine."

"You figure you'll marry that woman this time?" Tom didn't look up at his partner. He stirred busily at a pan full of dry biscuit makings and bacon fat.

"I ain't marryin' nobody," Sam replied. "What kind of fool question is that? What could I offer that woman?"

"What does she have now?"

"Self-respect, for one. And she's alive."

"What's that supposed to mean?" asked Tom, looking up at him.

"Ah hell, Tom!" Sam stared at his partner for a long moment, then looked away and spat, gazing off into the distance.

"What're you afraid of, Sam?"

"Cut it out! I ain't afraid of nothin'."

"Nothin'?" Tom stopped stirring. "I am."

Sam looked at him with a questioning lift of his chin. His partner went back to cutting bacon grease into the flour for a while, then finally plopped from his squatting position to his rump. He went back to mixing.

"You're a good partner, Sam. I guess we're practically brothers. Way I figure, you marry Nadia I'll have to go my own way."

Sam felt a rush of emotion, but he wasn't in the habit of letting others see that side of him. He was half Choctaw! He couldn't let on he had a soft side.

"I ain't marryin' nobody, Tom. You know what a bachelor is, don't you? A man that don't make the same mistake once. I ain't marryin'. Except maybe you. You spoke for?"

Tom laughed and flipped a spoonful of coarse flour at Sam. "Shut your mouth! My horse'll hear, and he's already got designs on me."

It took many days to cross New Mexico, and another week to travel through Arizona. Sam Coffey and Tom Vanse stopped at the bustling town of Tombstone for a few days, and there Sam made a last ditch effort to avoid going to Nogales. He thought the world of Nadia Boultikhine; that was just the reason he didn't want to see her. With the misfortune that had followed him all his life she would end up dead if he let her yoke her ox with his.

So in Tombstone at the Oriental Saloon Sam took the hard-earned cash he had made on the K Bar Diamond and tried to set himself up in the gambling trade. Of course his bad luck followed him;

he lost it all.

It was on Tom's money that they rode into the quiet burg of Nogales, Arizona Territory. Tom had never said much to Sam about losing his wages in Tombstone. He knew Sam well enough to know why he had done it, but he also knew that Sam needed to leave behind his ghosts, to forget the nonsense of being plagued by misfortune. As much as Tom hated the thought of losing his longtime saddle partner, Sam needed Nadia, and she needed him. It was not right to keep them apart.

The law in Nogales was Marshal Jared Lightman, and Tom and Sam called on him their first stop in town. They knew Lightman from when Nogales was a new town, and he had become, if not a friend, at least a friendly acquaintance. Jared Lightman was no *light* man at all. He stood an easy six-foot-five and must have weighed two seventy-five, a solid man, up in his years but still steady of eye and of hand, with an unruly shock of still-black hair that kept wanting to sweep forward at his temples. Against custom, he seldom wore a hat, claiming it would make him lose his hair.

Toting the badge had gained Lightman a watchful eye, but it had not dulled his sense of humor. He beamed when he laid eyes on the pair. "Well, I'll be! I thought alligators had ate yuh or somethin'! What in the world are you boys doin' back in town?" Lightman spoke with a deep, appealing drawl.

A wide grin broke the hard lines of Sam's face. "Howdy, you old coot. How've you been?"

Marshal Lightman clucked his tongue. "I can't complain, Sam. My eye's givin' me a little trouble. Nothin' I can't live with." He looked at Tom after shaking Sam's hand with a broad paw.

"There's some womenfolks hereabouts'll be awful glad to see you come back to town, Tom. But maybe their husbands won't be so glad." He chuckled and shook Tom's hand. "Shoulda warned us you was comin' back. We would have rolled up the streets and locked the doors." Again the big man chuckled, his eye corners crinkling with mirth.

In the brief six months that Sam and Tom had lived in Nogales, working on one of the local ranches, it had come to seem like home to them. More precisely, Tom had worked the ranch. Sam had broken his leg in an accident with a wild horse and had spent a couple of months recuperating at a local boarding house—the boarding house of Nadia Boultikhine.

It seemed in a big way like the stuff of storybooks how Sam and Nadia had fallen in love. She had made no secret of the fact that she was—or *had been* married. But when love came it was powerful, unstoppable, the makings of a Jane Austen novel. It was not something either of them had planned, yet neither could deny it. But when things had gotten too serious Sam had become scared and ridden away. It wasn't something he would have admitted to anyone but himself, but scared he was. Scared, first of all, of becoming involved with a woman who might still have a husband lurking somewhere. But mostly frightened of bringing his bad luck down on that woman.

Nadia was still living over on the Avenida Gomez, according to Lightman. She seemed to be a confirmed widow and was running the same boarding house she had been in when Sam and Tom rode out. Sam wanted to see her—he ached to. He could feel her presence in the air, and it filled him with longing.

But when they left Marshal Lightman Sam headed stubbornly for the cantina. Tom followed like a good partner, although Sam said nothing to him about his destination. It was his one last way to stall before once again looking into the beautiful black eyes of Nadia Boultikhine. As much as Sam wanted to hold her again, it was the worst thing he could do. He was resolved to die a single man.

Chapter Four

On a run-down chair shaded by the leafy roof of the ramada, retired prospector Abraham Varnell sat facing the plaza and dreamed. Through his fevered mind streamed visions of the Sonoran Desert and of the jungles near the Sea of Cortez, of cardon cactus sixty feet high, of beaded lizards and swarms of bright red and blue, yellow and green parrots. He saw the deep square tracks of jaguar and lush jungle-like growth and knife-like agave and an endless plain of desert that reached toward a rugged blue line of towering, mirage-like mountains.

He awoke with a start.

Here in the main plaza of American Nogales, Abe Varnell was alone. At the brassy-blue sky he squinted his eyes while pulling a thin leather case from his vest pocket and sliding out a little brown cigarette. He lit it with a match drawn quick across the cane-bottom seat.

The cigarette soothed Varnell's nerves, but neither it nor any other vice could erase the vivid images that clawed through his brain. He thought once again of the gold, of the desert, the Mexican mountains, and of Homer Erring, his partner …

Homer had been gone for a year now, lost on some nameless playa in the Sonoran Desert. A year had passed since the Yaqui Indians had imbued Varnell with the fear that haunted his every sleepless night.

Varnell pulled off his hat and mopped his balding pate with a gray striped sleeve. He stood up and looked around, seeing no one. Siesta was serious business in Nogales. Only a white man, a crazy one like Abe Varnell, would sit out in the heat when a nap was in order. Yet it was in this lonely, forsaken street that he found the only kind of hush that came anywhere near to peace.

Abe Varnell had just turned sixty years old, and his face was a road map of all the places he had been. He still carried his lean six feet ramrod-straight, and the six-gun on his hip was a well-known warning to anyone with the idea of robbing him of the gold he had risked his life to bring out of Yaqui country in eighty-four. No one knew how much gold was there, but it was enough; Abe Varnell had lived in comfort without one day's menial labor since his return from the desert.

Varnell hitched up his gun belt and wandered down the *avenida* to one of the rutted lanes that intersected it. He cut south until the familiar shade of the Vaquero Cantina's veranda caught his eye. Swinging the oaken door inward, he was greeted by the dark coolness, the rancid odor of liquor and the juices of meat soaked into pine tables.

A thickly accented Mexican voice lifted from the shadows behind the bar. Varnell could hardly see the speaker for the depth of the darkness, but he knew who it was. "*Hola*, Abraham. Have you no sense to stay off of the street in this day of heat? You will bake your brain."

Varnell drew deep on the near-forgotten cigarette, squinted and blew smoke toward one of the high, tiny windows that lit the place. "Chacho. Que tal?"

"Bueno, amigo." Varnell could hear the smile in the bartender's voice. "You? You ready to take me down to get that gold?"

"You ready to die?"

"But Abraham! I, I have the luck of the devil."

Abe Varnell chuckled, and in his dry, gravelly voice it sounded like a shovel scraping mud off a barrel. "Don't fool yourself, amigo. That *is* the devil down there. Cajeme."

"That old man?" Chacho teased. "That old man, I cut his throat and choke him on tiswin."

Varnell cringed at a vague memory of tasting that awful Apache corn liquor, tiswin. He looked Chacho square in the eyes. "That old man could kill you and every man in this town." His voice was flat and a little cold. He knew it, but he didn't care. Why did everyone have to talk about the old Yaqui, Cajeme, and the Yaqui gold? Yes, Abe Varnell knew a place where a man could go and become richer than in his wildest dreams. But thanks to Abe Varnell one man had already died trying to get rich. Wasn't one enough?

In reality, he ached to find partners who were tough and willing—and *honest*—enough to go down to that sun-baked country looking for his gold. But did such men as he needed exist? Tough, perhaps. Willing, of course. But honest? Not likely.

"Tequila, my friend," he told Chacho. "And please, no more talk of that cussed Yaqui or of tiswin. It unsettles my stomach."

"Bueno, amigo, I am just talking, just an old fool talking. You go sit down, you take a nap. I have glasses to clean."

Varnell took the glass and bottle Chacho gave him and wove among rough-hewn tables to his favorite chair in the dark corner. Besides the rancid liquor and meat juices, the dank air of the place bore tinges of its cool dirt floor and of old wood and straw and stale tobacco smoke. Varnell kicked at a cockroach bigger than his great toe as he sat down and filled his glass with tequila.

For two hours Abe Varnell intermittently sipped at his tequila and chased vague nightmares. Then, sounds from outside roused him. The town was resurrecting itself. As the cantina was on the west side of the street, long blue shadows would be pouring from the porch into the dust by now, and in that shadow Varnell liked to lurk, living the life of leisure. Not seeing Chacho behind the bar, he let himself out the front.

He plopped down in one of the shaded rocking chairs, setting his tequila on the ground. The changing scenes that came to Nogales after siesta amazed him. The streets were dotted with peons in white cotton and straw sombreros, vaqueros in boleros and conchoed wide-legged pants—*calzoneras,* they called them. Señoritas lazed here and there with obvious intent, and burros and horses seemed to shore up the corners of every business establishment. One did not have to wait long to detect the presence of a pig or a goat or a dog, either. The streets of Nogales were a menagerie.

Like a faithful clock strikes every hour, two men caught Abe Varnell's eye and cut across the street to him. Wherever Varnell went these kind of men found him. These two Varnell had seen before, hanging around the Ventana with a crowd of troublemakers headed by Burton McGrath, the son of an influential local rancher. One was a short, stout man with a narrow-brimmed hat coated with dust and overalls hung from tattered suspenders to half cover a checked gingham shirt. His mustache was so big Varnell could hardly see his mouth even when he was talking. His eyes, although crowded by rotund cheeks, were expressive and sparked with good humor.

The other man was taller, his face flat, his broad nose pushed to one side and its tip red and bumpy like a faded strawberry. A deep scar across one cheek ended at the corner of his nose and there was a split an inch long down from the top of his left ear. He wore flat-heeled ankle-high shoes covered with dust and a revolver tucked into the pocket of his pants with the tip of its scarred wooden butt protruding. The only thing incongruous to his overall appearance was the red paisley cravat hanging aslant down his shirtfront. Unlike his crony, distrust and contempt tainted the look in his eyes.

"You Mister Abraham Varnell?" the shorter man asked.

Varnell nodded, not liking the highfalutin use of his name nor the look of the speaker. His eyes, the same cool dirty green as river ice, studied the pair noncommittally. "I am."

"My name's Dexter O'Brien," the shorter of the partners said. "This is my partner, Temple Stratton. You can call me Caps and him Temp. That's how we're known to our friends."

Varnell studied the two, down to the gun in Stratton's pants, looking for other arms on either of them. He pulled out a cigarette and lit it, drawing smoke and holding it in his mouth until it came out as he spoke. "And why should I call you at all?"

He felt, more than saw, Temp Stratton's gaze go harder. But Caps O'Brien's eyes twinkled, and a toothy smile sparkled through the walrus mustache.

"Well heck, Varnell, you've pegged us. I can see you're too astute a man to wallow through small talk. Can we sit down?"

"I don't own the chairs."

Caps chuckled, letting his stout frame plop into a chair, which he scooted around to face Varnell. Temp Stratton stayed standing until Caps looked at him warningly and jerked his head toward one of the other chairs. "Your butt sore, Temp?"

The taller man scowled, then forced a little sardonic smile when Varnell looked up at him. He walked over and turned a chair backwards, sitting so the back of it acted like a shield between him and Abe Varnell.

Caps eyed Varnell for a moment with his eyes shining. Finally, he said, "Mr. Varnell, Temp and me are prospectors. We're also hell on wheels with guns, both of us. Maybe I shouldn't say we're prospectors, exactly, but we've prospected, and we're good at it. We've done a little of everything, truth be known."

"And you're good at it—of course," Varnell chimed in, his voice notched by an edge of sarcasm.

"I expect so," said Caps. His face had gone a little tighter this time, but most of the smile held. The twinkle in his eyes, however, had slipped away. "I hear tell, Mr. Varnell, that you get folks comin' to you all the time askin' can they partner up and go down to Mexico to get your gold out. Seems like right near everybody around here knows about that gold cache of yours. Point is there has got to be one perfect man, or a couple perfect men, who are just what your doctor ordered for this job. You've found 'em, sir. Or in this case they've found you. And wait until I explain our deal to you."

"Don't tell me," Varnell intoned. "You go get the gold, bring me back a third and you each get a third."

"You've heard that one before," Caps said, hardly missing a beat. "No sir, we wouldn't disrespect you like that. No, Mr. Varnell, we mean to give you a full two thirds, and we just take one third twixt the two of us. I'm thinkin' that would be plenty, if the stories are true about how rich it is. What do you say?"

"Sure, I might as well dream two thirds as dream a third," Varnell mocked. "A couple of boys—like you two, for instance—could sure live mighty fine down in Mexico on a full *three* thirds of that gold."

"Why, Mr. Varnell! You cut me to the quick. You think we'd cheat you?"

Abe Varnell blew a cloud of smoke toward Caps's face. "I don't think it. I know it. And don't call me Mr. Varnell again. I can smell a crook a mile away, and you two stink like a privy."

With that, Temp Stratton was up, and his hand clutched the grip of his pistol. Caps O'Brien upset his chair in leaping across to his partner, grabbing hold of his wrist and bearing down savagely. The taller man grimaced and swore. "Let go of me!"

Caps glared at him. "Keep your hand off that gun or I'll break every bone in your arm."

The two had a staring contest while Abe Varnell surreptitiously slid a Smith and Wesson forty-four from its holster and laid it across his lap, pulling his hat off his head with the other hand to lay it over the weapon.

At last, Caps let go of Stratton and turned back toward him. He couldn't fake a twinkle in his eye, and even his smile, which to the casual passerby might seem friendly, was forced. "You read us wrong—Varnell. We would sign a contract with you. You could have it written up by a lawyer of your choice."

Varnell chuckled, his eyes remaining cool. "Lawyer! Some folks pronounce that 'loyer.' Sounds an awful lot like 'liar,' doesn't it?"

Caps laughed. "Yessiree. I don't trust 'em either, my friend. Don't trust 'em much at all, just one of this world's necessary evils. But I hope you'll give thought to our proposition. I guarantee you won't be sorry." He held out his hand to shake. It was a big hand, scarred and oft broken, with dirty, jagged nails.

Varnell just lifted his hat to show the gun in his hand. "Sorry, boys. I can't shake with you."

Caps nodded, unable to meet Varnell's eyes this time. But though he tried to hide it Varnell could see the hate across Caps's face before he turned to go down the street with his hands swinging like he had not a care in the world. Temp Stratton had already walked away, his shoulders stiff.

Across the street at the Ventana, a little rougher cantina than the kind Varnell liked to frequent, he could see shadows moving about inside the open door. Judging by the tall grulla tied among the other horses at the hitch rail, the son of the area's biggest rancher would be found inside.

As if Varnell's thoughts had called him up, Burt McGrath came walking to the door and glanced out into the bright sunshine. The Ventana didn't have the Vaquero's shaded good fortune; in the afternoon the sun fell on them like a wall. But that didn't seem to bother Burt McGrath, who stood there until being joined by two of his friends.

Varnell had lived in Nogales long enough to know most of the white folks by name—at least nickname. In his mind, he ticked off those McGrath kept as company. There was Lug Colton, the big dolt spawned by Andrew Colton, owner of the mercantile. Lug never seemed to work, and it was apparent why. Knowing Andrew Colton, he had probably tried to teach him the family business, but Lug was such a ... *Lug* that he probably ended up losing more than the business could make up. So his best contribution to his father was to stay with Burt McGrath and drink all day.

Then there was Scrub Ottley, whose livelihood was to go from cantina to cantina and shop to shop, sweeping and cleaning the few glass windows and carrying refuse away from the storefronts. Scrub fancied himself a tough man, although only twenty-one. He had saved up enough money to purchase a pearl-gripped silver-plated Remington revolver that hung from his right hip. It was probably more dangerous to himself than to anyone else, but to judge by Scrub's swagger the boy imagined otherwise.

McGrath's friend Johnny Riles came out last and glanced around at his three cohorts. Johnny worked at one of the local livery stables, and Varnell had chatted with him on occasion. He seemed like a decent human being but for the constant bad influence brought to bear on him by the other three, who were always drinking and gambling and looking for trouble.

Burt McGrath's mother had died giving him birth, rumor had it. A doting maid and housekeeper had spoiled him like a bad horse right under the unwatchful eye of his father, Abijah. Abijah couldn't be faulted. He had ten thousand acres of ranch to oversee, and a crew of ten to twenty cowboys, depending on the time of year, who were wilder than a bunch of brush cattle. But when it came time to give any responsibility to Burt, his only offspring, Abijah had been disappointed time and again. Burt was nothing but irresponsible, and if he had any kind of heart it was hard to find swimming the whisky river.

Varnell was watching McGrath and his cronies when from the corner of his eye he saw a Chinese man he recognized as the slightly hunchbacked Ah Can headed toward the Chinese joss house. Ah Can was one of the few Chinese who still wore his little square hat and queue. Even on the rocky street he had on white slip-on shoes that might better have been called "slip-offs," as they tried to slip off his heels every time he took a step.

It was Ah Can's bad fortune to come down the street right after McGrath and his toughs stepped out of the cantina, and as Varnell could have predicted the foursome gave each other the eye and started out to intercept him.

"Hey, Chinaman!" McGrath yelled out. He, as the provider of whisky and gambling money for the other three, liked to be thought of as their leader. It was expected of him to roll the ball.

The Chinese man stopped midstreet and stared at the oncoming four with dread. It was obvious he had dealt with their ilk before.

"Can go joss house," the little Chinaman said with a nervous smile. "Can no time talk."

Scrub squinched up his eyes and looked over at McGrath. "Can go joss house? Is he askin' if he can go to the joss house?" The joss house was a new structure on the northern edge of town where the Chinese went to worship.

"I guess so," McGrath replied, but Johnny cut him off.

"No, his name is Can. Ah Can."

Ah Can smiled. Varnell grimaced and spat. He wanted to go out and rescue the man, but feeling against the Chinese all across the West ran strong, and it was no different in Nogales. Helping him would invite trouble on Varnell, and he didn't need any new trouble.

"*Ah Can?* Sounds like a south'nuh talkin'," said Lug Colton derisively. "Ah Can. You can what?" he said, laughing.

"Can go joss house," repeated the Chinaman, and he tried to skirt the foursome, but Scrub stopped him as McGrath motioned Johnny to maneuver around behind him.

Several people along the street had stopped to watch the spectacle, many of them with grins of anticipation. The Chinese came to America and worked for a pittance, doing jobs no sane American would, for like wages, and thus worked the Americans out of a living. For this the Chinese were hated. It was unlikely Ah Can would find a champion on this street.

Ah Can had one fist doubled up, but it wasn't out of readiness to fight. Scrub noticed it and said, "What you carryin', Chinaman?"

"Can go joss house."

"Shut up!" Scrub's face had lost any teasing look.

Burt McGrath stepped in. "Come on into the saloon and have a drink with me and my friends. Then you can go to the joss house."

Ah Can glanced toward the Ventana, then shook his head adamantly. "Go joss house. Go now."

Johnny Riles had positioned himself behind Ah Can, as directed to by Scrub, and now Scrub stepped forward and shoved Ah Can hard in the chest. The Chinese spilled over Johnny's foot and landed hard on his back, the breath knocked audibly from him. A little leather poke flew out of his hand when he lit.

At that moment two men across the street caught Abe Varnell's eye. He didn't know why, in the midst of all the excitement, these two should stand out of the gathering crowd, but they did. He had but a moment to look at them, however, before his attention was drawn back to the row in the street.

Scrub had stepped around the Chinese while he was scrambling up and dusting himself off. While Johnny, Lug and Burt kept him detained, Scrub picked up the leather poke, throwing it up into the air and letting it land in his palm with a soft jingle. He looked craftily at the others.

"You take Can money? You give back Can money!" Ah Can cried, advancing on Scrub.

"You accusin' me of stealin'? You been smokin' too much opium, Chinaman," growled Scrub, and he touched the butt of his fancy Remington.

"You no take Can money. Can need money!" The Chinese seemed to have lost all sense of danger as he came closer to Scrub.

Scrub suddenly tossed the poke through the air, and big Lug Colton caught it. "You're gonna have to be faster than that if you want your gold back, Chinaman," Scrub taunted.

The Chinese turned on Lug, running at him. Lug just tossed the bag over to Burt. It went from there to Johnny, who laughed and tossed it back to Scrub. But in the eyes of Johnny Varnell saw something the boy would not have wanted his cohorts to see: a twinge of guilt.

Scrub tossed the bag up into the air and caught it again, liking its jingle. "What'd you do, Ah Can? Rob a bank?"

"You no funny!" Ah Can said angrily, marching to Scrub. "You give back Can money."

Meanness had replaced the teasing light in Scrub Ottley's eyes. When the Chinese reached him he backhanded him across the mouth.

The Chinese backed up, shaken, then yelled at Scrub. "You give back Ah Can gold! Damn white!"

Scrub's eyes went hard, and he swung hard at the Chinese with the gold poke in his fist. With the added hardness of the gold, the blow cracked stiff on Ah Can's jaw, and his eyes rolled back in his head. As he went to his knees Scrub gave him a vicious boot in the center of the chest, knocking him

backward. Hurriedly, Scrub squirreled the poke away in his vest pocket.

Even as he was measuring a second kick, across the way Varnell saw the older of the two strangers touch the other one's arm and start forward. His partner, who stood the taller by perhaps two inches, stepped between Burt and Johnny like they weren't even there, and the first man stopped Scrub from throwing what would be a third kick, speaking to the little trouble maker with a voice full of rocks. "I think that's enough, partner. Why don't you just let him on his way?"

Scrub Ottley stood five-foot-seven at the tallest. He was a wiry fellow, and scarred fists showed he had joined in his share of fights. But this newcomer made Scrub look like a little boy. Still, Scrub was by a good twenty years the younger of the two, and proud. Besides, liquor did half his talking.

Scrub looked around at his cohorts, gauging their support. He spoke to the mean-eyed stranger. "Just who do you think you are? This is a stinkin' Chinaman. You want trouble, you just bought it."

The stranger sighed. "Never said I wanted trouble. I'm just tellin' you he's had enough. Let him go."

Scrub's left fist came out of nowhere and sank deep into the other man's stomach, and he followed it with a hard-driving right to his jaw. The blow made the bigger man take a step backward, but he didn't go down. Instead, he dropped a shoulder and then came up fast and hard with a fist to the bottom of Scrub's chin. Scrub's feisty expression did a turnabout, with a blink of his eyes and an utterly stupefied stare, and he fell sideways into the dirt. He started to come to his feet, facing the opposite direction, and it was all he could do. As he came halfway up, his opponent kicked him hard in the seat of the pants and knocked him down again.

By then Burt, Johnny and Lug had overcome their surprise. With hushed determination they attacked the two strangers. This time it was white men falling victim, and Abe Varnell contemplated getting up to help. But again, Abijah McGrath was a big man in that town; Varnell liked Nogales and didn't relish the thought of being forced to leave. So he swallowed his pride and stayed sitting. The rest of the onlookers didn't seem even that inclined to join in.

Varnell judged the bigger of the strangers to be pushing forty-five years old, and his friend must be fifty if he was a day. But

McGrath's bunch had made a bad choice in bucking them. The two were hardened by years of heavy labor, which showed in the veins in their thick hands, in their muscular necks and tight-drawn cheeks. They were not men to trifle with.

Lug was the biggest of everyone there, standing an easy six-foot-six. But he was soft from lack of labor and too slow to be of any consequence in a fight with men as experienced in fisticuffs as these two newcomers obviously were.

Lug went down hard under a blow from the bigger stranger, and this time it was the stranger's turn to use his foot. His boot toe caught Lug in the chest, and Lug grabbed his breastbone and gasped for breath.

In all the commotion, Scrub Ottley got to his feet, shaking his head. Weaving dizzily, like a coyote he skulked off down the street, leaving his three friends to the fight as a couple of Chinese appeared and carried the unconscious Ah Can out of danger's path.

Caps O'Brien and Temp Stratton were standing in the doorway of the Ventana now, but they didn't seem interested in joining the fray. It was obvious to Varnell that these two were real hardcases, not pushing, name-calling bullies like McGrath's bunch. Varnell kept his eye on them, seeing in them the danger of gunplay. If it came to that, he promised himself he would throw aside his neutrality. He couldn't allow the strangers to be shot down, not when they were apparently the only men with any guts in the entire town.

The fight ended almost as quickly as it began, with Lug lying face down on the street, Johnny backed up and nursing a bloody chin, and Burt holding up his hands, palms out in sign of surrender. The two strangers looked around for Scrub.

Burt heaved for air. "You ain't seen the last of us, mister," he spoke to the big stranger.

It was the dark-haired one who replied in his growling voice, "Then we'll finish it right now." He moved toward McGrath, the devil in his eyes.

"W— Wait!" McGrath brought his hands back up. "It's done for now. I'm done."

"You're done, all right." The stranger turned around, his wild eyes passing over his partner. Abe Varnell had seen some tough men in his time. But by the way this man had handled himself in the fight, and by the untamed look in his eyes, he would have bet he was seeing one of the toughest.

And he wasn't discounting the other one, either. He was big and broad of shoulder, and though he seemed to be of better humor than his partner, he had put on one dandy show, making short work of Lug, with whom a lot of the locals were afraid to tangle.

The two strangers stood and watched as McGrath and Johnny helped Lug up out of the dirt and retreated into the Ventana. Abe Varnell stood up from his rocking chair with his tequila bottle in hand. He made sure it was in his right hand, his gun hand. No use making these two any edgier.

"Buy you boys a drink," he said casually as he walked out into the street and stopped near the two strangers. "My name's Abraham Varnell. You can call me Abe."

The bigger of the two men rubbed a hand across his mouth. "Obliged. I'm Tom Vanse." Varnell swapped the bottle to his left hand so they could shake. "This is my saddle partner, Sam Coffey."

Chapter Five

Abe Varnell turned and held out his hand to Sam. The dark-haired man just looked at it then back up at Varnell without making a move to shake. "Hello."

Varnell reddened a little, thinking Sam must be mad at him for not joining in the fight. "Sorry I didn't help you boys out. I'm not as young as I used to be," he said half-heartedly.

Sam glanced down at the Smith and Wesson on Varnell's hip. In his eyes he had the wild look of a fighting Spanish bull. "We fight our own battles."

Varnell nodded. "That I can see. But I apologize just the same. It'd set my mind at ease if you let me buy you a drink."

Tom slapped his partner on the shoulder. "Sure, mister. Don't mind Sam. Takes him a while to wind down after a row like that."

Sam looked up and down the street, then back at Varnell. His eyes still glowed with intense anger. "Where'd that little Chinaman go?"

Varnell hadn't given Ah Can another thought, but now he realized he had vanished. "Looked like he was knocked pretty cold. I saw a couple of his boys come and helped him up. Probably took him down to the joss house. That's where he said he was going."

"Joss house, huh?" Sam said. "What about that other fella? That mean little one."

Varnell raised his chin. "That's Scrub Ottley. He lives back behind a saloon over on the Avenida de los Estrellas. You'll probably find him there nursing his wounds."

"All right then. You wanna buy us a drink so bad, take us down there," Sam gruffed.

Varnell hadn't let himself trust many people since his return from the desert. Everyone in Nogales knew he had gold stashed somewhere. And everyone knew about his treasure trove in the Bacatete Mountains of Mexico. Being a man of means, it was hard to trust anyone. But Sam and Tom, as far as he knew, had no idea that he was any more than a saddle bum. He liked that. And in spite of Sam Coffey's hard stare he found himself liking him and Tom.

"Come with me, boys. I'll show you the place."

With that, Varnell turned and started up the street, followed by the partners. Coming to the plaza, they crossed it and came onto the Avenida de los Estrellas, a street much like the one where the fight had happened. The little shops and brothels and cantinas each exuded their peculiar odors as the trio strode past. There was the fresh smell of tortillas and beans and bread, whisky, cigar and cigarette smoke, and someone was smoking a pipe. Two or three of the places smelled like leather, and one like lavender. One stank of formaldehyde. And all of these odors were tainted by the garbage that littered the streets at nearly every building corner. As in many towns, it was common practice to deposit trash on the street for the hogs and stray dogs to rummage through.

There was one nameless cantina, muddy white in color, that sported the blue door and windowsills common to southwest adobes. The color was supposed to invite good spirits and ward off bad.

Also like most adobes, the windows were high up in the wall and little more than a foot square.

"This is the place," Varnell said. "Raoul Cordones owns it, but he never named it, so folks just call it Raoul's. He rents a back room out to Scrub in exchange for him cleaning up the place. I suppose it's a little late to ask, but could you tell me what we're doing here? I would have thought you'd nailed Scrub good enough."

Sam grunted. "There is no 'good enough' for a turd like him."

Varnell looked over at Tom Vanse, who shrugged. He acted like he wanted to say more, but with Sam so close he abstained.

Sam stood for several seconds with his hand on the door, his eyes shut to accustom them to darkness. Then he pushed into the cantina and stepped quickly to one side. Varnell regretted not following Sam's lead; he couldn't immediately see anything in the dim light while Sam was already striding across the room.

"You got a runt here by the handle of Scrub Ottley?" Sam's voice filled the room.

"In the back." Raoul Cordones, standing back of the bar, pointed toward a closed door. "I think he's lying down."

"Not for long, he ain't." With that, Sam started toward the door. Tom and Varnell followed, Varnell assuming Sam meant to follow up the fight.

Sam didn't hesitate at the door. He just turned the knob and put his shoulder to it, and when he stepped inside there lay Scrub on his bed, his Remington pistol in hand, leveled at Sam.

Five seconds ticked by. Sam stared Scrub down, eyes deadly. But it was not the same look they had held when his breathing was fast and his lips contorted with anger. This was the quiet deadliness of a man who has had time to think, a man who is not afraid of the dark hand of death.

"You gonna use that or just lie there wastin' everyone else's breathin' air?"

Scrub had scared eyes, big and red and staring. He scooted up on the bed, still holding the pistol on Sam. "Wh— What are you doin' here? How'd you find me?"

"How dare you ask me any questions while you're holdin' that peashooter on me. Listen, boy. That ain't much of a gun." Sam edged a bit closer as he spoke. "If you plan on usin' it, I hope you're good. I've been shot before. Three or four times. And I'm still here—which is more than I can say for the fellas that shot me."

He was still closing on Scrub as Tom came in the room behind him and chimed in. "He's right, kid. He's got scars on his chest from other boys that wanted to kill him. I sure hope you're a better shot than they were—for your sake. That ain't enough gun to put this man down before he gets you, too. You're liable to get into more trouble than you can solve. Even if you get Sam, then you gotta get me and Varnell, here."

"You better give me the gun, boy." By now Sam was only five feet away from the muzzle of the pistol. He stared unblinking at Scrub. "You shoot that thing and it's the last sound you'll ever hear."

"Who said you could come in here anyway?" said Scrub, dropping the gun almost nonchalantly as he tried to sit up farther on the bed.

Sam reached out and grabbed the uncocked pistol around its cylinder so it could not be cocked. He jerked it out of Scrub's hand, then opened the loading gate. Putting the weapon on half cock, he turned the cylinder, slipping each of six cartridges out of the weapon in their turn.

"Cartridge under the chamber," he said, almost as if to himself. "You'll shoot your fool leg off." With a twitch of his lip, Sam threw the expensive weapon carelessly to one side, and it collided with the wall and rattled to a stop on the floor. As an afterthought, he flung the cartridges after it.

Sam took a sidestep to where Scrub's vest hung on a chair, and he reached into every pocket. Other than a plug of tobacco, they were empty.

"What are you doin'?" Scrub finally managed. "You got no right to go through my stuff."

Sam kept looking. While Scrub lay on the bed, staring as if paralyzed, Sam patted his shirt pocket, then the front pockets of his trousers. Scrub lay stiff and wide-eyed. Not once did he even glance over at Varnell and Tom, who waited in the doorway, not wanting to disrupt Sam's concentration.

Sam went the rounds of the little room, seeking out every rat hole that could conceivably hide gold coins. Then he went again to

Scrub while the little man gawked, mesmerized. Sam casually grabbed him by a boot with both hands and twisted so that Scrub had to roll to his left or risk his leg breaking. One glance showed there was nothing in the kid's back pocket. Sam put his hand hard on the back of Scrub's neck and turned to Tom.

"Yank off his boots." Wordlessly, Tom did as asked. Still nothing.

Letting go of the kid's neck, Sam took the edge of his mattress in both hands and heaved upward. Scrub went flying and landed with a jarring thud on the floor against the wall.

There on the board that supported the flimsy straw mattress was a little leather poke. Sam reached down and picked it up, oblivious to Scrub scrambling to his feet against the wall. He poured a handful of gold coins into his palm. Seventy-five dollars.

"Hey, that's mine!"

"It is, huh?" Sam sniffed the air, then held the bag up to his nose. He turned and handed the leather bag to Tom. "What does that smell like?"

Tom smelled it and raised his eyes back to Sam. "Incense."

"It sure does," agreed Sam, turning back to Scrub. "So that's yours, huh?"

"Well, some of it is," Scrub managed to utter. "You can't take it."

Sam just raised those dark eyes. A little smirk pulled at the corner of his mouth. "I can't?"

With no more than that he turned and walked out of the room, and Tom followed. Varnell met the kid's eyes, and for a long moment they stared each other down. Varnell fancied he could hear the beating of Scrub's heart from ten feet away.

"He's not a man to mess with." Varnell followed the other two out of the room, leaving the door standing open.

Abe Varnell had seen a lot that day. A day that had started out run-of-the-mill, even a little boring, had turned out quite eventful. He had met two men with whom in his younger days he would have been game to ride the river. Real men, like even the so-called "Wild West" did not see all that often. Both of them had patches on their pants. Sam Coffey had one probably five inches across on one of his elbows, and the faded yellow scarf around his neck was frayed on the edges and stained with old blood. Both of their boots had seen happier times, and sweat muddied their hats. All considered, and with what they had put themselves through that day, he couldn't blame them for taking the money from Scrub. And after all, it was not as if they had beaten him for it, like he would have if the tables were turned. They had stood up for the Chinese man. Maybe that was only because they had known about the gold and wanted it for themselves. But they had saved the Chinese from a good beating, and why shouldn't they have some gain?

When they got outside, Varnell thought they would part ways. But Sam's words stopped him like a sandstone wall. "Any idea where that Chinaman lives?"

Varnell heard Tom chuckling. He looked over to see Tom was watching him, enjoying the puzzled look on his face. "You have to know Sam. Once he takes up a cause he's like a bulldog for hangin' on."

Varnell looked back at Sam. "I don't know where he lives, but I can tell you where he probably is right now. Why?"

Sam cocked his head as if Varnell were a little slow. "*Why?* This is his money, ain't it?"

The joss house was a Chinese temple, of sorts. They might call it the Temple of the Saints as well, or Mao Temple. It was where the local Chinese came to worship, and it had cost them dearly to build it. It was a sign that they had come to Nogales to stay, that they had brought their famed industriousness here and would work their fingers nearly off to make enough money to provide for their families.

Varnell had been in the joss house once before. He was not a man completely void of curiosity, and he had Chinese he considered friends. One of them was the tall, stately man with white mustache and beard who came out of a back room when the trio entered the temple.

Burning incense infused the stifling air with a sickeningly sweet smoke. Blue rays of light filtered in through the smoke haze from windows on both sides of the long, hall-like room. At the far end there was a beautiful altar draped with rich red brocade embroidered with gold. In front of it were smoking pots and a couple of bowls filled with joss sticks, made of fragrant dried paste and burned as incense. A hanging lamp illuminated these things, four lanterns with trailing silk tassels and several sprays of peacock feathers.

Varnell dipped his head politely to the old man in response to the elaborate bow he offered the three of them.

"Hello, my friend Abraham. I can help you?" asked the old man. He pronounced his r's like l's.

Varnell turned to Sam and Tom. "Sam Coffey—Tom Vanse. Meet Quong Sing. He is one of the elders here."

Quong Sing bowed again, then looked back at Varnell inquisitively.

"A while ago there was some trouble out in the street," Varnell explained. "One of your people, Ah Can, was attacked by some ruffians."

"Yes! They tookee much gold—gold to send bones of our elders to homeland."

Varnell explained briefly to Sam and Tom the Chinese tradition of digging up the bones of their dead once it could be safely assumed the flesh was all gone and sending them back to the motherland. This was done ritualistically after about seven years for every Chinese citizen who had died in America and could be located.

"If they're missing so much as a finger bone they'll dig around until it's found," Varnell said.

Quong Sing smiled politely and gave a small bow. "You like talk to Can? I go lookee."

Quong Sing left, and Tom turned to Sam and said under his breath, "That thug was right about one thing: that name sounds like some Alabaman talkin'. Ah Can." He laughed outright.

"Ah so," Sam said with a lopsided smile.

Soon three more Chinese entered with Quong Sing. One was Ah Can, looking none the worse for having just been cold-cocked. The four of them came forward, all with bare heads. Quong Sing introduced two of them as Ah Ling and Kwong Wong. They were both up into their sixties, with eyes full of mirth and youthful good spirits. They bowed as Quong Sing introduced them.

"Ah Can you have met."

At the mention of his name, Can bowed. He glanced nervously back and forth between the two rough-looking strangers.

"We ain't met, just seen him. I think we have somethin' that belongs to you," Sam said to Ah Can. He held out his hand, the leather poke across his palm.

A huge smile leaped to Ah Can's face. "You— You find! You so good. You so good Ah Can. Thankee! Thankee!" He held out his hands, and Sam turned his palm over so that the pouch tumbled into them.

Ah Can quickly opened the pouch and counted the coins, then looked up with some confusion. "Is too much," he said. "Is too much, fifteen dollar."

Sam simply lifted one shoulder in a partial shrug. So Scrub had not been lying after all; part of the money *had* been his. Sam could have used the fifteen dollars for his own needs, but Ah Can was the one who had taken the beating and humiliation. For his own part, Sam would have paid money to take part in such a good old-fashioned brawl.

Even having thought this, Sam held out his hand. "Let me see the extra." Ah Can placed the fifteen dollars in gold and silver coin in Sam's outstretched hand, and Sam counted out five of it and returned the rest to Ah Can. "You keep the extra, pardner," he said. "Them fellers just paid you interest."

Quong Sing and Ah Can gave a huge smile, and Quong Sing said, "Because of you our dead now go home. Good go home, be buried. What can we do for you—pay for this? You come, you smokee pipe. Come!"

Tom was first to catch onto the old man's meaning. "You mean opium?" The old man nodded. "No, thanks all the same. We'll leave you to yours."

"Ah, you smart man. Is no good, opium." He put his hand on his chest. "No good, velly bad, make man think not so smart. Sometime man weak, you know?"

Sam allowed himself another crooked grin. "Yessir, he sure is."

But as Abe Varnell observed Sam Coffey and Tom Vanse, he found himself wondering if these two had any weaknesses. One thing he was almost sure of: there was a reason the three of them had come together the way they had. For over a year he had been watching for the right man—or men—to go after his secret cache of gold.

Fate had thrown them in his path.

Chapter Six

Sam Coffey and Tom Vanse seated themselves in a dark corner at one of the Mexican restaurants on the *Calle del Indio,* where Abe Varnell had requested they meet him. At that moment Varnell was off doing a small favor Sam had asked of him.

The smells of the restaurant were all Mexico, tortillas frying, frijoles and red peppers. Chicken was roasting too, and its aroma pervaded all, even through the cigar smoke from a table full of soldiers on the far side of the room.

A young Mexican girl brought them what she referred to as *vino.* She wouldn't meet their eyes, but she smiled shyly and said, "Gracias," when Tom told her in Spanish that she had a pretty dress.

"What do you suppose that old man has in mind?" Sam asked after the girl disappeared.

"Old man! He ain't much older than you. He's just bein' friendly, I suppose."

"Nah, he had a look in his eyes when he asked us to come here. Somethin's naggin' him."

Tom shrugged. "Well, we ain't sittin' on any high horses, pard. Let's just say we ain't flush. He offered to buy, and far as I'm concerned I wouldn't want to disappoint him."

A scowl crossed Sam's face. "Tombstone robbed us blind."

Tom didn't reply to that, although Sam had left himself wide open. "What's on *your* mind, that's the question," Tom said.

Sam raised his eyebrows. "On *my* mind? My belly thinks my throat's been cut. That's what's on *my* mind!"

"That's what I mean," said Tom with a laugh. "Poultry, porcine or bovine?"

"Porcine or bovine!" Sam scoffingly repeated. "You been memorizin' the dictionary again? How 'bout *fe*-line? Or *chick*-ine?"

The rattling of the front door bells cut off Tom's laugh, and they turned to see Abe Varnell scanning the dimly lit room. He came on over, his milky green eyes scouring the supper crowd for potential trouble.

"Howdy, Abe," Tom greeted as the older man stepped up. Sam merely nodded.

"I'm glad you made it," Varnell said with a half smile, and he sat down with his back to the room in the only seat they had left him. With Sam and Tom's eyes on the room he did not have much to worry about.

"You boys sit at my table you'll have to put up with smoke," he said. "I've been smoking since I was eight years old, and I *love* it!" He pulled out his little box and withdrew a cigarillo, then held the box out to first Tom, then Sam. When both refused he returned it to his vest pocket.

"You order?"

"Waitin' on you," Tom replied. He kicked back in his chair and glanced around the room. Two of the soldiers were looking toward them and talking, but they averted their eyes the moment he saw them. "You know them?" Tom asked Varnell.

Varnell shrugged. "I don't. But everybody knows me."

Tom appraised him, and Sam just raised his eyebrows—a full sentence, for him.

"Doesn't sound like a good thing, in this town," Tom said. "I'd as soon be nobody."

"Yeah. Me too," said Varnell, raising his finger for the serving girl to bring him something to drink. He turned back to Tom and Sam. "What's on the menu?"

Sam came back with, "Beef. It's what's for dinner."

Tom shook his head, looking with mock disappointment at Sam. "I've been tryin' to break him of this habit he's gotten into," he told Varnell. "But he's a cowboy from way back. He doesn't know they serve anything but beef. Don't ever ask him what's bein' served."

Giving a chuckle, Varnell looked at Sam "Maybe you ought to be a beef salesman."

The young girl came and went, bringing the customary wine. Water in Nogales and in many small desert towns was of such poor quality that alcoholic drinks were often used as a substitute. The girl memorized their orders, a pretty simple chore when the options were tortillas and beans with rice and chicken … or tortillas and beans with rice and beef. No *feline* or *porcine* available. Tom specifically inquired, with a big grin.

Varnell took a big puff on his smoke and blew it out the side of his mouth, chuckling dryly at some secret thought. He looked at Sam and Tom, who were waiting patiently for what he had to say about the errand they had asked him to run. "Well, it's done," Varnell said. "You should have seen Scrub's face when I walked in and handed it to him. You would have thought I'd punched him in the guts." The prospector was referring to the extra five dollars Sam had taken back from Ah Can. After some consideration, Sam had insisted on giving it back to the little man. Varnell wasn't sure if Sam had meant it as a concession or a slap in the face, since two thirds of it had been retained.

Sam gave an amused half-smile. "I'll just bet."

"And he thanked you profusely, I'm sure," Tom put in.

"Thanked me? Oh, sure. He said you're a dirty damn thief and he'll be coming for the rest of it."

Sam's expression changed little. "I'd love to visit with him again. What's on your mind, Varnell?" He watched the older man place his cigarillo on the lip of a stone dish.

Varnell looked up and studied him. Finally, he chuckled. "Your friend doesn't mince words," he told Tom. Tom just grinned.

"Boys, I like the way you work. I saw you come to the aid of that Chinaman when nobody else in the West would've. And to top it off you went out of your way to track down Scrub and get the money from him, then find Ah Can and give it back. And then the thing with giving some of Scrub's money back when you had to know you'd get no thanks for it. I'm honored to have been there and seen it all. You know you're a rarity—not just in the West, but anywhere."

"And you just feel kindly enough because of that to treat us to supper," said Sam brusquely.

"Not exactly, boys. You sure you don't want a smoke while you're waiting on supper?"

"We're obliged for the meal, Abe," Tom cut in. "But I can tell you we're both a little curious why you're doin' it. If there's somethin' else on your mind you'd best tell us. Give us a whole meal to stew on it."

Varnell emitted his gravelly laugh, looking down to snuff out his smoke and lean forward in his chair, his cool eyes going from one to the other of them.

"I find myself not trusting many people. Especially in Nogales. There's something about me that I don't think you boys know, which is what gives me this lack of trust. What would you think if I told you I was likely the richest man in Nogales?"

Sam just stared at him. Tom did, too, for a moment, as his eyes leaped from one to the other of Varnell's, trying to read into his glance. "Looking at your clothes, first off I would think you were pullin' our leg. Second, I would think you're the friendliest rich man I've met."

"Third," cut in Sam, "I'd know you were settin' up to use us for your own gain."

Varnell couldn't help laughing, but like Sam he wasn't the type to laugh long and hard. He reached unconsciously for his case of smokes, but his hand fell away to rest on the table.

"Well, boys, I'm likely the richest man in Nogales—maybe in southern Arizona."

Tom smirked. "You're pullin' our leg."

"I'm not pulling your leg. But maybe I am the friendliest rich man you ever met. I'm worth at least a couple of million, boys—a modest estimate."

"The millionaires I've met knew down to the penny what they owned," said Sam critically. "What makes you different?" He didn't know why, but he wasn't questioning Varnell's statement about being rich.

"What makes me different in that respect is most of it is not in my possession, and I am not in a position to count it."

Tom turned and nonchalantly looked over the room. All of the soldiers had their eye on the table until he caught them looking. "That's why those soldiers keep starin' over here, I take it."

"Must be. Listen, boys, I have a story to tell you. It's the kind of story that might be a little hard to swallow. All I ask of you is to just eat and listen. You don't have to say anything."

The Mexican girl arrived with three plates and put them on the table, chicken for Tom and Varnell and the beef for Sam.

Varnell picked up a knife and cut off a piece of chicken, biting into it and sighing with pleasure. "Good food," he said. "Set to eating, boys. Let me tell you a story.

"I was a prospector for a good share of my life. But I prospected different than the run-of-the-mill creek mucker. I went out of my way to talk to people, to learn the legends. Especially the legends of Mexico. I made friends ... well chosen friends. Especially Mexicans. And Indians. I'll bet you've heard of the lost mines of Mexico, mines claimed by the Yaquis or the Apaches or both. There was the Tayopa, the Naranchal. The silver ledge. A dozen more without names. Some of them unbelievable. Some with a big element of truth.

"I met an old Seri Indian once. He was blind—well, almost. He could see a little light, and shadows, out of his right eye. His wife, she didn't speak any English, and he didn't speak much. But he spoke Spanish, and so do I. His kids were killed by the Yaquis. He had four of them, three daughters and a son. And a fire those Yaquis hung *him* over was what blinded his eyes.

"I was prospecting down in his country, and I pitied the old man. I was nearby anyway, so I took to bringing him meat, helping him out all I could. One night he got caught out in a storm and turned all around. He ended up falling down in a hole, and he had his foot wedged between a couple of rocks and broken. He would have died there if I hadn't found him. I stopped my prospecting and took care of him and his little wife for a few weeks. I couldn't just leave them out there helpless. I took care of his corn and melons and squash, shot him some game. Carried water.

"I guess you could say that old man grew fond of me—and I did of him, too. He had a smile that would wrinkle up his old eyes and just melt your heart. One day the old man—I called him Paco because I couldn't pronounce his Indian name—he set me down in confidence, and he told me a story. It was a story of why the Yaquis had set upon him and his family. A story of gold."

Tom and Sam had been eating all the time Varnell talked. They had cleared half of their plates, and at that moment both of them, as if their brains were connected, put down their forks and knives and took a long drink of wine. Their eyes were both skeptical, but neither looked at the other. They continued to watch Varnell and wait for more.

"Well, after I had old Paco and his wife, who I called Susie, back on their feet, I talked to him again about the gold. He had told me about it for a reason, I knew. He wanted me to find it."

"You didn't tell us why the Yaquis set on the old man," Tom pointed out. "Don't drop a line like that and then not finish."

Varnell laughed. "Gets your attention, doesn't it? All right. I'll tell you. Old Paco, see, he had been in the mountains hunting, and he had seen the Yaquis go into this hole in the side of a mountain and just disappear. He was shocked enough that he stayed around to find out what they were up to. After they all cleared out, he went down to have a look, and he discovered this cave chock full of trunks of gold, obviously stuff they'd been stealing—coins, jewelry, bullion and the like. This cave was an old Spanish mine, and there was even still gold in it. Paco took a bunch of gold out, but he made the mistake of going back again. The Yaquis caught wind and followed him back to his house. That's when they killed all his children, and they cut off his one eyelid and hung him up over a low-lying fire, just enough to burn the skin on his face and destroy his eye. And then they let him go. He said they didn't warn him about going back. There was no need—he couldn't see enough to leave his yard."

Tom scratched his ear. Sam took a swig of wine and coughed. Neither dared look at the other. They were burning up with curiosity to hear more of the story, but they weren't about to let Varnell know that.

"The story gets in your craw, doesn't it, boys?"

Tom laughed. "I reckon."

Varnell clicked his tongue and cocked his head. "Well, it did mine, too. And when Paco told me he could direct me right to that mine, it *really* got in my craw. I asked if I could bring a friend of mine to help me, a man I had prospected with for many years. The old man hesitated, but once he understood what a good friend this man was he agreed. I came back up to Tubac, where my old friend Homer Erring was scratching out a living with a patch of melons and corn. He had given up on prospecting. But he had it in his blood. It didn't take much to convince my old pard to come down to Mexico and give it one more try.

"We went down and sat again with old Paco, and he gave us such precise directions to that hole in the mountain a blind man could have followed them." Here he stopped and chuckled. "As I guess a blind man would give! Homer and me, we had a few ideas on how to hide in Indian country. We'd been doing that for years. I had invented this little stove that would cook with coal oil and not smoke much. We also stocked up on jerky, so we wouldn't always have to have a fire. So we set out with a couple of packhorses up into the Bacatete Mountains west of Hermosillo, where this gold mine is.

"We didn't have to ride more than a day from the old Indian's place, and the directions he gave us were so easy to follow it didn't seem right. I had never imagined getting rich could be that easy. Well, it wasn't. Excuse me a moment, boys."

Varnell paused and wiped at eyes that were getting a little misty. He drank his wine, then poured himself another glass and drank that, too. Wiping a hand harshly down his face, he stared at the table. He blinked his eyes a couple of times and looked off across the room, but Sam had the feeling he wasn't seeing the room … he was seeing his past.

Varnell returned his gaze to Sam and Tom. "I started this story, and I'll tell it all. Homer and I found that mine. It was like finding eggs in a hen house. The easiest thing I ever did. And it was so rich we went crazy. I started hauling out gold coin, gold bars, jewelry, caching them in a couple of different places we would pass on the way back out of the mountains. I guess we must have cached at least a million dollars worth of gold. I know it sounds far-fetched, boys, but this place was rich. Richer than most people dream.

"We had emptied out all of those chests and started picking at the rich veins still in the wall. We'd been there for a couple days by then. That's when the Yaquis came." He cleared his throat loudly and stared over at the table full of soldiers. His eyes had started to grow a little red. "They grabbed onto us, took our horses and our guns. I thought they meant to kill us. Their leader is a famous Yaqui, goes by the name of Cajeme. José María Leyva. There's a name I'll never forget. He used to be some kind of a bigwig with the Mexican government, until they tried to treat him like they did all the other Indians. Now he's mad at the world, and mean as a badger with a toothache.

"But for some reason he was going to spare me and my partner. Of course he wasn't going to let us take any of that gold with us, and he was going to make us leave all of our supplies and two of our horses. But he was letting us keep our hair, our clothes, and the horses we were riding—although he took our saddles. That Yaqui spoke English, and he spoke Spanish without any Indian accent. He told us what would happen if we came back there. He said he'd skin the soles of our feet and send us out of there as naked as the day we were born. And there was no bluff in José María Leyva. So we left."

Both Sam and Tom had cleaned up their plates. Varnell's still sat virtually untouched. When he reached again for the wine bottle Sam growled at him. "All right, damnit, what happened?"

Varnell looked up at Sam, and for several seconds their eyes held. Sam had no intention of dropping his eyes, and it didn't look as if Varnell did either. At last, the older man's lips twitched, and he sank back in his chair, closing his eyes for a couple of seconds, then opening them again.

"We got as far as Hermosillo. We were pretty much home free, as far as the Yaquis, and I talked Homer into going back. He argued with me for hours—practically begged me not to go. Then almost fought me to keep me from it. But he finally realized I was going, so he came with me. We snuck back and got into one of the caches we had made. Took out maybe twenty thousand dollars worth. It was all we dared try to carry.

"We rode all night, carrying the gold in a couple sets of saddlebags we borrowed back in Hermosillo. But at first light the Yaquis were on us. I don't know how many there were, but a bunch of them had followed us. We ran for all we were worth. But I lost Homer." He clenched his jaw for a moment and looked down at his glass. "I lost him."

Sam and Tom were silent. Sam's face was expressionless, but Tom's eyes were full of sympathy. Neither of them tried to goad the prospector into speaking further. But Varnell went on voluntarily.

"I think one of their arrows or a bullet got Homer's horse, and he went down. I heard him scream. It just made me ride faster. And once I thought I heard him screaming a few minutes later. It was like they hurried right into torturing him, just so I could hear it. I wanted to go back for him, but I didn't know what I could do. I kept riding hard, hoping to get help. It took me a week to get back to Nogales. I didn't even stop at Paco's, or in Hermosillo. Them Mexicans are scared to death of the Yaquis. They won't set foot in the Bacatete Mountains. They know that's Cajeme's country.

"I rode until my horse was crippled, and then I walked. I walked, and I baked in the sun. My feet got bloody raw, and the skin was peeling off my cheeks in big pieces. But I still carried the gold—ten thousand dollars worth. And I still have it.

"I killed my partner, boys. Killed him as sure as if I pulled the trigger. And anyone who was to partner up with me now would be going down in that desert alone, because I could never go back. I still have nightmares about that place. I won't tell you any lies about it. It scares the devil out of me to even think about it. But if a man was to trust me and go down in there and follow my maps, and if he was to live and keep out of sight of the Yaquis, the Apaches and the Mexican bandits, well gentlemen, he might end up being one of the richest men in Arizona."

As if to punctuate his sentence, he reached into his vest pocket and pulled out two gold coins, both stamped with some Mexican design and Spanish lettering. He placed one each in front of Sam and Tom, *clacking* them loudly onto the tabletop for emphasis.

Chapter Seven

Sam Coffey reached out and picked up his glass, all the while staring at Abe Varnell. Not once did he look down at the gold coins in front of him.

Tom was the mouthpiece of the partnership, but Sam recovered more quickly than his partner and leaned back in his chair, eyeing Varnell speculatively. "Damn it, man, you don't know us. Why you tellin' us all this?"

"Because I can't go after the rest of that money, boys. The devil's looked me in the eye one too many times."

Sam glanced over at Tom, then back to Varnell. He raised his glass to the prospector and cocked his head a little. "Well, sir, I hope you find someone to help."

"Yes sir, Abe," Tom chimed in. "I'm sure you'll find the right men for the job. Thanks for dinner, and good luck to you."

Without another word, they stood up, nodded at Varnell and walked out. They could almost read each other's minds, after years riding the trail side by side. Neither one wanted or needed to hear any more about the Yaqui gold.

They stopped outside the restaurant door and scanned both ways along the street as if they were twin marionettes. "Well, Coffey, what do you say? You ready to go see Nadia?"

Sam raised an eyebrow and looked at his partner. He was amused that neither of them said any more about Varnell's story and the gold coins, for he knew the story was burning a hole deep in Tom's brain like it was in his own. "I guess. I've put it off long enough." In spite of his casual words, Sam was burning up inside to see Nadia. It had been far too long.

"You just gonna walk in there smellin' like a stale bear?" Tom asked.

"Is that what I smell like?"

"Not exactly. I'll take the bear."

"Well, last time I looked weren't neither one of us well heeled enough to go throwin' money away on a bath," Sam remarked.

"Then maybe you'd better go see Nadia by yourself. I can hardly stand to think of the look on her face when she lays her nose on you!"

"There's a water trough down the street. Maybe I oughtta go strip down buck naked right here in the middle of respectable society and take me a bath," Sam said sarcastically.

"Well if you weren't so uncouth an' ape-like, you would have taken notice when we first rode into town of a bath house we passed. *You* ain't well heeled, Samuel Coffey. I still got all *my* money!"

"If you think I'm takin' a bath with you I'll choose the horse trough any day."

"That's just what I was hopin' to hear, old man! I'll take my bath alone, thanks. You go drown your graybacks in another room, for all I care. I'll loan you the money, all right, an' believe me, stinky,

I'm not doin' it for you! I'd be embarrassed into next week if I had to watch Nadia try to give you a bearhug when you smell like a miner's boot."

"Stinky!" Sam stared at his partner, feigning disbelief. "Then since you're such an all-fired man of society, lead the way."

"All right, I will." Tom started off down the street. "And while we're at it, I know you can't help your chest lookin' like a ratty bearskin rug, but I would think you could take off that thatch on your face. No self-respectin' woman is gonna want to snuggle up to a bear, washed or not!"

It only cost fifty cents each for both the bath and the shave, and after toweling off their faces Tom forced some of the parlor's rose water on his partner, telling him to dab it on underneath the hair on the back of his neck. "Trust me, pard. It's well worth it. It's an amazing thing what the sense of smell can convince a body of. Hell, if I was to close my eyes I might just think you were a woman."

Sam scowled. "Uh-huh. You'd think a raccoon was a woman if I left you in the woods alone long enough."

With a laugh, Tom clapped his friend on the shoulder and steered him out the door, tossing two dollars at the proprietor of the bathhouse as he told him in parting, "There's a woman who's been waitin' some time to see this sweet-smellin' critter."

So they walked off down the street, past the quiet, dusty adobes with the skinny, big-eyed children and their dogs, past hogs rooting in refuse, and Mexican "maidens" sitting on stoops waiting for the right man with the right morals and the right pocketbook to walk by. Past the smells of chilies and beans and simmering meat, tobacco smoke and liquor, and the overriding smell of mesquite smoke from the evening cook fires that began to crackle in people's houses and out under ramadas.

They made their way to the sights and sounds of laughter, and chattering Mexican women and chickens clucking in contentment; and doves that settled their delicate frames on the green branches of the paloverde and cooed in soothing warm voices; and the mockingbirds who sang their repertory of a dozen songs and tried to drown out the crickets tuning up their fiddles here and there. The soles of their boots landed in the soft, cottony dust and made its scent rise into the air to mix with that of the rose water, and the dry coolness of the desert breeze felt good on their necks and picking through their newly washed hair.

And then there was the house, isolated and forlorn, with native paloverde and ironwood growing around it and a big sycamore spreading its branches from the dry creek bed behind. The white paint was cracking, and stucco had dried and decayed and unshipped itself from the walls in places, exposing bare adobe brick. The windowsills and shutters and door were painted blue, but it too was wearing off under the constant onslaught of sun and wind and the hard monsoon-like rains of summer. The walkway was of native stone, some of the individual rocks coming loose to create dangerous footing. The little bantam chickens that roved the yard pecking at insects also made for hazardous travel.

"Looks like Nadia could use a man's hand around here," Tom commented.

"You leave the poor woman alone," growled Sam in return.

Tom was just as quick with his rejoinder: "You already did that."

Sam grunted and gave his partner a disgusted look. He was good at both, but neither the grunt nor the look meant a thing to Tom; he knew how his partner felt about him.

Sam stopped at the door and pulled off his hat, running a hand back over his close-cropped hair.

"Ain't nothin' to mess with, Sam." Tom flashed his dimples, spitting a stream of tobacco juice into the dirt beside the door. "You already scrubbed off the sand and snake dung."

Sam gave Tom's trail of tobacco juice one of his practiced scowls and then spat on top of it. "You oughtta give that up. It's a disgusting habit." As if his words had reminded him, he hurriedly slipped a finger inside his cheek and raked out his wad of tobacco, flinging it into a nearby brittlebush. He wiped his fingers on the seat of his fresh trousers, ran his hand over his hair once more, took a deep breath, and knocked loud and ponderously on the door.

The passing seconds mimicked hours while Sam tried to look the hard-eyed, unconcerned man most people knew. But his heart hammered away clean down into his stomach, it seemed, and he could hardly breathe. He thought he heard footsteps approaching from inside and hoped it was some housekeeper or tenant. But the door opened, and all his false hopes fell on the threshold.

Before him stood a woman in her late thirties, with rich brown hair piled thick on top of her head, straight eyebrows over the deepest black eyes in Arizona, and a full, pouting mouth that matched the curves of her body. The latter were evident even through her floor-length olive-green dress, with its nickel-sized designs that looked like a thousand eyes staring him down.

Nadia Boultikhine had lost no beauty. Sam stared at her, she stared at him, and Tom enjoyed looking at both of them and letting his dimples try to saw through the sides of his face.

"Sam …" The name was almost a whisper brushing past the woman's lips.

He wet his own lips with his tongue. "Nadia. I come to see you."

Tom tried to hold back a laugh, but its beginnings escaped him, so he figured he might as well save face in speech. "Well now, Coffey, if that ain't the most obvious thing all year! You gonna kiss the woman, or do I have to show you how?"

A grin tickled Sam's lips, then broke over his face and lit up his eyes. Nadia practically threw herself against him with a laugh of glee, and Sam drew his arms tightly about her, trying not to break her but not wanting anything to come between them.

Finally, they stepped back from each other, and Sam held her by the shoulders and gazed her up and down. "Woman, you're a sight for sore eyes."

"Oh, that's the oldest line in the book!"

Sam grinned and hugged Nadia again. This time when they parted she lifted her eyes a couple more inches to Tom. "Look what the cat dragged in."

"Now *that's* the oldest line in the book!" said Tom with a laugh. "How've you been, Nadia? You look mighty good."

"Thank you, Tom. It's so good to see you." She walked to him and put her arms around his middle, and he squeezed her and pushed her away. "Don't get me started, lady. I haven't seen a woman as good-looking as you in months, but Sam and me don't share *everything.*"

"Why, you—" Nadia stared at Tom with her mouth open in

mock dismay.

Tom just stood there with his teeth shining under his mustache. He loved to tease the women with his smile.

Later, the three of them sat around the table in a dining room that, unlike the outside of the boarding house, was well-kept and decorated with the amenities of a well-bred woman. The curtains were clean and bright, yellow with red roses. The cupboards had no doors, and their contents showed the world what an organized woman Nadia was. On one end of the room was a porcelain sink, a big Franklin stove on the other. Photographs of farmer-types hung on one wall, images marred by age. Two doors led from the room, both closed. The centerpiece of the room was the table at which they sat, a big oaken monster with carved chairs to match. The place was set up to feed a house full of guests.

The door to the outside opened, and a young boy stepped inside, looking around excitedly. His dark eyes lit up when he recognized Sam behind his big mustache. "Sam!"

"Howdy, Nikolai!" Sam beamed.

The boy ran to him, and Sam engulfed him in his arms. Nadia could not contain her broad smile. She gazed at them and glanced over at Tom, who was also grinning. Yes, it was good to be home.

It wasn't until later that Nadia admitted how poorly she was doing with the boarding house. She only had two boarders now, hardly enough to keep the place open. It was a time for hoarding what little she had, hanging on until times changed or she was forced to sell.

Sam rued his bad luck—and more so his bad planning—in Tombstone. If he had kept any of his ranch wages he would have given it all to her. But only Tom had any left, and being Tom he gave her half of it, which came to forty dollars. That left them only forty on which to live until they were able to find work.

"You'll stay here, of course," Nadia told Sam and Tom later when they appeared to be growing restless. The two men looked at each other, then back at the woman.

"*Please,*" Nikolai chimed in.

"How could we say no to that?" Tom said. Sam just grinned.

They slept in small but immaculate rooms furnished only with a bed, a small dressing table, a nightstand with one drawer, and a full-length mirror. On the nightstand stood a ewer and water basin, and beneath the bed was the ubiquitous chamber pot, its lid closed tightly although, knowing Nadia, it was spotless.

There was a small window looking out from Sam's room, and from it he could see the light that glowed in Nadia's chamber, in the other wing of the house. Her drapes were drawn tight, but he could see her shadow whenever she passed before the lamplight. He sat on his bed, back against the wall, and stared longingly that way.

Tom and Sam both enjoyed feminine company, but beyond that they were not like most of the other men they had worked with over the years. As for Sam, he had found the only person he figured could ever be his life mate, if he had been so inclined. And Tom had lost his life mate and his children to disease years ago. Women of the saloons were a mere temporary diversion Sam and Tom enjoyed in public, never something to be taken out into the dark netherworld of the brothels and cribs that accompanied most saloons of consequence in the West. To Sam, that was one of the things that drew him most to Tom: his undying loyalty to his dead wife. Any man with a loyalty like that was a man who would stick by a partner till death. And even then Sam was not so sure his friend's ghost wouldn't return to guide him on his way.

That was some woman over in that room, though, a woman who would draw the glance of any man, provided he was right in the head. She was perfectly shaped, even at the ripe old age of … thirty-eight, or whatever she had turned the past December. She was hardly wrinkled in the face, and her hair was as full and shiny as a girl's, matching the shine in her black eyes. But her looks were far from everything. Sam had always been a firm believer that the way a woman carried herself, laughed, and talked was what made her beauty either go on beneath the surface or die a hard death in the first hours of knowing her. And Nadia had a voice that, though a touch on the husky side, made his insides dance, particularly when she sang. Her favorite song was "Silent Night," and he swore she could melt any drift of snow within miles when she sang it. What was more, she knew who she was. She was sure of herself without being proud. She carried her shoulders back and her stomach in, without the need of a corset if she chose not to wear one. She met a man squarely in the eyes, making him understand that she was a match for anyone, male or female, and she could use a rifle alongside most men, better than many. Her hands were slender, but strong and callused, and her lips, though they could cut a deserving man down, could meld to a lover with a softness known only to the gods.

Sam would have given anything to take Nadia's hand in marriage, to provide for her the rest of his life. But around every turn bad things happened. First it was his own family. Then every job he ever had ended in disaster, every good horse he ever rode broke a leg or died. He was the one who led his horse to the poisoned water holes or put his friends in the path of Indian arrows. The death of Trina Sward was just one in a long line of tragedies for him. It was not fair to add Nadia and Nikolai. He loved her with everything in him, and every time he rode away a part of him died. But he could never make himself take her hand. He would not spend the rest of his life with her death on his conscience.

Rustling mesquite branches against glass made him look over at his window, and he stood and slid it up. The breeze played at his curtains and the edges of his hair, cooling the sweat on his face. There is a scent in the night and in the wee hours of morning that whispers magic to a desert dweller. It is the desert's reward for enduring another of her oven-like days, a conglomeration of all the varied vegetation and a honeyed sweetness permeating the atmosphere itself.

It was pitch black outside, inviting myriads of stars to bristle across the swath of sky. Somewhere in the far-off distance a coyote yapped—happy or forlorn, no man could truly tell, but certainly with careless abandon. In the foreground rang a chorus of crickets, one of them hidden under a tile in the floor, and an owl hooted out in the trees. Heaven was this nighttime Arizona. The only thing missing was the angel in the room not far from his. And then he heard her softly start to sing "Amazing Grace," and heaven was complete.

In the morning Tom and Sam were out with first light, looking for work. A man had to be out of the house and busy in that part of the country at an early hour. It was late June, and the temperature could reach a hundred and twenty. A man didn't dally in the early morning when it was a cool eighty-five.

Employment in Nogales was scarce, beyond local ranches, and neither Sam nor Tom felt ready for that. There were a few far-flung mines, but they had each had their go at that. The Chinese and Irish were willing to do the work for less than they were. If a man were to work for a pittance, just as well he be on horseback in God's sunlight, with the clean sweat that is cooled by breezes, and in the shade of a hat brim, rather than the darkness of the devil's lair that was a mine.

Sam's first labor was at a local livery stable. He knew it was temporary work, but it became even more temporary when a mule front-kicked him in the thigh and took a board between the ears to show it the error of its ways. He was planning to quit, but the owner had seen his treatment of the mule and fired him. He walked away from the stable without the thirty cents he had earned for his two hours swamping stalls.

Tom was content to load sacks at a local granary. But his contentment lasted only until the Danish owner made it plain he was going to follow him around all day, prodding his heels like a lazy mule. A man could only be expected to take so much supervision before he could not consider himself a man. Tom earned one dollar that day before they closed the business at six o'clock. It would be his last dollar there.

"At least you made it a whole day," said Sam, sitting at a dark table in one of the cantinas and massaging his bruised thigh. "Hell, if they'd pay you four times those kind of wages, only eleven and a half more months and you'd be set for the rest of the year!"

Tom gave him a sarcastic grin. "You just sit and chew on that mustache and be thankful I'm willin' to share my hard-earned dollar with you. That same glass of beer would cost you half a dollar back east, you know."

"They don't have this kind of beer back east!" Sam said, allowing himself a half-grin. "I don't know why you're so all-fired proud of it. You want it back?" He hurriedly guzzled the rest of it down and set the mug on the table. "You'll have to wait half an hour."

Tom laughed, and sticking two fingers through the foam of his own beer he flicked the smelly dew in Sam's face. "There's all the beer you deserve. See if I spend my hard-earned cash on you again!"

Sam licked one drop off his lower lip, his day's whiskers burning the underside of his tongue. "There, that's about the amount of that stuff a man should have to stand."

Tom wiped a sleeve across his mustache, clearing it of foam. "I've been thinkin' about mustangs, Sam. The army still buys 'em, don't they?"

"So?"

"So what do you say we go out and round up fifty or so?"

"I been lookin' at horses' butts all day—some of 'em the two-legged kind. Now you wanna go out and chase 'em all over the desert?"

"Why're there so many more horses' butts than horses?" Tom asked with a grin.

Sam laughed. "You beat me to that one. You serious about huntin' horses?"

"There has to be a better way to make a livin' than haulin' grain for a horse's butt and gettin' kicked by mules," Tom replied.

Sam raised his chin contemplatively. "Reckon you got a point there. And we'd be workin' for ourselves. But it ain't so different from chousin' cows. And you seen where that got us."

Tom's response was to take another drink of beer and stare into the mug. "What about the law? Maybe Lightman could use a deputy."

"Maybe. But not two."

"How about the army?"

"They wouldn't take a couple Methusalehs like us."

"Not for soldierin', but they might take you for a scout. You can track a fly across a dead cow, Sam, and you can survive on nothin'. Besides, you smell just like a dirty sock—you'd fit right in."

Sam grunted. After a moment he raised one arm and sniffed beneath it. He grunted again and gave Tom one of his patented half-grins. "Well, those are flies buzzing you too, not bees. You sure don't smell like no rose."

"Hey, maybe you could open up a barber shop out of Nadia's house!" Tom said, with a look of feigned excitement turned quickly to disillusionment. "But I suppose they wouldn't trust a barber as scruffy as you. You'd have to get a haircut, too, and then you'd put all those fleas out of a home."

"They'd do all right. They could just move into your armpits with their kin."

Tom gave another chuckle. "Well, thanks to you and your no-good ways, you spent a day not making one cent, and my dollar is half gone on stale beer. You either go scout for the army or you're gonna have to don a skirt and some war paint and start singin' and dancin' for a living. I say huntin' horses beats that. Unless of course we can get the town to loan us a grubstake to keep you out of sight!"

"You're too cheeky, Curly. Pay the man, and let's go home."

Sam got up and walked out, pausing a moment in the doorway to glance up and down the street. What was a man to do to earn a stake in a no-account border town like this?

As Sam walked away a man stepped from the building next door and started down the boardwalk. The man was short and obviously powerful, with a pleasant face and a huge walrus mustache. Sam had seen him hanging around with Burt McGrath and his bunch. The man seemed to be overly interested in Sam, and Sam, who normally would have ignored him, couldn't help but turn his head and follow him for a ways with his eyes. After a couple of seconds, the man just smiled and nodded cordially, then turned away.

Sam's next encounter was not quite so calm.

He was just turning his head back to the front when he ran into a barn wall. At least it seemed like a barn wall. It was another man who had just stepped from the same building where the first had been, and Sam took a couple of steps backward. The other man, caught off balance, stumbled to the side.

He was a big man, a little bigger than Sam, and to a man who had spent as much time in roughneck saloons, mining towns and cow camps as Sam had it was immediately apparent by the man's battered, scarred face that he liked to brawl. He whirled to face Sam, his eyes narrowing.

"You always try to run over everyone that comes down the pike?"

"Hold on," Sam said evenly, putting up his hands placatingly. "I didn't see you."

The big stranger, another of the men Sam had seen attached to Burt McGrath, seemed emboldened by Sam's easygoing response. He took a step closer. "Didn't see me! Damn, boy, would you have seen a plow horse?"

Sam took a deep breath to settle his nerves before he replied. He knew his temper after fifty-odd years, knew his proclivity to explode. There had been a time he would already have been in a fight if someone had broached him this way. But today it was hot, he was tired and discouraged. The last thing he wanted was a fight. There wasn't a doubt they would both get hurt.

"Mister, I was lookin' the other way. Simple as that. Sorry I bumped into you."

Sam honestly thought the altercation, such as it was, would end with his apology. But the big man took another step forward. "You ain't sorry enough."

"Let it be, mister," came Tom's voice from the side. "You're playin' with a rattlesnake."

The big man laughed. "A snake, huh? I don't see no fangs." With that, he brought up his hand and punched two stiff fingers into Sam's breastbone. "Get outta my—"

He never finished his sentence. With the old fire leaping into his eyes, Sam dropped a shoulder and brought up his right fist, too fast to dodge. The big man's teeth snapped together, and he dropped sideways back into the doorway of the store he had come from.

Sam heard the footsteps of the man's partner rushing back over to them. He would have turned on him, but he knew Tom was there, and the man on the ground was likely to be like a wounded badger, savage and deadly.

For a drawn-out moment, the big man lay there on the stoop shaking his head and blinking his eyes, as if he did not know quite where he was. His partner reached his side just as his eyes cleared, and he looked up at Sam. "Why you—" Cutting off his own sentence, he went for his gun.

Sam's hand was rising to his own pistol butt, although it was obvious the fallen man would have beat him to the draw. But neither man cleared leather before the stocky partner crouched and locked his grip on the bigger man's wrist, making his mouth twist in pain.

"You fool!" the shorter man growled quietly. "What the hell you think you're doin'? We don't need this kind of trouble now, not here." He leaned in closer to him and tried to make his next words quieter. "We got somethin' goin' in this town, man! You wanna land back in the pen?"

"Let go of my arm," the big man said vehemently. The other man relinquished his grip, leaving four white indentations where his fingers had been. He stood away, putting his hand to his gun butt and staring hard at his partner.

"It's over, mister," the man said to Sam out the corner of his mouth. "My name's Caps O'Brien, by the way, and this hell-raiser is Temp Stratton. Don't mind him, he's just havin' a bad day an' lookin' for somethin' to step on. Best you get on your way 'fore you git hurt."

Sam didn't move. "Somebody was sure about to get hurt. I wouldn't be too sure who. You'd better keep your dog on a tighter leash."

Stratton started to sit up and pull his gun again, but his eyes flickered over to Caps, and with a surly grunt he let go the piece and struggled to his feet, dusting off the seat of his pants.

Caps O'Brien laughed. "All right, boys, fun's over. My dog's calmed down. Come on, dog," he said to Stratton. "Let's walk."

Stratton threw off the calming hand O'Brien put on his shoulder. He whirled and stared fire arrows into Sam. "It ain't finished, old man. You best be lookin' for me, 'cause one day I'll be there. Temp Stratton don't take gettin' knocked down by no man, 'specially not an old buzzard the likes of you. I *owe* you."

Sam was too mad to reply; his only answer was to stare down the bigger man, wanting with everything in him to lay him out cold again. But it wouldn't be so easy a second time.

"Sam's a patient man," said Tom, off to the side. "Just take the rest of your life to pay back that debt, if you're of a mind."

Caps laughed. "Ah, don't worry, boys. Temp's just blowin' off steam. Come on, Temp, shake the man's hand."

Stratton blew derisively out his nostrils and turned to walk stiffly down the boardwalk. Caps turned to Sam and Tom. "Sorry, boys. Some people just ain't got no sense of humor."

*   *   *

Later, in the Ventana, Burt McGrath, the rancher's son, sat drinking a whisky and playing cards. There were five at the table—his partners in laziness, Lug Colton and Scrub Ottley—and the two toughs, Caps O'Brien and Temp Stratton. In the two weeks since O'Brien and Stratton had begun to hang around the Ventana with him, Burt hadn't noticed them going to any regular job. But Burt had so much money, thanks to his old man, that he didn't really care. The two were a constant source of entertainment, especially Caps, with his stories gleaned from all over the West, his jokes, and most of all the tricks he performed with his six-gun.

Both of the men, though older than Burt and his bunch by at least ten years, seemed completely taken with Burt and even laughed now and then at Lug and Scrub's inane wisecracks. Burt liked having followers—liked it enough that he was willing to buy them drinks and food and loan them money just to make sure they stayed around. It was especially flattering, and perhaps a little amazing, that they were older men who had seen the elephant and still thought a small town rancher's son worthy of their company. Burt could not understand why his father would not give him responsibility for the ranch. It was obvious grown men were more than content to let him be in charge and show them where the bear squatted in the woods, so to speak. That was his major source of contention with Abijah McGrath, and it was why he chose to spend the majority of his time in Nogales. He wasn't going to stay out on the ranch just to be bossed around by some foreman who had no stake in the ranch beyond his month's pay.

The only missing player in the game was Johnny Riles, who worked the livery stable. Once evening set in, Johnny showed up, and the game was complete. The livery swamper sat in and prepared to lose his day's wages.

This was no high stakes game; they were only playing for nickels. McGrath was the only one who could have bragged of high stakes, and he was too busy buying drinks for everyone to think of loaning it all to them to lose in the game.

"Say, did you all hear about the ghost?" said Caps suddenly, during a break in the game's momentum. "Yeah, some feller was in the paper claimin' he seen a ghost in the road the other night. He walked up to it, feelin' pretty brave on a load of tequila, and poked it. Next thing he knew he was sittin' in a sycamore tree with a busted arm."

"Dang!" Lug exploded. "If that don't beat all. Ghosts can throw people?"

"Naw! The moral of the story is, don't go pokin' no white mule in the rump in the middle of the road at midnight."

The others paused for a moment, then guffawed. Even Lug laughed, hoping, now that he was aware he had been caught in a joke, that the merriment kept him from being teased for his gullibility.

Temp Stratton was staring at Lug, and it was plain that some dark thought was bouncing around behind his eyes. He finally just smiled, without any real humor, and looked away, taking a long slurp of his beer.

"Let's play some cards, boys!" Caps said, picking up the cigar Burt had bought him and stuffing it in the corner of his mouth. "I'll show you how the big boys in New Orleans play the game."

Stratton spent a lot of time staring at Johnny Riles, and after a few rounds he said, "Boy, you smell like horse dung. You wash your boots before you came in here?"

Johnny laughed nervously. "I guess not. I'm used to the smell."

"Yeah, Johnny, you stink!" Burt enjoined. "Wouldn't hurt you to spend some of that hard-earned cash and go to the bath house once a month. Or at least take a dip in the horse trough!"

Everyone laughed. Caps O'Brien poked Burt in the ribs. "Dang, you're gettin' funnier every day, boy! Good thing you decided to hang around me."

"Boy smells like the south end of a north bound bull," Stratton muttered, sipping his beer.

Caps looked over and kicked his partner under the table. "You still on Johnny? Come on, let 'im alone! When's the last time you had a bath yourself?"

"Yeah, well I ain't wallerin' in horse dung all day."

"At least hoss dung is hidin' the sweat smell on young Johnny. You smell like man-sweat, Temp! Ain't much that smells worse than that, exceptin' maybe the underside of an outhouse. And sometimes you smell like that too."

Stratton scowled. "I fold. I'm down to one dime."

Burt, seeing that Stratton was miffed by having his teasing turned on him as Caps often did, fumbled into his pocket, pulling out two bits which he tossed Stratton's way. Stratton grabbed it out of the air, nearly catching Lug Colton in the mouth with his elbow. "I'm still through. I'm hungry."

"Well, you ain't gonna eat on no thirty-five cents," said Caps. "Why don't you stay and try to win back some of yer stake?"

"Ah, don't worry about it," Burt cut in. "I got a little extra. 'Tween me an' Lug we can stake anyone who's broke to a meal. Let's go down to that Chinese restaurant. Maybe we can find one of them other Celestials throwin' his gold around."

"Supper!" Caps turned and winked surreptitiously at Stratton. "Now that's a good idea, Burt. Thanks. We sure owe you one. You, too, Lug!" he said to the bigger man who still sat there dumbfounded, just realizing he had volunteered to buy.

"You don't owe me a thing," said Burt smugly. "Glad to do it."

"Celestials, huh?" Caps went on. "Maybe you oughtta think along bigger lines." He scooped up the change on the table in front of him and stood up, letting it trickle down into his coin pocket. "Them Chinamen don't have all that much. There's bigger games to be had."

"What do you mean?" asked Burt.

"Well, take that prospector Abe Varnell, as a for-instance. You were to get on his good side you'd stand to make a lot more than stealin' a few bucks off a Celestial." In the West Chinese were referred to as Celestials.

Burt laughed. "That old man hates our guts! He wouldn't give us a kick in the butt to throw us out of the way of a stampeding horse."

"That's why you gotta work on him, son, don't you know? But who am I to say? You'd obviously know him better'n I do."

With that, they all filed out of the cantina, Burt in the lead, his shoulders back and chest puffed out. Life for Burt McGrath was good.

Chapter Eight

Out under the stars sat a swing. It screeched like a startled bat every time it reached its rearward apogee and lurched forward again. But Sam Coffey didn't mind the noise. In fact, he didn't even hear it.

Under one of his arms sat Nadia Boultikhine. Under the other, Nikolai.

Through the mesquite branches the stars sparkled like gold dust in firelight. The owl adorned its tree beyond the back yard again, its *hooo! hoo-hoo-hoo* muffled by the walls of the house. The crickets chimed on as loud as ever, and Sam sat and longed for Nadia's voice to join in.

Tom had politely excused himself and gone to bed, for although a good wagon needs four wheels, this swing didn't. Little Nik was somewhat of a third wheel himself, not yet old enough to know it. But finally the time came for the little one to retire, and at his mother's soft command he got up without complaint, hugged Sam goodnight, and disappeared inside the house.

Sam moved closer to Nadia until any closer would have found him sitting on her lap. "He's quite a boy, Nadia. I don't know how you do it alone."

She did not reply for ten or fifteen seconds. Finally, she said, "Thank you," and then was silent again for some time. But he could almost hear her mind churning. "I don't have to be alone, Sam."

Sam swallowed, and in his mind he swore. He had let himself in for that. "Your husband's still out there somewhere."

With a sigh, Nadia twisted and rested one arm on the back of the swing, looking up to meet Sam's eyes. "You know and I know Niki won't be back, Sam—not after all these years. He's dead."

Sam had never met Nadia's husband Nikifor—which she had told him in Russian meant "victorious"—so he couldn't judge the man. But Nadia was only voicing what Sam, too, believed: Nikifor Boultikhine was dead. No living man would voluntarily remain far away from this woman.

"All right, Nadia. I got a gut feelin' you're right. He would've come back. But that ain't everything."

Confused, her eyes searched his. "Everything?"

"Look at that," Sam said suddenly, pointing at a shooting star that plummeted unusually slowly down the sky.

Nadia turned in time to see the tail end of it. Its ethereal beauty left her speechless, although it was plain she had much she wanted to say.

As for Sam, he was silent of his own choosing. He had never spoken to the woman of his fear of bringing bad fortune to her, and he did not know how to now. But the time was coming when he must. Some day she was going to come flat out and ask him what was making him wait on marrying her. Maybe then he would tell her. For now he wanted only to bask in her nearness.

Back at the Ventana, the hour was late. Caps O'Brien and Temp Stratton had eaten their supper and were standing at the bar with Burt and his friends entertaining them with stories of their days in Mexico and New Orleans. O'Brien had been an explosives expert at one time and had used that expertise in the mines of Mexico. Stratton was a gunman without conscience. He didn't care who he used his gun on, just so he used it well. If he was telling the truth, he had killed seven or eight men, he could not remember which; Burt and the boys had no reason to think he was lying.

It was not too long before the subject came back around to Abe Varnell.

"That ol' boy carries a lot of dough around on him," Lug said. "I seen 'im spendin' it in my daddy's store. I did shore enough."

"They say he's rich," commented Caps. "But I reckon everybody knows that. He's sittin' on a gold mine."

Burt had drunk too much. His eyes were bleary, and he swayed in tilting away from the bar. "He's a highfalutin old man. Too good to talk to me."

"He ain't all that old," said Caps. "He can't be sixty."

Burt and Scrub laughed, then Lug and Johnny joined in. "Hell, some of us aren't twenty!" Burt said. "If he's fifty he's old!"

Caps laughed hard, slapping Stratton on the shoulder and jarring a laugh out of him, too. "You're funny, Burt. Hey, I'm empty."

Without hesitation, Burt shot up his finger and set them all up again.

Caps thanked Burt and took the beer, downing a fourth of it, then wiping his mouth. "I wonder where that old man hangs out," he said with a smirk. "Maybe we oughtta go ask him again if he'll let us join up with him an' go lookin' for that gold. Sure as shootin' he can't spend it all."

"What if we just ask him where the gold is that he carries?" Stratton said with a sneer. He looked hungry, like an alley dog at twilight. The dull thud under the table was Caps kicking him in the leg.

Lug grinned. "Why, he carries a money belt around his waist! That's where his money always is!"

Caps laughed heartily again. But he was not near as intoxicated as the casual onlooker might believe. "A money belt. You don't say!"

"Sure, I seen it two or three times when he come in the store."

"How 'bout that," said Caps with a smile. He looked over casually at Stratton, who was eyeing him. "Yeah, a man with that kind of money must hang around in one of the fancy joints in town."

Burt shook his head quickly. "Naw. He always just hangs around in the Vaquero, right there across the street. He don't spend much of that money that anyone knows of. Just keeps it and counts it, I guess."

Nonchalantly, Caps nodded, purposely not looking at Stratton, although he knew he was watching him. "Well, I reckon it's his business what he does with his own money," he said. Caps stood suddenly away from the bar and clapped Burt warmly on the shoulder. "Well, Burt, I appreciate the drinks an' all, but I think I'm about done in for one evenin'. It's about time to hit the hay."

"Yeah, that's right," Stratton agreed. "Long day huntin' work tomorrow."

"You boys don't stay out all night," Caps chided. "And don't do anything I wouldn't do, now." He grinned and walked unsteadily toward the front door. But the moment he was outside he straightened up, and all unsteadiness left him.

*   *   *

Early the next morning Sam Coffey and Tom Vanse were standing at the opening of the Perro Borracho Mine (which in Spanish means Drunk Dog), watching the Chinese, Mexican and Irish miners come and go. It was dark as a bear's brain cavity inside, and the stench of dank hot air reached the surface from deep inside the steamy belly of the earth. They could smell hot rock, too, and hear the echoes of the ore cars that crept with clanking, clicking doggedness out of the throat of this dragon to deposit their loads. The men who came out were bedraggled, covered to the inch with black soot and grime, even their lips and the hairs protruding from their nostrils; no telling what was in their lungs. The men who plodded in were spiritless, or muted dread filled their eyes. The Chinese trooped in hunch-shouldered, stone-faced.

Finally, the crew boss, Dowdy McGill, came up behind Sam and Tom. "Well, you boys get enough just lookin', or you wanna sign on? I'll tell you again, four dollars a day is better'n you'll get anywhere's else hereabouts. An' you won't have no eight hunnerd pounds o' horse fallin' on you neither."

"Nope. Just five thousand tons of rock," Sam retorted. "I reckon not, Dowd. We both done our time in the bottom o' one of these pits. It's like I figured—once you leave a hole like this you can't ever go back."

McGill gave a grunt and spat tobacco juice at the mine opening. "Uh … yeah. I thunk the same thing. But I been at it too long to walk away. That five thousand tons o' rock at least would make a tolerable grave, and it wouldn't stove a man up like a horse might. Comes to bein' crippled or bein' dead, I'll choose dead—any day."

Sam mulled over Dowdy McGill's words all that morning as he scoured the streets looking for some sign of hope, some way he could make even a dollar and a half a day. Carpenters made good money, six dollars in one day if they were good, but it seemed in Nogales most folks did their own building. Most of the town was adobe, so there was no fancy woodwork needed, and most down-to-earth folk had learned to make do, to use the skills their fathers and mothers had taught them. He might be able to tend bar. He hadn't looked into what that paid—if anyone even needed a barkeep. But he had seen saloon crowds, and he was sure it was not how he wished to spend any great fraction of his life.

That afternoon he and Tom came back together, and they ran into Marshal Jared Lightman. He treated the two of them to a drink at one of the cantinas.

"You boys happen to hear what come of Abe Varnell last night?" Lightman asked between sips.

The partners glanced at each other, then back at Lightman. "Somethin' bad?" Tom asked.

"He got beat up—yeah, pretty bad. Somebody caught him walkin' down an alley and slugged him over the head. They got his money belt and a couple hundred dollars."

"I take it no ones knows who done it," Sam said.

"Nope. No witnesses."

"It's never easy bein' a lawman, is it, Lightman?" Tom asked. "Say, you wouldn't be needin' any deputies, would you?"

"Meanin' you two?"

"Sure."

"Well, I'll be honest with yuh; the idea seems pretty tempting. But we just ain't got enough to pay any new help, boys. Otherwise I'd've already hit you up."

"That's what I figured, but it doesn't hurt to ask."

"No, of course not. So I take it you've had no luck diggin' up work."

"None."

"Well, I'll keep an eye out. Couple of hard workers like you, a man'd think there'd be somethin' out there for yuh. You stayin' out at Boultikhine's, I assume?"

Sam nodded. "Hangin' our hats there for a while."

"Then that's where I'll look if I come across anything. Well, I reckon I oughtta get back out there. It's a rough town, yuh know." He winked at the partners, turned and walked away. His shoulders filled the doorway as he walked into the sun.

After the lawman left, Sam and Tom retired to their customary table at the back of the room and made themselves a plate from the victuals offered at the bar—limp flour tortillas they used to gather up beans, rice and shredded chicken. As long as a man was drinking, the food came free.

"Too bad about Abe," Tom mused.

"Too bad," agreed Sam. "Seemed like a nice old feller."

"Old!" Tom laughed. "Hell, he can't be ten years older'n you!"

"Just so."

Tom laughed again. "You're right. I reckon neither of us is any mornin' rose! Not too bright, though, him carrying around that kind of money."

"That's for sure. Not near as bright as a couple o' entrepre—however you say that word again—like we are. Rhymes with 'ornery manures,' don't it?"

"Yeah, he sure ain't as bright as the two of us ornery manures," agreed Tom with a laugh. "But then I've never had two hundred bucks to carry around anyhow. Maybe I would've done it, too, just to show I was well heeled."

"Reckon that means they got off with them two shiny coins he set out in front of us, too," Sam mused, only half hearing what Tom said.

"I reckon. I guess we should've picked 'em up."

"Sure, an' then we'd be obliged to listen more an' maybe even go down in that forsaken desert lookin' for fool's gold. No thanks. I c'n think of more immediate ways to get my throat cut."

A shadow filled the doorway, and they looked over to see Abe Varnell standing there, his hat sitting strangely high on the crown of his head. When he came more fully into the room they discerned the white bandage wrapped around his head.

"Howdy, boys," he said.

"Howdy, Abe!" Tom stood up. "Have yourself a seat." After Varnell sat down, Tom said, "Marshal Lightman told us about your misfortune."

"Oh, that. Yeah, they jumped me. I figured it was a matter o' time. But I still ain't broke. Reckon they didn't want my gun." On a whim, he pulled the pistol out of his holster, and while the two of them watched curiously he cracked open the cylinder, then tilted it to let five or six nuggets of gold along with five shells plummet into his hand. The gold had come out of the chamber under the hammer. He grinned up at them. "End of the chamber's plugged."

"Oh, here we go again," Sam said.

Varnell didn't flinch as he began to load the pistol and deposit the nuggets into their safe chamber. "You boys oughtta reconsider. Word around town is you're lookin' for work. You wouldn't have to work again if you partnered up with me."

"That's true," Sam said. "It don't do dead men any good to work."

Varnell laughed, wincing as a twinge of pain reached his brain. "I can't blame you. I know it sounds bad."

"You *made* it sound bad," agreed Tom.

"I wouldn't ever want you to go down there not knowin' what you're up against."

"What made you choose us anyhow?" Tom asked.

Varnell eyed him long and hard, one eyebrow raised. "If you don't know then maybe you're not smart enough to partner up with. You ask me that question after how you handled yourselves in that fight, then went out of your way to get that Chinaman's money back for him? You even gave some of Scrub's money back. Cut the modesty routine—you boys are a rarity. But even saints have to eat. How long can you go without work?"

"What we know is cows," replied Sam. "We'll end up back on a ranch, soon as we get desperate enough."

"I got the feeling the other day you weren't keen on ranch work right now. You're running from something."

Sam was able to work up a laugh, taken aback by Varnell's savvy. "Runnin' from ourselves—like always."

"Thirty dollars a month suit you boys?"

Tom shrugged. "Better than a poke in the tail with a frog sticker."

"Huh! Not much better. Imagine making a million dollars in two weeks. That's what you'd stand to do with me."

"*For* you," corrected Sam. "You won't go."

"I could go as far as Hermosillo."

"But not up into the Yaqui stronghold you wouldn't. It'd be just me an' Tom an' a desert full of Injuns and Mexican bandits. Don't seem like a winning proposition."

The barkeep came over and brought Varnell a drink, and he pressed a coin into the Mexican's hand, then turned and winked at Tom and Sam. "No, those two gold nuggets are not all I have left, either. I have not even been tapped yet." He settled back in his chair and took a swallow, favoring each of them with a long, searching glance. "I hear you boys been stayin' with the widow Boultikhine. She's a mighty fine woman."

Sam's eyes lost all humor. He stared at Varnell, trying to read any meaning behind what he said. "She is that."

"You'll have to find a different place to stay before long, though," Varnell said nonchalantly. "Word around town is she's going to lose that place."

"Word has it," Tom put in. "Lots of rumors in this town. It's like a holey bucket full of cows; some bull has to leak out every now and then."

Varnell shrugged. "That woman sure could use a champion. I don't know what you boys think of her, but if I were younger I'd be her champion—if I could afford to."

Sam smirked. It was obvious Varnell knew a lot more than he was saying outright. He must know everything that happened in this town—with the exception, perhaps, of who had hit him over the head.

"Well, the woman don't need no dead champeens," Sam said gruffly. "Finish up this grub, will yuh, Abe?" It was the first time he had called Varnell by that name. "I think Tom and me're gonna start makin' plans to go horse huntin'. That's the *other* only thing we know."

Tom and Sam sat at Nadia Boultikhine's dining room table over fresh coffee and a map Sam had scratched on a piece of paper bag. The town of Nogales was central on the map, surrounded by a series of mountains signified by little inverted V's. In that part of the country they would call them mountains, anyway.

There were a few streams and springs outlined on the map—but very few. There was a ranch scratched in here and there. But even Sam, adept enough at making a map, could not portray the desolation and aridity of this corner of the world.

Sam drew upon his experience hunting the wild *mesteños,* as the vaqueros called the mustang, as he dragged his callused finger around the map. "I've gathered herds here … here … and here.

There's a good spring there. That's almost a sure bet."

"What kind of critters?" Tom asked. "The army ain't lookin' for scrubs."

The older partner gave a big shrug and one of his hard stares. "I wouldn't give a plug nickel for most of 'em. One in ten will be a good mount. Ranchers may take a lot of 'em—but *they* won't give *us* a plug nickel!"

Nadia stopped to refill Sam's cup—Tom's was still full—and rested her hand on his lean shoulder. She looked up from the map to meet Tom's eyes, and for a long moment they held each other's gaze. Sam finally cranked his head around to see her. "We'll do all right, woman, don't you worry. We'll make enough for a while to get you by. Feed some o' them broncs the right feed you'd be impressed what we make of 'em."

"Sam's right, Nadia. There's no cause for you to fret."

"I'm all right," the woman said, nodding bravely. "I'm worried about the two of you. After what happened in Texas … mad horses can't be much friendlier than mad cows."

Sam smiled crookedly and looked at Tom. "She's got that right!" He looked back down at his map, seeing it in his mind's eye covered with dirt and rock, cactus and desert scrub. Little water, little graze, and little hope. But they had to try.

Sam was leaning against the corral as evening bled up through the bold sky, fanning out a blanket of red emblazoned with golden tufts of cloud. Little Nik came to stand beside him and watch Gringo and the other horses quietly chew their hay in the enclosure, standing hipshot to rest one leg at a time.

"Do you think you can help my mama?" the boy asked with the supreme innocence of a tender child.

Sam looked down at the boy and tousled his hair with his sunburned hand, its veins stark like twisting vines. "Nikolai, your mama could survive in a burning house. That's one tough woman in there, an' don't you ever forget it. She'll do everything she can to make sure you grow up tall and strong. But yeah, son, I'll help your mama. She's a good woman. An' you're a good man."

Nik looked up with a bashful but proud smile. Together they

stared out across the landscape and could see Tom ambling far out in the cactus, wearing shotgun chaps to protect his legs. The big cowboy had his thumbs hooked in his waistband, and he seemed to be studying the ground with all intentness. They watched him for five minutes in total silence, and several times he stopped to gaze off to the south.

A realization suddenly struck Sam, and he straightened up, his eyes narrowing. He stared for a long time at Tom before his gravelly voice broke the music of doves cooing in the paloverde.

"Damn. He's thinkin' about Mexico."

Chapter Nine

Early next morning, the sky was pale and leaves draped serene and still. A thrasher made its music from an ironwood tree, while a Gambel's quail crowed from a paloverde and mockingbirds and grackles vied for attention. An early rising cicada buzzed from under a brittlebush, and one lone coyote lifted its voice in shrill, broken melody, trying to reunite with its mate. All of these sounds melded into one resonant tone of perfect tranquility in keeping with the coolness rising off the sand and the exquisitely aromatic scent of the southwest. A roadrunner picked its way nervously among the scrub, and the quail darted like dry-land tadpoles, looking for insects that would soon take cover from the heat of the day.

Sam Coffey and Tom Vanse saddled their horses on that idyllic Arizona morning without discussing it. It was time they went for a ride, for a horseman always thinks better from the back of a good saddle horse. The other horses sucked loudly from their trough, fighting each other halfheartedly for the dominant place near the grain. The mourning dove made its melodic *coo-oo, coo, coo, coo*, then waited for a response. The harsher call of an Inca dove was its only reply. Into this devil's paradise rode Sam and Tom.

They had ridden for two miles, following an invisible line that paralleled the Mexican border. Sam chewed tobacco, silently offering a chunk to Tom, who took it without comment. Tom's bay blew out its nostrils and shook its head, and the disturbance broke Sam's tongue loose.

"You're a fool, Vanse."

Tom looked over, little creases of humor playing along the edges of his mouth. "Just now come to that conclusion, did you?"

"You're changin' your mind."

"About what?"

"Horse huntin'. Your mind's on Mexico."

Tom offered a sheepish, close-mouthed smile, displaying his deep dimples. He spat past the bay's neck onto the caliche soil. "You always were smarter than you look. Yeah, I been thinkin'. We're not bein' fair to Nadia, pard. There's a reason for everything. There's a reason we came back down here when we did. You think about it: there's a reason we saw those boys pickin' on that Chinaman, and a reason Varnell saw us come to his rescue. God didn't send us down here to hunt wild horses."

"God! What makes you so all-fired sure God sent us down here at all?"

"There's a reason for everything, Coffey. And He comes up with the reasons."

"Say we go. My luck goes with us. Say we dodge the Yaquis. We run into bandits. Say we dodge the bandits. We run into 'Paches. Say we dodge the 'Paches. We run into snakes, sandstorms, flashfloods."

"Or lightning," Tom put in.

Sam looked at him sharply. "Yeah—lightning." There were few people who knew how deeply Sam detested lightning. And of those few none but Tom would have dared mention it. Long ago, lightning had killed Sam's family.

"So what's your point?" asked Tom.

"Are you a bald-faced fool? My point is, we go down to Mexico and we don't come back. *Some*thing will kill us. Death's followed me since I was nine years old, and it all started in Mexico. Call it destiny—we cross that border, death catches up."

"You're actin' like an addle-brained kid, Coffey! You think you're safe on this side of the border? They have Apaches here, too. And bandits. Snakes, sandstorms. Herd studs that will stomp you into the dust just for lookin' at their mares. Here's how I see it: Nadia needs a stake, and she needs it now, or she goes under. Then where does she go? We stay here and hunt horses, maybe we make a little money. We don't know if it'll be enough. And maybe we die—and what for? For a very little bit we stand to gain. On the other hand, we stand to make at the very least a few thousand dollars in Sonora. Sure, we could die. But at least the stakes will have been worth the risk. Look what happened in Texas—for thirty bucks a month, Coffey! A measly fifty for me. We both near wound up dead."

"My bad American luck kills our friends," said Sam, spitting savagely across the top of Gringo's head. "Call it a gut feelin' or whatever you like, but I'm tellin' you—my Mexican bad luck will kill *us*."

For ten seconds Tom stared at his long-time partner while humor battled concern across his features. Finally, he shook his head and spat. "You're serious, aren't you?"

"You bet I am! I've had gut feelings before."

"So have I. And my gut feelings about Mexico say we'll come back with enough money to go into whatever business we please. Ten bucks says my gut feelings are stronger than yours."

"Oh yeah? How you gonna prove it without gettin' one of us killed—or *both* of us?"

"I'll make you a wager."

"You never win wagers. What're you gonna do, bet how many holes I have in my drawers?"

"I already know that. Last time I lost a bet I had to wash 'em for you, remember?"

"Then what?"

"I don't know. I'll think of somethin'."

They kept riding in silence. After several minutes, Tom jerked his horse to a stop without warning. He looked over at Sam. "I got one."

"One what?"

"A wager."

Sam eyed him suspiciously. "I sure don't like that look in your eyes."

"Well, you want the wager, or not? Six bits?"

Reluctantly, Sam nodded, then chuckled. "Six bits—against me goin' to Mexico with you if I lose. Well, you never were any too bright."

Tom nodded toward the outstretched limb of a saguaro cactus. "See that scorpion?"

Sam squinted his eyes. "You dreamin' again?"

"No, you're just blind. Look there, on that cactus limb pokin' out there."

"Good molly, Tom! You got the eyes of a buzzard!"

"I know. Now, whoever can hit that scorpion with a knife wins."

Sam looked back at the arachnid in disbelief. "Sure, Tom! That's fifteen feet off! You couldn't hit it if it was *six* feet away, and I don't know if *I* can even hit it at fifteen."

"So if neither one of us hits it, we're back where we started."

Sam gave one of his half smiles. "You're on, Curly."

They both got off their horses, and Sam pulled out his knife, the very same knife he had used to win many a contest against Tom. Tom looked from where Sam stood back to the cactus. "You goin' first?"

"You bet. I don't want you scarin' it away before I get a chance to throw. Besides, if it's pinned there that'll improve your odds. You oughtta be happy."

"You're still thirteen feet away," Tom said. "Is that where you wanna throw from?"

"I don't see why not," Sam said with a smirk. With that, he drew back the knife, gauged his target carefully, and threw. The knife twirled through the air, hitting the cactus with its side and bouncing off into the dirt.

"Well I'll be—Sam, that's the first time I've seen you miss!" Tom said, grinning.

Sam wiped his hand across his mouth to erase his sour expression. "Well, I might have missed, but you haven't thrown yet, and we both know you've never beat me yet."

Tom stood there smiling at Sam for a long several seconds. "All right, smart boy." He turned and walked over to the cactus, keeping an eye on the scorpion all the while. As he reached it he stared at it calculatingly, then bent over to pick up Sam's knife. Taking one look back at his partner, he turned and with a swift motion stuck the knife blade through the scorpion's body, pinning it to the saguaro just as it was starting to move out of nervousness.

Still grinning as if the expression had never left his face, Tom turned with a great big shrug. "Guess I win."

"What the hell was that?" Sam growled. "You won nothin'!"

"Sure I did!" Tom folded his arms across his chest.

"How you figger?"

"I bet you I could hit that scorpion with a knife. I hit it with a knife."

"Oh, no! You're not drawin' me in with *that* one. I said from right here." He jabbed a stiff finger at the ground.

"I asked you if that was where *you* wanted to throw from. I didn't say *I* was gonna throw from there!"

Sam glared up at Tom. "You son of a—"

"Uh-uh!" Tom stopped him, shaking his finger in mock admonition. "Leave my mama out of this, Coffey. I thought you liked her."

"I did. But I didn't know her only son was the devil!"

"Come on, partner. I beat you fair and square."

Sam stared hard at his partner. "You're a stinkin' cheat."

"That may be," admitted Tom. "But you're goin' to Mexico, ain't you?"

Sam Coffey stood in the shade of the sycamore and bit chunks off a big juicy piece of cantaloupe. Tom and Nikolai were over by the house spitting watermelon seeds at each other and laughing. Sam faced south, staring Mexico in the face. It was Sonora, Mexico, where his entire family had been killed. He couldn't help wondering if it had always been destined to claim him, too.

Sam thought back over all the years, back to 1842. Amazing how time galloped away! He was a nine-year-old boy then, son of an Irish father and a Choctaw mother. Headstrong he was, just like his father. But lazy, unlike his father. His father liked to tilt a bottle, but he was never lazy. And no one, including Sam himself, could ever guess where the trait came from.

His father and he argued often over silly things like cleaning up his plate, soaping his saddle, putting away his clothes, feeding the cows. The stubborn and lazy streak was his alone. His younger brother, Henry, was ambitious enough. He had even gone into business for himself, making rawhide whips and reatas for local vaqueros. And Sam's Choctaw mother was anything *but* lazy. She worked from dawn to dark, providing good food and a clean environment for her family. She was constantly smiling, and sometimes she would sing while she worked.

The memory of that August afternoon was painful. They had gone down into Sonora to do some trading, a few cows for some melons and corn, perhaps some fine-woven Mexican wool cloth. They paused to make camp and let the cows graze, but they wandered too far. Sam's father was constantly after his oldest son to learn to make his own way in the world by fostering ambition in him. It wasn't working. That afternoon, a lightning storm loomed ominous on the horizon, so the senior Coffey sent his son after the cows. As usual, they argued about it. Sam did not want to go. And when he did it was only with the intent of seeking out a good fishing hole along the stream.

An hour later, the storm which had hovered for some time along the horizon suddenly advanced on them with new power. Sam was sitting up in some rocks, looking out at the desert and watching the lightning dance and sparkle on the horizon. He could see their camp from there, but to anyone in camp he would be but a speck. He saw his father and brother leave camp, looking for the cows—and for him, too, of course.

So he made up a lie. He would say he had not been able to locate the cows—even though his father, knowing what an accomplished tracker his Choctaw grandfather had taught him to be, would know he was lying. Sam was too lazy even to think up a believable lie.

He climbed down out of the rocks after he saw his father and brother locate the three cows and start driving them back toward camp. He followed along at a safe distance, screened by the brush. By the time they neared camp he was only a dozen yards away from his father and brother, still hidden in the brush. He saw his mother come out to greet her husband and her one responsible son.

Suddenly, she looked over and saw his face peering out from the brush. "Sam!"

His father saw where she was looking and turned. His eyes went angry when he saw his oldest son. "So where have *you*—"

Whatever Sam's father was going to say came to a sudden stop. An eerie sensation gripped them all. Sam had no idea what it was, but his hair crawled up on the back of his head and neck, and his body tingled. A strange look came over the face of his mother and father, and his father looked up at the sky. He had only the time to yell, "Get down!" But all of them were still standing as a bolt of pure white fire plummeted out of the dark cloud overhead.

Sam remembered waking up lying on the ground in the pounding rain, his clothes soaked. He remembered running toward camp, seeing the charred places on the bodies of his father, his mother, his brother. He recalled sitting in shock, though he could remember no tears. There were images of digging and filling three graves. And he could see himself riding aimlessly, one wagon horse beneath him and another in front, which he drove along with the one cow that hadn't been killed by the lightning strike. He rode until he could go no more, then felt hands lifting him from the horse gently, the hands, as it turned out, of Tarahumara Indians.

The Tarahumaras became the only thing Sam could call a family. They taught him all about the plants of the desert. They taught him how to create fire with a bow and drill. They showed him the magic of flint and steel. They demonstrated how to snare a rabbit, spear a javelina, shoot an arrow through the heart of a mule deer he had been able to creep to within twenty yards of without its knowing he was there. They taught him everything there was to know about the desert.

And then he walked away.

He left the Tarahumaras with the ability to run more than forty miles in a day (no mean feat but nothing compared to the seventy miles and more some of the young warriors could travel), to track a rattlesnake across a rock field, to find life-giving moisture in the desert where to white man's frantic eyes there would appear to be none. He also left with the desire never to return to Mexico, the land that killed his family.

His drastic lesson taught Sam to work—to toil at times until his hands bled, until long after everyone else quit to play music or cards, or to drink themselves into a stupor. Working hard, sometimes seemingly beyond human endurance, was the only way he could ever pay his family for not being beside them, for not sharing in their deaths.

Sam had stopped slurping on his cantaloupe. The rind lay on the ground, already drying in the heat. His face and hands sticky, Sam came to awareness staring across the face of the Mexican desert. Well, considering the strange ways of destiny, perhaps he would die down in Mexico. But maybe death was the only path to true freedom. And if by his dying he allowed his blood brother Tom Vanse to become rich and bring back a fortune for Nadia, then perhaps that would be enough. Whatever happened, at least one of them had to escape that desert—for Nadia.

Sam sat down under the sycamore with his forearms resting across his knees and watched Tom and the boy. Tom's family came from Norway, and the Norse were hardworking people. So Tom had come by his ambition naturally. He was a handsome man by anyone's standards, outgoing and a provider. Perhaps he, not Sam, was the man Nadia needed, a man strong enough to tame this land, strong enough to stand beside her in good times, or to hold her during those times when the elements or fate made her weep.

The more he watched Tom, and Nikolai and Nadia, the more he believed that even if he died things would work out. Tom was right. God had brought them here at this time. God had sent them Abe Varnell. And perhaps, indeed, he had sent the yellow bull and the one-eyed cow.

It was time to go have a talk with one craggy prospector.

They met in the cantina, and Abe Varnell listened quietly while Tom spoke. "How serious were you about a partnership, Abe?"

"As serious as an arrow in the guts," the older man said evenly. "You boys having a change of heart?"

"Let's say we are. How would we line out the particulars?"

"We'll find us some place private, first off." Abe looked mildly toward a table full of locals who had come in about the same time as the three of them and sat down too close. "Then I'll draw you a map and shake your hands, buy you all the supplies you need, and wave goodbye to you at the border. There won't be any attorneys involved in this deal. I don't need a signed piece of paper. I've seen your integrity at work."

"That was less than a hundred dollars," Tom pointed out. "What makes you think we'll feel the same about thousands?"

Varnell met his gaze levelly and gave a little shrug. "Anybody who would go out of his way for the good of a Chinaman he never met and give back money to a no-good little thief would not cheat an old man like me."

Tom shrugged. "I reckon."

Then Varnell looked over and met Sam's gaze. "You're awful quiet, Sam. What do you say about all this?"

"I just hope the gold's there. A year's a long time for them Yaquis to haul it away."

"There's very little Cajeme needs gold for now," said Varnell. "He just doesn't want white men or Mexicans to get it. Those Yaquis survive on their wits and next to nothing else. Besides, they're raiding all the time. If anything, there's more gold now." He glanced back at the other table with its curious patrons. "Let's walk on over to the livery stable, boys. I keep my horse there—and a few other things. It's a whole lot more … *lonesome,* if you catch my drift."

In the bright shade of the livery stable floated the scents of nesting pigeons, damp horse bedding, leather and hay. The only noise within was the quiet, contented cooing of the pigeons in the rafters. Once in a while the sounds of the town would reach them, or the restless stirring of horses out in the corral. Otherwise, the afternoon was still.

Looking around to be sure no one was watching, Varnell pulled off his hat. He slipped his fingers behind the sweatband, loosening the red satin lining inside the crown. From there he pulled out a neatly folded piece of soft leather, looking up at Tom's understanding grin.

"Treasure maps don't keep well in money belts," he said with a wink. Then he motioned with his head to a stall and walked over to unfold the piece of white leather and smooth it against the side of the stall.

"This map is so simple it will surprise you, but I guarantee you won't get lost unless you're absolute fools. This is Nogales." He pointed. "This is the border. This is the Sierra Bacatete—the Bacatete Mountains. Over here is Hermosillo. It will take you maybe three days to ride down there. Plan on restocking up on supplies in Hermosillo. Five miles west of Hermosillo is the home of my friend Paco. The gold is six or eight hours' ride farther, through some of the most hellacious country you ever came across. Mountains straight up and down, and full of critters that might like to have you for lunch. Not to mention the Yaquis, Apaches, and bandits."

"Not to mention," repeated Tom, "but you already did."

"Just so you know. Now. My daddy always said to never put all my eggs in one basket, so … There's another half to this map. Paco has it hidden. That old Seri is my friend, boys. I'm telling you that, and don't you ever forget it. Go to him and show him this." He pulled out a small, beaded pouch that contained dry specks of tobacco. "His wife made this for me. No one would know that unless I told them. You make sure you tell him where it came from. If you are my friend, you are his. Tell him I sent you for the other half of the map. His half leads you from his place to the gold, which is almost smack-dab halfway across the Bacatete range. These two maps will guide you exactly, but you won't need them most of the way. It wasn't like whoever found the way in there had much choice of trails. You go where the trail is or you end up looking like a cactus—or a piece of coyote meat, whichever your luck calls for." He missed Sam's scowl, but Tom was expecting it and looked over just in time to catch it full in the face.

Varnell looked back and forth between the two of them, his eyes serious. "Now, if—"

A sudden distinct stirring in the adjacent stall stopped Varnell cold. Alarmed, he practically jumped sideways to the edge of the stall. Sam and Tom joined him there, crowding around. There, crouched in the straw, looking like he had been caught with his hand in someone else's gold poke, was one of the toughs Tom and Sam had interrupted picking on Ah Can, the Chinese.

"What the hell are you doing in there, Johnny?" Abe Varnell growled.

Johnny Riles straightened up slowly, looking from Varnell to Sam to Tom, then back to Varnell. "D— Don't tell my boss I was in here, will you? I had too much to drink last night. I was tryin' to sleep it off."

"Little young to be hittin' the firewater so hard, aren't you, Johnny?"

Riles smiled nervously. "Well, I don't know. It didn't seem like it last night."

"You're a liar, boy!" Sam's voice was as harsh as the desert. "If you hadn't slipped and kicked that pile of straw over we wouldn't have even known you were in there. You little turd—you were spyin' on us!"

"No sir! I was asleep, I swear."

"Get out of my sight," ordered Varnell. As the boy brushed past him, headed for the door, he kicked him hard in the butt, shoving him on his way.

Sam gave Varnell and Tom a hard stare. "That boy's lyin'. He heard every word you said."

Varnell glanced after Johnny, then back at Sam. "I'm afraid you're right, Sam." He swore. "Nothing to be done for it now. He doesn't know when you'll leave, though. You'll have to plan that carefully. Surprise them."

"*Them?*" repeated Tom.

"He won't make a move without telling his partners in crime— Burt McGrath's bunch. If we have to deal with Johnny we'll deal with them all. But I wouldn't worry about it. Even if he heard us nothing will come of it. Those boys don't have the spine to go down into that desert, no more than ninety-nine percent of the people in this town. They can talk all they want, boys. But whether our deal's out or not, by the time anyone knows what we planned you'll be long gone. And I defy any of those crow-headed dough brains to find their way to Hermosillo, to say nothing of the gold."

"Yeah, well a chance at a few thousand dollars' worth of gold can buy an awful lot of luck," Sam said with a scowl. "And that's all they need to find us."

"Sure, as long as it ain't your kind of luck," Tom cut in. Sam handed him a scowl.

* * *

Caps O'Brien wiped both ways at his walrus mustache. The corners of his blue eyes crinkled up with mirth as he watched Burt McGrath prepare himself for the next shot. It was an easy affair, a straight shot at the six ball into the corner pocket. Any amateur could have made it. The trick was not to scratch.

Burt had too many warm beers under his belt. He belched loudly and blinked his eyes as the fumes assaulted them. He studiously ignored the room full of people who watched him. Finally, he struck forward with his cue, hard and crisp, bringing the cue back at almost the same moment it struck the ball. White ball struck green with a solid clack, and the green ball went straight down the hole, the cue ball retreating back. Burt stood up and grinned triumphantly. He took the chalk off the corner of the table and rubbed it over the end of his stick as if it were an exact science.

Lug Colton, who could not have sunk a ball on any bet in less than two tries, just stared in awe. Scrub Ottley was less impressed. He stood and sipped his beer with the weight of his pistol hanging at his hip, trying to look nonchalant.

Temp Stratton took a big draw on his cigar. This was one of his few cordial moments. "I'm tellin' you, Caps. This kid's a natural! Bad day when you took him on, pardner."

Caps shrugged. "Should've recognized my betters."

Burt leaned over and lined up on the eight ball. If he sank that one it would leave only stripes on the table. "Don't feel bad, Caps. I've been doing this for years."

"Ain't no shame bein' bested by an expert," Caps returned, and he watched Burt sink the ball and stand away from the table a victor.

"Reckon I owe you a beer," Caps drawled.

Burt just laughed. "We're playin' for fun anyway, right?"

"That's right, but it's only fair!" said Caps with a big grin splitting his mustache.

He tossed a tiny gold coin through the air, which Burt caught. "Seems like you're feeling flush today."

Caps hesitated for the briefest of seconds, his eyes flickering over at Stratton. Then he cleared his throat. "Yeah, Burt. The strangest thing happened last night. On our way back to the room we decided to stop in at another cantina, and we, uh … ran into this whisky drummer there, drunk on his own wares. He was a nice feller, but that gent couldn't have beat a jackrabbit at cards! We won a nice little stake off 'im."

"You have the luck of the devil," Burt said with a grin. "That's the kind of odds we like around here."

They all moved up to the bar and ordered their drinks, and Caps eyed Burt up and down. "I didn't have any idea you could play billiards like that, Burt. You sure excel at a lot of different things. Where'd you get all that talent?"

Stratton looked around him at the others. "He must've took Lug and Scrub's!"

Lug laughed. He was too stupid to know the joke was on him. Scrub gave a little chuckle, unsure if he dared act offended.

"Say, Burt," said Caps, "somebody said your old man's in town. Think he'll be lookin' for yuh?"

"He might," said Burt, squaring his shoulders as he took a swig of beer. "But he doesn't run my life."

"I don't imagine so. Man as tough as you, I imagine you do pretty well what you please."

Burt turned and spat into a cuspidor, the liquid making a low tinny sound. He smiled, basking in the praise of this man who was at least ten, maybe fifteen years his elder.

Burt was impressed with these two. In fact, no one had impressed him much more in the year it had been since he had taken to frequenting Nogales to avoid his duties at the ranch. His first encounter with the two men had been neutral, but since he had started hanging around with them he had gained a healthy respect for the men they really were.

Caps O'Brien, although not a tall man, looked impressive in his barrel-chested stockiness. He had cleaned up today, wearing a white shirt with black stripes, tailored trousers and a gray wool vest with four pockets, one dangling a gold watch chain. But all of his clothing could not hide the grace of the man, the wary, feline way he watched the saloon crowd while to the casual onlooker he seemed at ease. O'Brien's feet were small, which to a cowboy lent bragging rights, and his hands were well able to maneuver a pool cue or a deck of cards. McGrath had also seen them handle the forty-four Colt he wore in a cross-draw position on his left hip. But in spite of their finesse, Burt was also guessing that if Caps laid a hand to something it did not get away, for in shaking the man's hand he had felt his vise-like grip. Burt had no doubt; Caps O'Brien was a man who had seen the world, taken his bite of it, and come away with meat in his teeth.

Then there was Temple Stratton. Caps's partner had enjoyed a haircut, and his brown hair was now cropped close above his ears. He wore a revolver in a cross-draw holster like his partner's and another on his right hip. Stratton could be surly at times, but he was no slacker in the department of tough. Unlike Caps, who might have been considered a pleasant-looking man to some, Temp was a broken-faced brawler. His flat, scarred face and broken nose with its strawberry-like tip would have made no favorable stir in a feminine world, but it won its place of respect in a realm of saloon brawlers and tough customers. The man was broad across the shoulders and narrow in the hips, his fists flat-knuckled and big as whisky jugs. He had fought some, and he had taken some blows, but Burt figured he had hurt more than he had been hurt, and kept coming back for more. His outstanding brutish toughness made him a man to be admired in a crowd clamoring to be top dog.

A couple of hours later the five of them had shared some long drinks, not only beer but hard liquor. They had played a few hands of cards to kill their boredom, another game or two of billiards. But the alcohol was starting to have its effect on them, at least on Burt, Scrub and Lug. They were itching for something else to do.

It was at that moment that the cantina door opened and spilled light across the floor, and Burt recognized the quick, nervous steps of Johnny Riles before he heard his voice. "Hey, Burt, you ain't gonna believe this!"

Burt turned, trying to look casual even though the excitement in Johnny's voice sparked his interest. "What's up there, Johnny? Find a penny in one of them cowpies you like diggin' through?"

Everyone else laughed. They had to—Burt was their bankroll.

Johnny flushed. "Come on, Burt, listen to me!"

Burt sighed. "All right, what's up? You look like your mama married the saloon owner!"

"Naw! It ain't nothin' good or bad, just pretty funny. I guess the old prospector finally found his suckers."

No one else noticed, but Caps and Stratton leaned their ears closer to the conversation. Any mention of the "old prospector" was reason enough to listen in.

"You mean Varnell? What're you talking about?"

"Them two drifters who ... well, them two we had it out with. They decided to throw in with him and go after his gold! Guess they won't be around long. I can just see their hides a-hangin' from some cactus!"

"Yeah, the Yaquis will make short work of them," Burt agreed. "Gold! It didn't work for the old man, why would they think it'd work for them?"

Caps stepped away from the bar, closer to Johnny. "Hey, Johnny, keep your voice down there, pard. Let's go over to a table. I wanna hear more of this." He jerked his head at Stratton to follow them.

The little parade made its way to a corner table, where everyone pulled up chairs and gathered around to hear Johnny tell them how he had lucked into his information while out cleaning stalls in the livery. Burt, Lug and Scrub, even Johnny, had nothing to do but laugh at the stupidity of the two drifters agreeing to go after the gold, but Caps and Stratton were silent throughout.

"I don't know how stupid they are," Caps said after the mirth had died away. The comment drew the quick glance of everyone. "Yeah, that's right. I mean, rumor has it there's so much gold down there that ten men couldn't carry it out. Boys, that must be more than a million dollars. Imagine what you'd live like for the rest of your life!"

Scrub scoffed. "Yeah, but imagine what the rest of your life would be like if the Yaquis got hold of you and skinned you alive and tied you over an ant hill! You know, they got these poisonous little ants down there that eat flesh like it's goin' out of style!"

"Ah hell!" Caps gave Scrub a hard look. "I'm livin' proof, boy, there's nothin' in this world as bad as folks would have you think. Temp and me, we been in Yuma. Even that wasn't the hellhole they claim. Not for tough men, leastways. We've both lived in Mexico, and it ain't any worse than Arizona or New Mexico. Same Injuns, same bandits, same snakes. What's the difference between ridin' around down there or between here and Tucson? I'll tell you what the difference is—a million dollars in gold!"

Caps's optimism put the others to silence. For fifteen or twenty seconds they sat pondering, nursing their drinks, then one by one began to look around trying to discern what everyone else might be thinking. Finally, Johnny broke the silence. "But at least them two boys have a map. We don't have anything!"

Caps sank back in his chair, folding his hands on the table in front of him. A huge grin sparkled within his mustache. "We don't need a map! That's the beauty of it, my friends! All we have to do is follow those two and let 'em do all the work. Then we take it from 'em and go on our way. But, it's too bad we don't have any money. No way we could go down without havin' somethin' to buy us an outfit with."

McGrath had a crafty gleam in his eye. He could sense everyone starting to gravitate toward Caps and his friendly, confident attitude, and he was quick to jump at this opportunity to save the day, knowing what kind of prestige his offer would bring him with Caps and Stratton, not to mention the boys.

"Who says we don't have any money?"

"Ah, Burt." Caps waved him off. "You don't wanna go spendin' your money on the likes o' that idea."

Burt looked quickly around. "What do you mean?"

"Ah, I was wrong. It's too risky." Caps leaned back farther in his chair.

"Risky! What do we look like, a bunch of dudes?"

"Well, no, you're a pretty tough bunch, there's no doubt about that." Caps chuckled as a thought came into his head. "That would right enough be a good sort of justice though, wouldn't it? We saw the way them two thrashed you out in the street. 'Course they wouldn't have been able to if they didn't take you by surprise," he added quickly. "But it sure would be somethin'—let 'em work their butts off, then just walk off with everything."

Burt looked around excitedly. "Caps is right, boys! You talk about justice! How'd that be? Those two stuck their noses in our business, pulling that Chinaman out of his tight spot. We were just having fun! What do they think they are, some kind of guardian angels? And then they walk around here like nothing can happen to them. Can you imagine the looks on their faces when we take their horses and the gold and ride away with them standing there in the desert? Shoot, it'd be worth every mile!"

Even Scrub had a smile on his face when Burt finished talking. The little man had always had a mean streak, and of course he felt like he had more reason than anyone to hate the partners, especially Sam Coffey. Sure, they had given him back part of his money, but that didn't compensate for making him look bad in front of the whole town. "How much you really figure is down there?" Scrub asked of the group.

Caps seemed about to answer, then stopped, and they all looked at Burt. "You boys have heard the stories. Millions. Maybe billions!" he exaggerated in his drunkenness. "Enough to make us all rich—and humiliate those two highfalutin do-gooders in the process."

Johnny was shaking his head. "I've heard bad stories about Mexico. Them Rurales!"

"Shucks, Johnny! You heard Caps. Mexico's no different than here. You know how big that place is? We could be there and gone without them even knowing we'd been there. I say we go!" Burt stood out of his chair, swelling his chest as the image of himself leading this group of men into the desert filled his brain. He swayed a little from the effects of the liquor but steadied himself against the edge of the table. "Come on, boys. You with me?" He looked around at his friends, at his new cohorts, Caps and Temp. Both of them shrugged.

Caps said, "Sure, if you'll lead the way there, Burt! No way I could do it without you." Underneath the table, he knuckled Stratton's leg conspiratorially, and a big grin broke over Stratton's face, making his eyes gleam.

"You can count me in," chimed Stratton, and the others followed suit. Even Johnny gave up his misgivings in the face of all the excitement.

"We'll show 'em they can't take on the four of us without consequences!" Burt boasted.

They spent the rest of the evening sitting around the table planning their big adventure. They would need to outfit themselves with supplies for the journey, with extra horses and ammunition and plenty of good guns. That would have to be Burt and Lug's department, as they were the two with the only easy access to funds. They would have to obtain maps of the country, and talk to anyone they could find who had been down there.

And Caps planned to pick up a few dozen more sticks of dynamite. If there was one thing in this world he was good at, it was explosives; they had saved him from more than one tight spot.

Young Burt McGrath was a big man that night. His father's influence was far away, and the men in this cantina looked to him as their leader, something he had always sought. He started planning what they would do, listening patiently to any suggestions, but always the last one the others looked to for a decision. That was how a man in charge of an operation like this had to be.

Caps sat back in his chair, a full mug of beer in front of him, fingering a shiny gold double eagle underneath the table, and gave young Burt McGrath one of his most contented smiles.

Chapter Ten

Goodbyes had never been easy for Sam Coffey. He sat with Nadia under the canopy of the porch swing that night and dried her tears. She was a tough woman—she didn't shed many of them in his presence. But enough that he knew she was scared.

"It'll be all right, woman." He didn't say *he* would be all right, for that he could not promise. He put his arm around her back and held her close. He thought of the little boy asleep in the house, and of Tom. Happy-go-lucky Tom. He seemed to think they were going on some kind of lark.

In reality, Sam understood Tom well enough to know most of his attitude was a show. Tom was aware of the dangers that faced them in Arizona. He was no fool. In fact, he was one of the most canny men Sam had ever known. But he would play out his act to the end, hoping to set Sam at ease.

A thought came suddenly to Sam, and he looked out across the yard, to a spot under a paloverde tree. There he had long ago planted for Nadia the stem cuttings of the mysterious night-blooming cereus, also known as queen of the night. It was a strange flower, exquisitely white and beautiful, many-petaled, with a bundle of pale yellow emerging from its center. It bloomed only one night of the year, in June or July, then was gone. Not since his childhood had Sam seen the queen of the night bloom.

"Did your flower ever show up?" he asked, trying to sound nonchalant.

It took Nadia a moment to catch up to his train of thought, but then she glanced quickly over at the spot they had chosen for the flower. "No. It lies there and waits—perhaps for you to come home."

Sam swallowed hard. He had always wanted to be there with Nadia when the cereus came into flower, to see the look he knew would light her face. But it was a one night thing. The chances were next to none.

"I ain't seen one bloom since …" He paused, and she looked at him questioningly.

"Since when?"

"Since my folks died. Ma, she loved that flower. She used to wait for it every year, and there was always a big celebration the night it came out. But yours doesn't bloom. Must be some kind of sign." He didn't say it, but the sign he got from it was that he was never meant to be in the presence of that kind of beauty again. And perhaps he had never been meant to be in the presence of beauty like Nadia's, either.

Nadia laughed. "A sign! Yes, it's a sign that it's too dry down here. Why, what kind of sign do you think it is?"

Sam was usually good at keeping his thoughts to himself. This time he said something he knew he might regret immediately. But perhaps it was a good time to have it out there before them.

"I'm thinkin' maybe it's a sign we're not supposed to be together."

Nadia looked up quickly at him, about to speak. But whatever she wanted to say was lost in the desperate silence, and instead she took his hand and buried her face in his chest.

To keep from being followed as easily, Sam and Tom rode out one hour later, just the two of them and their horses, leading three pack mules through the night. Tom was carried by a lifetime of dreams … Sam, burdened by a lifetime of doubts—and the haunting memory of the night-blooming cereus that would not come to flower.

Nadia Boultikhine sat alone on the swing after Sam and Tom had gone. It was late. She had no idea what time, but stars had dazzled her eyes for hours. Still, she could not sleep, and she sat there on the silent swing and stared in the direction Sam and Tom had ridden away.

Nadia considered herself a smart woman. Perhaps not one of instinctive intelligence, but certainly one who learned from past experience. She could not say she had foreseen her husband deserting her. When she had awakened to find Nikifor gone it had worried her, but she had first assumed he went to town. The day went by, and he did not return, and then she suspected foul play, feared that perhaps he was hurt somewhere … or dead. The day turned into a week, and weeks into months, and all-consuming fear eventually turned to numbness. Then came the day she received a letter from Nikifor, and enough of a stake to buy the boarding house.

The letter was written simply and with little emotion, the way Nikifor Boultikhine would write it. He told of how he loved her and Nikolai, but he had decided being tied down was not for him. He had gone to Mexico to search for treasure. He recounted how he prospected until finding a vein he thought would make him rich, a vein that netted him three thousand dollars before playing out. He sent her fifteen hundred in the same letter. The money and the letter were the last sign she had heard from him.

That experience was one of those which taught Nadia to be the smart woman she was. And tonight, with the stars sparkling like diamond dust, and the wind worrying the tree branches, and the crickets making their night song around her, Nadia knew Sam was not coming back to stay. She had sensed it in his every word, in the very way he carried himself. Did he intend to help her keep the boarding house? Yes! There was no doubt in her mind about that. If he and Tom made good in their quest, and if Abe Varnell's stories were true, she would never again have a material need. But Sam, if he returned at all, would not stay. He would leave his money and he would be gone.

Nadia could not say why she knew this. Instinct was the only word to explain it. But that was all she needed. She turned her eyes to gaze over at the spot where Sam had so lovingly placed the night-blooming cereus, queen of the night. Oh, how he had wanted to see it bloom with her, though he had never come out and said that. It was one of those emotions she had been forced to read behind his eyes. Now it just languished there under the paloverde as time dragged by, showing no color, and little life. When the hard realization struck Nadia that she was finally, *truly*, alone at last, she lowered her face into her hands, and she wept in silence.

Strange noises ring in a Mexican night. The yelping of a kit fox and bird cries, magnificent and strange, wing through air unbelievably clear. The cries rise from everywhere … and nowhere. A man can strain his ears, his eyes … still he sees only the dull black images of giant saguaro arms prodding the sky, menacing the crackling stars. He hears the wind chittering in the mesquite branches, the creak of saddle leather and the soft plodding of many hooves that in time fades into the mists of subconsciousness. And he hears again the fox, and those strange birds that only come out in the dark, joined now and then by the cries of coyotes, an owl or a wolf. The Mexican night engulfs the traveler, and soothing air whirls down to cool the sand, hypnotizing the human mind with an ethereal beauty that will evanesce with sunrise.

Neither Tom nor Sam spoke, each entertaining his own thoughts. Tom yearned after the family he had long ago lost. His wife, Beverly, his children, Tom, Jr., Sarah, Leah and John. He had only meant to help that family traveling across the desert alone. Their own wagon train had left them because they were sick. And the train the Vanses were traveling with had no intentions of stopping. But it was in the Vanses' blood to stop and help. The family had scarlet fever. Tom never contracted it, passed over by some bizarre twist of fate. But under its cold, callous grasp his family now lay in shallow, rock-covered graves on the Camino del Diablo.

Sam's recollections were of his own family, his hard-working father who would have done anything to see his children succeed. His mother, the best cook that side of the Northwest Territory. His brother … he hardly even remembered him now.

When the lightning began to play on the distant horizon, Sam bunched his jaws and tightened his grip on the reins. He sensed death in everything around him.

Tom was able to remove the halters of the pack string after a while. They were far enough away from home by then, and the mules would follow. The sun loomed high, shadows deep but short. In the distance ragged ridges gnawed at the underside of the sky, blue only because of space, not because of any magical coolness in the air there. Heat simmered off the sand, and except for circling vultures the world was still. Only the two white men and their animals were willing to move on a day such as this.

"Where do you suppose all them Yaquis are?" asked Tom, jogging up next to Sam.

"If they were in your ear you'd know!" shot back Sam.

Tom laughed and spat. "What's that supposed to mean?" He got no answer. "Still worried?"

"Somethin' like that."

"What are you gonna do with all that gold?"

Sam gave his partner a queer look. "Give it to you."

Shaking his head, Tom dropped his eyes to his saddle horn. He looked up and scanned the brush, the three vultures—no, four—that rode the brassy sky. "How far you think them buzzards can see?"

Sam glanced up, raising a forearm to guard his eyes from the sun. "Into next week, I reckon."

"Then I reckon they can see us rich," Tom remarked with a big grin.

"Yeah … rich."

Tom cranked his hips around in the saddle so he was sitting there half-cocked. "Pard, I've never seen you more surly. There really is somethin' in your craw. You wanna go back to Nogales?"

"Hell, we're here now."

"Yeah, we're here all right. And you're just about as sociable as a tailed-down bull. Say, why don't you sing me a song? 'Rock-a-Bye Baby' or somethin'. I need a nap."

Sam had to fight to hold back a grin, but his eyes belied it.

"Careful, you might crack that stone face!" Tom said with a big grin. "I'm sure thinkin' about a blue-eyed gal I saw in El Paso. Purtiest gold hair I ever saw. Big blue eyes. Incredible figure. But she sure had some big paws!"

At last, Sam had to laugh. Tom nodded with satisfaction and turned his head back toward the front. He had succeeded, but it was time to fold; making Sam laugh took too much energy.

Caps O'Brien had always been good at holding in his emotions. He might be madder than a jilted prostitute, but a man looking at him would never have known it. Temp Stratton was a different story. When they heard from Johnny Riles that Sam Coffey and Tom Vanse had left in the night, Caps just laughed. But Stratton shook the hotel with his curses. He shattered the ewer against the wall, even pulled his pistol with intentions of shooting out the mirror until Caps stopped him.

"Ain't the end of the world, pardner. Simmer down. We'll just have to rethink it."

Stratton turned with the cocked pistol in his hand, tilted upward. "Rethink it! We could rethink it for two weeks! If they *out*think us we'll still come up empty."

"It might work to our advantage. Why let 'em just lead us to the gold? Why not catch 'em on their way back out—when all the work's done?"

Unconsciously, Stratton let his pistol slide back in the holster. He scratched his jaw, then looked over at Caps with the anger draining quickly out of his eyes. "Now there's a plan I like even better."

"Only now we've gotta find us somebody that can follow them boys. I never was much of a tracker, especially in rocky country."

Stratton scowled. "See? There's always something!"

"Damn, you're a pessimist. You know what your problem is? You got a negative attitude." Caps nodded. "You wanna sink your own ship 'fore it even gets out of the harbor!"

"It's sunk," Stratton said sullenly.

"Come on," Caps ignored the comment. "Let's go hunt up the kid. He's the brains of this outfit."

"The hell he is!"

"Well, he's sure the cash!" Caps corrected with a wink. "If he got out of the house without bein' caught, that is."

Burt McGrath had headed back to the home ranch the evening before with a promise of raiding his father's safe and coming back with enough money to fund their venture. Caps was all for the idea. The kid might not have been too bright, but when it came to finding money he sure had a knack!

They put on their hats and wandered down to the Ventana, which even at eleven o'clock in the morning was inhabited by a couple of dusty drifters. Caps walked up to where the bartender was swabbing glasses.

"You seen the McGrath kid today?"

"Si! He was looking for you."

"Well, I'm lookin' for him! Where'd he go?"

"I don't know. You check the *calabozo?*"

"Hell, that boy's a saint," said Caps. "What would he be doin' in jail, volunteerin' his time to cook for the prisoners?"

The bartender guffawed. Then he looked beyond Caps. "Ah! He is here!"

Caps and Stratton turned in unison to see Burt come through the door with all three of his cronies, Lug, Scrub and Johnny.

"Where you been?"

"We must have crossed paths," Burt answered Caps. "We were just over to your hotel. They said you moved out."

"Yeah, we moved out! We gotta make dust, kid. I never expected them gents to head out so soon. They make more snap decisions than a ruttin' bull in a cow pen! We gotta find us a tracker, kid. Pronto!"

"Oh." Burt was obviously taken aback. "But I thought— You mean you're still goin' after 'em?"

"What do you mean, boy? Of course we are! Ain't you?"

Burt looked quickly about. "Well, uh, yeah, sure. Sure I am, Caps."

"But we need a tracker. Know anybody?"

"I don't," said Burt, perhaps a bit too quickly.

A big grin crossed Lug's face. "A tracker! Shoot, Burt! You got one of the best trackers in this whole country working right out at your ranch." Lug turned to Caps. "This gent even goes by the *name* of Tracker!"

Delight covered Caps's face, and he shared the look with Stratton and slapped him on the back. "There yuh go, Burt! So where is this great tracker?"

Burt looked uncertainly at Lug. "Well, he's …"

Stratton glowered at Burt. "First you don't tell us about 'im, now you won't tell where he is. Well, it don't matter. You think we got time to ride out to the ranch an' look for 'im? We gotta ride now or it's gonna be too late."

Instead of looking disappointed like Caps thought he might, Burt suddenly swallowed hard. Drawing up his shoulders, he shared a self-important look with the two of them.

"All right," Caps said. "Well, where is this boy?"

Burt, still seeming to enjoy his moment of importance, hooked his thumbs in his belt and looked back and forth at Caps and Stratton, his eyes narrowing cockily. "Well, boys, it just so happens that Tracker is down at the gun shop. He just got back from selling a herd in Prescott, and every time ol' Tracker makes a bundle of money he buys a new gun. He's got no use for women or booze or cards, but he's got a collection of guns you wouldn't believe. So I expect he's picking out the latest model as we speak. My old man just paid him off yesterday … with the cash Tracker brought back from Prescott. Which the remainder of," he added, taking a deep breath and letting it out with a sigh, "a little mouse tells me might be riding in my hip pocket about now."

Caps slapped Burt hard on the shoulder. "You got it! Hey, Burt! I'd ride the river with you any day." Caps turned and winked at Stratton. "You see? What'd I tell you?"

Burt clucked his tongue. "Anything for my pards. Especially if it gives me a way to show those two saddle bums they aren't going to treat friends of mine like that and not have to pay the consequences."

Burt turned from the saloon with a sick feeling beginning in his stomach. Ever since hearing Coffey and Vanse had ridden out, he had sort of hoped the entire deal would fall through. He knew he had talked big last night. Perhaps too big. But with the partners gone out of town on an unknown trail … Now Lug had foiled his hopes! Where would this trail eventually lead them? Burt was afraid to guess, but he wasn't so sure he shouldn't have stayed out at the ranch. His thoughts were interrupted by Caps.

"Burt, you sure are a good man to have around. Hell, we prob'ly oughtta figure half of whatever we get goes to you, since you're the one financin' the trip, and findin' this tracker and all. We sure couldn't do it without you."

The others echoed him, Lug slapping Burt hard on the shoulder. Even Stratton seemed pleased for once with Burt's performance. Before long, they had Burt forgetting all about his misgivings.

As they walked toward the gun shop, Burt, Caps and Stratton shoulder to shoulder with the other three trailing behind, Burt told the two ex-cons more about Tracker. He was a black man, his real name Abraham Winborn, and he had been born a free man. The man who had fathered him, at an advanced age, was none other than the famous mountain man, Esau Winborn, who had been adopted into the Shoshone tribe and proved himself enough of a fighting man to rise into position as one of their leaders. Esau was most well known for bringing down, in his last days in the mountains, the huge white bison bull the Shoshones called White Mountain. His son, Tracker, was thirty-some years old, lithe as a bobcat and able to track a speck of dust in a whirlwind, or so Burt bragged. And just as importantly, he could take a pine cone out of the crotch of a tree at a hundred yards. Tracker, although not much good with people, unable to read or write even his own name, was the ideal outdoorsman, a progeny of which old Esau Winborn could be proud. They would surely find more than one use for such a man in the country into which they were headed.

They met Winborn at the gun shop with a brand new Marlin in his hands. He stood six-foot-two, with muscle that advertised itself even through a hickory shirt and wool vest. Lean of hip, his shoulders rounded and muscular, his presence would draw attention in any crowd.

For no outwardly apparent reason, Tracker Winborn tensed as they came into the store. He turned his head and met Caps's gaze with eyes as intense as the sun but as dark as night, and between the look and the eagle's beak he wore for a nose he made even Caps pause in his step.

But Caps never stayed daunted for long. "This must be Abraham Winborn."

The black man turned fully to him, letting the rifle ease to his side. "And you'd be …?" His glance flickered to Burt, paused on Stratton, then went back to Caps. Even though shorter than Burt, Lug and Stratton, the intelligence of Caps shone through his eyes. Proving himself a sagacious observer, Tracker knew the true leader of this group.

"My name's Dexter O'Brien, but my friends call me Caps."

In a voice as deep as a well and rough as a cavern ceiling, the black man said, "Mornin'—O'Brien. My friends call me Tracker. You can call me Mr. Winborn."

The façade that Caps guarded so well froze for a moment, and a darkness showed through the deep blue of his eyes. His glance flickered over Tracker's muscular frame, gauging him. Then he smiled, followed by an outright laugh. "I'll be. A darkie with a sense o' humor. Well, *Mister* Winborn, you're the first colored man I ever called 'mister' and mayhaps the only one I ever will. But I believe you might have earned it."

Tracker gave him a ponderous nod and looked at Burt, moving only his eyes. "Mornin', Burt. Why you in town?"

"Came lookin' for you," said Burt. At that moment, he faltered, and after searching for words he turned sheepishly to the others. "Ummm, do you think maybe you boys could leave me alone here with Tracker for a few minutes?"

The storekeeper was looking at Tracker expectantly. "Well, Mr. Winborn? Is this the new toy this month?"

"Drop it in the box," said Tracker as he glanced back at the man. "And a couple boxes of shells, too. You say these shells c'n be bought anywhere?"

"Oh yeah! This rifle will be the rage, you can mark my words. Winchester'll have to do some fancy stepping to keep up with John Marlin."

The black man looked at the rifle with a satisfied nod. "Just so," he said. He turned again to Burt and his party while the shopkeeper went to the storeroom to pull out the long wooden case that came with the rifle.

Tracker let his eyes slide over all those present, finally resting them on Burt. "You can say whatever you got to say when I get outside."

Burt nodded, then turned again to look at Caps pleadingly. Caps gave him a reluctant glance, then jerked his head at Stratton. The five of them filed out the door. Caps paused in the doorway to let the other four pass. "We'll see you down at the Ventana, Burt." Burt gave another preoccupied nod, waiting nervously for Tracker to finish.

Once the black man had purchased his rifle and they were outside standing in the partial shade at the side wall of the hardware store, Burt gave Tracker a searching glance. "I need your help, Tracker. I got me a big deal."

Tracker grunted. "A big deal? I heard them words before."

"No, really! I have a chance to make a fortune—and you, too, if we play our cards right." The black man held his tongue. "I'm serious about this, Tracker. We have a fool-proof way to go down in Mexico and get more gold than you can imagine."

With only his eyes Tracker smiled, looking at this young man he had known since Burt was only eleven years old, when Tracker had first hired on with his father. "I've heard o' them 'fool-proof' ways, boy. Mostly, it's only fools that believe 'em."

Burt laughed nervously. "I knew you'd say that, Tracker, but I'm dead serious. There are two men who have a sure-fire map to Mexican gold. They got it from Abe Varnell, and you know *he's* got money!"

For the first time, Tracker gave Burt a real, studying look, and for the first time paid him real attention. "All right, Burt. All right. Who are these fellows?"

"Just some men we met," Burt said, ashamed to admit how. "But Varnell took a liking to them and hired them to go after his gold. And there's way too much for just two or three men!"

Tracker didn't often laugh, but he gave a soft one now, then went serious again. "Don't you be fallin' for a tale like that, youngster!

The road to hell is paved with skel'tons o' men that believed that kind o' bull."

"No, Tracker, this one's for real!" Burt insisted. "But we need you to track these boys down to the gold so we can get in on it."

Tracker grunted. "I had me one day o' rest, Burt," he said with a tone of tired dread in his voice. "I ain't about to go off on a wild goose chase after all them days I just had on the trail. Besides, what if them two boys take it all?"

"Uh, well ..." Burt hesitated too long.

"You gon' take it from 'em?"

"Well, no, Tracker! Nothin' like that." As much as he tried he couldn't keep the doubt out of his eyes. In fact, he wasn't completely sure what drunken words he'd said the night before, but he was half afraid he had already agreed to something like that. But he had enough sway over the others to talk them out of doing any harm.

"Well, you don't sound too sure of anythin', Burt," said the black man. "You can't even be sure o' them boys you're goin' with."

Burt was disappointed. How could he not be? He was going to be made a fool of if Tracker wouldn't go!

Burt's jaw hardened. "Well, you're entitled to your opinion, Tracker. Tell my father where I went. Tell him I'll be back, with enough money to take care of everything."

"Take care of everything? What you talkin' 'bout, boy?"

"Ah, it'd take too long to explain," said Burt uneasily. Of course he couldn't admit he had taken money from the safe, not until he had enough to pay it all back, with interest. "I'll see you when we get back."

Burt started to turn away, but Tracker grabbed him by the shoulder.

The black man sighed. "You're bein' a fool, Burt. A true fool."

"Think what you want," Burt retorted, eyes flashing hurt anger. "I'll be seein' you."

Tracker's broad hand clamped harder on Burt's shoulder. "When you goin', boy?"

"Now, Tracker. Right now."

"No way to talk you into stayin'?"

"Too late for that," Burt said flatly.

Tracker scowled. "How much you figure they'd pay a man to follow tracks down into Mexico and get shot at by every human scorpion in sight?"

Burt turned fully back to Tracker and eyed him speculatively for several seconds, the first sign of hope beginning to come into his heart. "You looking toward another new shooting iron, are you? We come back with that gold, you'll have enough money to buy five of them rifles—and more."

Tracker measured the boy with his eyes. Finally, he just shook his head. It was plain to see he was disgusted with himself. "I'll go, boy, but it ain't for a new shootin' iron. I'm goin' only because somebody with half a lick o' sense has got to go keep you from gettin' your fool head blowed off."

The black man started to turn back toward the store. "Come on with me, boy. Guess I better go tell the storekeeper to hang onto this here new rifle 'til I get back."

Chapter Eleven

"The wind that day made a horrible moan, out through the chaparral. While Claudus McKnight, with a beat-up spade, dug a grave out for his pal."

Tom Vanse's voice rolled almost melodically as he recited the poem he had memorized one long winter night in a line shack in the Texas panhandle. Sam Coffey could actually feel himself being lulled to sleep in the saddle.

"Then there in the dirt, the very dirt, that his friend would forever hold, lay the shiny devil that had brought them here—the Sierra Madre gold." Tom glanced up at the sun, then over at Sam. From the corner of his eye he could see the thunderstorm looming nearer on the horizon. He suddenly cleared his throat and resumed his recitation with a different poem.

"Thirty miles back is Arizona, and down below is hell. Seven hundred is Mexico City, and the sound of the mission bell ..." Tom paused, his eyes squinted up in thought, then went on. "I'll give you a cup of pure water if you'll dig me a twenty-foot well, but I fear it might be boilin'—you'd be diggin' right through hell!"

The rhyme struck a chord in Sam and woke him up. He twisted in the saddle and speared his full attention at his saddle partner. "Where'd that come from?"

"I made it up."

"Made it up! When?"

"Just now."

"Oh, so now you're a poet?"

"Not so's you'd know it."

"I'll be—" Sam stopped and shook his head. "I liked you better when that snake bit you back in the panhandle and you swelled up so bad you couldn't talk for a week."

Tom laughed. "Well sir, you're losin' your mind, ol' Coffey! You're the one that got bit by that snake!"

Sam grinned, spreading his big black mustache out to the sides. "Ah hell, that's right. And my ears swelled up so bad I couldn't hear you. Either way I liked you better."

Time passed, and the clouds began to darken. They soon became glowering, and it was fortunate they still heaped moodily on the distant horizon. The cottony drifts and dunes from earlier and the glowing yellows and hints of orange had turned to blue and purple-black humps of raw, nervous power. It was impossible to tell how high the thunderheads raged, but easily thousands of feet. They did indeed look like fortresses at that moment, as Beverly Vanse would have called them. Beleaguered fortresses with secret passageways and courtyards preparing for one final battle that would see their walls cave in.

"You oughtta hear the song I'm workin' out," Tom offered.

Sam looked dismayed. "Now a song, too?"

"Sure. It's about the time I first fell in love with you."

"Watch your tongue, Curly, or you might be lookin' at my south end headed north."

"That's a scary thought. Kind of reminds me of the time—" The first of the lightning flickered like fireworks across the underbelly of the cloud, which showed a burnished color through the gargantuan celestial fists swollen purple with rain, or if not with rain then with enough energy to tear the distant mountain range in half.

The storm was too far away to hear, but Sam had no doubt there was more to come. He bunched his jaws and tightened his grip on the reins, despising the menace in those clouds, hating how it made him think of his parents' end.

Tom took a deep breath and let out a sigh. He sank his fingers into his horse's mane, then drew them out, pulling gently to loosen tangles. He wished he could comfort his partner, but what tortured Sam was buried too deep.

The horses and mules plodded on, so far unperturbed by the approaching storm. Tom started to speak again, recalling the first poem he had ever written, the winter after he buried his family. A hunting trip for bighorn sheep up in the high Beartooth country of Montana had inspired him to pen the words.

"I traveled to the top of the world, where eternity unfurled. Yet time stood still, and always will, up at the top of the world." The next lines seemed to play right along with the moment as a wind picked up and hurled dust along before it and rustled the grass and the branches of the mesquite. "The wind made the only song, cold as it whisked along. Glaciers bold guarded tales untold, far from the hurrying throng. Nothing moves at the top of the world, where the granite is pink and purled. I felt God there, in the flawless air, up at the top of the world."

His face creasing in a half smile, Sam looked over appreciatively at his partner. "Not bad, pard. Always did like that one."

Tom smiled in return. He knew how hard these storms were on Sam. They might have been magic to poets, yet when the thunderheads bulked on the horizon and began to glower, they held no magic for Sam. For him, they bore only memories of hell.

The scent of rain, propelled by increasing winds, vitalized the desert. Clouds whisked out the sun, and brush and mesquite uncloaked the dust from their shoulders, flinging tiny projectiles of sand at the travelers. Sam and Tom were no strangers to this country. More than one person had referred to them as desert rats. They had tried their hands at the so-called profession of prospecting before, and prospecting took men into wild, barren country timid men dared only read about. Sam and Tom had seen their share of lightning and sand storms, flashfloods and barren country so dry they had found themselves longing for jobs in town. But those foolish notions never lasted long.

In spite of the lurid temptation of all its modern contrivance, pretense and vanity, its smoke, vice and vile feculent stench, civilization is no place for a man.

A spider web of lightning dipped and jagged and swirled along the horizon. This time it brought a distant rumble eight or nine seconds later. But it was the harbinger of closer, fiercer strikes. Soon, streaks of white fire hammered the mountainsides every half a minute or so.

"You worryin' about me again?" asked Sam when Tom cast him a look. "You act like a mother hen."

With a big grin, Tom spat tobacco juice into the brush. "Reckon we oughtta be huntin' a hole? After all, you can't be dyin' on me till we've pulled out enough of that gold to make me rich."

"The only hole around here's the one you're diggin' yourself." Sam tried to smile, but his eyes flickered in the direction of the storm, his face tightening.

The thunder's grumble over the western mountains cut off Tom's intended response, and he glanced at the looming bank of cloud, then tried to catch Sam's reaction. Sam's eyes returned to the trail, his jaw set.

"Better at least pull down the packs and cover ourselves and all these supplies with a tarp. If that rain makes it over here we'll lose all our flour."

Sam nodded agreement, and without a word he was already swinging his leg over the saddle. They had reached a place where the trail had washed out, with crumbling sides and a fringe of brush. It was going to take a few minutes to find a crossing anyway, and there was no better place to wait out the storm—not that this one was good, but any place close by was equally uniform in its lack of shelter.

They tied the animals in the brush, away from the taller trees, and piled the packs together a few feet out from a limestone face, then crouched against the stone and pulled a tarp over everything. There was one dark blue veil of moisture sweeping to the earth northwest of them that bode their supplies no good.

A couple of back to back lightning strikes made prolonged fluorescent light flicker on the outside of the tarpaulin. Moments later the crash of thunder drowned out the beating of Sam's heart. "Why don't you finish that one about the highwayman?" he suggested to Tom.

The bigger man looked up, surprised to hear him speak. "I stopped when I quit rememberin' what came next. Must have been a sad ending."

"So? Didn't stop you from tellin' the one about Claudus McKnight's partner dyin'."

"Sure, but that was really a *happy* ending," Tom said exuberantly. "Yeah, his partner died, but he found the gold when he was diggin' his grave. What could be happier?"

"Your mother ever tell you you was a mean s.o.b.?"

"My *mother*? No, I don't reckon she ever did mention that!"

Another crash of thunder consumed Sam's retort. It was close, and he cringed and crammed his eyes shut but opened them immediately, avoiding Tom's gaze. In Tom's mind, he cursed. It was not fair for Sam to have so vivid a reminder of such a tragic accident. There weren't many lucid mementos of a disease such as the one that had killed Tom's loved ones. There were certain smells, or the taste of rye whisky such as what he had consumed that fateful day. He still could not drink rye whisky. But he had no souvenir so violent and soul-rending as his friend did with every crash of thunder. Nothing he could say to Sam would ease his mind, not after the decades that had already passed and brought no salve to his heart. If Tom had known of a cure he would have slapped down everything he owned to spare his friend such torture.

The rain arrived in pounding sheets, and for a time it seemed like the thirst of the desert was being slaked. A flash of light now and then showed through the tarp, followed by a sharp clap and roll of thunder, and at those moments the rain seemed to drive much harder against them, almost stinging through the canvas. Yet it didn't take long for them to realize the storm consisted mostly of wind, lightning and thunder. What rain there was served only for show. They had seen storms in east Texas and even in Denver that had sent down several inches before ceasing. This was not such a storm. The water left standing from this one would be gone in a day or two. But it was yet late June. The wet storms of July and August could turn the desert into a flower garden and bring out dormant aquatic life in droves.

A roar and a flash of light seemed to come at them together as if tied to the butt of a huge, severed tree, slamming the rock against which they crouched. Of course nothing but sound had struck the rock, but Tom would have played hell convincing Sam.

With his back to Sam, Tom felt a tremor go through his partner, and he gritted his teeth. He hated to think of the fear that must be upon Sam. He hated that worse than this moment itself, and this feeling of being trapped like a helpless animal under the canvas while the mountains seemed to disintegrate around them.

He heard one of the horses scream, and a mule brayed in answer. He lifted a corner of the tarp and looked out, and through the driving rain he saw the mule tear loose its tether from its smokethorn mooring and wheel away, careening back down the trail. He swore and jerked the canvas over his head, drenching himself with water.

Before he could say anything, he heard a muffled groaning that seemed to arise from the mountain itself. He paused, and Sam half-turned toward him, then was still, listening. Another peel of thunder momentarily drowned the noise, but when the thunder rumbled off it was hard to tell where it ended and the mysterious groaning noise started back up. The sound grew louder, and louder still. It turned to a solid, sustained roar.

The mountain was coming down on them!

Chapter Twelve

Both men tore the canvas from their heads in time to see the surge of brown water boil down the draw not three feet below them. The head of the flood was frothy foam laden with dead brush, rocks and a huge log that tumbled along like a mere a toothpick. They watched in awe as the waves rolled and crashed on down the mountain, making the horses strain against their tethers and shrill out in fright.

Within minutes, the rain had ceased, and only a hint of the wind remained. The two men were soaked clean through their clothes. The flash flood had captivated them so the thought of taking shelter under the tarp again had not crossed their minds.

Where the flood had passed, the rock was bare—scoured clean of dirt and grass. Anything that might have tried to grow there that spring had been robbed of life, as Sam and Tom might have been had they known the desert a little less and taken shelter under the inviting banks of the washout. It had looked like good shelter, but the desert will deceive and destroy a foolish man. It would never do to forget that.

Sam stood up and stretched. The canvas fell to the ground, making water that had pooled on it seek fresh pathways and escape in tiny runnels down into the rocks. The target of the biggest lightning strike was obvious across the draw. Only sixty feet away a sprawling mesquite still smoked, its crown shattered and branches strewn afar. Tom covertly studied his friend. He reached down and picked up a corner of the canvas, raising it to free more water.

"How you feelin', Sam?" he asked in a casual voice.

Sam had walked over to Gringo. By all outward appearances, he was trying to calm the animal, running a hand along his rain-drenched neck and talking softly to him. He didn't even look Tom's way, and it might have appeared to the casual observer as if he hadn't heard. But Sam was only six feet away.

Dragging the canvas, Tom started toward the pack mule. As he came alongside Sam, he laid a hand on his shoulder. Sam pivoted toward him with a blank look. "You all right, pardner?"

Sam sucked a deep breath and nodded. "We made it through another one."

Tom clapped his friend's shoulder. "Reckon we better find a place to sleep close by. It's gettin' too late to look for that mule today, and if he comes lookin' for us he'll come back to this spot."

They threw out their bedrolls among the boulders, although it was almost impossible to clear enough rocks to make a decent bed. At least the nest of boulders would camouflage them should enemies wander by, and out here *anyone* could be their enemy.

Sam lay on his back that night and stared at the stars, so dazzling in the desert, and tonight more than usual. Maybe he just noticed them more—maybe he noticed *everything* more—in the wake of such a storm.

He listened to Tom softly snoring and was comforted. There had been nights in bunkhouses and line camps, box cars, and one night snowed in at a stage stop outside of Red Lodge, Montana, when that snoring had nearly driven Sam through the roof. But now he was as soothed by it as a baby must be by the trill of his mother's lullaby.

The two of them had not spoken much since the storm, or before it, for that matter. And it sure wasn't Tom's doing. How Sam despised his fear! Alone he had fought Apaches on the Mogollon Rim. He had beaten back a posse of angry Mexican vaqueros intent on hanging him for stealing cattle—of which he was only *technically* guilty, since he had killed the calf only out of hunger. He had brought down a bear once with a .45 pistol, saving Tom's life. He had trekked alone into a blizzard to save a hapless family of immigrants from certain doom, and it would have astounded most men who knew him to learn he was not completely fearless. So why should lightning scare him?

Sam sighed. That one star—was that a star, or a planet?—it burned so bright and powerful. What was up there? Angels and a God? Or just vast emptiness with tiny campfires that gave no warmth, and little light? Was his family up there somewhere?

Again, the thunder of that nearby lightning strike crashed through his brain, and he shuddered. In that instant, he could see the blinding streak, as big as a tree trunk, crash once more into his world. Not the strike of today, but the strike of years ago that had taken his family out of the world. What had saved his life that afternoon, and why? He was close enough that by all rights it should have taken him, too. Yet he wasn't even scathed. The lightning had only hurt his eyes and ears, and even those had healed, in time. Well, there was one thing that would never heal—his soul.

Sam had never told anyone, even Tom, how much he hated lightning. He had only told Tom the story, and Tom had watched him and surmised the rest. But it hurt knowing anyone *had* to know this secret. Sam was over fifty years old. Yet he had the fear of lightning that a six-year-old might have—and even most of them didn't. It made him sick in the pit of his stomach, yet after all these years it would not go away.

Somewhere out there, maybe from somewhere like that bright star overhead, Sam liked to believe his folks still watched over him. He had labored harder his whole life than any other man, trying to make them proud.

When Tom blinked his eyes and sat up in his blankets there was a band of subtle gray above the eastern horizon. The morning star still hung bright, and bats flitted through the half-dark, seeking out their last nourishment before the world became too bright to endure.

The morning birds chirped, and flitted through the brush. Sam was asleep. It had probably been a long night for him. But the horses and mules were awake, and restless. His own mount stared at him and stomped a foot. It shook its head, rattling the metal pieces on its halter.

Tom gathered wood and built a tiny fire under the overhang of a boulder. Although a larger warming fire was tempting, too many mountains loomed over them, with too many eyes possibly looking down. He cooked a breakfast of cornmeal gruel. It was not much, but it would put something in their bellies until they could find a better place of concealment.

It was getting lighter now, but even with the eastern sky pale blue, the morning star shone. Tom watched it for a time. That was his wife's star. He had playfully "given" it to her the night they were married. He didn't know anything about the stars, so when she asked him its name he made one up. Cinderfire, he had called it. Cinderfire. She had promptly named her horse after it. Now both of them were gone. Too many years ago. He had never spoken the name of the star aloud again, but Cinderfire lived in his heart. It was where his sweetheart had gone to await him.

After eating his portion of the gruel, Tom walked out into the rain-damp brush and looked downslope. The first thing he made out in the growing light was their wayward mule, grazing without care about four hundred yards below them. Once, it lifted its head to gaze their way. He would not even waste his time going after it. It would come when they started off.

With no mountains in the east to obstruct it, the sun swept early over the Mexican playa. Sam was up at almost the same moment the sunlight struck him, looking bleary-eyed around. It was a good thing Indians had never attacked them in the morning; it took Sam a few minutes to get his senses back about him.

"Sleep good?" asked Tom.

His partner looked over at him, blinking. "Sure. Ain't every night you get to sleep on a rock pile."

Tom gave a lopsided grin. "Why don't you grab a plate? You can add some fine fixin's to the hospitable accommodations."

Sam started to get up, then lay back down and threw an arm over his eyes, letting out a groan. Shaking his head, Tom laughed. "We oughtta make Hermosillo by afternoon today," he guessed. "We've made good time."

Sam sat up. He ran a hand back through his silver-edged hair and picked up his hat, snugging it to its accustomed place above his ears. Shaking his boots out, he pulled them on and staggered to his feet, looking around.

Still smirking at his friend, Tom waved a hand toward the little cove where breakfast waited. Sam ate from the frying pan in silence, seated up on top of the big limestone boulder looking out over the world. He sat there for some time before he noticed the mule standing down the slope grazing.

"That's one stupid mule," he heard Tom say. "Could've been

halfway back to Nogales by now."

"At least you admit he's stupid," Sam shot back mischievously. "We could've been, too. And if we don't get a better cook in Hermosillo we *are* goin' back!"

"Sounds like you just volunteered," replied Tom, drawing up hard on his cinch.

Climbing up on the boulder, Sam looked around. He had to admit it was good to be back in the mountains. The songbirds twittered around them in a melodic chorus. Once in a while he would see one flit from one bush to another, looking for a new crop of seeds, or just moving out of nervousness. The horizon cradled the glaring white globe of the sun, and its fresh morning light bathed the rocks and the vegetation that still sparkled with rain. It gave the massive peaks of the Bacatetes the look of gilded castles on the horizon. And it made yesterday's storm seem like a distant dream.

Tom fit the skillet Sam had scoured clean with sand down in an empty space he had left for it in a pack, then finished drawing up the diamond hitch on the pack and slapped the mule's rump.

"There's millions of dollars waitin'," said Sam. "We best get."

Tom whipped his head around, but it took only one glance at Sam to wipe the surprise from his face. His partner was looking at him with that dubious look of good humor.

"No, I ain't changed my mind. I still think it's a fool's errand. But it's your show."

Tom laughed. "Then let's go—pard."

They had to be close to Hermosillo. Every arroyo taunted them with the expectation of seeing it unfold on the other side. They were riding through the brushy foothills of a branch of rocky mountains with pines fringing their upper ridges. Suddenly, Sam drew Gringo in and waved for Tom to stop.

"Pull into them trees there," Sam ordered. Even without seeing the cause for his concern, Tom obeyed. He had long since learned to follow his partner without pause.

Sam pulled out his field glasses and gazed through them to the west. Finally, he motioned Tom over. Tom took the binoculars and brought them to bear on the object of Sam's interest. Not three hundred yards away were ten or fifteen men dressed in a mixture of short-tailed bolero jackets or vests, and either tan or white cotton trousers or flare-legged *calzoneras*. Atop their heads were flat-crowned hats or big sugar-loaf sombreros. Near them were tied a matching number of horses.

"There's your first look at them banditos we been hearin' about," Sam said. "Mean-lookin' bunch."

"Suppose we ought to ride over there and introduce ourselves?" asked Tom.

Sam looked askance at him and saw that he was joking. He took back the binoculars and stared through them again. "Good idea, pard. Find me in Hermosillo an' let me know how it goes."

The bigger man put his hands on his saddle horn and pushed, stretching his back. He looked up at the sun halfway down the sky.

"I'd sure hate to run into a bunch like that," Tom said.

Sam held up his hand urgently. "Wait."

Coming on the run was a rider. A cloud of dust funneled up behind him as he came through the gray line of mesquite trees. He jerked his mount in, and Sam watched him gesturing back the way he had come, up toward the pine-fringed ridge.

Sam handed the binoculars to Tom again. "What do you make of it?"

While Tom studied the scene, the whole group mounted and started at a good clip toward the mountains.

"I don't rightly know," Tom admitted, "but I say we make tracks toward Hermosillo. I'd say there's somebody up there, and I sure don't want to be between the two of 'em when they meet."

Sam frowned. "I'm curious. These horses need a rest, Curly. Let's take a breather in that patch of mesquite."

With a shrug, Tom stepped down from his bay, followed by Sam. They led their horses over to the trees, well off the trail, and watered themselves and the animals from the water barrels one of the mules was carrying. Tom stretched out in a shady spot, while Sam kept watching the direction in which the bandits had gone, his fingers sweaty against the field glasses.

Twenty or thirty minutes had gone by when he saw movement up the hill again. For the distance, he couldn't make it out clearly, but it appeared to have been made by someone other than the Mexicans, someone coming down from the ridge. Without warning, something flashed mid-slope, accompanied by billowing dust and smoke. Three seconds later there followed a brief leaden report, and Tom swore and sat up, blinking his eyes. "What was that?"

"Dynamite," Sam said, bringing his glasses to bear on the spot again. He saw a couple of horses, hardly more than specks, go racing off in opposite directions. Then there was another cloud of smoke and dust from the trees, and three or four seconds later another loud report.

Tom was standing next to Sam now. "Give me those glasses. What's goin' on?"

"Nothin' you can see. I think you were right—let's get outta here." Another cloud of smoke mushroomed on the mountain, then the ensuing boom.

Suddenly, they heard the clattering of many wings and looked over through the tree branches to see a flock of jays taking off from a copse of mesquite that lay along a gully in the direction they had planned to go. Sam ran for Gringo instinctively and hissed at Tom to do the same. They reached their horses and covered their noses with their hands. Both men looked apprehensively at the pack mules at the same time, but neither man spoke. They turned their heads and gazed toward the trees from where the jays had flown.

In the trees appeared a handful of Indians, copper-colored specters. Their knee-length moccasins with the round toe tabs, their long, straight hair banded by colored cloth, and their wide, flat faces told Sam Coffey these were Apaches, reputedly the deadliest guerilla fighters in the world. And some of the fiercest white man haters known to man. They seemed close enough to hit with a frying pan ...

Chapter Thirteen

Sam and Tom stared toward the Apaches. Pushed to the edge, driven from lands they themselves had stolen at the cost of much bloodshed, now desperate and starving, the Apaches hated white men and Mexicans with the fiercest passion. Sam and Tom were screened by the brush around them, catching only glimpses of the warriors through the trees, but any move was apt to attract attention, and if spotted there would be no mercy.

It was another explosion on the mountain that saved their lives. One of the Indians, for some reason, had turned his eyes in their direction. He didn't appear to see them but seemed to sense something wrong. Then the sound of the explosion came from the mountain, and the Apache whipped his eyes that way, gigging his horse with his heels.

The timely explosion and whatever made the pack mules just stand there quietly and watch the Apaches go by saved the partners from sure death. The mules must have been satisfied with the company of their own companions, and probably the smell of the Indians and their scrubby mountain horses was strange enough to make them lose interest in saying hello.

Not half a minute later Sam and Tom watched as the last of the Indians vanished in the gray desert brush, headed in the direction of the dynamite blasts on the mountain.

Abraham Winborn was not as black as obsidian, but he was near as dark as the eyes of the buckskin horse he rode. His eyes *were* as black as obsidian—black and hard and sharp enough that Apaches might have thought to use them for arrowheads.

Winborn, the man they called Tracker, crouched among the wind-tortured pines just below the ridge top and scanned the environs. Around his neck hung a pair of field glasses his employer, Abijah McGrath, had given him as a gift. But he was loath to use them. He was in dangerous country here, the land of murderous Mexican bandits, Apaches … and the dreaded Yaquis. Binoculars, like a piece of mirror, could make a flash that would show forever through this clear desert air. And Indians, with eyes like eagles, might travel many a mile to investigate something shining out of place.

Their view below was obscured by the trees, but Tracker did not want to leave that screen just yet. He wasn't ready to expose himself to whatever dangers might lay beyond.

Caps had different ideas. He watched the black man as long as he could stand it, then stepped up alongside him. "If you ain't gonna use them glasses, darkie, give 'em to me. I don't care if you got the eyes of a buzzard, you'll see more *with* 'em than without."

Tracker's gaze could have bored postholes. "Ain't nobody takes my glasses, mister. They'll be used, but not till there's no other way." At that very moment he saw a flash of light from below. He jerked his eyes that way and for a long time stood staring, Caps forgotten at his right shoulder. Finally, his lips parted. "You wanna see why I don't like usin' these?" He pointed down the ridge, where to him several dark shapes were plain against the gray mesquite branches. "They're usin' glasses."

Caps and the others had all seen the flash of light, too, and they strained their eyes to see whatever Tracker was looking at. "Go ahead." Tracker slipped the strap of the binoculars over his head and handed them to Caps. "They're already watchin' us."

Looking sharply at the black man, Caps raised the glasses to his eyes and scanned the rolling hills and rocky gullies. At last he spied the dark knot that eventually materialized into five animals tied in the trees. Then the binoculars below made their flash again.

Suddenly, Tracker swore and reached for his rifle, slipping it with a sucking noise from the scabbard under his stirrup leather as his horse shied away at the sudden movement. Tracker, ignoring the startled looks of the others, ran to an upslanted, flat-topped boulder and fell onto it, his sharp eyes picking through the trees. One of the horses let out a long whinny. Almost instantly it was answered by one, then another, perhaps two hundred yards down the ridge.

Burt's eyes snapped over to Scrub. "Damn, that boy's got ears like a wolf! He heard them horses coming!"

Scrub didn't reply, just pulled out his pistol and scrambled to where Tracker had bellied down on the rock.

"Hola, amigos!" The cry rang up through the air, reverberating off the uneven rim of rock at their backs.

The would-be thieves all looked at each other, startled. Tracker's face was expressionless as he scanned the trees. He picked up a movement, then a brown face. Soon, a man dressed in a white shirt and tan calzoneras, the fancy Mexican pants with flare legs, stepped out from the trees, his rifle held aloft in one hand.

"Amigos! Let me see you."

"There's only one man," Tracker heard Lug say, from off to one side. He frowned but made no comment. He did not know how many men were down there, but he had heard a lot more than one.

"Should I shoot 'im?" Scrub piped up.

"Yeah," Tracker growled sarcastically out the side of his mouth. "Shoot him an' the other dozen with him."

"There ain't no—"

"Shut up!" Caps cut Scrub off. He was looking through the trees at a light buckskin that had moved its head in the pines and revealed the dark eyes of another bandit standing next to it. "I see another one."

"Four," said Tracker. "I see four, and I heard a lot more. I guess you better start talkin' fast, Caps, or we gonna be in a shootin' match."

Burt's eyes flashed at the black man, miffed that he would single out Caps as the group's spokesman. He stepped forward, trying not to reveal too much of himself beyond the rocks. "We ain't lookin' for trouble!" he yelled down.

A chuckle rose from the trees. It wasn't the man who had spoken before, but now that one laughed, too, and his big white teeth nearly sparkled in the sunlight.

Lug exclaimed, "Them teeth are whiter than Tracker's!"

The black man ignored him as the speaker of the Mexicans opened up again. "Of course you are not looking for trouble, amigo! Nor are we! It is just *mi compradre* and me here. We are hunting some cattle that have wandered away. You have seen them?"

"Blow the liar's head off!" Scrub growled.

"You shut up or I'll blow yours off!" Stratton said sharply.

Scrub gave him an angry look, but the killing light in Stratton's eyes kept him silent. As fast as Scrub liked to think he was, he sensed he was no match for Stratton.

"Well, what're we gonna do, Burt?" Johnny Riles finally found his voice.

No one seemed to hear Johnny. It was plain the Mexicans were up to no good, and they all knew they were in trouble. The Mexicans were lying about how many were down there; why would they do that unless they intended on setting a trap?

Caps caught a movement in the trees beyond the Mexican. Looking there, after a moment he saw a man creeping up the slope on his belly, screened by brush. He scanned to the left, and after ten seconds' scrutiny he found another one there, or at least the foot of one that slipped behind a patch of vegetation.

"It's now or never, Burt," he said casually. The tone of fear that was in Burt's voice, and Scrub's, Lug's and Johnny's, was curiously absent in Caps's. "They're tryin' to flank us, my friend."

Burt yelled down again. "We're just waiting for our ten friends to catch up. We're going to Hermosillo to pick up some cattle from a Mexican friend of ours."

Caps smirked at the back of Burt's head. Who did the boy think he was fooling? These were bandits! Even if Burt's words were true it would mean nothing to them; Burt obviously thought having a Mexican friend was going to put him in their good graces. But bandits were as likely to kill their own people as any other race.

Shaking his head, Caps walked over to his saddlebags. He pulled out five sticks of dynamite, then started fishing in his vest pockets as he went at a crouch farther along the ridge. He would show these little boys in a startling way why he was known as Caps!

Pulling from his pocket a handful of little wooden plugs—blasting caps—with fuses already hanging out of them, Caps began to push them into the previously excavated ends of his dynamite, compacting them as deeply and solidly as they would go. With a smile, he removed a match from the same pocket where the blasting caps had been. He scratched the match across a piece of limestone and touched it to the end of a fuse. Sitting up, he counted to ten, then threw the dynamite down into the trees.

There was a brief pause. Then the mountain seemed to explode in thunder, and debris spewed everywhere. Horses screamed, startled yelps rose from the timber, and the bandit spokesman turned and almost fell in his haste to escape. A horse took off galloping across a sidehill clearing to the left. Another ran to the right. Others could be heard crashing down through the trees.

There was a big smile on Caps's lips as his second match touched a fuse, and fifteen seconds after the first blast another shook the mountain. There was no firing back. One man below was crying. The cries soon turned to a whimper.

A spiteful shot broke the air, and bits of rock scattered beneath Burt McGrath, so Caps gleefully lit another stick of dynamite and sent it spinning downslope. He watched its dangerous arc, and a laugh that reeked of pure pleasure shook his chest. A man gave a dull cry as the miniature bomb exploded. By the sound of his voice it was the last cry he would make.

There was no more shooting on the part of the bandits, but Scrub Ottley sent a few bullets snipping down through the trees, more out of fun than in expectation of hitting anything. "Whoo-ee! You showed them greasers!" he yelled.

"Shut up," Temp Stratton said, his eyes hard as gun butts. "You better go clean out your drawers. You're just a scared pup barkin' at wolves."

Caps looked at Scrub and knew Stratton spoke true. Scrub was scared, all right, not only of the Mexicans but of the white man standing before him staring at him like he was gutter swine.

To break the tension, Caps laughed again. "Ol' Temp's just funnin' yuh, kid! You're right, we showed them greasers we won't be messed with." He held up a couple of the wooden plugs he had pulled from his vest. "Any o' you boys ever wonder why they call me 'Caps?' Heh heh. Blastin' caps. I always say you can't carry too many." Without warning, he primed another stick of dynamite and said sharply, "Temp!" and tossed the dynamite up into the air over the trees where the Mexicans had been.

With unbelievable speed, Stratton drew his pistol and from the hip shot the whirling dynamite in mid-air. The explosion shook the trees, spattering the lot of them with tiny, harmless fragments as a gust of hot gas pushed them back, almost making Johnny fall.

"Last town we was in, they took to callin' us Caps and the Gun," he said. "He's the Gun."

The four young men stared at Stratton as the last of the smoke drifted out of his gun barrel. Scrub swallowed hard.

Chapter Fourteen

Caps O'Brien sat on a boulder and rolled a cigarette, looking down the mountain at the rocks and ragged tree tops. After twenty minutes or so he saw a knot of riders straggle out of the lower tree line and make their way into an arroyo, disappearing from sight.

Temp Stratton smoked his own cigarette down to its most miniscule stub, then flung it into the brush carelessly, its tip still aglow. His eyes hard and brooding, he studied the back of Scrub Ottley's head.

Tracker Winborn hung off by himself. He was a loner even back at the McGrath ranch, but even more aloof with this group. His hat hung from a thong at his throat, and he watched, expressionless, as the Mexican bandits disappeared into the gulch.

Finally, Caps stood up. "Well, I reckon we know where our boys are now," he said. He motioned toward where they had seen the flash from the field glass lens earlier, along with the dark shapes of the horses.

Stratton was studying the grove of trees where the horses had been, grayed with the distance. "Well, they ain't there anymore."

"How fur you figure they could have got?" asked Lug Colton.

Caps looked over at the black man. "Well, darkie? How far?"

Tracker's eyes cut to Caps. Black fire glowed deep within them, but a perceptive man would also have observed the wariness not far beneath the surface. "You forgot. It's Mister Winborn. Your guess is good as mine … whitey. Ain't been half an hour, and they got pack mules. Hustlin' up, they mighta got five miles behind 'em."

Caps stared at Tracker. There was humor around his mouth, but the same humor did not surround his eyes. Finally, his gaze softened, and he chuckled. "Five miles maybe. Well, that's good. We gotta

give 'em enough lead to take us to that gold before we tip our hand—
Mister Winborn."

Tracker's eyes narrowed. They jumped to Burt, then back to Caps, then Stratton. The entire trip down here Caps and Stratton, and even Burt, had been acting real careful about their intentions as to the two men they followed. But the more Tracker observed Caps and Stratton, the way they talked between themselves, the way they acted with the younger men, he knew this was a bad situation. No matter what Burt and the others might have been lulled into believing, Caps and Stratton had no qualms about killing the two strangers when they got that gold. No qualms at all. Could young Burt really be so stupid as to think they intended only on sharing the gold?

Tracker's gaze scanned to the horses. He was still holding his rifle, and now he walked over and shoved it down into the boot.

Caps took the cue. "Let's make trail, boys. Who knows when them Messicans might come back with help?"

Burt quickly spoke up, afraid of losing his imagined status as the group's leader. "Yeah, come on, boys, mount up!" He didn't catch Caps's amused smirk. But he caught the warning look in Tracker's eyes.

They rode off down the mountain in single file. Caps halted in the trees to stare at a puddle of blood in the grass, and farther along lay the remains of one bandit who had been too close to one of the sticks of dynamite. It had torn him nearly in two.

A couple of minutes later, with all of them mounted and moving downhill, Tracker pulled alongside Burt and spoke nonchalantly in a voice as quiet as he could make it. "We gotta talk, boy. An' we gotta talk soon. You're in with a couple o' rattlers here. There ain't a bone in my body that doubts they're gonna kill them two boys we're followin' the second they get hold of that gold. Whether you like it or not. I know you like to feel you're in charge o' this bunch, Burt. But you ain't. You better start thinkin' real hard an' fast of a way to get us outta this, or it's gonna come to shootin'. And somebody's gonna—"

"What you whisperin' about, nigger?" Temp Stratton growled suddenly, coming alongside the two of them.

Tracker looked over at him, careful because he knew Stratton could jerk his pistol much faster than he could maneuver his rifle. "We're just talkin' about home ... whitey." As much as he knew he shouldn't have called Stratton that, he couldn't resist. Without another word, he gave Burt a last look of deadly warning, touched spurs to his mount and rode to the head of the group.

Tracker led the way straight toward the trees where they had seen their quarry and the horses. He kept wary eyes on the country around them, but his main goal was making it to that mesquite grove so he could get on some kind of trail to follow. Only now he knew he couldn't lead this group all the way to the gold, and to the two gold hunters. He was going to have no part in any killings or thievery, and he was positive that Caps and Stratton were set on both. But right now there was another fact glaring him savagely in the face: to try and back out was as good as suicide. Caps and Stratton would never knowingly let him ride off, not when he was their ticket to finding those two.

The last stretch of the mountain before they came down into what could be considered foothills consisted of a massive garden of broken granite boulders and scrub brush. A few sizeable trees clumped among the rocks, but mostly the larger stuff could find no hold in the callous ground. The six men got in line and picked their way through the rocks, watching for snakes while they scanned ahead to the flatland where they had last seen Coffey and Vanse.

They had nearly reached the bottom of the rock cluster when a familiar voice rang down to them from above.

"Hola, amigos! We meet again!"

Surrounded on all sides by rocks, brush and cactus, it was pointless for the six manhunters to try and run. One look around told them there were Mexican bandits everywhere. Their leader was standing on a boulder fifty yards above, where he had secreted himself until just the right moment. The Mexicans had no horses in sight. They must have tied them beyond the rocks, then worked their way back to wait for the little cavalcade to come down the mountain.

Caps's eyes shot back and forth, gauging the enemy's strength. The Mexican who had spoken to them before seemed to be the leader.

He was the only one doing any talking, and he had the look of a leader, as well. There were at least ten others in the rocks around them, all standing and holding rifles either pointed casually at the riders or nestled in the crooks of their arms. The lot of them appeared relaxed, but in their eyes were the looks of brown tigers ready to pounce.

"So, amigos, you like to use the dynamite, eh?" spoke the Mexican leader. "You think you pretty smart. Let me see you use that dynamite now. Can you throw up this hill?"

Caps's mind flashed to the rest of the dynamite in his saddlebags. He had at least a couple dozen more sticks. He had packed plenty, knowing the demoralizing effect even one explosion could have on a group of would-be foes. But the wily Mexican had planned his ambuscade carefully; there was no way he could throw the dynamite to any good effect up this slope, even if he could have pulled it out without getting shot. Caps sighed. Ever since Yuma, he had known he would die on a hot day in the desert. He just did not know it would be today. But this had come down to a question of who had more firepower—specifically rifles. And there was no way he and Temp Stratton were going to best these Mexicans, not with the four rank amateurs they had to back them now. Caps had never been one to roll over. He would make a fight now, and he would die. But he would take the bandit leader with him.

"Hey, amigo!" Caps smiled at the leader of the bandits. "There's a lot of gold where we're headed. You come with us, we'll split it with you. Maybe we could help each other—keep the Yaquis and Apaches back. What do you say?"

The Mexican leader let his eyes jump to a couple of his comrades, then back to Caps. "Ohhh. You are very smart, señor! Gold! Very funny, no? This is country for silver, not gold. You are not dealing with a fool!"

"I don't think you're a fool," Caps retorted amiably. "But I'm tellin' you, there's a cache of gold in these mountains that would make us rich. All of us! We only have to find two men we've been followin'. They have a map that will take us right to it."

"Oh, yes. I have seen such maps." The Mexican burst into a fit of laughter. "I think you really believe what you are telling me. It is a shame that we cannot share all of that gold, you and I. You will be dead, and then unfortunately I will not be able to find any gold. Such a shame!" He laughed again. Then his face went hard. "Amigo, you killed my compadre Anton. For this you must die."

He started to raise his rifle.

Caps had survived a long and arduous career by being cunning and adaptable, practicing moving fast and doing the unexpected. He didn't try to draw his pistol and shoot at the Mexican. The pistol would have been the fastest weapon to get in his hand, but the Mexican was too far away, and not handicapped by sitting on a horse. Caps was not in the habit of bucking unbeatable odds like a rifle at fifty yards.

Throwing himself against the horse's neck, he rolled sideways off the saddle, at the same time jerking his rifle free of the scabbard. Barely keeping his feet when he landed in the rocks, he slapped the horse's rump to send it clattering away from him.

Rifle shots exploded all around. Lug Colton, caught completely by surprise, took at least three bullets in the first round of fire. He was a big man, but half an ounce of lead beats two hundred seventy pounds of human flesh. The bullets clutched Lug and carried him from his saddle and dashed him against the rocks like a wet towel.

Caps aimed at the Mexican bandit as the man's rifle centered on him. He squeezed his trigger first, and as the cloud of smoke erupted from the barrel the Mexican bandit pulled himself up straighter, then dropped his rifle and plunged over the side of the rock. Bullets whined everywhere, one dangerously near Caps's head, showering him with rock fragments. He spun and wasted a shot toward the new threat, then ducked into the rocks.

There are few sounds as terrifying as the ricochet of rifle bullets in a rock quarry. But without warning one more harrowing rent the air: the screams of Apache warriors.

Caps looked up through the rocks in time to see a rush of copper bodies clad scantily in breechclouts and moccasins, colored cloth holding back their hair. He saw one, then two Mexican bandits fall in the onslaught, and then he stopped watching. It was one thing to fight bandits with the knowledge that he would die. It was altogether another to fight an enemy who would do his utter best to keep him alive only to suffer the worst tortures the human mind could conjure up.

With the ring of Apache yells in his head and the glimpse of another Mexican bandit catapulting backward off a rock with an arrow in his chest, Caps turned and fled.

The sleepy town of Hermosillo was no place to be in the summer of 1886. It was hot and dusty, barren and dry. With the Yaquis making war, commerce was slow in Sonora, and the quiet streets of Hermosillo at first glance were devoid of any sign of life.

Big Tom Vanse rode his bay past the entrance to the town with the easy, slouched posture of a man with years in the saddle behind him, too many of them just that day. His dirty wide-brimmed hat shaded his green eyes and whiskered face, and the Spencer carbine in his scabbard sawed back and forth beneath his thigh.

Beside Tom, Sam's red-rimmed eyes scanned the lifeless streets of this somnolent adobe town. He brought a hand up to scratch his jaw, whiskered so thickly his face looked blue-black well up past his cheekbones. Watchers on the street took in this hard-looking rider with scars on his hands and his face and a dark gaze that appeared almost fiercely intense. In truth all Sam Coffey wanted right now was a quiet corner table, a meal and a long drink of water.

They rode into the drowsy plaza with an orange fireball of sun striking sideways at them from the west. Their hats and linen dusters, horses, rifle butts and boots all carried a coat of white dust lifted from the desert. On the far side of the plaza, on an undistinguished square adobe, a sign heralded them: CANTINA. Without exchanging words, they rode that way.

The town did not appear much different than most Mexican towns. It hosted the usual array of scattered adobes and brush *jacales,* the standard refuse scattered like broken bones, and a pair of hogs rooting in the dirt, heedless to the passage of the two men and their mules. They stopped at the unassuming adobe cantina. Five huge bundles of red peppers hung there from protruding rafters, one of them intertwined with garlic.

The sign on the door that read, Cantina, was small. The larger word was written below it: "BIENVENIDOS." Welcome. It was written in a dainty hand across the incongruous slabs of oak that had been used to fashion the door.

Alongside the quiet cantina was a corral, where the partners loosened their cinches and turned in their horses where water waited in an inviting trough. They did not bother to remove their rifles or any other piece of gear before stepping inside the establishment.

It was dark in the smoky shadows. The only illumination came from two small windows set high in the wall for smoke to escape. The walls were foot-thick adobe brick, allowing little light and less heat, and making it comfortably cool in here after the harsh glare of the sun.

There was a long bar built of oak planks at the left side of the room, and only four tables set about the small room. There was a sturdy oaken back door like the one in front, with a dog-eared saddlery advertisement tacked askew in its middle.

Sam and Tom ordered drinks from a bucktoothed, emaciated bartender who eyed them a bit suspiciously and spoke little. The dead silence of the place impressed Sam. It was so quiet he could hear the tinkle of liquor as it spilled into his shot glass. The only other person moving around in the room besides him and Tom was a señorita wearing a thin white cotton dress, of which only the top part showed above the bar.

This black-eyed señorita was the most beautiful Mexican woman Sam had seen since a little cantina in El Paso where Tom's charms had inadvertently almost gotten the two of them killed, ending with them running into the New Mexico badlands, a gang of vaqueros hot on their trail. The last they heard of the vaqueros, they were laughing in glee, nearly too drunk to steady themselves in the saddle, as they rode back toward the *"Paso del Norte."*

Tom was a big man, six-foot-four in his socks, and broad across the chest and shoulders. This physique and his sharp nose, thick brows and big green eyes, the dimples that creased his cheeks, and the carefully groomed mustache had always drawn women. Sam laughed at how they looked at him as if longing to run their fingers through his curly brown hair and be a … a mother to him. At least it seemed that way to Sam.

Tom didn't have a whole lot of use for feminine company, however, although he would share a friendly drink with them. His true love was his Beverly, and when he had lost her he seemed to have lost the better part of his soul.

It did not take long for Sam to see the young señorita had set her eyes on Tom. They had no more than sat down when she came to their table.

"What could I bring you?" she asked in her own tongue. Her voice had a strong, appealing accent.

Sam answered in Spanish. "Please bring us *frijoles y tortillas*. We are very hungry."

From off to the street side of the establishment a wizened little Mexican man with crevices scratched along the sides of his mouth came toward the table and caught the woman's sleeve as she was turning away. "Wait just a moment," the old man said. She turned back around, and he went on, "I would like you two caballeros to meet my little friend. This is Anjanetti Silva."

Tom and Sam looked at each other, then back at the old Mexican, stunned momentarily by his interruption and by the mouthful of name.

The old man smiled broadly, lighting up his eyes and revealing his broken teeth. "Americanos who come to Hermosillo just call her Anna."

Anna Silva smiled as each of the men took her hand in greeting. Her eyes lingered on Tom's face until Sam spoke, when she turned her glance on him. She said in her native tongue, "What a voice!" Then, blushing, she walked away.

The old Mexican sat down abruptly across from Sam and put his hands on top of the table. "You two are loaded heavily, I see from your animals. You are here to prospect for silver, no?"

Sam raised a brow. "Who are you?"

"I am called Hector Ramón Calvaza. Here they call me the old loco who sees everything and knows nothing." His eyes hooded slowly over, until they were mere slits. They flickered back and forth between the partners. "But Hector Calvaza knows everything of importance in Hermosillo … in Sonora … in *Mexico!* There is a thing you would like to know, you caballeros Americanos, you ask Hector Calvaza."

"I don't believe you know what we need to know," said Sam conversationally.

"One thing I know: I made a misjudgment. You do not come looking for the silver like all of the other caballeros Americanos. No, you two Americanos, you come looking for the gold of the Yaquis."

Tom and Sam sat completely quiet. Hector Ramón Calvaza could not have fastened their eyes to his face any more effectively with a bucket of tar.

"Do not sit with your mouths hanging open. You will catch flies." The old man's eyes crinkled as Sam and Tom sank back in their chairs. They both looked at the Mexican in a new light. He was more than just a meddling old man, it seemed.

"This Yaqui gold—there are a lot of people who know about it?" asked Tom.

The old man laughed. "*Every* Mexicano in Hermosillo knows about it. Only one or two foolish Americanos look for it. There were two others one year past who come looking for this gold. Only one man came away, and he did not even care to stop again in Hermosillo. He rode fifty miles to the north, where only some vaqueros saw him. This man, he ran for the north like el Diablo he was chasing him." Abe Varnell …

"So why do you tell us this?" Tom queried.

"Because in Hermosillo we know not to go near this hidden treasure. The Yaquis guard it with their lives—and with your deaths. And if you get past them you contend with the banditos who claim these mountains. Beyond them, waiting, are the Apaches. You try to find the gold in those mountains, you die. By one means or another, you die. And then perhaps you bring disfavor upon Hermosillo as well."

"We came here looking for an old blind Seri Indian and his wife," Tom offered. "Do you know him?"

"Yes, I know of him. He is an old fool who would commit suicide with his stupidity."

"He is still alive then?"

"Si. He lives miles from here. Toward the mountains. But you must not pursue your journey, my two nuevo amigos. I am not lying to you. The gods do not favor a man who goes into the Sierra Bacatete. If you do not die you will very likely wish that you did."

Stubborn because he didn't like being warned away from anything, Sam said, "We are looking for this old Seri Indian. If you would show the way to him we have a message for him from a friend."

The old Mexican shrugged. "The choice is yours, amigos. But I am quite certain in telling you, if you go on with what you seek, you will die in Mexico. And only the wind will be there to bury your bones."

Chapter Fifteen

Caps O'Brien ran for all he was worth from the battle that had become Mexican against Apache. He fell once and scraped up his face but got up and kept running. It was five minutes before he made any attempt at trying to figure out his whereabouts. Five minutes punctuated by the occasional ring of rifle or pistol shot, occasionally a scream.

Finally, the day was still. He crept on through the rocks, his fingers bleeding from the tiny wounds made by prickly pear spines. He didn't find the others, but they found him.

Tracker and Johnny Riles came upon Caps while he was sitting on a boulder trying to pluck stickers out of his knee, where his pants had been ripped by the rock he had fallen on. One moment Caps was looking down, intent on a stubborn spine, and the next he felt eyes upon him and whirled to see Tracker. Then Johnny appeared from the rocks behind him, shaken and white-faced.

"We gotta move," Tracker said, as if they had been together all along. "Those Apaches will be lookin' for us. No doubt they're about done with your Mexican friends."

Caps came off his boulder seat as if spring-loaded. "Where to?"

"Back in them rocks. I got our horses."

Caps perked up. If he had never realized Tracker's value before he certainly did now. *Too bad you're colored,* Caps thought, stopping short of saying it aloud. *You might have made a good partner.* Tracker was definitely a good hand to have around, but Caps would never have admitted that to any of his "equals."

They climbed down through the rocks in silence, only looking back once in a while. When they reached the horses, tied securely in a patch of mesquite, Caps glanced around. "Where's the rest of our boys?"

"Don't know that," said Tracker simply, going to his horse and drawing the cinch tight. "And I don't know's we better stick around to find out. Those 'Paches be breathin' down our collars soon. Them boys are old enough to watch out for theirselves."

Young Johnny studied Tracker's impassive face. He spoke for the first time since the black man had found him, his face filled with apprehension. "You … you reckon any of them lived?"

The black man shrugged, looking understandingly at Johnny. "Sorry, boy. Don't know that neither. Not Lug. I seen that."

Johnny's face paled, and Caps nodded. "Yeah, he took a few hard hits. Well, what do you know about this country, nigger?"

Tracker looked over sharply at Caps. "I know I ain't no 'nigger', first off." He took the saddle horn and swung into the saddle without touching his stirrup, then looked down at Caps. "And otherwise all I know is Hermosillo is yonder way, and that's where we best be headed if we wanna live."

"Fine by me," said Caps. "Me an' Temp decided if we got separated we'd just keep on like we would if we was together. Sooner or later we'll meet up if we're able."

Johnny swallowed hard and fought his trembling fingers to stuff the end of his latigo into some form of a knot. Then he and Caps climbed aboard, and they started southeast.

Temp Stratton stood beside his horse with Scrub Ottley and Burt McGrath sitting in the shade of a boulder. He squinted across the desert, then back into the high rocks where the battle had taken place. No movement. What were the Apaches doing? Were they on their way? Perhaps they didn't care about the white men. Perhaps the Mexicans had left enough booty to satisfy them. A nice thought, but Stratton was no optimist.

"Get your carcasses up." He flashed his scorn at the two younger men, whose shirts were soaked with sweat. None of the three had been wounded in escaping the fusillade, nothing short of a miracle.

Burt and Scrub stood up. Burt forced his melancholy thoughts about Lug Colton out of his head and looked at Stratton. He had something to say, but before saying it he caught Stratton's hard stare. His eyes flickered around for a moment while he dug up nerve to try and recapture some of his leadership. "We'll head home, I reckon. That's probably where the rest of them are headed, if they're alive."

"Head back if you want to," replied Stratton tersely. "That's the way the Apaches are waitin'."

"What else can we do?"

Stratton's hard blue eyes pierced him. "Caps and me already talked about that. I ain't worried about my pardner. Him and that darkie will be canny. They'll head downhill and wait for us. If we don't meet up with 'em they'll start to head toward Hermosillo. It should be off to the south and east somewhere, according to what that nigger told us. If they're alive, we'll find 'em there. If not, they'll start lookin' for them fellers' trail and keep goin' after the gold."

Burt shrugged. "Well, I'm all for finding out where the others went. I've been with Johnny for a long time. I'd hate to leave him down here if there's a way to join back up."

Stratton smirked. "Me, I'm all for findin' them two boys with the pack mules. I didn't ride all this way to go back without gold."

Out of Hermosillo the following morning, Sam Coffey and Tom Vanse rode in search of the homestead of Paco, the Seri Indian. In the unwelcoming foothills of the Bacatete Mountains, they found it. It was the only spot with any real greenery as far as the eye could detect.

Tom and Sam rode up to the house and stepped down. They glanced around the quiet yard, where chickens clucking and scratching at the lifeless dust seemed to be the only life until a roadrunner scampered across a clearing twenty yards away.

"If the old man ain't around maybe we'll be eatin' chaparral rooster for dinner," said Tom.

"Not with these plump chickens standin' around here gawkin' we won't." Sam turned to the front door. "Hello the house."

There was a muffled scraping inside. Then the gray wooden door creaked open, and a man aping a curled brown piece of leather stood in the doorway. Scar tissue surrounded one of his eyes, and behind its lid was merely a dark slit. The other eye was there, but he didn't appear to see much out of it, either. This must be the "Paco" Abe Varnell had told them about.

"Can I help you?" asked the old man in Spanish. He seemed at ease with the sudden appearance of the two strangers, as if the thought of death didn't frighten him at all.

"We came from a friend of yours," said Sam in his rough imitation of the Mexican language. "He told me to show you this."

Knowing the old man could hardly see, Sam walked close to him. He stopped three feet away and stretched out his arm toward the old Seri, holding the pouch.

For a moment, the man stood there, sniffing the breeze. He must have smelled the buckskin and the tobacco that had been kept there. Perhaps he smelled the scent of his wife, whose hands had made it. Whatever it was, a smile engulfed his face, and he reached out and took the buckskin pouch, fingering it to confirm his suspicions.

"Ah! My friend Abraham!" he beamed. "You know Abraham!"

"Yes sir, old man. Abraham Varnell is an amigo of ours." Sam turned and looked at Tom, whose soft smile belied how the old man's obvious fondness for Varnell touched his heart.

"Come into my home," said Paco. "Enter. Enter!" He let them go before him, then slipped through the doorway himself, leaving the plank door open. "You would like something to eat? To drink?"

"Just water," Tom replied. "Water would be mighty good."

Sam looked around the room, searching for sign of any other inhabitants of the place. There were none. Where was the wife Varnell had spoken of?

While Sam and Tom sat and sipped water, savoring the cool feel of it wetting down their throats, the old man was silent, fondling the buckskin bag, sniffing it, rubbing it against his cheek. Finally, he sighed. "You have come for the gold."

Sam and Tom looked at each other in surprise. "Well ...You are right," Sam replied. "Abraham was afraid to come back to Mexico. I guess you do not know what happened to him after he left here, but it was bad. He found the gold, but the Yaquis caught him and his partner. His partner did not live, but he did. Only now he lives in fear." He struggled with the Spanish, knowing it must sound stilted and unnatural.

"I have heard," said Paco. "The Yaquis, they come, they tell me what happened. Then…"

"*Que?*" Tom asked.

"They took my wife. I have not seen her since."

Something gripped Sam's throat. It must have struck Tom, too, for both sat silent, staring at the old man. "*Lo siento,*" said Tom. "I am sorry for your loss."

"I do not think you should stay in Mexico," Paco went on. "In the Sierra Bacatete you will die—in a horrible way."

Tom and Sam glanced at each other again. Sam couldn't speak, but Tom seemed to be doing fine. "*No quedaremos,*" the bigger man said. "We will not stay. But Abraham told us you could direct us to the gold. We will take only what we can carry one time. Then we will be gone."

A tight smile came to the old man's face. "You *Americanos* all are alike. You think once is enough, but never is it enough. Once, you will take the gold, then you will come back again and again until you are caught. But if you want the gold so bad, stay with me today. Eat this noon, again tonight. In the morning I will show you the way. But the way to the gold, it is also the way to your graves."

As the old man had promised, they ate a good dinner, spent the day keeping him company, then ate once more, at supper time. At dawn they woke to a filling breakfast, and then Paco pulled down a dusty old box from the mantle of his fireplace. The box came open with a creak, and his wrinkled hands shuffled around inside it until they touched on a folded piece of buckskin, which he took out of the box. Turning, with the leather in both hands, he walked to the partners. He paused, then laid the buckskin on the table top, unfolding it and spreading it out before them. There it was, the missing piece to the puzzle held by Sam.

Paco sat with them to explain the wriggly and sharp lines, and the words on the map, and to tell them the way to the Yaqui Gold. Sam couldn't help the nagging feeling that by giving these directions Paco was placing his own life in jeopardy. But the old Indian showed no hesitation.

Before they left, he pointed off in the direction they would travel. "There is another one up there."

Sam and Tom looked at each other questioningly, then Sam looked back at Paco. "I'm not sure I understand."

"Another one. Another man, perhaps younger than you. Three weeks before, he passed this way. He also searched for treasure, but I did not tell him about the gold. He is seeking silver. This one, he drove a wagon with two strong oxen. He was a kind man. Perhaps you will look for him when you are in the mountains. Maybe it will be that you will come out together."

Sam spoke in English to Tom. "How about that? More than two fools out here at once!"

Tom just grunted. "What was this fellow's name?"

"He called himself Silas Ranstrum."

Tom smiled, although he knew the old man really couldn't see him. "Well, *viejo,* we'll look him up."

Of course neither Tom nor Sam really thought they would run into this Silas Ranstrum, but it didn't hurt to appease the old man.

They followed Abe Varnell's carefully drawn maps and the instructions Paco provided them. Old Paco had a grasp of life, Sam figured. Perhaps he was just fatalistic, but he seemed completely at ease with everything around him, even the chance that he might die for this transgression. He surely knew the danger in giving them directions to the gold; the Yaquis had proved their fetish for torture.

They startled a basking rattlesnake on the trail early in the morning. Sam's horse balked, and he reined him wide around the big serpent, looking down with his skin crawling. "Big ugly thing," he said. The snake coiled there on a rock, its rattle going wild. Its head seemed to fill with air every time it breathed in, and what a pair of eyes! Tom had killed a rattler once after they had been out in the desert for two days with nothing but water. He had tried to convince Sam to partake of it, but he had no interest. In the end,

Tom just threw it away. He didn't have the appetite either.

Around mid-afternoon, perhaps thirty miles from Paco's place, they crossed a dry wash and witnessed a startling sight: the remains of a wagon with debris collected around its wheels. They were too surprised to say anything, but the partners stopped at the wagon as if on signal. They looked up one end of the draw, then down the other.

They could see the wagon had not been here long, so it seemed obvious who it belonged to: Silas Ranstrum. What would possess a man to bring a wagon out here? It had been a canvas-covered wagon, but there had been a fire, and the front half of the canvas had burned. The rest, oddly enough, was still in good shape.

Tom looked over at Sam. "Indians, you figure?"

Sam shrugged, nudging Gringo in closer to the wagon bed. He peered in through the front of the wagon, where a few pieces of canvas fluttered from the scorched ribs it had been attached to. Inside was a single crate and a few other jumbled items, none of them of much obvious value. Intrigued, Sam looked over the wagon a little closer until something struck him hard. There was a large, splintery hole in what was left of the wagon seat, and leaning up against the front of the seat, reduced to rusting metal and a little charred wood, was a rolling block rifle.

Sam swallowed hard, looking up involuntarily at the sky. "This wasn't Injuns," he told Tom. "It was lightning." He pointed out the hole in the seat, and the rifle that looked like it had also been struck, then burned. "Rain must've put out the rest of the fire. It burned that big hole there in the front of the bed, but the back part and that canvas ain't touched." Then he noted the lack of substantial supplies in the back of the wagon, along with the lack of human remains. "Well, Injuns might've found it later and taken anything they thought was valuable. But I'd still bet this feller's end came long before any Injuns happened by."

Tom was studying his partner's face. Sam felt it and looked over, and for several seconds their gazes held. The mutual thought was plain: lightning, the bane of Sam Coffey's life.

Sam scanned the lightning storm's battleground once more. In front of the wagon, some still inside the tree and mingled with the rotting and chewed harness, were a few large bones, and under a catclaw bush a little ways off bleached an ox skull. Sam's eyes caught boots protruding from the far side of the off front wheel, then looked farther to see, among rumpled clothing, the grisly remains of a human skull picked clean by scavengers. He turned with gritted teeth and touched spurs to his horse, saying, "There's what's left of Ranstrum. You don't outrun lightning."

Tom lingered for a moment, riding around to gaze at the skeleton. What this sight must have done to Sam! He sighed and spurred away, pulling alongside Sam. For a while, he watched the relaxed bob of his horse's head, the twisting back and forth of its ears.

Abhorring the eerie quiet, he said, "Some people are born with bad luck. You figure he knew what hit him?"

Sam sighed, the side of his face twitching. "I doubt it. Looks like that off wheel was broke an' he was down there fixin' it." Prospecting, thought Sam. With no sure knowledge of any treasure. What a sorry excuse for being here. And no excuse whatever that was intelligent, in his opinion—which also applied to him and Tom!

The going became rougher. The wagon would not have made it much farther. The trail took Sam and Tom through canyons and narrow passageways and over the tops of craggy, broken ridges that would kill a careless man or horse. The wayward mule lagged forty yards behind, swiping leaves from branches for a morning snack as he passed by. Even thorn bush leaves were good enough. But he made sure he did not lose sight of his companions.

Some of the canyons they passed through were so narrow they made eerie echoes as their horses' shoes clattered across the stones. Sometimes their passage accentuated the silence so fiercely it was as if they were the only beings in the vast world. The echoes ascended endlessly and lost themselves in the harsh, cloudless sky where the sun boiled like a molten brass ball. Nothing else, not even a bird, made any noise once the sun reached its zenith and began again to wring the sweat out of them, from under their hat brims, down their sides and backs, against their saddles.

Sometimes Sam had to turn around and look behind him to make sure he was not alone. Always, Tom greeted him with a smile. Sometimes he would even tip his hat, until the brutal sun really began to sap his energy.

It was a lonesome and wild and strange land. Goblins and ogres, trolls and dragons must haunt these fastnesses, if one believed the lore of childhood. Elves and fairies must scurry and flit in these cavernous halls of stone and beneath these canopies of oak and sycamore and cypress. Giant serpents must—and probably did— slither down these rocky arroyos and in crevasses where a man could fall so deep and far he would not even hear his own dying cries.

Thorn brush and scaly plants of all kinds seemed to fill each empty space, making gloves a necessity. If a man relaxed in the desert, he would die; and this desert was as bad as Sam had ever seen.

As they rode Sam attempted to impart to Tom all of the things that would be of use to a man lost in the desert. This was part of his training with the Tarahumara people, to know the desert like a Bostonian might know his pantry, and he wanted Tom to have every edge in case they were somehow separated.

For moisture there was the agave, the barrel cactus, the bee or wasp, whose path might lead a man to some *tinaja* or seep in the rocks. Wild horses or burros were also a sure sign of water nearby.

For nourishment, again the agave. To start a fire there was the yucca to use as a hand drill, or here and there a piece of flint or chert that, used against the shank of a spur or a belt buckle or firearm, might yield the needed spark. Cover—that was the difficult part. In most environments one might find leaves to use as an insulating blanket. In this country, once away from the watercourses, any leaves that did grow were too small to be of any true value as cover. A man would just have to hope he could find sufficient bunchgrass to cover himself when he needed to conserve his body's heat. The sand, while warm during the day, was cold at night and would actually rob a body of heat.

They were riding up over the rim of what Sam knew instinctively was the four-mile canyon Abe Varnell and Paco had told them about. They were tired. They were hot. They were thirsty.

Then, like a ghost, they saw the lone Indian in the high-up rocks, watching them in silence.

Chapter Sixteen

When Sam Coffey and Tom Vanse drew in their horses, the Indian was gone.

They stared up at the rocks a hundred yards away where they had last seen the image of the Indian with straight, bobbed hair and a long breech clout that caught the wind as he turned and leaped from sight. He had been wearing some kind of tunic, revealing only his arms and legs, deep copper in color. A piece of blue cloth was tied around his head.

Sam steeled himself before looking over at Tom. "Told you this was a bad idea."

"How far you figure to the gold?" Tom parried, acting nonchalant.

Sam scowled and looked down at the second half of the map, which he had kept in his hand for the past two miles. He scanned the surrounding rocks, picking up a couple of landmarks Abe Varnell had carefully sketched. He was a little surprised they were actually there. It seemed like the entire trip had been too fast, too easy.

"Half a mile, maybe. Could be less."

"What are we waitin' for then?" asked Tom. "Let's get it while we can."

For several seconds Sam gave his partner a hard stare. "You're loco. If we had a lick o' sense we'd turn tail and head back *that* way—" he jabbed a finger "—and get back to Nogales as fast as we can."

Tom just grinned, showing his deep-sunk dimples. "And leave all that gold?"

With a scowl, Sam pulled an 1881 Marlin rifle from its scabbard and opened the lever, blowing into the receiver. Other than a coat of dust, it was clean. Sam honored a simple code: a rider of the wild lands cares first for his weapons and his horses, so they will care for him.

Always one to blaze new trails, Sam had bought the Marlin when it first came on the market and made it out to Texas in 1881. He liked the heft of it, liked its balance. More than that, he liked its power. The Model '76 Winchester had once been touted as the best repeater to come down the pike. But when the Marlin made its play, chambered originally not only in .40-60, but in .45-70 as well, it was the best thing ever to happen to lever action guns, in Sam's mind. Of course the .45-70 bullets dropped like rocks once they got around two hundred yards. The reward was that anything they hit also dropped like a rock. And no lever action arm had ever been strong enough to pack these massive cartridges until the Marlin.

Closing the rifle's lever made a shiny new brass cartridge slide into the chamber. Sam was glad to see them making casings of brass now instead of copper. Copper had presented a weakness a man in battle could ill afford. Such problems had come to light especially after the Battle of the Little Bighorn, where frantically trying to dig swelled copper cases out of the breeches of Springfield carbines had been the death of many a cavalryman while Sioux, Cheyenne and Arapaho warriors waged battle with Winchester and Spencer, bow and arrow, lance and tomahawk.

Sam grimaced and spat. Too much thinking about Indians. Right now the subject did not set well.

Just as he was touching spurs to his horse's ribs, he heard Tom's rifle clack shut. They were both as ready as ever. But were they ready to die?

From that time on they saw no more Indians, but nothing else was on Sam's mind. He spent his time trying to think of ways to save his and Tom's life. At least one of them had to get back to Nadia, or she was through. And it was only Nadia that kept him going now. If not for her, he would have turned around after seeing the Indian. They were not going to have much time if and when they found that cache of gold. It was going to be a question of getting in and out, fast.

Neither man spoke. Scanning everything, they rode between the silent walls of the constricting canyon. The rocks magnified and flung every sound back at them. The din assaulted their ears. The heat drove down, invisible fire. Sweat dampened their cheeks and backs. Sam's pulse drummed against the inside of his round-crowned gray hat. His palms were sweaty on his rifle butt and on his reins.

This deep in the canyon, no breeze sifted dust or loose hair. The day was quiet, quiet as death, and the shadows of four vultures gliding loose along the ground accentuated Sam's sense of impending doom.

They rounded a corner in the canyon, and there, alongside the gravelly stream bed they paralleled, stood two giant sycamores, looming proud with handfuls of leaves hanging lackluster on their last living branches. The two trees were four feet apart at the bottom, but as they went upward, they came together for one brief moment, ten feet up, then branched out slightly again, creating what looked like a tall, skinny X.

Sam stopped and stared. Almost involuntarily, his eyes shot to the left, where in the cliff side appeared three holes, two of them side by side, a third below these. It resembled the face of a clown … or a ghoul. The tall X and the face in the cliff were the crux of Varnell's story. They were the final piece to a puzzle the prospector's painstaking directions had made very easy all along … *too easy.*

When you find these two landmarks you have found the Yaqui gold.

Sam had not known until that very moment if he completely believed Varnell's tale. Even now, he didn't know about the gold. But a surge of excitement welled up in him from deep inside, and just for a moment he believed everything. He could almost feel the gold in his hands. He could see himself and Tom riding back across the desert, triumphant, headed home to a new life.

And then, in his mind, there were the Yaquis …

Tom clattered up beside his partner, still holding his carbine, a beat up Spencer. Tom could not hide the excitement in his face. He did not look directly at Sam, but the eager look in his eyes nearly made them glow.

Sam had let his mind wander now and then while riding. He had tried to come up with reasons why Varnell would point them toward the Yaqui gold in the first place. Try as he might, he could come up with nothing but the obvious or the completely far-fetched. But the gold Varnell had been spending in Nogales was real enough, so some gold was there, or at least had been once. Perhaps not in the quantities Varnell liked to remember, but there all the same. Getting it back to civilization would be the trick …

Skirting to the left of the X as Varnell had directed them, they traveled another fifty feet. Here, a sort of alleyway fifty feet wide that almost appeared to be hand-hewn branched off the main canyon, ending forty yards in against a broken wall of rock that angled steeply upward for five or six hundred feet, unscalable. He could see the scars in the crumbling rock. He could see bold slashes of quartz, just like Varnell had described. Sam's chest constricted until he could hardly breathe. *Everything* was just as Varnell had described it.

And when he looked closely enough, there was a dark crack in the stone wall that at this angle looked deceptively like a fissure in the cliff, not the passageway driven into the mountain that it was.

Sam remained a-horseback, watching Tom slide down the side of his bay. He would have laughed at his partner if he had not been so delirious himself. Tom's knees seemed to almost buckle as his feet settled on the ground, and he grabbed onto the saddle horn and stood there for a moment, looking toward the dark crack in the wall. He turned and glanced up at Sam with such a look of expectation and hope that Sam prayed the gold would really be there, that it would be as rich as Varnell had portrayed. He could not bear to see the hope in Tom's eyes turn to ashes.

Sam did not get off his horse. They had come so far. *So* far. And all the while his cynical side had whispered to him, *There will be no gold.* He had told himself over and over he was a fool for coming here. He had numbered all the reasons he and Tom should have stayed in town. Never had he truly believed there would be any gold, although deep down he had wanted to. He had wanted it more than anything.

Now here they were. Everything from the beginning had been as described, down to the deathly silence of the canyons. Sam's hope was so fervent now he didn't dare dismount and go any closer, only to find out they had been complete fools. The numbing excitement was so all-consuming that both men had forgotten for the moment about the elusive Indian.

Tom was walking toward the rock wall, his footsteps uncertain on the jumbled rocks. He slipped once, looking like he would twist his ankle, but he kept on, eyes glued ahead. There were huge boulders strewn about the foot of the cliff, dislodged from far above and somewhat masking the entrance to the cave. When Tom stopped in front of the crack, his face was expressionless. He turned toward Sam, staring numbly.

Sam regained enough of his sense to study the surrounding rocks. He half expected to see the Indian from earlier—or more likely a couple dozen of them. But even as dangerous as their position was, it was hard to keep his mind on the Yaquis. He stepped down from Gringo and started toward his friend, with one last scan of the rocks.

When he stopped, Tom was still standing there looking like he didn't know whether to laugh, cry or scream with delight. Sam's eyes were drawn inescapably to the black crevice in the side of the cliff. There was only one place where you could see that the crack went deep into the mountain: the place where they were standing. A bird could see the hole, but the cliff that loomed across from it was so rugged and steep and broken that a man would play hob working himself to a position where he could see this far down into the canyon. From farther along the canyon all a man could see, until mere yards away, was an inconspicuous looking fissure in the rock. It was no wonder it had startled old Paco to see the Yaquis disappear into the mountainside. It must have seemed like the work of evil spirits.

Tom looked at Sam, then followed him over the broken rock and boulders to the yawning mouth of the cave. It appeared to have begun as a natural hole in the cliff, but from the rock lying outside it was plain it had been enlarged by the hands of man. And just inside the opening there was a frame of heavy timbers built to support the rock above. Sam did not know much about the Yaqui people, but this did not appear to be the work of any Indians. Perhaps it was some old Spanish mine the Yaquis had assumed possession of when they took back their country.

Just inside the doorway Sam found a stack of torches leaning against a timber. With his heart thudding, he took a match from his vest pocket and scratched it on the beam, holding up the pitch-covered end of one of the torches so that it picked up the flame. Fire licked across the black surface until the entire head of the torch was burning, giving a dancing burnished glow to the far wall.

With his left hand on the rock face to steady him, Sam stepped into the shadows, followed closely by Tom. He looked around warily, up at a handful of bats dangling from the ceiling, unmoving and quiet, down at the floor scattered with their droppings. Here and there was a shiny scratch in the stone, most likely quartz.

Footing was treacherous in the bouncing shadows. Sam stepped on a rock and rolled his ankle, catching himself against the wall. A little laugh escaped Tom, but he quickly went silent when a wrong step put him in a depression and almost tipped him over.

Sam had no time to return the laugh at his friend's expense. Before he could even think about laughing, the torch light and his eyes fell at once upon a line of boxes at the rear of the room. He threw a glance at Tom, then started forward.

The boxes were wooden. All but one of them were simple crates, lined with what appeared to be canvas or some other type of rough material that showed between the slats. The other was a chest made of heavy oak and reinforced with three thick metal bands. All of the boxes had lids, and all of them were on, but none of them was locked, although the big chest had a hasp.

Sam's cynical side took over while he held the torch and reached for the lid of the big chest with his left hand. The boxes would be empty. This place had no road signs leading to it, but it was not hidden, either. He could not imagine anyone leaving all that gold lying around for long, especially after Abe Varnell had made his escape. The Yaquis, of course, had no way of knowing if the prospector had made it back to civilization. If he had made it then all of their riches were in jeopardy. Why would they be foolish enough to risk that? Unless they left it here simply as a way to lure new victims into a trap …

Forcing that thought uncomfortably aside, he lifted the lid with some effort and pushed it up, making its stiff hinges creak. In the bottom of the chest was a shiny filtering of goose feather gold. Otherwise it was dark and empty.

Sam's heart fell. He looked over at Tom, who looked like someone had kicked him in the belly. Sam sucked in a deep breath and sighed. He looked at one of the crates but made no move. Tom's trembling hand reached out and tilted back the lid of the crate. The canvas inside the empty container was dark and dirty and littered meagerly with more shiny bits of gold no larger than the head of a pin.

Tom's hand fell to his side. He looked over and met Sam's eyes. Sam was trying to tell himself he did not care, that he hadn't expected anything and that riches would only have led to heartache. He was trying to believe he could go back and find some other way to make a living, and that somehow he could save Nadia's boarding house for her. He was strong enough to believe this for a moment, to believe that all his pain and disappointment was for Tom. The look in Tom's eyes truly did make him ache inside. Tom had wanted this gold so badly. He had prayed for this dream to be real. Now they both feared they had made the trip for nothing. Who could tell how long these boxes had been empty? The Yaquis had probably come and taken everything right after Abe Varnell headed north.

"We ain't lost yet," Tom said. His words shook Sam, and he stared. "Ain't lost?"

"Hell no! You can see these walls. Look at that quartz! There's still gold here. We'll just have to work a little harder for it."

"That's a real nice idea, Tom, but in case you ain't thought about it at least one Injun already knows we're in here. How long do you think it'll be before they're all down on us? This deal was supposed to be fast. Get in, pick up the gold, get out. If it comes to diggin' for the gold and pickin' it out of these walls, we ain't gonna get out without gettin' caught."

Tom swore, but he quickly chased it with a smile. "Sam, we came this far!"

He turned and kicked at one of the other crates they hadn't tried yet, a crate forty inches or so long. The hollow wooden sound they should have heard was instead the sound of something solid. Tom swung his eyes to Sam, and he reached down and threw back the lid of the crate.

Sam expected to see the crate filled with chunks of ore. But it wasn't ore. It was full of brand new 1886 Winchesters.

Tom looked over at Sam, whose mind was already working. "I guess we know what they used the gold for."

"Yeah. I wonder who they gave it to."

Sam shrugged. "I don't know, but I know one thing. These rifles can stay right where they are. At twenty-five bucks or so each it wouldn't be worth our lives to try an' drag 'em out of this hole."

"I might take one," said Tom, trying to hide his disappointment at his fading dreams of gold. "If I can find a case of cartridges to go with it."

Sam looked down at the first small case that sat just beside the big chest. He had to pry the lid off, and sure enough it contained individual cartons of cartridges. All of them appeared to be .45-70 caliber.

"Hey, what do you know!" Sam said with a grin. "We'll be twins, brother." He set his torch against the rock wall and reached down to pick up a rifle, turning it so he could look down the bore. "There you go, pard. Forty-five seventy. You could have used my shells. Now we can both stock up. I've been hankering to get these two rifles side by side and see how they shoot. This is supposed to be Winchester's answer to my Marlin."

"You don't have to tell me," Tom parried. "You don't even hardly know how to read. I'm the one that read those flyers to you."

Sam grunted. He held the rifle up to his shoulder to test its balance, nodding with grudging admiration. "Feels good. But not as good as my Marlin."

Tom, who really had no loyalty to any rifle although he had carried his Spencer now for fifteen years, reached down to pick up a rifle of his own. He hefted it in one hand, held it up to look through the sights, worked the action. He raised his eyebrows and pursed his lips thoughtfully. "That's all right. I think I'll trade."

Sam gave another grunt. "Let's get out of here. I got a bad feelin' about this place."

"You've been havin' a bad feelin' since we left Arizona, Gran'ma. Why don't you go make us up a platter of hush puppies while I chop some of the gold out of this rock?"

"You'll have a time doin' that. What're you gonna use, your knife?"

"I got my camp axe," Tom retorted. "That oughtta work."

Sam shrugged. "Well, tarnation, I don't care about my hair, Curly. You lose yours, though, and you'll be whinin' about it till next Christmas."

"Maybe longer," said Tom with a grin. "But I got nobody in particular that wants to run their fingers through it."

"Think I'll bring the animals in here out of sight," Sam decided.

"This place is big enough."

"Right! And how am I supposed to dig with all those horses' butts in here stickin' in my face?"

"Horses' butts? Well, you oughtta fit right in!" Sam growled, his face breaking into a big grin as he turned away. A few yards away he turned back again. "You do whatever you're gonna do, Tom, and let's get outta here. We ain't savin' Nadia anything if we're both dead."

After Sam left, Tom sighed and looked down at all the crates lined up along the wall. There were a bunch of smaller ones, apparently more cartridges for the Winchesters. He figured he would take one or two full ones with him when they left. That would keep him in ammunition for a few years to come, even if he spent a lot of time practicing. You could never have too much ammunition. He tried to push thoughts of the Indian they had seen earlier out of his head. Chances were he was a lone wanderer anyway. Besides, as far as they had come for the gold, he was determined not to leave empty-handed. After all, if the Indians were going to give chase, they were going to give chase.

One of the other crates was a little larger, and he flipped it open casually. It was a little dark within, and he had to pick up Sam's torch and hold it over the case to see what was inside. What greeted him made him shrink back, aghast. Then he looked closer, to make sure he wasn't imagining things. The case was full of wizened, hardened body parts—mostly ears and fingers. A couple of the pieces appeared to be noses. A rancid, greasy odor rose up from the box, and he quickly shut it, his stomach queasy. What kind of people were these?

He knew he should grab a rifle and a box of ammunition and get out. But it was the devil making him stay to the bitter end. Running his tongue around inside his dry mouth, he looked at the next crate, the last one. This one was about half the size of the big chest, probably two feet wide by a foot deep. He was half afraid what mementos he might find inside. But curiosity had always been his downfall.

Reaching down, he took the lid and tipped it backward.

* * *

Outside, Sam had decided one thing. Whether they were to make a run for it or not, these animals absolutely had to be rested. They had made it a long ways that day, and they couldn't be expected to turn around and make it out of the canyon without some rest and without a chance to let their backs dry out. Only a fool with no knowledge of horses would think it a good idea to turn and flee because of the sight of one Indian. After all, it wasn't that uncommon for Yaquis *or* Apaches to travel alone. There might not be any other Indians within a hundred miles of this place.

With that false comfort, he started to remove the packs from one of the mules when he heard the cry from inside the cave.

"Sam!"

The alarmed sound of his friend's voice made Sam drop the pack and draw his pistol, running toward the cavern. He stumbled on stones as he came up to it, catching himself against a timber.

"Tom! You all right?" It was silent for a moment while Sam waited for his eyes to adjust to the dark in the cave. But soon he could see the torch glowing dimly on the floor, lighting up the crates and Tom sitting there on the big chest, staring at him as if in a trance. "What'd you do, go and get snake-bit?"

Tom started shaking his head. "No, but if this had been a snake it would sure have bit us both." Saying that, he held out his hand, and the metallic rustle of coins sliding across each other reached Sam through the stillness of the cavern.

Chapter Seventeen

The torch Tom had dropped in the sand began guttering back to life, but it took Sam walking over to pick it up before its flame licked high enough to give decent light. He looked down at the gold coins in Tom's hand, then pivoted the torch so its light shone down on the contents of the last crate. The container brimmed not only with gold coin and ore, but precious stones, including some mounted in necklaces, brooches or rings. Originally, the gold within the walls of this place might have drawn the Spanish to it, but the Yaquis apparently used it now only as a cache.

Speechless, Sam stared at the treasure, as did Tom. But the sight of it triggered a thought, and he walked over to the crates of ammunition and pried one open. True to appearances, it was full of smaller boxes of .45-70 cartridges, all wrapped in a sheet of oiled yellow-brown paper. The crate of rifles, on the other hand, revealed a different story. Sam began carefully to unpack it, leaning each rifle against the rock wall. He saw when he was only halfway down that the crate contained more than rifles. The bottom of it, or at least as much as he could see, was filled with chunks of gold, gold coins, gold bricks, chain and jewelry. It resembled some massive trunk of pirate treasure straight out of a child's storybook. Only in his imagination, in fact, had Sam ever seen anything to match this. So absorbed in it was he, he didn't even feel Tom standing beside him, staring in wordless awe at the incredible treasure before them.

Abe Varnell had not been dreaming. The value of what lay in this room had to be at least a million dollars, and as far back as the corridor appeared to go on their left, who could tell what other treasures it led to? Sam and Tom had truly found their fortunes.

Yet it didn't take long for Sam's cynical side, or at least his practical side, to surface. It was this transition of mind that freed his tongue. "I wouldn't go dreamin' just yet, big boy. You think them Yaquis just went off and left this unguarded? If we're lucky, that Injun we saw a while back is alone. If we're not …"

"If you're worried, let's go."

"*Go?*" Sam stared.

"I mean let's pack as much of this as we can hold and go. It isn't gonna be like we thought. We won't be diggin' in the ground or choppin' in these walls. The gold is here for the taking, Sam! Let's put it in our packs and go while we can. We can put enough of this away in ten minutes to retire on."

Sam's eyes flickered toward the outside. His partner wanted him to think he actually believed that by the mere act of loading their packs and riding out of this canyon they would appear safely back in Nogales. But Tom was smarter than that. Many miles and many hazards still stalked between them and freedom. Neither Tom nor Sam could ever believe they were safe until they crossed the Mexico line. A man who has just discovered himself rich beyond his wildest dreams can push a lot of dread to the back of his mind. But Sam and Tom could not forget the Indian and the smell of death in this cavern.

Yet the gold was what they had come for. They returned to the horses and with their saddlebags in tow they began loading all they could of the richest of the bounty, all the while having to remind themselves that this was not, indeed, a dream.

How does a man who has never had anything estimate the point at which he is rich? When does he cross the magical line where first he will never again have to work for a living, and then, where he has gained enough wealth to live anywhere in the world in style? Sam loaded gold coin and nuggets and jewelry until his fingers hurt, pushing away the knowledge that every minute here placed them in greater danger. He stowed gold until it began to look like any other rock, like something seen and touched by him every day.

And when there was no more room to put the gold, they started thinking of places they could hide more and come back for it later—just like old Paco had told them they would. They made three caches along the trail back toward Hermosillo before deciding they were pushing their luck too far.

It was on their way back to the cavern after their third trip that they saw the second Indian. They first heard the little stone, tipped off the rocks above and clattering into the quarry. The rocks around them magnified every sound, even the drumming of Sam's heart in his head. But the little rock might as well have been cannon fire. Sam and Tom jerked around at the same time.

The Indian was standing up on what appeared to be a narrow ledge, staring at them with only his lower legs concealed in brush. He was at least seventy feet above them, with the same shoulder-length hair as the first one, lifting in the gentle breeze, and the same tunic tied with a belt and piece of cloth around his head.

All these details Sam could account for, and he knew his imagination was not strong enough to conjure up such detail. But in the next moment he was gone. Sam looked over at his partner, scowling. Tom's gaze started to swing to him, faltered, then finally made contact. Of course it was not as if Tom had asked the Indian to appear there, but his sheepish glance made him look guilty.

"I didn't imagine that, did I?" drawled Sam. "Just to make me feel better about my mind not slippin' on me, tell me what you just saw."

Tom scoffed. "Your mind's not slippin', Sam. He was real. Or *it.*"

"It?"

"Looked like a woman," Tom said.

Sam laughed. "A woman! You'd see a woman in a stove-up burro if you were alone long enough. I'm rollin' tight in my blankets tonight."

"I'm serious," Tom rejoined. "That was a woman."

Sam looked at the horses and scratched his jaw. He didn't admit it to Tom, but he had a feeling his partner was right about the Indian being a woman.

He looked back at Tom. "If it *was* a woman, there must be a camp around here. Personally, I think the long hair just has you fooled. Man sees what he wants to see."

Tom started to protest, then caught the gleam in his partner's eye. His answer was a grunt. "Do we go out tonight?" Tom said.

"Tonight? How about right now?"

"What about the old saying that an Injun won't fight at night?"

"An *Apache* won't fight at night—or at least they don't like to. How do we know Yaquis believe the same? That might be their favorite time to kill us," Sam said dryly.

"So we go now then."

"How about tonight?" countered Sam.

Tom stared at him, then frowned. "That's what I just said."

"I'd rather be the one sayin' it," said Sam with a half grin. "You know them horses gotta have rest. More than half a day, if they could, but that sure ain't in the cards. I'd say we're in the best defensible position we're gonna find—right here. We got shelter and no tellin' how many rifles and cartridges. If they catch us, I'd rather they catch us here, especially if it's daylight."

"Abe said there was a spring close by here," Tom recalled. "Reckon we oughtta find it and refill these barrels before it gets dark."

Sam grunted his agreement. "Go find it. I'll stay back and cover you." With those words Sam went and drew his Marlin and came back to Tom's side. He looked at him for several seconds, trying to read what lay behind his partner's eyes. Then, a tilt of his chin was enough to get Tom moving.

The water was easy to find. Moss cushioned the rocks where it coursed down out of the cliffside, giving life in that shadowed nook to bright little ferns and sedges. There was tiny aquatic life bouncing to and fro in the pool, and the rocks over which the spring water trickled were thick with green ooze. But it was the best tasting water Tom had tasted in days—far better than what Nogales offered.

Many dippers full recharged the water barrels, and several more Sam's and Tom's bellies. By then the sun had disappeared behind the high rock walls, leaving them in bright shadow. No telling how long until nightfall—five, perhaps six hours. It was going to seem like eternity.

The shadows purpled, and the sky above turned a blazing orange. Strange birds called, and somewhere a fox made a little yap, inviting nightfall. The west-facing cliffs, still in sunlight, lit up like gold, and even the pines that mimicked a hairline along their highest crags seemed to blaze in the encompassing light. Nighthawks performed acrobatics down the chasm, and one by one the crickets began to chirp. The air cooled, bringing back scents of the desert that sunlight had stolen away. There was no Indian to be seen, but their aura filled the falling twilight.

Sam and Tom waited at the mouth of the cavern, rifles held in taut hands, scanning the rocks. The closer it got to evening, the more tense they became. For hours they had tried to calm each other with teasing banter, but each had his secret dread not far below the surface. They knew they were in dire circumstances here. They also knew if the Yaquis caught up to them while they were riding away they would have to let go of the pack mules, losing everything they had come down here for. But it was better than losing their lives. Besides, they both had enough gold in their saddlebags not only to make sure Nadia did not lose her livelihood, but that she lived for many years in style. That, after all, was what really mattered now. It wasn't like they had worked a lifetime for this gold. If they lost it now it wouldn't change their lives.

Shortly after finding the gold, they had taken the saddles off their horses and unpacked the mules. Being ready for sudden flight was a nice thought, but a savvy horseman does not with good conscience leave his animals hot and burdened. They had to recover from the day's travel to carry the two men far out of the Bacatete Mountains. Now, with darkness fast approaching, they saddled back up, and the first thing they put on their saddles was the bags full of bounty—a boon and a detriment, for while it would make them rich it would also drag their horses down.

The darker it got, the more Sam believed perhaps they would make it out of this canyon of death. Perhaps his bad luck had been broken.

And then the world came down.

The clatter of many hooves began as a distant rattle, and Sam's eyes leaped to Tom. Tom stared up the canyon as the noise grew until it filled the canyon like thunder, reverberating between the cliffs to mimic hundreds of horses.

Side by side, sharing the same feeling of dread, they scanned the twilight, seeking images to match the sounds. And they were there, weaving like ghosts in the cool, rocky chasm. Horses blew, leather creaked, a man spoke in a guttural whisper.

It became plain to Sam that all egress from the canyon was blocked by a tight group of horsemen, hair fluttering at their shoulders.

Sam's heart battered his breastbone. He took a deep breath to try and still it and stepped into his stirrup, swinging his leg over the saddle. Tom followed his lead. Sam held the ropes of all three mules in one hand. At least until their situation grew too desperate he would try to keep the animals up with him and Tom. Deep inside he had the hope that these mules and horses had been grained well enough the last few days that they could outrun the grass-fed Indian mounts. And if that wasn't in the stars at least turning the mules loose behind them might create enough confusion among the Yaquis for him and Tom to make it to some other defensible place. But all of these thoughts he tried to comfort himself with did not begin to set Sam's mind at ease. Danger loomed far too near tonight.

The horsemen came to a standstill, and a false silence descended on the canyon—false because the animals still breathed, some blew out their nostrils, and crickets had again struck up their music.

"I am called Cajeme."

The deep, resonant voice from the dark had an eerie effect. Sam clenched his jaws and stared toward the man who had spoken, obviously an Indian. Although he was speaking English, an oddity this deep in Mexico, his voice had that Indian quality that only those who are far removed from their kind for many years can disguise.

Sam could feel the presence around him of many bodies as the voice came again. This time he could make out the man's lips moving. He spoke in a guttural tone, and his English was not perfect, but it was better than anything Sam would have expected. "My true name is José María Leyva. This is my country. And that—" he motioned with a rifle barrel toward the mules "—is the gold of my people. Yaqui gold."

So these were indeed the Yaquis. By their dress and their wide flat faces they could have just as easily been Apache. Even in all his years in Mexico, Sam had never seen a Yaqui. He would have known no difference even in full daylight.

"They call me Coffey," said Sam, his voice louder than he had intended. "My partner there is Vanse." He had pulled a cigar from his vest pocket and put it nonchalantly in his mouth, his heart thudding so hard that just before opening his mouth to take the cigar his teeth chattered together. Drawing a match from his pocket, he struck it and put it near his face to light the cigar. The yellow flicker of the match licked across Sam's face, revealing his beard, his tired eyes that knew and almost expected death. He said nothing of the gold in his packs. What was he to say?

"You need not speak," said Cajeme. "You come from the other white man, the one we believed perhaps had died. He was called Abraham."

Sam hoped his surprise didn't show in the darkness. This man was no fool, and his memory was sharp. He drew deep on his cigar, making its tip glow crimson. "Was that his name?"

Cajeme laughed. "Sí. Unless you would call him Varnell. I told him what happens if he let anyone know about this place."

Sam remained silent. He could almost hear Tom breathing beside him, even over the sound of his own heart drumming in his ears.

"It surprises you I speak your tongue, no?" said Cajeme. "I speak five. Do not let my appearance fool you, amigo. I have fought with the Governor Pesqueira against the armies of the French, and I speak some of that tongue also. I have been alcalde mayor of all of the villas of the Mayos and the Yaquis. I speak Spanish—*perfecto*. I speak English, as you hear, because those Spaniards who made me a leader spoke some. But I am Yaqui, before all else. And you are in my country."

"I reckon we are. We were fixin' to leave."

Cajeme laughed heartily. "Amigo! You cannot just *leave* Yaqui land! You have come here to steal from my people. And now you know where I keep our fortunes. You cannot leave here tonight, tomorrow … ever."

Sam had heard of Cajeme, of how he had been one of Mexico's most loyal subjects, how he had fought with the Mexicans against the French and been placed in control of all the Yaqui River country. Later, the treacherous Mexican government had attempted to subjugate him. He had defeated them in several major battles until losing the Fortress of Anil to the Mexicans and then two hundred people dead and two thousand prisoners at a place called Buatachive, here in the Sierra Bacatete. After smallpox swept through the Yaqui Valley and brought death to many of the survivors, the bulk of the Yaqui rebellion had ended. But not for Cajeme. With his force of Yaqui warriors and a handful of women and children he haunted the Sierra Bacatete and kept the Mexican military on its toes, striking, raiding and killing in guerilla fashion. Cajeme's war against the Mexican people would end only with his death, it was said.

And for all Sam might have believed of Cajeme, this José María Leyva, he could not doubt he was a man of his word. Unless a miracle interceded, Sam and Tom would never leave this lonesome canyon alive.

Taking a deep breath, Sam coiled himself. Then he sprang, flinging his cigar at Cajeme's face and wheeling his horse. There were Yaquis to every side, but none expected either man to run. Gringo plowed into the middle of them, towing the mules behind. Horses screamed and pitched in the confusion, and one of the mules bawled and kicked an Indian horse in the leg.

Halfway free, Sam had to let loose of the mules, and Gringo broke through the Yaqui ranks with a loud, frightened grunt.

Then he was free and running. Even in the darkness the black gap by which they had come to this place yawned like an enormous defile.

Laying his spurs to Gringo's sides, Sam and the buckskin sprinted for the gap.

Chapter Eighteen

Sam Coffey could hear yelling—not the cries of angry riders chasing him, but of one man barking orders.

Sam had grown up in an environment not unlike this alongside the Tarahumara people. He knew the ways of this wild desert. Already, with the madly surging horse between his knees, he was planning how to survive. Perhaps more important, though, was to get Tom back to Arizona alive. Where *was* Tom? The moment he realized for sure that his partner had not made it out of the Yaquis' grasp, Sam knew he could not keep riding.

Ahead was a dark cove gnawed by the elements into the side of the canyon, perhaps by years of erosion or one violent shaking of the earth. He had noted it as they rode past, and now he saw it looming as his horse breathed savagely up the slope. In desperate hope, Sam veered Gringo into the cove, instantly screened by ghostly brush and cactus. Gringo grunted as thorns speared his side, the same thorns that pieced Sam's right pant leg. But neither Gringo nor Sam cried out, and when the rush of Indian horses thundered past, he and Gringo sat listening like rats lurking in a hole.

The sound of the Indian horses had just faded away when Sam whispered Gringo out of the cove and trotted back the way they had come, Marlin in hand. Along the way they passed the three places he and Tom had hidden gold coin and nuggets earlier in the day. But now his mind merely touched on the treasure. All of that money was no kind of exchange for Tom's life.

Long before the cave, he slowed Gringo, then finally brought him to a standstill. It was almost pitch black, but many years prowling dark trails gave him the ability to discern shapes and recall what those shapes represented. Nothing moved. No horse, no man. Where was Tom? Where was his horse?

Leaving the buckskin ground-reined, Sam removed his spurs and slipped along the edge of the canyon wall. He hated his tall-heeled boots right now. Although a blessing when riding or during a chance encounter with a rattlesnake, they were a detriment on these slick rocks.

When he neared the mine, he made out a dim light emanating from it. Glancing back toward Gringo, he could see only darkness. He sipped deep of the cool night air and moved on. Crickets became still as he neared them; he hoped the Indians did not take note of that. Somewhere an owl hooted, a haunted and hollow sound up high in the rocks.

He had jacked a shell into the chamber of the Marlin and let the hammer back down. He was tempted to re-cock it, but the slightest slip on a stone with these despicable boots and it might be his last mistake.

With every ounce of Indian he had ever possessed, Sam stole up to the mouth of the cave. Peering around the corner, he saw light coming from back in the corridor and heard a voice rise and fall. The silence resumed. With his heart pounding inside his head, he slipped off the boots and set them against the cliff wall.

Fully confident the Indians would never expect him to be back here after his miraculous getaway, he stepped into the cave. He ghosted through the sand, pointing his toes and sliding them along the floor to feel for loose stones. Once, a rock started to tip away from his toe, and he sucked in a breath and waited as it teetered back in place.

Acrid was the smell of torches, the scent of pitch and burlap. The dust had been stirred up, and that, too, was pungent. Beyond that, Sam smelled horses. And Indians …

Five more steps ... four ... three ... two. A hard voice stopped him. It was Cajeme.

"Your compadre, he will not go far. My men are of this desert. They have the good spirits with them. It is a matter of time only."

Steeling himself, Sam stepped around the corner. There sat Tom, on the ground staring up at Cajeme. There were three more Indians standing by, one behind Tom, the other two to Cajeme's left. One of the latter two was a woman—the woman they had seen standing in the rocks watching them.

Sam's eyes ran up and down Cajeme in the torch light. The Yaqui chief was powerfully built, although not as tall as Sam. His chest was flat and wide, striated with sinewy muscle. He wore the same cloth band around his hair as those with him.

Sam brought his Marlin waist high and thumbed back the hammer. The rock walls magnified the sound, and Cajeme and the others whirled.

"You were right," Sam growled. "I won't go far."

Cajeme stared at Sam for a long moment. Tom wore a big grin of relief, shadow from the lamplight making his dimples into crevices. "'Bout time you got back," he said. He walked between two of the Yaquis and over to the cave wall, where he bent down to pick up his gun belt and holstered pistol. He strapped it on and turned to Sam.

"Where're their horses?" Sam asked.

Tom jerked his head farther down the corridor. "They got a spot back there."

"Go get 'em, and hustle up. Them others'll be comin' back."

Sam held his rifle on the Indians while Tom disappeared down the dark corridor. Sam had a feeling he was only beginning to comprehend the immensity of this cavern. Soon, he could hear the echoes of horses blowing and of hooves striking stone, and Tom smoked back into the lantern light leading his bay and four Yaqui horses.

"Gringo's out toward the gap," Sam said. "Take them animals over to him while I decide what to do with this bunch."

Cajeme was silent, his dark eyes hooded. But it took little guesswork to discern his fury at being caught off-guard. Tom led the horses past Sam. As he walked by, the look in his eyes was one of utter thankfulness. Sam had plucked him from the very hands of death, and they both knew it. Tom would have never expected any less of his partner, but he would never forget it, either.

As Tom faded out, Sam turned back to Cajeme. "You can keep your gold," he said. "We just want out of here. In fact, you can keep the mules, too, and all our supplies. I'm askin' a day without bein' followed. I promise you we won't be back this way." Cajeme's eyes narrowed, looking not angry but amused. Still he said nothing. His silence rankled Sam.

"I reckon we were wrong to come after your gold. But it's a cinch you took it from somebody else yourself." Cajeme's nod was so slight it was hard to see.

Suddenly, a horse screamed outside, followed by a pistol shot. With incredible swiftness, Cajeme caught up one of the torches that glowed against the wall and dove into an alcove, flinging the torch toward Sam's feet as he did so.

Sam pivoted back toward Cajeme, who had disappeared from sight, but one of the other braves struck him hard at the waist, knocking the rifle sideways.

Down Sam went, the solid weight of the Yaqui on top of him. The Yaqui jerked the rifle away from him and flung it aside, and for a moment they struggled hand to hand. The Yaqui was powerful and sure of his strength. He let go of Sam's wrist long enough to strike him back and forth across the face, then rose up and jammed a knee into his groin. Sam grunted with pain, struggling to roll away. The Indian rolled with him, allowing him to go to his side, then giving him a hard shove to help his momentum carry him over on his face. A hand ground into the back of Sam's neck, ramming his face against the sand. He strove to pull his head free, but this man had him. Soon, other hands clutched him, and he heard another horse scream outside, and then the faint pounding of hooves. A pistol shot split the night, met by the *boom* of a rifle.

Sam struggled against the weight on top of him, but now they were jerking him to his feet, nearly tearing his arms loose at the shoulder. The Indian who had held Sam made a jumping kick from the floor, taking Sam in the chest and knocking him back to the ground. Even in his agony, helplessly sucking for breath while he fought the sand in his eyes and mouth, he could see one Indian holding his Marlin rifle, another his pistol. Cajeme had gone to the mouth of the cavern, but now Sam heard him striding back, and he stopped in front of Sam.

"Soon your foolish friend will be dead. He cannot escape this canyon."

Sam's lungs caught and seemed about to burst, then sucked in a much-needed rush of air. Unfortunately, they carried sand into his windpipe as well, and he bent double coughing. While in this moment of torment, one of the Yaquis struck him a savage blow to the side of the head, and he went down hard against the cave floor, his ears ringing. The whole place seemed black and eerie. The walls were spinning, and little flashes of light zoomed across his vision like shooting stars. The metallic taste of blood was strong on his tongue, but even in his agony all he could think of was Tom.

Someone came in from outside, and harsh words were exchanged between the newcomer and Cajeme. Finally, Cajeme whirled away and spat. Sam had sat half up and watched him out of the one eye that wasn't full of sand. He felt blood trickle down the corner of his mouth.

Sam could of course understand none of the Yaqui tongue. But he understood unspoken language, and Cajeme's voice and expression said Tom had made his escape.

Eternal was the night. A fire glowed orange in the center of the cave. Smoke wisped up along the ceiling and was drawn by the air outside, so the environment in the cavern stayed tolerable. But every time Sam started to drift off to sleep one of the Indians would walk over and kick him, or poke at his stocking feet with the point of a knife or a hot ember, or throw a handful of sand in his face. The Yaquis took turns sleeping. There was only one awake at a time. And his—or her—single job was to keep Sam from drifting off.

Somewhere in the hours before midnight, the other Yaquis came back in, speaking in low tones. Their report angered Cajeme, and they seemed completely humiliated when he pointed to Sam and made it clear he had eluded them and come back while they were out chasing him.

After the interminable night, daylight skulked down the canyon walls. It was still dark back in the cave, but with first light they dragged Sam out to the cave's entrance and extinguished their torches.

Outside, a fire chittered at the cave opening, and the smell of roasting meat taunted Sam. He guessed what they were cooking over the fire when he saw Tom's horse lying twenty feet away with a large portion of its hip hacked out.

A quick glance around told Sam his buckskin, Gringo, was not here. Since Tom wasn't here either, they must be together. Tom could not have found a better horse. And the two of them had better be far on their way to Hermosillo by then. How often did second chances to escape fate come along?

Gnawing on a hunk of blackened meat, Cajeme came over to Sam after half an hour. "Amigo, your friend has escaped—because of you. Of course we could find him, but why? We have you. Besides, this man called Varnell will send others after my gold if he sent you. The time has come to move it."

Sam stared his defiance.

"You know, amigo, I was going to kill you. I was going to hang you over a fire and let you cook to death very slow. But I have a change of my heart." Cajeme put the last piece of horse flesh in his mouth and licked his fingers, putting one of them all the way in and drawing it back out with a satisfied sucking noise. He leaned to wipe the remains on his knee-high moccasins.

"You, amigo, are one brave man," Cajeme said. "You could have run and kept running. You would have lived. But to save your compadre you came back. Brave, amigo. A thing of courage a Yaqui would do—not a white man. Because of this, I choose not to kill you. The desert maybe, but not me or my people."

Sam's eyes flickered around at the others, the first glimmer of hope rising in his chest. Cajeme must have read the hope, and he chuckled mirthlessly. "Do not let this make you happy, amigo. This desert hates you, as it hates every white man. The chance you survive is not so very good."

But Sam knew his chances *were* good. He knew the desert. Even on foot it was but a playground to a man trained intensively by the Tarahumaras.

Cajeme studied his captive. His eyes were narrowed, but there was humor in them as he discerned the continued hopefulness in Sam's eyes. He seemed to draw sadistic pleasure in trying to take away that hope. "We will take everything you have, amigo. *Everything.* You will leave this canyon the same as the day you were born, with one difference. My compadre there"—he pointed at a big, sadistic looking warrior with a crooked nose— "he is going to make sure your time is not easy. You see, he is going to give me two little skins for my woman to make a bag of great medicine. These skins, they will come from one who must be of strong powers.

"They will be from the bottom of your feet."

In the high rocks, surrounded by oak and juniper, dark sweat soaked Tom Vanse's shirt. Twenty minutes earlier he had left Gringo tied to an oak tree, knowing the horse could not make this climb. Tom sought a way around, a way to get back to the hidden canyon where Sam was being held captive.

Tom sat to rest on a limestone boulder. With sweat trickling into his eyes, he looked down at the bullet burn across his left thigh. The Yaqui last night had been good, good enough to miss being hit by Tom's pistol shot while at the same time managing to almost put a bullet through him, a bullet that went on to mortally wound his bay. Tom had been lucky and fast enough to scramble into Gringo's saddle.

The bullet burn didn't hurt so much now. More than anything, his legs were numb, hard to move after the steep climb he was not used to. Every step up the rocky, pine-covered slope was a chore, and every step threatened to be his last. But that was his blood brother down there, the man who had risked his life to come back into the jaws of hell after him. How could a man ride away from that? He refused to run off like Abe Varnell and regret it the rest of his miserable life.

Yet what could he do? It was daylight, and there were at least a dozen seasoned warriors down there holding his friend. Tom had fought all night and morning trying to foster some plan of rescue. But it seemed futile. Still, he could not just leave, not with Sam in the grasp of the Yaquis. Tom sat on the rock gazing down into the maw of the canyon. Somewhere down there was Sam, begging rescue. And Tom could do nothing.

Then, as if invoked by his thoughts, an eerie wail rose from the canyon depths. The rocks made sound bounce back and forth until losing itself in the sky. It was unmistakably Sam's voice, although Tom had never heard him sound like this before. The noise was that of agonized screaming. Tom had seen bad things happen to his friend. He had seen him with a knee horribly infected by a mesquite thorn. He had seen him thrown butt-first into a cholla cactus, and thank his good friend Tom at the same time he was cursing him to the devil for pulling those vicious thorns out of his south end with pliers. He had seen him in a fight when some Mexican in San Antonio had tried to take off his ear with his teeth. But never had Sam sounded much more than annoyed … until now. Whatever the Yaquis had found to inflict on Sam, it must have been the worst pain he had ever had to endure. All Tom could think of was going for help before it was too late. If it wasn't already …

Chapter Nineteen

Tom Vanse stared out across the twisted, time-rent rocks of the Sierra Bacatete. He knew the direction he had to travel, and even if he hadn't, Gringo did. But how to elude the Yaquis who would be watching for him that way? Wait for dark? What would happen to Sam in the meantime? And what if he waited until dark and they found him anyway?

He decided to make his best shot for Hermosillo immediately. It seemed a vast distance across the Bacatetes to the dusty little villa. To Sam it must have seemed like it was back in Texas.

Tom rode Gringo alongside the trail in the brush when he could. One thing he was sure of: he did not want to get caught out in the open. But staying off the trail made for slow going, and sometimes, when the canyons were particularly steep-walled, there was nothing to do *but* ride the trail. Fortunately, it was not on one of those stretches when he saw the dust ahead.

Tom's heart leaped. This was a large cloud. An optimist might have hoped for wild horses or burros, but wild animals in dry country instinctively move slowly to conserve water. What caused them to move so as to raise this amount of dust? Whatever the reason, in this lonely country a party of riders as large as this could bode him no good. Chances were it was Apaches, Yaquis, or Mexican bandits. Whoever it was, it was not wise for him to let them see him out here alone riding a good horse and with a good rifle in his scabbard. Men had died for much less.

Turning the buckskin, Tom wove his way down into the nearest draw. He had to concentrate on moving slowly to keep from raising too much dust of his own, but at the same time quickly enough to get under cover.

But the Yaquis appeared before he was out of sight.

Tom had just stopped the buckskin, seeking a stand of trees in which to secrete himself. He looked back up the draw as the first of the Yaquis hove into view. One let out a wild yell of discovery. Tom cursed and snapped his eyes around him. No place of concealment! No way of escape but to outdistance them! Laying low across Gringo's withers, he put spurs to his ribs. The horse bunched its muscles and took off like a roadrunner down the sandy draw.

Sam Coffey was filled with anger so all-consuming his soul seemed to be digesting itself. He lay naked in the rocks and sand in front of the Yaqui gold mine. The sun shot arrows down at him, coursing through to his inner core. Baking him. Killing him.

The Yaquis were gone, as was the gold. They had left only what a man would have to dig out of the walls, unless, that is, they had not discovered the caches he and Tom had made. The mine in itself was rich, but if Sam could choose he would never come back to Yaqui country. Only it was too late to choose.

An hour had passed since Sam looked down at his feet. The pain had not lessened, but he had forced his mind to numbness. He had been made to watch them after they tied his body to stakes driven into the ground. They held his head up by supporting it with rocks and his eyes open by propping prickly pear spines against his lids, then the sadistic looking Yaqui took a layer of hide from the bottoms of his feet like skinning a squirrel. He was lucky. They might have trimmed off his eyelids, too. He had heard of such things from the Apaches. Rustlers did the same thing to cows to keep them from seeking refuge in thorny brush. The sun made short work of their vision, but the cruelty served its purpose, for the cattle stopped diving into cover at every chance. In comparison, the prickly spear spines were mild treatment, and only there long enough to make him observe his own torture. Afterward, the only reminders were burning sores beneath his eyes and under his upper eyelids.

Blood caked the sand at Sam's feet. Flies buzzed the sand and congregated on his wounds, walking, tickling him, tormenting him. The hum of their wings was almost overpowering. But he hurt too bad to move. Three of the Yaquis had beaten him with stout limbs of mesquite, rendering his arms and legs red and swollen. They would be horribly bruised by the next day … if he was still alive.

At last, Sam rolled over onto his stomach, and it was as if the blood moved in his feet and brought them back to life. The pain rushed back all over again, and he cried out and beat the ground with his fists. Finally, he gritted his teeth, and with a prayer on his lips he raised up on his elbows. The sunlight was horrific. The entire front of him was already seared, and the pain would grow worse. The only way for him to move would be on his hands and knees, no better than an animal. Worse, since animals at least had hardened pads or hooves meant to travel on. Sam continued to clench his teeth and force himself to think of something else besides his pain and the pain that lay ahead.

The first thing he needed was water. No man lacking it in this country could survive. The thought almost made him laugh. It had taken a day to ride here from Hermosillo. A hard day. His mode of travel now was crawling like a baby in the broiling sun wearing nothing but a sunburn. *Survive?* The notion was ludicrous. But because he was Sam Coffey he would struggle east until he died. He would not torture his soul in hell with the knowledge that his ghost had flown from right where the Yaquis left him.

Sam had not been to the spring, but he had observed the direction in which Tom traveled to get water, and he had his senses about him enough to remember most of the instructions Varnell gave them. With that in mind, he started crawling.

The pain was almost unbearable in the soles of his feet, his knees, his hands. Every sharp rock seemed to lie there in wait for him, and every time his foot bumped the ground the vibration shot all the way through to his wounds. At one point he almost wished he were a child again and could lose himself in tears. But his Choctaw blood drove him on relentlessly, and soon his clenched teeth began to hurt as bad as his feet ... as if anything could hurt that way.

Once Sam found the spring and quenched his thirst, he scooted into the shade of a big boulder and lay there hurting, wanting to die. He couldn't even look at his feet anymore. It brought back too much pain. So he lay there gathering his strength. Just from the crawl of a couple of hundred yards his knees were scuffed and burning and bloody. He forced himself to think of the Yaqui, Cajeme, and of the big ugly brute who had skinned his feet, laughing now and then and finally holding up the grisly trophies for him to see. He pictured the lithe, gracefully muscular Yaqui who had beaten him in the cave, whose every muscle rippled with power, with large veins down his biceps, along his forearms and hands, and a groove down his belly that made him look like some anatomy student's model, the ones made with no skin in order to clearly define the muscle structure beneath. These were the three men he remembered most. Three men he could have killed with a smile on his face.

Sam had never felt so strongly about killing someone. There were men he had run across, and even a woman now and then, he figured did not deserve to take up their allotment of flesh and skin. But he had never figured it was his place to do anything about it. Not until now ... Now he would have killed with great satisfaction.

There was a half hour or so during the heat of the day when Sam decided he should just stay where he was. Here was water, and he had what was left of Tom's fly-blown horse lying out in the sun. Maybe in a few days he could heal up enough to travel.

But that half hour was fleeting. By the time it passed he started thinking more logically. His feet were not going to heal enough to walk in a few days, and perhaps not even in a few weeks. If he was to survive this desert, it was up to him alone. Maybe Tom would make it back with help, maybe he wouldn't. Sam couldn't rely on that chance. He had to go, and tonight he would. He would travel in the dark, safe from the sun and perhaps safer from prowling predators, especially the human kind. He knew his chances of surviving the trek were improbable. But if he stayed here he was as good as dead, and Sam had never in his life rolled over and given up.

After resting for another half hour, Sam rolled liberally in the mud, caking himself to protect his skin, and headed back out into the sunshine, crawling toward Tom's horse. When he reached it, he cut out a large hunk of the tepid flesh with a sharp rock, devouring the first of it raw. He needed nourishment now, not later, and if the meat poisoned him he would just deal with it.

Once he had taken the edge off his hunger he began to hunt around for prospective tools. He would only be able to carry so much away from here, so he would have to be selective. Planning out in the grueling sunshine would be detrimental to his thoughts, so he crawled into the cave and up against the wall where the empty crates lay scattered. Once he was there, and the searing pain in his feet again began to turn to numbness, he wanted nothing more than to sleep. But that would have to wait.

Fire Sam could make. His skills were such that he could fashion himself a bow and drill fire set, which was just one step back from a flint and steel. Alternately, he could break one of the steel hinges off the big trunk, and with luck he might lay hold of a chunk of flint or chert and graduate to that method. He didn't know the chances of finding flint, but he knew he could find yucca or cottonwood to make a spindle and make enough cordage from the sinews of the horse to use on the bow. A rock to use for a hand-held spindle socket was something he would hardly have to cast about to find.

The more he planned, the more optimistic he became about his chances. Sam Coffey could make it out of this desert if any man could. No man was going to put him down as effortlessly as that!

There were several things he must have. First was water. And how to carry it? He would fill a section of intestine with water and tie it on the ends like a sausage, slinging it over his shoulder like the Tarahumaras had taught him to do. He had to have cordage, and the horse's sinew would provide that. For nourishment he would cut some horse meat into strips and lay them in the sun to start drying or make a fire back in the cave, away from prying eyes, and smoke it. The Indians had taken much of the best meat, but there was enough left to last him a day or two if he ate sparingly—more than he could carry, anyway. And last, he had to have shelter, which in this case would consist of any crude clothing he could make from the horse's skin. He couldn't tan it. That would take far too long and too much energy. But he could cut it out too large and put it on green, and at least when it dried it might be in a shape that fit him. Even the thought of the flies and yellow jackets that would swarm him with his raw set of clothing on was a torment, but that was better than the alternative, baking raw in the sun.

He also had to have some kind of weapon. If he could not find a good enough club of wood, one of the horse's leg bones would serve.

Having made his plans, Sam set out. He moved gingerly at first, but soon he learned to force his pain from his mind. Also, once the blood started moving, some of the stiffness seemed to seep out of his bruised appendages.

Waving off the swarming flies, he first wrenched out the horse's stomach and a six foot length of intestine, hacking them loose with the edge of a stone he honed by striking another against it at an angle, chipping the smooth edges away a flake at a time until he had a serviceable tool. Before he finished hacking at the intestines, he had been stung four times by yellow jackets.

He took a length of tendon from the horse's back and cut loose large pieces of hide which he would use to make his rough vest and apron, several pairs of pads for his knees and hands and a pair of moccasins. Through that part of the process he only got stung two more times, and he was happy to kill the responsible yellow jackets.

He felt a little guilty hacking on Tom's horse. Old Tom and his poor horses! If the cayuses had any way of knowing who was getting their mitts on them they would have turned outlaw to keep from packing Tom Vanse around. Seemed any horse beneath that man was destined for a violent death. When he remembered that Tom was now riding Gringo he had to force those thoughts out of his mind.

Sam put all of his booty into the bay's stomach, then dragged it back to the stream, battering all the while at the swarms of flies and yellow jackets. At the stream, he rested for a while, breathing in gasps like some fat-jowled city boy. He could feel gas building in his stomach from the sour meat he had eaten. He hoped it would get no worse.

Re-coating his body with mud, he then went to work washing all the horse parts in an area far away from the source of the spring so as not to poison it for future travelers. He fleshed the horse hide as best he could, then hacked out arm holes for a vest and slid it on with the hair side in. He cut another piece of the fetid hide off for an apron and wrapped it about him the same way, tying it on with lengths of horse tail braided together. The flies were immediately all around him, and one vicious yellow jacket stuck him in the arm when he tried to wave it away. He despised those little devils and always had, but they played second fiddle to the Yaquis now. At least the sun wouldn't get to his tender skin now, so the little devils appeared to be one of the necessary evils of life.

The rest of the afternoon he worked on his bow and drill set. He made cordage of the sinew from the horse's back after it had dried out sufficiently, a spindle of a dried yucca stalk, and the base for the spindle out of cottonwood. He found a round rock that fit nicely into his palm for the spindle socket and ground a hole into one side of it. Last, after cutting off the rest of the horse's tail and most of the mane, he rolled them up and tied them tightly, stuffing all of his precious accoutrements into the horse's washed stomach.

His last abuse of Tom's poor horse was hacking its upper leg loose and scraping it clean of meat, then smoothing off the last of the flesh with sand until the bone shone starkly white in the fading light.

As the sunlight disappeared from the cliff tops, he crawled back to the spring and glutted himself on cold water, then filled the length of intestine, sealed it with horse hair, and slung it bandoleer-style over one shoulder.

At last, he gave the cavern one final look of regret and started his long crawl east, dragging his bounty with him. He estimated a crawl of at least four days in front of him. Would Tom come back for him before he made Hermosillo? Or would he be found by Yaquis?

Apaches? Mexicans? God alone knew the answer to that. And God alone walked with him as he made his way up that hollow sounding canyon that only the day before he and Tom had ridden into triumphantly to claim their fortunes. There was no sound. Even the prayer on his lips was silent.

Chapter Twenty

Nadia Boultikhine had never been one to stay still. Especially not when a loved one faced mortal danger. She was no woman of great power. Other than a knack for shooting that Sam claimed she had, she possessed no special skill that might have made her seem a valuable asset in a manhunt. But Nadia had heart.

She was first shocked, then angry, when Abe Varnell came to her shamefully to tell her Sam and Tom were trailed out of town by would-be thieves. Because of him, Varnell said, not only did the partners face dangers before them, but behind.

Nadia was aware of Varnell's misfortune in the desert, and she intuited his encompassing fear of Mexico. But in spite of this fear, he was determined to use the last of his treasure to ride to Hermosillo, hire help, and go to Sam and Tom's aid.

Varnell had not intended on company. He had meant to face his shame and his fear alone. But he did not know Nadia. Varnell was a tough man, but it would have taken one much tougher to hold back Nadia Boultikhine from riding to rescue her man.

The road to Hermosillo was arduous. And for Varnell and Nadia the first third of it was marked only by horse hooves clopping in the sand and rocks, wind in the trees and the occasional cry of a bird. The two humans who might have spoken were both too busy fighting their own misgivings ... and fear.

The Yaqui who had wrestled Sam Coffey into captivity sat a dun horse blending dust-like into the colors of the desert, its eyes making large, dark pools in its head, its mane and tail hanging long and tangled. The Yaqui wore a white breech clout that revealed legs deeply copper, lithe but as deeply muscled as his arms. He was shirtless, and the square muscles of his chest rippled above a deep-cut groove running the length of his belly. The Yaqui's hands were not huge, but the sinews and veins that sculpted of them a road map testified of crushing strength. His neck and well-formed head, his intelligent eyes and wide, phlegmatic mouth, his black hair that lifted in the desert breeze—it all painted a portrait of a man born to the desert, a hard man to take down.

A faint tightening of the Yaqui's knees signaled the dun to move forward with the graceful pace of a horse bred in the wild country, able to travel a hundred miles a day. The smooth motion made the two of them seem as one, gliding like ghosts through the sand.

Down below, the Yaqui watched the Americano with the heart of steel. He now had clothes, water and weapons, and with these he could survive. But Cajeme's instructions were clear: no luxuries for the Americano.

Another unseen signal made the horse pick up pace, and with a grim look the Yaqui rode down the slope, gravel and sand sliding down as they made their careful descent.

It was growing too dark for Sam to see. He sat up to rest his knees and the palms of his hands, thinking of the blood he had left behind. If anyone wished to follow him he had drawn what was tantamount to road signs behind him. Even a child could have tracked him, by the queer indentations he left … and by the blood.

In spite of pain that made him want to scream, Sam laughed with the knowledge that he could have traveled no more than three or four furlongs. It seemed like five miles! He was bloody, bruised, exhausted. But he was not whipped. He would allow no man to put him under.

Nearby was a big sandstone boulder, and he dragged himself over and leaned up against it, his legs spraddled before him. Before leaning back, he pulled off the horse gut he was using to transport water, and the horse hide tunic, and laid them aside. It was good to be free of them.

Sam didn't like to look at his feet. He had seen bad injuries in his time, and some that healed up as good as ever. One time a horse he had ridden had yanked off its entire hoof in a crevice between rocks. He had not believed it possible, but the hoof had grown back, and the horse had gone on to become one of the fastest he had ever ridden. Yet looking at his feet he found himself wondering if he would ever be able to walk like a normal man again. The pain served one purpose. It drove him on, so intense it was almost impossible to sleep. But beyond that it was easier to will out of his mind than to dwell on.

He knew what he needed to start its healing process: agave. The stout-leaved desert succulent, known by many different names depending on the species, names such as maguey, lechuguilla, century plant, yamp, bacanora or mescal, contained rich healing juice in its leaves that he had seen work what some might have considered miracles. There were many different kinds of agave, some too slender to do any good. But on this trip he remembered pointing out to Tom some of the tall thick agave that brimmed with medicinal pulp and could be used as a source of moisture. But finding them would have to wait until tomorrow, so he decided to rest here until dawn.

Using the iron hasp he had taken from the Yaqui mine, and a chunk of flint picked up along his route, Sam made fire in a grass bundle. It was so dry he was able to dispense with the customary char cloth generally employed for such fires. He made the fire small, and hidden on three sides by the big boulder and several clumps of brush. The glow on the rock and brush would be invisible to anyone more than a hundred yards away.

Unfortunately, the Yaqui was not a hundred yards away.

Since leaving the cave, Sam had been more keen to the sounds of the desert than ever. But coaxing the fire into life distracted him, and he did not hear the hoof falls of the horse. As the flames rose a little over a half-foot high and he searched around for a rock on which to roast a hunk of the horse meat, he felt eyes on him. Instinctively, he whirled.

The sky silhouetted a mounted Indian, to all outward appearances relaxed, holding his reins loosely. The horse, too, stood statuesque, its misshapen mustang head moving ears and eyes alone, piercing the night in search of danger.

Sam's mind raced. Foremost in it was the thought that he had made it only half a mile from the scene of his torture, only to die here. Was this a Yaqui, or Apache? If he was Yaqui, did that mean Sam would be spared? Not all Yaquis thought alike, and not every Yaqui would know Cajeme's plan for Sam. To some wandering tribesman he would be nothing more than another intruder.

Seconds mimicked minutes while Yaqui and white man faced each other down. Then the head of the horse started toward the fire. He came in a slow, rhythmic plod, and stopped just within the firelight. It was then Sam recognized the Yaqui. The man stared, eyes shaded from the firelight by his horse's head. Yet what Sam could see in his eyes was not malevolence. It was musing. He was reading this white man like a student of medicine would ponder a cadaver.

The Yaqui rode over to a big bush and tore branches from it, then kneed the horse to the fire and threw them on. The flames raged high, lighting up both the Yaqui and Sam like bronze statues. The Yaqui scanned Sam with his eyes. Faint humor hooked the corners of his mouth, and something about his eyes revealed a deep intelligence belied by his barbaric appearance.

The Yaqui nodded. Then he pulled a rifle from its sling on his horse, and with the barrel he motioned toward Sam and looked down. Sam followed his eyes to the horse intestine water vessel on the ground. The Indian made a motion with his rifle barrel that could only mean to throw it aside. Dismayed, Sam stared. But when the Yaqui jacked his rifle lever, he picked up the intestine. Then, staring straight at the Indian, he untied the bow knot he had made with horse hair to hold the bag together, and putting one end to his lips he drank long and deeply, until his belly could hold no more. He expected to hear a rifle shot at any moment, to feel the slam of a bullet.

When at last he raised his eyes, the look of humor around the Yaqui's eyes had deepened. He nodded again, slightly, as Sam threw the intestine bag off into the brush.

The Yaqui looked down again, and for just one fleeting moment Sam thought he saw in his face something like mercy. But it quickly vanished. The Yaqui pointed once more with his rifle barrel, making a sweeping motion to indicate Sam's horse hide attire. Sam, heart falling, looked down at the vestments.

The Yaqui, face once again impassive, made the same motion with his rifle barrel for Sam to discard it all. Bunching his jaw muscles, hating this Yaqui with every ounce of his being, Sam stripped off the hide apron. Like the tunic, it had already started to harden, and was hard to remove. He flung them both into the brush after the water bag.

The Yaqui nodded again, then pointed to the east as by some unseen leg signal he made his horse back up a few steps.

Sam, heart thudding soddenly, tried not to think of the clothes, the water, the flint and steel. He tried not to think of the chunks of hide he had planned to use as moccasins. Thinking of them would not make them his.

Dropping back down to his hands and knees, he started again on his arduous trek with gritted teeth. Many things he had left behind him in the brush, but two things he had not: his will to live—and hatred of the Yaquis.

Gringo was an admirable horse, and the desert was his home country. He had been oat and corn fed not only in Nogales but from the stores Sam and Tom had brought with them. So even with gold in his saddlebags it had been with relative ease that he outran the Yaqui horses. And although Tom was fairly certain they would keep after him, he doubted they would catch up. His only worry was how he would find his way back to the trail with enemies crawling all over the desert in search of him.

With a sour glance toward the eastern sky, which lay on the far side of a jagged maze of canyons, Tom continued on down the draw. Not knowing for certain if the Yaquis had turned back, he could not take the chance on going back to the trail before the morrow.

He spent the night in a thicket of mesquite, afraid to start a fire, shivering to warm himself. It was one of the longest nights of his life.

Chapter Twenty-One

Taking cover during the day and traveling at night was common practice in the fiery southwest. Nighttime travel was safer and more convenient for a number of reasons. First of all, many Indian tribes shunned battle in the night, not for fear of the night itself, but because of religious taboos. Second, even for those Indians not inclined to superstition or religion, locating an enemy in the dead of dark could prove difficult. Third, it avoided temperatures that sometimes soared into the hundreds, and a sun that not only racked down from the sky, but from the rocks and sand.

Yet in spite of every reason to travel in the night, in reality sometimes the night itself spelled death to one with no path to follow. There was the obvious possibility of getting lost, and there were the nocturnal prowlers of the desert. Mexico was home to several species of rattlesnake, along with coral snakes, poisonous scorpions and centipedes and beaded lizards. The warm-blooded creatures could also pose a threat, the mountain lions, jaguars, wolves and an occasional wandering bear. And if all of that were not enough, there were dozens of dangerous plants that could bring on pain and suffering.

The truth was night travel made sense in a land of well-traveled roads, but in the trackless desert there was only one choice: sit out the night and travel under the watchful eye of the broiling sun and whatever *human* predators might be waiting to exact their toll.

Sam crawled until he was well away from where he had left the Yaqui, along with all of his tools for survival. He was too angry, too vastly furious to be weary. He had actually been able to convince himself, back at the Yaqui cave, that he would survive, that no bloodthirsty band of Indians was going to bring down Sam Coffey. But this incident had set him back, as stripped of the instruments of human invention as when he left the womb. At least his belly was full of water.

Sam was too infuriated to ponder the amount of blood he had lost on the last stretch of trail. But when at last he sat up to rest he realized it had to be considerable, from the raw feel of his hands. So unfeeling had been his anger that he had had no realization of the rocks and spines and sand that had savaged his palms. And of course his knees would match them, but he hadn't bothered to feel them yet. He sat there stunned at the height of his own fury, wanting nothing more than to kill the Yaqui. For that matter, *any* Yaqui! They had made a lifelong enemy, although it was growing more and more doubtful he would live long enough to be much of a threat.

Sam had nothing. No tools, shelter, clothing, food or fire. No water. As far as he knew no living friend, either. It was a big desert, and for Tom to make it out alive with the Yaquis on his trail would be tantamount to an Old Testament-style miracle.

Sam had only two weapons, two prospects for survival: his own Choctaw stubbornness and the sudden realization that he did not know how to die. And then he realized he had a third: his love for Nadia.

He knew what his next aim had to be. If he could steel himself, numb his body enough to keep crawling, he would reach the abandoned wagon of Silas Ranstrum. There he was sure to find articles a resourceful man might make good use of. Remembering the wagon brought the first large glimmer of hope Sam had experienced in some time. With grim determination, and with the wagon as his beacon, he crawled on.

When the exhaustion caught up, it set in like the cold of sundown on a wintry Colorado evening. Even while Sam's mind still churned with murderous intent, and the pain in the soles of his feet sometimes made him want to beat his fists against the ground, he felt his will to stay awake ebbing, and desperately he peered into the dark for some kind of shelter. All he could find was a stand of mesquite, and he crawled to it and lay down, oblivious to the dead branches that had fallen beneath the canopy, their thorns gouging him, piercing his weary flesh. He was likewise unaware of the centipedes and tarantulas that crawled through the neighborhood, and the big hot-blooded, yellow-eyed beast that padded dangerously near him when the Big Dipper was nearly level in the depthless black sky.

A healthy man traveling well clothed, well fed and well supplied might never notice the chill of a desert night. But wounded, naked and unsheltered Sam felt every shift of breeze. He was only lucky enough to have the strength left to shiver, and the vibrations of tooth against tooth served to remind him he had not died.

Even exhausted as he was Sam slept fitfully, waking a dozen times, once to the call of coyotes, and once when an owl stopped its hunting long enough to moan hauntingly in the mesquites while it preened its feathers. It must have been near four in the morning when lobos began howling in the near distance, and the mournful cries lifted the hair on his neck. He had never heard of a man being attacked by free, healthy wolves, but what if they found a man in his condition? If they ate him and scattered his bones he could never tell that he had been attacked, so the statistics would remain unchanged.

Every part of Sam's body ached as he lay and wondered if the wolves would come. His bruises throbbed, to say nothing of the soles of his feet, although he had grown used to the pounding of the bruises by now. The pain in his feet was still exquisite, but he managed at times to drum his consciousness of it away.

He had been forced to spend nights without shelter before. Always he was able to find sagebrush or leaves, boughs of fir or grass to cover himself and preserve some of his natural body warmth. But in the Mexican desert everything grew fierce, sharp and wicked. How did one make cover when doing so would be as detrimental as being exposed to the cold? Besides, bare branches, short of being burned, would be worthless for preserving warmth, and the desert plants were pitifully short on leaves, this being their very defense against the sun.

Sam dozed off, but not long before dawn he came sharply awake. At first, he heard nothing, but he sensed that something had awakened him, something more than just the cold. He strained his ears into the dark, his eyes and nose, too, senses largely ignored by "civilized" humans for detecting danger in the nocturnal world. Still, it was his ears that first served him. He heard stiff brush crackle, then the ever-so-faint sound of a canine sniffing out a scent. Breathless, he waited. Then it came again, only now he was sure it was from a different direction. Then he could see a dark shape, darker than the darkness itself, or perhaps only so because of the starlight behind it.

Wolves.

Nothing to do but wait. They knew where he was. If they wanted they had but to take him. Perhaps more by instinct than anything, he gradually became aware that five or six of them had come to surround him, all of them snuffling quietly in the brush, reconnoitering this invader of their domain. He heard a low, almost inaudible growl, what might have been considered a groan, and then in moments he heard brush crackle again as the wolves whispered off. They made no haste, but they had no further interest in him for the moment, either.

Sam knew some time around dawn, when the sun below the horizon was busy casting brass and pinkening the eastern sky, that he was going to die if he had to face many more nights such as that. There seemed to be no warmth left in him. The cold rose from deep inside, and even his fiery hatred of the Yaquis no longer heated him. The only good thing about it was how it had dulled the fierce pain in his feet. He turned toward the pink-gray horizon and started on, anxious to use the soft candle of Aurora while he could, before Apollo, god of the sun, made this Sonoran waste into hell.

Sam found himself praying for sunlight after an hour had dragged by. Motion didn't warm him, and he still ached through and through from the cold. Then he discovered breakfast stretched across the hard-packed soil before him, and just for the moment he was glad the sun had not come.

The seven-foot rattlesnake in the trail liked the cold even less than the man who was about to eat it.

Sam had never believed he would eat a snake. He remembered turning his nose up the time Tom had offered the meal, and he would have scoffed then if anyone had suggested he might not only eat snake but eat it raw.

The snake was torpid, too cold to put up much fight when Sam collected several big stones into a pile five feet from it and then pelted it to death. With the knowledge that food and water were all that could see him through this day, he took the snake while its nerves still made it writhe and bit through its scaly hide. He ripped with his teeth, stripping away a half-foot long piece of skin before it tore off. Then he bit into the flesh, pulling it from ribs. He thought of the last rack of ribs he had eaten at a Texas barbeque his boss, Chet Sward, had thrown for Trina when she turned sixteen. He had never had better ribs. Never a better feed of any kind. It would sure be nice if a steer had as many ribs to gnaw on as this rattler.

Sam almost grinned at the thought of a long sway-backed steer with this number of ribs. Now *that* would be a barbeque! He thought of many things, the last night with Nadia, the taste of salt spray off the gulf on Matagorda Island. He thought of lemonade and Scotch whisky and a hot apple pie Trina had made them one night when they got back from recapturing a runaway filly of hers. He dreamed of many things trying not to remember he was eating raw rattlesnake, but not one of them left the same impression on his tongue and throat and in his mind as the stiff pink flesh of the snake.

Sam glutted himself on serpent, eating far more of it than he thought prudent, the way a wolf will for not being sure of its next meal. When he had finished he stared at the remains of the reptile long and hard before throwing it away. Among his quiver of tricks was that of manufacturing poison, at which the Tarahumaras excelled. They would use a deer spleen, a rattlesnake head, sometimes even a little urine, crush it all together to make a paste, which they hung in a rawhide bag or in the animal's gall bladder in a tree for several days. Once it had cured the requisite amount of time they would dip the tips of arrowheads into it. The poison was so potent that even if they only scratched the leg of a deer with the arrowhead it would die.

Sam contemplated the prudence of using such poison, should he be able to fashion himself any kind of weapon, but in the end he threw the snake away out of fear. The poison was too lethal, and he would die a horrible death himself should he get any of it on his wounds. The poison would make up for a lack of skill in throwing a spear at a rabbit or whatever game he came upon, but like the serpent from which it was made it could also turn on him, a chance he was not willing to take. He had seen two Tarahumaras die after accidentally slicing themselves open on their treated arrowheads; it wasn't the kind of death a man would envy.

The sun topped the eastern mountains and quickly began its punishment. It didn't take long before he began to sweat, and that scared him. If he sweat he lost his body's stores of water. His tongue would begin to swell, his eyes would start to grate in his skull ... and then his mind would begin to go. He had seen it before. In fact, he had felt it once. It would be no way to die. A poisoned arrow would be preferable. Faster, anyway.

But at least in full sunlight he could avoid some of the other hazards. The bits of gravel partially embedded in the hardpan were a source of pain he would have to live with, too numerous to avoid. But he could skirt the dead cholla with their nests of evil spines, the rattlesnakes, prickly pear and ... *agave!*

There it was at the edge of his path. Agave, although in some forms, such as the aptly named shin-dagger, was as much of a hazard as any cactus, now seemed like a miracle from heaven. Further miracle was the fact that, out of all of the species of agave his adopted Tarahumara people had shown him, this agave was one of the sweetest. Not only that, but its raw juice, very caustic to the skin in some species of agave, was relatively mild.

Instinctively, Sam scanned the terrain all around, looking for his Yaqui nemesis. It would hardly do for the Indian to see him harvesting agave. For one thing, it would tip Sam's hand to the fact that he knew more about desert survival than any of the Yaquis had likely given him credit for, and for another, the Yaqui would probably take it away from him. Of course, if he followed his previous pattern he would wait until Sam had gone through extensive pain and preparation before confiscating it.

Sam saw no one, but he had no misgivings. The Yaquis, masters of battle and desert survival, would be every bit as good as the Apache at camouflaging themselves. The Yaqui could be watching his every move—but he had to try.

Preparation for harvesting the agave took nearly as much time as the harvest itself. He made a sort of long chisel out of a mesquite branch, which took more than an hour and a half. Then, putting the chisel end of the stick against the base of a fat plant, he drove a fist-sized rock against its handle. After several blows, the agave broke off at its stem.

Next, he had to trim the spines off the leaves with a sharp piece of chert rock he had picked up earlier to have on hand in case he could harvest any steel from the abandoned wagon to make the other half of a flint and steel fire set.

The slightly caustic juice in the agave caused his hands to itch, small cost for the moisture, the nourishment and the healing power he knew the agave would surrender. Now, before he could partake of the plant's goodness, came the hard part: he had to make a fire. The way the Tarahumaras had taught him to tame the plant's caustic juices, to make its meat edible, and to make it yield the moisture agave was famous for, was to roast it. He had dreaded that part all morning, for right now, with no steel, and no longer having his bow and drill set, making a fire meant twirling a wooden rod between his hands fast and hard and long enough to create the requisite spark. And that, considering the raw and bleeding condition of his hands, was sure to call up the most exquisite pain he had felt since the Yaqui took the skin from his feet.

Pushing aside his dread, he crawled to a yucca and cut off its stalk to use as a spindle. He found the dead branch he would need to turn the spindle in, hacked it in half lengthwise and made a notch in it for the coal to fall through, and then, four hours after first laying eyes on the agave, he bent over his spindle and a pile of bark fluff he had peeled off a mesquite. With a rapid rubbing motion, he began to rotate the spindle back and forth. His hands, already sore and raw, almost immediately began to paint the stick red with blood. His wrists ached maddeningly from the beating the Yaquis had given him. Sam gritted his teeth, suppressing a cry of pain. He used that energy to bear down even harder on the stick, to spin it faster. But his own blood kept making his hands slip down the stick, so he had to grip it harder.

Sam prayed for a fire, but his bleeding, aching hands kept sliding down the spindle, greased with blood. The palms of his hands were all that seemed to be catching fire.

Chapter Twenty-Two

Sam sat for many minutes slumped over what could have been his fire. His heart beat soddenly, and his haggard spirit seemed to puddle like swamp water in the depths of his chest. But in time another stimulus came into his heart, and that was Nadia. He had to escape this desert, and he had to escape it in one piece … for Nadia.

But why? He had nothing for the woman now. Any riches he had gained had been fleeting, and now he would return to her only the shell of a man. How could a man be so self-centered as to burden a woman like Nadia with what he had become? He couldn't, not unless some sign came to him, some sign too powerful to dismiss. He had sworn not to carry his misfortune to Nadia and her son, and it was a vow he had to keep.

Taking a deep breath, he looked down at his agave leaves. The pieces he had chosen were about a foot and a half long and five inches wide. They were the thickest of the bunch, full of soft, succulent pulp that could be used to nourish or to soothe. Other agave were used for cordage, and some of their roots for soap.

Sam had seen Tarahumaras eat raw agave, although it was not common. They almost always roasted it in rock-lined pits to turn its starch into sugar and make it palatable. But raw agave was better than no agave. Tarahumaras had been known to survive on its moisture for many days, weeks—even months—without needing to hunt water, which even for a Tarahumara could take a miracle to find during the dry season.

Steeling himself, Sam peeled the hide off one of the biggest of the pieces of agave and downed it quickly. His mouth didn't feel any wetter, but he was happy to know the rest of his body would have the moisture it needed.

The sun pounded down, and across the desert nothing moved. Sam needed rest, but first he had to find shelter. The 1880's, the Victorian Age, was not a period when anyone went around exposing much skin. Even appearing in shirtsleeves in public was frowned upon. So Sam's once white skin was raw and red. His butt, for one, had never seen sun for more than the brief moment it might have taken on a cattle drive to dive into a hole along some river, and usually he did that still clad in long johns. It was obvious he would hurt for a long time just from the sun he had already endured.

Sam could see the top branches of a big ironwood tree growing in a gully a hundred yards away. He didn't want to travel that far, but he had to shade up if he wanted to rest. After downing as much agave as he could hold, he started crawling. When he reached the tree his palms were bleeding and caked with sand and bits of gravel. Sam would normally have been sweating from the pain, but sweating had mostly ceased since earlier that morning. Until he absorbed the juices of the agave there was little more for him to sweat.

The shade under the ironwood was broken, but it was the best Sam could do. He curled into a ball and was almost immediately asleep.

When he awoke he had no immediate idea why. He sat up and looked around, feeling like he was on a three-day drunk. The desert was still, except for grasshoppers clattering in the brush. On the far horizon a mass of cottony-bright thunderheads had accumulated, packed tightly together like sheets in a sack. The sun shone blindingly off them.

Sam caught movement out in the sunlight toward his agave patch. He stared that way, but whatever had been there was gone. But *something* had been there—something big enough to catch his eye at this fair distance. Perhaps a deer, a peccary. Perhaps … the Yaqui?

While the sun climbed the rest of the way into the sky, Sam sat in the shade of the ironwood and contemplated his odds. Considering the skills and knowledge he had learned with the Tarahumaras he still thought that, even naked and starting out with no tools, he had a chance to make it to Hermosillo. He thanked God Tom had been the one to escape. Tom was a capable man, a good hand to have around. But he had never lived with any people of the desert. He could not have survived this ordeal. Sam just hoped his friend remembered the few things he had told him about desert survival.

Sam's first order of business was fire. He had about decided to use the raw agave on his feet, which cried for soothing moisture, but as badly as his hands and face itched from the juice, it was not an idea he relished. There was one more chance, something he had been too exhausted to think of earlier. He looked down at his scabbed hands. Simply contemplating the coming task made them ache. But it had to be done. He took a ragged stone and roughed up the wooden spindle so badly it could not slide through his hands even if they were slick with blood. Then he turned to the dreaded task.

Taking the spindle between his throbbing hands, he put the point of it on the carved-out indentation in his fireboard and bore down, starting to spin it back and forth. He clenched his teeth. The fire was already there—in his hands. He growled out loud, cursing his own pain. His hands started to bleed again, but the splintery wood kept them from sliding down, so his pressure on the spindle served its purpose. Minutes went by. Then magic began to happen.

First, a fine little smoke, as fine as steam, curled around the spindle's base. Sam ached with the strain, his body weak from lack of nourishment. But he could not stop, or he would have to cut a new notch in his baseboard and begin again. He drove the spindle back and forth, forcing it with agonized determination against the base.

More smoke appeared, and more, tempting him to stop and check for a coal. His breathing was labored now, not only from exertion but from the mental stress of contemplating failure. With his hands crying at him, he stopped. Quickly and carefully he laid the spindle aside and picked up the base board, which had a flat rock underneath it. The board protected a little mound that appeared at first to be ashes but contained within it a tiny coal. He eased the coal into his bed of bark and began with slight puffs to breathe life into it. He could not lose control now. He had to be careful to not blow the ember away yet blow hard enough to coax it into life.

A miniscule puff of smoke twirled within his pile of shaved mesquite bark, then once again. He blew gently, unworried about spitting on the coal as there was no more moisture in him to make spit. And then, like a tiny miracle, the bark burst into flame!

Sam hustled the burning ball under a pile of dried grass and brush he had collected, then added stouter and stouter sticks to it until he had a fire he could span with his hand.

His heart pounded with elation, and a big grin split his face, literally cracking his lips. He felt the blood trickle down his chin from his bottom lip, but he didn't care. In fact, he was glad of it; it proved his blood had not dried up!

Within minutes Sam's fire crackled beneath the tree, whose intertwined branches served to break up the smoke column. He had carefully picked his fuel, only the driest grass, bark and branches. Between their dryness and the net of tree branches, there was not enough smoke in the air to warn anyone he was within miles.

He put several of the agave leaves on the fire to roast. It was best to do this in a deep pit, but he had no such luxury. His main goal was just to deaden the caustic property of their juice and render the plant useful for food, water and a healing poultice. He sank back on his legs, exhausted both emotionally and physically.

Damn the Yaquis! No bloodthirsty savage was going to bring down Sam Coffey *that* easy! He had never been beaten yet.

Fighting the urge to doze, Sam tended his little fire, adding sticks as it died down. The largest of the branches he put on was perhaps an inch around and burned quickly into coals. After two hours of this process, he pulled the agave off the fire to cool, letting the fire abate. He had been lucky so far in keeping the smoke down, but it was not as if he needed the fire's heat, and it had outlived its usefulness.

While waiting for the agave to cool, it struck Sam that he would need something with which to attach his soothing poultices to his feet. This realization had only set in when he thought of two things at once. One, the material for making cordage was immediately at hand; from where he sat he could see fifteen or twenty clumps of the same yucca he had used for his fire spindle, and its leaves made for some of the best cordage a man could find in nature. Two, he could have saved himself much pain and agony and possible infection in his hands by using the same cordage to create himself a bow and drill set instead of using the difficult hand spindle method. But it was not worth wasting any effort regretting his lapse now.

Sam's first order of business was to make the cordage for tying the agave to his feet. Next he would create himself a bow and drill set. With his raw hands he probably could not stand to make another fire with the hand spindle, but he could still work a bow.

Crawling back out into the sun, he cut off several spearlike leaves of yucca, then returned to the shade of the ironwood. His knees were raw and bruised, as were the palms of his hands, but if he let himself dwell on the pain he could easily give up.

Before doing anything else, he gorged himself on agave, leaving the biggest one to treat his feet. Then, since he was not wearing pants and therefore could not use his leg as a table on which to work the yucca leaves, he set one up against the bole of the ironwood, holding it with his left hand, and shaved the green outer membrane off, then turned it over and did the same on the opposite side. Remaining were long stringy fibers that had served admirably for hundreds of years when indigenous American people wanted cord or sewing thread. In fact, if one left the sharp point of the yucca leaf intact, it worked beautifully as a needle, the natural thread already attached.

By braiding strands together, Sam made several cords out of the yucca and laid them aside, then roughly hacked the agave leaf in half with the chert knife. When he applied the roasted agave half to his mutilated, sunburned foot, it was the next best thing to putting it in cool water. He sighed and closed his eyes, soaking in the relief. He used the cordage he had made to crisscross over and under his foot, effectively "sewing" the agave poultice in place. He did the same with the second piece. Then he rubbed the gelatinous substance liberally on his knees and hands, and on his raw, sunburned shoulders. Before it was gone, he made mud by mixing it with some of the soil under the ironwood tree, and this he smeared on his body as further protection from the sun. It soothed his skin, although at that point there was little that could comfort it very much.

It was while smearing on the mud that he had the idea of making a loincloth out of yucca cordage. It would take some time, but what did he have that day but time? His rear end stung so badly from sunburn he didn't consider *not* taking the trouble to protect himself.

It took several hours to manufacture enough cordage to weave together a very basic loincloth, like a small diaper. It was full of windows the sun could peek through and would never completely protect him, but compared to what he had had before, with little more hair on his back and butt than a snake, this loincloth would be a boon. It would certainly be itchy, but far better than hanging free in the Sonora sun!

Next he set to work on a bow and drill set. Braiding several strands of fiber together, then enjoining these thickened strands twice more, he had a stout piece of cord about two feet long. He found a branch a foot and a half in length and sawed a groove into both ends with his rock knife. To one end he tied the yucca cordage, then arced it and tied the other, creating what looked like a miniature archer's bow. He would make use of the same spindle and base piece he had used for his hand drill, and to use as a socket for the top of the spindle he found a flat rock that fit his hand nicely and drilled a depression in it. The smaller items he put down the front of his yucca diaper.

The stop had cost Sam seven hours by the time he crawled away from the ironwood tree. His bow and two fat agave leaves dangled down from cordage around his neck like a huge, garish necklace. His feet were clothed in agave leaves, whose moisture seemed to have already soaked deep into the raw flesh, soothing and beginning to heal it. His yucca diaper sagged down in front with the weight of his only other possessions, his palm stone, spindle and wood base. Comfort was far from the order of the day.

Sam's next destination was the wagon. Even though it had meant nothing more than a tragedy to him and Tom before, there were things at that site that might save his life now. If only he could keep out of sight of the Yaqui long enough to use them …

Sam's hands were bleeding. His knees were raw. Embedded in them both were dust and sand, tiny pebbles and thorns. Behind him he left the oddest of trails, one that might give even a seasoned tracker pause. Indentation of hand, of knee, marked by blood, and once in a while the scrub where a toe had dragged. Most of the time, except to a highly trained tracker, the ground was too hard to document anything but the blood.

Sam had company now. Seven black vultures circled above, patience their major virtue. And an obsession with cleaning, not themselves so much, but the land. If fate was their friend, scattered on the sand they would soon leave Sam's bones.

In the west, huge thunderheads glowered, and Sam kept a leery eye on them. What he did not need now was a lightning storm, along with its threat of flash floods. The gods had dished out enough already.

Sam used all of his agave for sustenance and to make more mud to cover his body. His makeshift diaper made his burned skin itch horribly, but it beat the alternative. He took cover several times when he found shady patches he couldn't pass up, but paused no more than a half hour at a time. He was driven to get back to the wagon.

Long in the afternoon he left the eerie canyon country, and late in the dusk he arrived within sight of the wagon, too tired to crawl farther. Ironically, it was sight of the wagon that made him collapse, and in the cooling sand he faded unconscious.

But he slept not the sleep of the dead. Movements in the night disturbed him. Once he thought he heard deer, other times it was noises in the brush he could not identify. Some were tiny scratchings—desert packrats or kangaroo rats, perhaps, or some other rodent. Another time larger, fur-covered bodies ghosted through the brush.

The sky crackled with stars, gallons of them splashed to and fro in clusters and vast trails like errant mists of sea spray. Giant cactus loomed faint against the sky along with trees, one containing the eerie silhouette of an owl that watched him when he fell asleep and was still there when he awoke.

Sam's mind went unbidden to Nadia. His heart ached for her and her loneliness. She would be sitting there in that lonely house, Nikolai her only company. She would long for him and wonder how he was, for she could have no idea he was in trouble.

He allowed himself to think of Tom, too. Tom had a good horse under him, in Gringo. That animal knew the desert, and if Tom gave him his head, and if there was water anywhere, he would find it. But had Sam told Tom enough about the agave, how it held vast stores of moisture? Or the barrel cactus? Had he shared with his friend enough of the little morsels of knowledge that might spare his life in this hostile land? He believed he had—if Tom had listened.

Brush whispered very close. Sam thought he heard the sound of an animal sniffing. He held his breath. Silence. Silence that ran on into eternity. He breathed out and back in, out and in, and still there was only that dead desert quiet, and even the nearby crickets made no music. Sam lay literally naked and helpless, and his instincts told him that very close by lurked mortal danger. But with no moon and starlight that hardly touched the earth, he could see nothing but the silhouettes piercing the sky.

Movement again, then a musky animal odor. Something was there, something very near. And big. Bear? Cougar? Wolf? Indian? No hoofed animal would be so stealthy nor have reason to be. This was an animal either with pads on its feet ... or moccasins. This was something predatory, something that smelled his blood, sensed his weakness, and now was weighing its chances.

Sam knew holding still was not his best option. Whatever this animal was, it knew he was here. It could probably see him. And if it believed him helpless that might make the only argument it needed to close in. So he moved, scraping purposely as loudly in the gravel as he could.

Brush crackled, signaling the animal moving off. It was not panicked flight, but cautious, a slow padding away. Perhaps it was mere flight of fancy, but he seemed to feel the vibrations of feet hitting the ground. This animal was no coyote, and he didn't believe it was wolf, either. It was bigger than either of those, and its movements were smooth and graceful. Bear, perhaps. Indian ... maybe. But he would bet cougar. Nothing moves so gracefully as a cat.

Sam made his way over to the wagon, where he crouched low. He did not crawl beneath the box, not wanting to be caught lying down. Instead, he propped himself against the near front wheel, and his eyes strained into the dark. The clear air and his nakedness made Sam shiver violently—that, along with fear of the unknown and his very weakness. But shivering was good, for it was the body's mechanism of staying warm. If his body had that in it then he was far from dead.

Even knowing something was out there possibly stalking him, Sam felt sleep drawing him down. For a time he fought it but finally decided he had to let it come or exhaustion itself would take his life. Before letting go, he crawled under the wagon to the other side and wrenched a spoke from the broken wheel. He returned to his former place, away from the dead man, and with the spoke as his only weapon he faced into the night and felt his eyes closing over.

The last thing that touched his senses was a strange, luring scent, a hypnotic scent that called him far, far back—back to his childhood …

Chapter Twenty-Three

The chaparral cock was first to awake, when it was barely light. Nervous and spry, the roadrunner darted into the rocky creek bed where Sam and the wagon lay. It stopped not far from him, cocking its eye curiously his way. He thought of throwing his club at it, but it must have read his mind. With a hard twitch of its tail, it was gone again on its morning race, hunting up some hapless snake or lizard.

Exhaustion had taken the place of weariness for Sam. He was slumped over in front of the wagon wheel when he heard the roadrunner, and it was all he could do to raise his eyes and watch it. He probably could not have killed it even if the bird had walked over and offered itself to him.

Sam looked down at his bloody knees. He turned his hand over and stared at the gory mess that was his palm. There was a large thorn broken off dead center, and although he thought of raising his other hand to pluck it he didn't have the energy. He fought to keep his eyes open. He wondered if there was any agave nearby. He needed moisture now, or he would never shake free of this exhaustion. He needed moisture, he needed sleep … and he needed meat. Of the three only the sleep seemed attainable.

Turning his head, Sam looked under the wagon. There on the far side of the broken front wheel lay what remained of the skeleton of Silas Ranstrum, broken among his clothing, which scavengers had shredded. His skull was still there, picked clean, but the bones of both hands had been dragged away, along with his forearm bones. It didn't take long for buzzards, maggots and desert ants to clean a corpse.

Beside the body lay a spare wagon wheel, which Sam assumed the man had been preparing to put on when struck. But he could see no lug wrench near him. Apparently whoever had sacked the wagon later had seen some use for that, too.

Speculation told Sam the lightning had hit either during or just before a rainstorm, and after Ranstrum and the oxen lay dead the downpour had extinguished the flaming canvas. Yet it appeared as if at least part of the fire had continued to smolder, for much of the front of the wagon box was charred, and in one place there was a hole burned clear through it, perhaps six or seven inches around.

Leerily, he glanced upward, searching for storm clouds. The sky was clear and pale now, and in the east light was gathering. He would have liked to crawl away, to make some time before the onslaught of the sun. But he had to have sleep, or his trek today would be short-lived. Swallowing his uneasiness, he crawled underneath the wagon and lay down to sleep, his club clutched close to him.

But sleep did not come. He was lying there, feeling absolutely exhausted, when a scent touched his nose, and with it came flooding memories. First was the memory of the same smell wafting in as he drifted to sleep the night before, and then again the memories of his childhood. This was an odor Sam had experienced only three or four times, back in his childhood, before his parents died. But it was a scent one could never forget. Hurriedly, he rolled out from under the wagon and looked around. Within seconds he spotted it, there in the shade of a nearby acacia, its white brilliance nearly aglow in the dawn: night-blooming cereus, the queen of the night! One night, and one night only, this beautiful white flower bloomed, and then was gone. And here was Sam to behold it! Glory, but it was beautiful!

How he wished Nadia could see this flower, and his thoughts flew to the one he had planted beneath her paloverde tree. He had convinced himself he was not meant ever again to see the cereus in bloom, that he was not meant to be in the presence of such beauty. But there it was, staring him in the face. The queen of the night!

Sam's eyes blurred with tears, and he felt the blood charge through his veins. The sight of the flower was miraculous enough in itself, but this early dawn it was only a trigger—the trigger that changed his life.

At that fateful moment, Sam Coffey believed one thing more powerfully than anything he had ever known. He was tired of running from childhood fear. He was ready to move on with his life, to take his chances on what the future held. He would survive this desert, and he would return on his own two feet to Nogales. Sam had discovered once more the queen of the night, but Sam's own queen waited for him back in Nogales. He meant to marry Nadia Boultikhine. Bad luck and fate be damned.

He crawled back beneath the wagon bed and lay down. He remembered feeling surprised when sleep actually stole down to claim him.

Nadia Boultikhine sat on the straw-filled pallet on the floor of what passed for a hotel room in Hermosillo and fought back bitter tears. Where did she go from here? Abe Varnell was out at the bar trying to beg assistance of some of the Mexican men there, but so far they had reached an impasse. The Mexicans remembered two Americanos who had come through, yes. But they had no interest in going into a desert filled with Indians and bandits to help rescue them. The two gringos had come for gold, and they had been duly warned. What happened to them now was no concern to the residents of Hermosillo. That was the last word Nadia had gathered before withdrawing furiously to the room. She knew her presence in the bar room could only hinder Varnell, angry as she was.

Nadia steeled herself and scooted over to her saddle, drawing a single shot Remington from her rifle scabbard. She slid a handful of rifle shells out of a leather pouch and studied their shiny brass. *Be sure to keep one for yourself,* Sam had always told her, educating her on dealing with hostile Indians. She would do as he said, because Sam knew about that kind of thing. But the other shells were going to bring down as many bodies as they could before she used one on herself. She would attempt whatever she had to to get Sam home safe.

Instinct told her that somewhere out there her man was lost or hurt, calling out for help. He had no idea help would come from her, but did it matter where it came from? Nadia would never have it said she had let her man die alone if there was anything she could do.

A wistful look came into her eyes as she thought of Sam, of the last time they had been together. His kiss had been so gentle, so full of promise, even as she believed it was his last. What she would have done to keep him there with her that night and forever! Had he stayed one more night, one of his dreams would have come true. As the shadows had stretched long across the yard, and she had sat with Nikolai out on the swing, the night-blooming cereus under the paloverde had donned its beautiful white gown. Sam should have been beside her for that.

Out in the main room, Abe Varnell slammed his calloused hand down on the bar, cold green eyes boring through the Mexican behind it. "There must be at least one real hombre in this town," he said. "I'll give you the day and night to think about it. I'll be up before the sun, and I'll be here waiting for an answer. Twenty dollars in gold, amigo. That is a lot of money. Twenty dollars in gold if you will go with me. If *anybody* will go with me. You convince three or four men to go, I will pay each of them twenty American dollars, and you as well."

With that, Varnell turned and brushed past the onlookers, stepping soundlessly into the room where Nadia waited. The woman, eyes hopeful, looked up at him. Varnell met her glance softly, shaking his head. He would have given all of his cursed gold to have a different answer for her.

Caps O'Brien, Tracker and Johnny Riles had made Hermosillo, but they had not stayed. It was not worth debating, not for Caps. He had come to Mexico seeking gold. He had come here intending to get rich. His partner, Temp Stratton, was convenient because he was good with a gun, a good man to have around in a fight. But he was not what Caps would have called a friend. Stratton was much too surly. Caps preferred men around him of better humor. But lacking humor, ability to fight was an admirable quality. Now, however, he had no idea if Stratton was still alive. He did not know about Burt McGrath or Scrub Ottley, either, and at this point it did not matter. The chances of their getting back together were slim. What Caps wanted was the gold.

In Tracker, Caps had an able companion. He did not like the black man, because the black man did not like him. But Tracker was good with a gun, and he understood the rudiments of surviving in this desert. Johnny, he was an amusing enough kid, and relaxed, too, now that Stratton wasn't around. He could carry on a decent conversation, and that filled Caps's gregarious need. All he wanted more was the Yaqui gold.

So now, only three men strong, they set off into the desert looking for the abode of an old Seri Indian, the Indian who, according to the story Johnny had overheard in the livery, had led Abe Varnell to the gold.

It was pure good fortune that led Temp Stratton, Burt McGrath and Scrub Ottley to the homestead of old Paco, the Seri. They had wandered off the main trail leading down to Hermosillo, and in trying to relocate it they stumbled on the oasis looking like a garden there in the scabrous brown rocks. Upon meeting the owner of the place, it was Scrub who recalled Johnny Riles's description of the old Seri who had shown Abe Varnell the way to the gold in the first place.

After several tense moments trying to explain to Paco how they had come looking to rescue their two friends, Coffey and Vanse, Burt, with his smooth talk, was able to convince the old man of their honorable intentions. They left the homestead not only with the old Seri's blessings, but with his description of the country through which they must travel.

Burt was strongly titillated by what they had learned from the Seri. He had told them he was concerned about the safety of the two friends of Abe Varnell he had already sent on ahead. Why? Because the gold they sought had been kept loose in crates and trunks, and they should have been able to load up plenty by that time and come back through his place.

Loose in crates and trunks! The very image of this kind of fortune almost made Burt's head spin. The chance encounter with the old Seri had turned into a dream! Shortly after their brush with death at the hands of the Mexicans and Apaches Burt had wished fervently they could turn and run for the Arizona border. In fact, that thought had come to him many times since leaving Nogales. But this mention of gold in boxes urged him on so strongly he could not have thought of leaving now even if it meant he had to continue on with the surly Stratton.

A sudden rush of guilt hit Burt so hard he had to strive to push it aside. Before parting the old Indian's homestead, he had told them he had a feeling things had not gone well for Tom Vanse and Sam Coffey. Burt swallowed hard as those words struck home once more. Even if things had gone well for them up to this point, they would not when Stratton caught up.

What would come of Coffey and Vanse when they found them? He couldn't help reflecting on how big he had talked back in the Ventana about revenge. But from what he had seen of Stratton, to him "revenge" would mean only one thing: killing. Burt wanted no part of that. Thoughts of the gold stirred his soul … but murder? Heaven help them if it came to that. He would simply refuse to take part in it. But what if they forced his hand? He couldn't help feeling any leadership he had enjoyed over Stratton had long since eroded into oblivion. Not only would they not listen to him if he tried to stop a killing, but … would they turn on him as well? Again, he pushed the thoughts away. He must take things as they came. But as the miles dropped behind, and he had more and more time to contemplate what lay ahead, the more he feared the end of this trail, gold or no gold. Could he live with himself if by gaining the gold he allowed two men to die?

Tom Vanse was lost like a feather in a tornado. Since running into the Yaquis two days earlier, he had dodged them and wandered the desert. Even using his two canteens sparingly, he had run out of water. He was at the point of desperation when they had seen a herd of burros, which led them to a *tinaja,* or natural tank in a sandstone depression. They had slaked their thirst and filled both canteens, then traveled on, satisfied. But Tom had eaten nothing in twenty-four hours and the horse had taken in only what meager bunch grass he could find.

They were riding through a sandy wash that snaked between mesquite stands too thick to maneuver when a searing pain exploded in Tom's right leg. He cried out without meaning to and dropped his eyes to see the protruding shaft of an arrow in his thigh!

Tom laid spurs to Gringo, who had already gathered himself to run. The sand, for a moment, seemed to suck on the buckskin's feet, but when he got moving he thundered down the wash like a jackrabbit, kicking up sand and gravel behind. Tom knew he was in trouble. But he was also smart enough to realize if he didn't outrun whoever had put the arrow in him he might never need worry about how badly damaged his leg was.

He never saw who was behind him. He just let Gringo run and run until he began to flag, when he realized he had better slow him down or they were both going to die. He had the handicap of carrying gold in his saddlebags, which no Indians would. He had been lucky enough to outrun the first bunch, and maybe this one, too, but with the arrow in his leg he was afraid his luck had run out.

Sam Coffey awoke with a start. He almost sat straight up, which he realized upon getting his senses back would have been a bad error; the underside of the wagon box might have given him a concussion. He was lying in the best spot of shade he had enjoyed since leaving the Yaqui mine. But the comfort of that shade did not come to Sam's mind. Something was dreadfully wrong.

Instinctively, he threw himself sideways, grabbing for the club he had made of the wheel spoke. Even before laying a hand to it he found himself face to face with two living fire opals—the yellow-green eyes of death.

Chapter Twenty-Four

Sam Coffey was stunned to immobility. He stared into those deadly eyes, four feet away. There crouched a full-grown jaguar!

The cat's gigantic, blocky head had powerful jaws that could crush any bone in Sam's body. Its front legs rippled with muscle, equivalent in the cat world to those of a Clydesdale stallion. Jaguar, the cat whose very moniker in one Indian tongue meant "the cat that kills with one leap." Jaguar—el Tigre!

The fact that the cat was crouched where it was, staring straight through Sam, its tail twitching, was ominous. Most cats would have fled at sight of a man. But this one seemed to sense Sam's weakness. This was the animal he had sensed stalking him!

Gathering all his courage, Sam flung a handful of sand at the cat's face and yelled, "Git!" The cat dodged its head and blinked, emitting a soul-numbing snarl. It slashed at Sam with a retaliatory paw, and if Sam hadn't rolled it would have laid his arm open.

The jaguar made a dive, claws bared. Sam jabbed at its face with the end of the wheel spoke. The cat sank back, showing its fangs with a loud hiss. With fangs a respectable inch and a half long, it was a safe bet this animal was not here out of inability to hunt for its own food, thinking Sam an easy meal. This fiend was here simply to kill.

The cat feinted to one side. Sam started to move that way, but the cat leaped the other. As its left paw came down flat, Sam drove the end of the spoke into the top of it. The cat screamed and slashed with its right foot, ripping the club from his hand, sending it skittering off across the streambed.

Sam's only weapon was gone …

With deadly intent, but seeming uncertain if Sam was still armed, the jaguar started around to the other side of the wagon. Feverishly, Sam started to roll that way, cranking his head about to watch it. The cat swapped ends and came back at him from the front. Sam was almost too slow to back away.

He searched around him desperately. There were a few medium-sized stones mixed with the sand, and he snatched them and let fly—too fast! One bounced off the cat's head with a thump, but it only seemed to infuriate the animal more. When he was down to the last one that looked like it would have any effect, he tried to steady his aim, to coordinate his hand and his eyes. He let fly, and if he had not been forced to throw sideways because of the wagon bed overhead, this one might have driven the cat away in pain. As it was, it struck the animal on the bridge of the nose, and the cat shook its head and backed up, letting out a furious roar.

Sam Coffey is dead, the voice inside his head told him. But he clung desperately to life, trying to hide the fear in his voice as he spoke. "God, you got any miracles for me you better drag 'em out." There came no clap of thunder, no heavenly light, no bells—no sign that his plea had been heard.

Sam's eyes dodged back and forth as the cat stepped forward, and he leaned back and kicked a healthy dose of sand in its face, hardly making it pause. He backpedaled to the hole that had burned through the wagon bed, thinking to pull down one of the weakened boards. Reaching up through the hole, he bore down hard and came away with hands full of brittle coals. Simply because he had them in hand, he threw them at the cat, but it dodged with ease.

Desperately, Sam tore at the boards, and this time, when he broke two large chunks away, a wooden crate started to topple down through the hole. In his attempt to roll away from it, Sam inadvertently missed being torn by the cat's grasping paw. He turned and yelled loudly at the feline, throwing more sand in its face. It simply shook its head, and the deadly look in its eyes flattened out. The cat was tired of being held at bay by this mere human.

Without warning, the box fell through the hole and cracked Sam on the skull. He rolled to one side as it lit and tipped, spilling its contents in the sand. Fumbling at little boxes and jars, he started throwing them at the cat with as much force as he could muster, his head still ringing from the blow. The jaguar, however, had gotten used to that game and become deadly efficient at dodging his missiles.

A few of the articles struck the cat in the body, but again it only made him more furious. As a last-ditch effort Sam threw another handful of sand and yelled as loud as he could. Not the sand but again the yell seemed to disorient the cat long enough for Sam to turn back to the fallen crate, digging frantically for anything to throw.

The only thing left was a little canvas sack not much larger than Sam's fist.

With a deep-digging fear that made him more determined than ever, Sam smashed the crate with his fist, breaking one board loose from the nails that held it to the box end. He savaged it loose from the other end.

By the time he could whirl with the short piece of wood the cat was coming under the wagon box with him, its fangs bared for the kill.

Sam stabbed hard and fast with the splintery board, aiming for the jaguar's eye. The jaguar ducked, so the board rammed it in the forehead instead, but at least the big cat didn't have the wits to react with a paw. Shaken, it scrambled backwards out of the quarters it had suddenly found to be too close.

Low and fierce, a growl rumbled like thunder out of the animal's throat. In the pulsating desert sun, the cat's coat seemed to shine like jewels, its black rosettes a thing of beauty against the tawny orange hide even as the beast was trying to kill him. The cat made a dash around the other side of the wagon, and Sam had to spin to get his feet out of its reach. It was so hard to maneuver underneath the wagon box that the cat's black claws almost reached him. Sam suddenly felt a burning in his eyes, and the powerful urge to sneeze, which he couldn't hold back. Two violent sneezes shook his body, leaving him temporarily helpless while his eyes were forced shut.

When the urge to sneeze was gone, Sam opened his stinging eyes and scrambled from under the wagon. He rolled a few feet out into the sand before coming to his knees. The cat, as if it had springs on its feet, leaped up into the wagon box, took one more half-jump, and paused, its front feet now on the wagon sideboard, facing Sam. It hovered above him now like some demon gargoyle. Sam knew he had done the wrong thing. He was in the open, with only a short piece of board to serve as a weapon. This three hundred pound cat had but one jump to make, and its weight alone would crush the weak man from his kneeling position into the sand. One quick bite.

Then it would all be over.

Unless ... Sam's mind groped. What if, when the animal leaped, he could drive the board down its throat? It was his only chance, if it was a chance at all. The jaguar's ears were flat against its head, making the head seem even larger. The yellow-green eyes glowed, intense, and its fangs seemed almost to glint in the sun. For the first time Sam noticed the animal's scent, like musk and fetid flesh stirred up together with dust. The lip curled, making the teeth glisten in the sun. That mouth, that throat looked huge, but when it came to the board clutched in Sam's hand they seemed like an awfully small target. The cat's muscles bunched. Sam's coiled, too ...

In desperation, Sam lost his nerve, threw the board at the cat's face and dove for the underside of the wagon. He skimmed the top of his head along the wagon's sideboard, so close was he, but once more in the shade of the wagon he rolled, just in time to keep out of the cat's grasp.

At the worst possible moment, his eyes began again to burn fiercely, and he fought off another sneeze. Something pungently powerful was roiling through this air, strong enough to taste. He started to whirl back toward the cat, but then he couldn't help but whip his eyes back to the little bag that had fallen from the crate. It had come open, and part of its contents had spilled onto the sand, which he had rolled into. It was a red powder, and Sam suddenly recognized that smell.

Ground red pepper! God's answer to his prayer?

Instinctively, he snatched the bag and rolled to his left. The cat's jaws were there, ready to close over him, and even though he rolled out of their path two big paws managed to clutch his arm, dragging him back toward the waiting canines. Without having to think about it, Sam dashed the contents of the bag straight into the cat's face and partly open mouth.

The animal lurched back, cracking its head hard against the underside of the wagon. Whipping its head to and fro, it spun away from the wagon, pawing at its eyes and snarling. It let loose with several sneezes, each fast on the heels of the one before it. It spun around in a full circle, facing Sam again but unable to see him. Frenzied, it wiped at its face with its massive forearms, trying to drive away a new enemy the cat had never encountered.

Sam thought about trying to reach the wagon seat and grab the remains of the rifle to use as a stave, but he was about as incapacitated by the pepper as was the cat. For those five or ten seconds he was blind, eyes burning horribly, and he knew with his feet as they were he could not make the wagon seat anyway.

But then he realized there were two stout weapons close at hand, weapons Sam could grasp and wield like a berserker. The thigh bones of the prospector!

Before he could make a dive for the prospector's remains, another sound broke the now deadly quiet afternoon. Half whine, half growl, it rose from the far edge of the draw. Sam looked up, too surprised to recognize the sound.

Behind the cat, motionless on the bank, perched a wolf.

Sam stared at the apparition long enough to see three more of them pad into his blurry line of vision, shoulder to shoulder on the dry bank like spectators gathered at the brink of the Roman Coliseum.

The cat, with tears and red pepper running down its face, and red smeared all around in its fur, whirled toward the new sound. It seemed to forget the helpless man-creature as it backed up to the wagon, back arched and tail twitching hard. Sam could have grabbed its tail—if his mama had raised a fool.

As he pawed at the pepper on his own face, he could see enough of the cat's profile to tell its mouth was shut. Its tongue came out nervously to lick its lips, and its eyes, while they would not look directly at any one animal, flickered back and forth. Its ears now lay so far back against its head they gave the appearance of being angled downward.

The cat sank back from the edge of the wagon, shaking its head violently at another attack of the lingering pepper. Its tail twitched again, and those eyes kept scanning, and then it began to sidle toward the cover of brush on the far side of the wagon.

The wolves closed in, gliding off the dusty bank and trotting around and past Sam and the wagon, their mouths open, panting, as they moved almost playfully in on the jaguar. The jaguar, however, was not in a playing mood. It beat a retreat into the brush with one last snarl and a strange, forbidding whine that conveyed its intent should any of the canines be fool enough to follow it into the thicket.

The big male wolf paused at the edge of the brush, looking after the cat with his tail shot straight out behind him like an oar. He pushed his nose forward and snorted at the brush, seeming, by the bright, hungry look in his eyes, to consider further pursuit. The other wolves looked at him for guidance. When he hesitated, they converged on him, some with tails wagging, some between their legs. There were seven of them altogether, fawning all about him until he snapped at one. Then slowly he turned his head and his eyes toward Sam.

Sam, meanwhile, had not moved. He still held onto the pitiful little half empty bag of ground pepper, the prospector's bones forgotten. What good would such weapons do against seven wolves? If he felt helpless with the jaguar, he felt like a kitten in a dog kennel now. One bite from such an animal as these, should it choose him as foe, could snap his thigh—and there were seven!

Yet in the eyes of the wolf he saw no malice, no intent to destroy him. He was not a menace to any young of theirs. He was not after their food supply. In fact, they seemed to perceive him as no threat at all. Even so, they began to circle.

The big male walked straight at his face, its nose working his scent over on the throbbing desert breeze. It didn't look into his eyes, it never put its ears back, and its tail never left its horizontal position. The others came around him in a gamut of postures, from complete distrust to open curiosity, disdain to apathy. The younger ones were almost fawning, licking their lips, dipping their heads like water ouzels. One that appeared to be an older female, probably the pack leader's mate, pretended to ignore him, looking away, sniffing the air.

After a couple minutes of this, the big male turned his tail and trotted west up the wash as if he had smelled enough human filth. The others followed him, one of the younger ones frolicking alongside a sibling and mouthing its neck.

Sam's heart had given up trying to escape his chest. The strain had gone on too long, and maybe the poor thing knew Sam did not have enough blood left in his battered vessels for it to afford such frenetic jouncing. As the last of the wolves left its dust to settle in the wash, its wagging tail seeming to propel it out of sight, Sam wanted to collapse against the hot sand and sleep. Never had he felt more exhausted, both in body and spirit. But the encounter with the jaguar, which he knew would have ended with his death if not for the opportune arrival of the canines—and of his Maker—made Sam more aware than ever how vulnerable he was. He had to make what he could from this wagon, and now. God could not smile on him the same way twice—although the past two days had certainly been fortunate ones for him. He smiled wryly at his own dry humor. Fortunate, indeed!

If the deserted wagon had not been sacked, Sam believed his luck would have changed. Surely this Silas Ranstrum would have had a knife, perhaps changes of clothing, and who-knew-what other implements he might make use of. But Sam already knew whoever had come by had left little unturned. Yet what about a toolbox?

It was an act of pure self-torture to crawl up into the wagon bed, and once up there he saw he had wasted his strength, for the toolbox was empty, hanging open on its hinges.

With a ragged sigh, Sam sank back. But he was not defeated. He was a man of the desert. There were still things here he could use. He would not go away empty-handed.

The first thing he must do was make clothes. The protective coat of mud was mostly gone from his sun-blistered skin, and although the canvas rubbing against it would be painful, at least it would not let him turn to charcoal, and it was better than the yucca diaper he was wearing now.

The agave pads which he had saved from his last fire and which he had carried tied around his neck would serve as poultices, with canvas moccasins to hold them in place. With that thought in mind, he cut into the wagon sheet with a piece of chert to make himself a serviceable tunic and moccasins. He went one step beyond a loin cloth by making himself another apron, then climbed back down out of the wagon with enough cloth left to fashion himself some sort of a hat. He would look like nothing less than a Mexican version of Robinson Crusoe before he was through.

With one strand of hope left, he crawled around the wagon to Ranstrum's remains but found quickly there was no knife, and his pockets were empty. Whatever human scavengers had wandered by had been as thorough as the animal kind who had picked the dead man's bones. The things he had been throwing at the jaguar out of the crate were all items more or less useless to the Indians. Sam's lack of fortune did not surprise him. On the contrary, he would have been worried if any wealth of food or supplies had fallen his way. The gods had long since set out to test Sam Coffey. He determined to meet their test—every inch of the way.

Gloves stretched tight over his big hands, Tracker lay on his belly studying the shack down below through his field glasses. Patches of green that must be melons and corn checkered the surroundings, and one spot so verdant it could only mark a spring colored a niche among the rocks fifty feet away from the back wall.

Caps O'Brien looked from the black man to the shack, waiting. Johnny Riles, back another fifty yards from them both, held the three horses.

"There's a man down there," Tracker finally said. "Sleepin' in the ramada. Ain't moved since we been here."

"One mule. No barn for other horses," Caps mused. "Judgin' by the looks of that mule, I doubt the man's a threat to us. More than that, I'm bettin' it's the Injun."

Tracker pushed up to his knees and let the binoculars swing from his neck. He brushed himself off as he stood up. "Let's go find them boys," he said. "I'll be lookin' for another job if I let that bird brain get hurt."

The black man had long since decided something. When he located Burt he would quit this outfit. He would give Burt and the other young men a chance to go back with him, of course. If not for that purpose he would already have turned back. If they chose to keep on with Caps and Stratton, that was up to them. In that case he figured on drifting over toward the Texas coast. Or maybe he would ride on to the Sea of Cortez and live on fish and mescal the rest of his life. One thing was sure. In spite of his disappointment in his son, it was doubtful Abijah McGrath would let Tracker come back to the ranch if he didn't bring the boy.

But Tracker saw no point in telling Caps his plans. For now let them think he intended to keep looking for the two strangers. Caps and Stratton were dangerous men, and if they did not think he was going to lead them to the gold they might decide simply to kill him. Eventually, he would have to face that. But it would be nice to have someone else on his side when that time came—*if* he could talk Burt into coming back with him.

When Johnny brought up the horses, the three of them climbed on board and worked their way down the brush-choked hill, making sure to stay in plain sight of the ramada. If this was indeed the old Indian they had been told about in town he would not see them coming. But if it was someone else it would not do to have him think someone was sneaking up on him. All Tracker needed was a rest and a drink of water, maybe a tortilla and some beans to fill the gaping hole in his stomach. Aside from that, he wanted just one answer: had Burt and his cohorts passed this way?

Paco did not see them coming, but he heard them long before they were halfway down the hill. He walked out to greet them, hands hanging at his sides. Three horses, moving slow. No voices, as of yet. Indian? White? Mexican? The old man waited.

He had long since stopped wishing he had his vision back. The Yaquis had taken care of his eyes, but in so doing they had caused his hearing to sharpen to an incredible degree. He could hear things he had never heard before. Things such as rabbits hopping lightly across the gravel. His ears would pinpoint them precisely enough that seven times out of ten he could kill them with a hard-flung stick. He could hear mice in the corn bin, and those, too, he could snatch with his hand and squeeze the life from. One thing being blind had taught him, since he could not travel far from the house and hope to find himself a deer, was that mice were a tasty dish, when properly prepared.

The horses were in the yard now, and a deep voice hailed him. He smiled and motioned them down. The voice had spoken in English, but he spoke back in Spanish.

"You are the three men of whom I have been told."

Tracker looked over at Caps, surprised. He looked back and spoke in very broken Spanish. "That depends on what you were told. We search for three friends of ours."

Paco dipped his head, reconfirming his first statement. "You are the three men of whom I was told. Come inside and have a drink of cool water. You would like something to eat also?"

Tracker grinned broadly. "I hoped you would ask. The road from Hermosillo, it is long and hot."

Caps smoked a cigarette and offered it to all the others. He was generous enough to trade spit with them, but not enough to give them a cigarette of their own. He was full of smiles and jokes while they sat in the little shack. His Spanish was horrible, but the others understood it enough to laugh at his humor, or perhaps they just laughed at his laugh. Some men said it was contagious.

Being split off from Temp and the others had worried Caps a bit at the beginning. But things seemed to be falling together. In Hermosillo they had had no trouble gaining the information they wanted, which had led them here. Now the old Indian had been expecting them, and he was going to send them on their way with enough information to reunite with the other three … provided, of course, that Stratton stuck to the path. If his ineptitude or an unforeseen danger turned them away from the directions the old Indian had given, then it was going to be up to Tracker's skill. But that didn't worry Caps. He had seen enough of the black man's ability to know he could take them straight to the others with as much ease as a school kid finding "chapter two."

Sam Coffey, now covered in as much canvas as he could comfortably wear, lay propped in the shade of the wagon box as the sun burned a notch in a western ridge. He had been able to use yucca leaves as needle and thread to stitch these clothes, and his experience with the Tarahumaras had shown him it would hold up remarkably well. He had made himself a small fire under a tree, roasting agave leaves which he feasted on until he was sated to the point of sickness. Agave poultices nursed his feet, ideal for such a purpose now that he had negated their caustic properties by roasting them. Sam was in good shape. He would have liked to have meat, but he did not need it, at least not at the moment. And if the proper creature presented itself, he just might have it, for now he was armed. He had created a spear from the brake handle of the wagon and a piece of strap iron sharpened against sandstone. The spear was going to be awkward to take with him, but it was more a necessity than a hindrance.

Still, he didn't intend on leaving here until morning. He was hoping that by then some hapless creature wandered into the wash, for he had made himself an arsenal of oxen bones and wheel spokes. Any quail or rabbit, snake or desert tortoise that blundered into his path would learn the wrath of a Choctaw half-breed.

Through a window in the storm clouds towering along the western horizon, the sun set with a fierce scarlet ire. Its molten rays erupted over the cloud tops to splash like sheets of Mexican gold against the upper cloud fringes floating like galleons away from the bulk of the thunderheads. Sam loved to watch a beautiful sunset. But this was the first evening he had been able to enjoy one in days. He stared at the clouds, too far away to feel threatening, and their beauty brought Nadia Boultikhine to his mind.

Temp Stratton had always been told he was lucky. It hadn't held true when the posse caught up to him and took him back to be tried for cattle theft. It hadn't held true when they sent him to the pen. But it had when he ran into Caps O'Brien in the Yuma penitentiary and became his partner, and it had also held up in every venture he and Caps had undertaken since.

That same dumb luck had led them to this wagon on such a fine, sunny morning. Even though none of them could be considered trackers, they noticed how the ground around it had been disturbed. They even made out what appeared to be big cat tracks intermingled with those of wolves.

The part that intrigued Stratton most, however, was the torn pieces of canvas, and the scattered bones of some small animal, freshly gnawed and lying near the remains of a fire that, judging by the fluffy white ash that had not blown away, could not be an hour old.

The intelligence of Burt and Scrub was so far beneath Stratton's that it rankled him having to talk to them. But they were the only ones handy. He pointed at the strange dragging track that left the scene. "I don't know what all happened here, but that's a man crawlin' away right there. I'm wonderin' if it ain't one of them two suckers of Varnell's."

"If that's so, something bad happened," said Burt. "And they don't have any gold."

Judging by the look that came over Stratton's face, he didn't like the idea of that at all. But he made no audible reply.

"Whoever it is," went on Burt, "he sure won't make it far out here."

"You got that straight," Stratton agreed, climbing into his saddle. "He won't get far if it's one of them two, for sure. Let's go find him." He flashed what for him had to pass as a smile, albeit a sinister one, and started off on the strange dragging trail. Someone was hurt. It was only common courtesy for Stratton to find them … and put them out of their misery. And if it happened to be the bootlicker that had knocked him down in Nogales, so much the better. He had sworn to pay that one back …

Chapter Twenty-Five

From the concealment of catclaw bushes, Sam Coffey saw the three riders go by and envied them their horses. He also envied them their guns, canteens, and shade-producing hats. But one thing he did not envy was their consciences; these man had none.

The desert heat had not made Sam so delirious as not to recognize the rancher's son, Burt McGrath, and his bellicose little friend, Scrub. With them was the gunfighter, Temp Stratton. Sam would not soon forget their run-in in Nogales. Nor would he forget the man's promised threat. It was a debt Sam hoped in his current condition not to hold him to.

Sam had no illusions as to what the three men were doing here. Johnny Riles had obviously carried word to them that Sam and Tom had come down here for Varnell's gold. But where was Johnny? And where were the other two—Lug Colton and Caps O'Brien?

Sam considered his chances. He could hope these three missed the wagon and continued on west up the canyon. But of course that was vain hope. If they had made it this far they either had powerfully good luck, or one of them was more than an average tracker. He could wait for them to come back, then try to overpower one of them and get a gun, but in his condition that would be like a mole winning a paw to paw with a badger. No, Sam's only defense lay in stealth and knowledge of the desert. He took to the deepest, thorniest growth, which was effective at concealing him but kept him at not much more than a stinkbug's pace.

Forty minutes after the three riders passed, he spotted them returning through a thin spot in the wall of brush. Now there were just two of them—Stratton and Burt McGrath. Where was Scrub?

That question was answered shortly. Sam detected a man's muffled cursing, the grunts of a horse, and the crackle of branches as someone fought through the brush Sam himself had been negotiating. It would be a tough time for anyone riding a horse in that growth, but not impossible, and he had left enough sign for anyone with half an eye to follow him once they knew he had taken to the undergrowth.

Even if Stratton and McGrath rode right past him, Ottley was eventually going to catch up. Sam had one chance. Right now he had two of them out in the open, unaware how near he was. He had to move. Now. *Immediately.* One more minute and it would be too late. The spear was no good; Sam was no spear thrower. He had learned to use a spear by thrusting, not throwing, and in any event this one was not sharp enough to make a sure kill.

A more accurate arsenal was right underfoot—the rough chunks of granite that littered the ground—and Sam scrambled to find one that weighed three or four pounds and fit his hand. Within seconds, the riders were alongside him, Stratton the nearest. That was fortunate, since Stratton was the one to take out. With all his might, the rock in both hands, he took aim and launched it out of the brush. Rock throwing for precision and force was a game Sam had enjoyed not only in his childhood but as a warrior-in-training with the Tarahumara. He had learned to be not only precise, but deadly. His present weakness was a detriment, but his aim was still accurate.

The missile sailed true, and before Stratton had any idea it was coming it struck him high in the chest with such force that he was thrown sideways off his horse. He was too stunned to even grab for the saddle horn, and as his foot left the right stirrup he hung up in the other, and his horse started to lunge away. If not for McGrath's fast reaction, he might have been trampled. But the younger man reached out and succeeded in grabbing a loose rein, and he fought the animal to a standstill.

Sam left the brush in a lunge, numb to the pain in his feet. He had to reach Stratton's pistol while he was down, for without it this temporary victory meant nothing. Even as he thought better of it, he dove under the belly of Stratton's horse, grasping for the holstered pistol. The frightened horse kicked at him instinctively, striking him in the ribs. Sam sank back, and as he went for the gun again the horse bolted forward, knocking him down as Stratton's left foot came free of the stirrup and he landed in a writhing heap. Sam scrambled for the fallen gunman, focused on the grip of his pistol.

With no warning, something popped in Sam's brain, and a loud ringing ensued. His elbows buckled, and he dropped forward onto his face, rolling over to look around. His head was spinning, and the clanging sound in his ears grew louder.

As he looked up, it was at the grimacing leer of Scrub Ottley, and into the barrel of his cocked gun. Ottley was unnaturally excited, looking over at Stratton and McGrath, then back down at Sam. It was a moment before he found his tongue.

"Boot toes don't feel so good, do they, mister?" he said with an affected growl. His boot lashed out, striking Sam on the opposite side of the head from where he was now becoming aware of a powerful ache. Sam grabbed at his head to protect it. He was in such pain he had to cram his eyes shut, and Ottley was not finished. He felt the next kick catch him under the ribs, the pain excruciating. The boot next came down on his belly as he felt a trickle of blood go down his face from the initial kick.

Then he heard a sharp cry. "Scrub! Leave him alone!" It was Burt McGrath. Scrub kicked him again, and Sam opened his eyes in time to see a hand reach out and give the little man a hard shove in the chest, knocking him back.

"He's had enough! Let him alone!" Head still spinning, Sam looked up to a blurry, wavering picture of McGrath.

And then he heard a third voice, a weak, gasping one. "Wrong! He ain't had close to enough."

With feelings of doom crashing down, Sam recognized the voice of Temp Stratton. At the moment it had that weakened edge to it, but he was recovering fast.

Sam cringed. Lying there on the hard-packed soil, he truly looked like the Robinson Crusoe he had earlier imagined, complete with his vest, apron, shoes and fallen canvas hat, his agave leaves and half of the jackrabbit he had killed at first light adorning his waist from a makeshift belt of yucca fiber. Resourceful he was, but Indian he must not be. He had let himself be taken—by white men!

The click of a pistol's hammer swayed Sam from any thought of getting up to fight. His only chance now was Stratton's lust for Varnell's gold. If he could convince them he knew where it was they would not want to kill him. But if he showed any more fight he could tell by Stratton's voice that vehemence would take the place of his greed.

Sam pushed himself to a sitting position. He felt like throwing up, and his head spun madly, throbbing as if in a vise. Stratton came around and stopped in front of him, his chest still heaving a little with each breath. Sam blinked his head to clear it and looked up. The sight of the big gunman fired up the same feeling of dislike that had roiled up from deep in Sam's guts at their first meeting. It was with great satisfaction that he recalled knocking him down on the boardwalk, and taking him out of the saddle with the rock. Now he feared both acts would be his doom.

Sam had known many men, and in some he found it hard seeing anything to like. But none had a worse aura than Stratton. Visible evil seeped out of this man at every pore.

Stratton looked Sam up and down, one corner of his mouth raised in a sneering grin as he took one last heaving breath to settle himself. Instinctively, Sam clamped his teeth together half a second before Stratton's boot struck out, catching him in the chin. He went down on his back, instantly struggling to rise.

"You'd better just stay down," he heard McGrath say, followed by Stratton's sharp retort: "Shut your mouth!"

A hand grabbed Sam by the hair and jerked him up, and he

struggled to sit, knowing Stratton would yank until he jerked the hair out of his head.

"You're supposed to be packin' gold!"

"I lost my pockets," Sam replied stonily.

With eyes meaner looking than any rattlesnake, Stratton scanned Sam's meager attire. "Lost *every*thing, I'd say. All right, mister. You got one more chance. S'pose you tell us about the gold."

One side of Sam's mouth ticked up, and he gave a little shake of his head. "Gold?"

Stratton's impatience flooded up, and he raised his leg and shoved Sam backward with the bottom of his boot, knocking him onto his back again. "*GOLD!* You heard me." Stratton's eyes had no mercy, and looking into them Sam had no doubt that attribute was beyond him. The big convict's face was scarred by a life of war, and hatred of the world hung there like a shroud. "Where the hell is it?"

Sam's first instinct was to tell Stratton the Yaquis had packed the gold off and ruined everyone's dreams of being rich—which was the truth. It would have given him satisfaction seeing the look on the other man's face. But his only chance lay in fooling him into thinking the gold was still where he had found it.

"I wasn't in much shape to pack it out."

Stratton's eyes scanned him up and down. "Now *that* I can see." He did not seem overly interested in how Sam had ended up this way. "Well, guess what, tough man. We're just gonna take us a ride back where you come from and pick it up."

A surge of dread rose up in Sam at the thought of going back to the Yaqui canyon. But then what could be worse than what he had already been through? Besides, going back would take time, and he might at least have a chance at one of their guns. Then he could get their horses, too. And he would leave the three of these human coyotes in the desert like they planned to leave him.

But it was not to be that easy. Not with Temp Stratton. And not with Sam's stubborn nature, which spurred the killer on.

"Let's go then," Sam said, straight-faced. "I hope you find what you been askin' for." His sarcasm was thinly veiled.

Stratton's eyes bored into his battered foe, and he growled, "We ain't goin' yet. First I'm makin' good an' sure to wash any fool notions out of your head." He stared at Sam for a sign what he said was sinking in, and then his face turned even meaner, uglier. "DO I LOOK STUPID TO YOU?" Stratton screamed the words so loud Sam's ears rang, and a livid flush boiled over Stratton's cheeks. His face shook with the height of his anger. "DON'T PUSH ME, BOOTLICKER!" His voice dropped to an even more deadly sounding level. "Boy, you even contemplate double-crossin' Temp Stratton you'll wish the Injuns got you instead."

"I wish that already," Sam said.

Stratton swelled up, and for a moment Sam prepared to take another boot. Hate boiled in Stratton's eyes. There were too many incidents, too many of Sam's inflammatory comments bottled up in the big man's head. Sam had pushed too hard.

No kick came. Instead, Stratton looked over at Ottley and McGrath, his face swollen with the height of his fury. But his voice came out quieter than before. "Get up some brush and make a fire. Right under that tree will do."

Sam glanced at the tree, a stout ironwood with one big branch arcing out several feet. His heart started to thud harder in his chest as he began to grasp the extent of this man's madness. His torture had only begun.

"A fire?" Burt stared at him. "Fire for what?"

"A FIRE!" Stratton screamed. "A damn fire!"

McGrath swallowed hard, only breaking eye contact for a moment, to look down at Sam. His shaking hands came up, as if to calm the big gunman. His obvious fear fell beneath his sense of mercy. "All right, all right. Can't you just tell me what it's for?"

Stratton's glare could have ignited fireworks. The day went still, and he turned with deadly intent on McGrath, stabbing him with his full attention. "There ain't a spot of respect in me for you, boy," he said in a voice gone strangely quiet, and more despiteful than ever. "Not one little jot. I'll tell you what I want you to know. Now you either get over there with your friend an' start pickin' up some sticks—" (Scrub Ottley was already almost frantically gathering kindling, avoiding even the appearance of looking Stratton's way) "—or you can guess what's gonna happen to you in the next five seconds."

It was out there before them now. Sam knew, Scrub knew, and Burt knew, without any direct statement from Stratton, exactly what he meant. Burt either did Stratton's bidding or he took a bullet.

His face taking on a pale cast beneath his sunburn, Burt turned numbly and started picking up sticks and brush. He and Scrub piled a good supply of it under the ironwood, then stopped and stood watching Stratton and Sam, entranced.

Stratton walked over to his horse and climbed up. Guiding it toward Sam, he looked up at the ironwood limb, which hovered eight feet above the ground at its highest point. Without looking down, he unbuckled the leather strap that held his lasso to the fork of his saddle and threw it over the limb, feeding it slack until the loop came down to lie like a frozen snake on the ground. "Put your feet in there," he growled.

Sam had decided he was safe as long as he played along with Stratton and led him back toward the gold. But now it was plain Stratton would not care even if he was only the remains of a man. And once they had the gold he would kill him. But what was Sam to do? Putting his feet in the loop let him in for certain torture, but at least he might live. And as long as he was alive, there was still a chance. If he tried anything now Stratton would shoot him, gold or no gold.

Sickness washing through his chest, he crawled over and placed both of his feet through the waiting loop.

Stratton sawed savagely on the reins, forcing his horse away from the tree as he dallied around his saddle horn. The slack of the rope disappeared, and the force jerked Sam sideways, slamming his head against the ground. He felt himself being hoisted into the air, the grass rope biting into his ankles with all the pain of a bear trap, slicing his hide, grinding his ankles together. He gritted his teeth, forcing himself to make no sound. Stratton would kill him before he heard him cry.

Keeping tension on the rope, Stratton rode to the other side of the tree, out of Sam's sight. He rode once around it, ducking to clear its branches. Then, keeping the rope taut by friction against the bole of the tree, he tied its end securely to a branch.

Burt and Scrub had gingerly come in to pile more branches below

Sam's head. The pile was large, and Stratton swore at them. "Knock some of that out of there! You light that off you're gonna kill him too fast."

Almost shaking like a whipped pup, Burt moved in close and kicked some of the branches away. He avoided touching Sam as if he were poison.

Sam just hung there, his face turning livid as blood flooded into it. Trying to push all thought from his mind, he steeled himself for what was to come.

"Now tie his hands," Stratton ordered, throwing a piggin string from his saddlebags to Scrub. The little man obeyed, his own hands shaking as he tied Sam's together behind the small of his back.

"Light it," he heard Stratton say. There was a certain pleasure in the words.

"But … What about smoke?" Burt dared ask. "What if there's Injuns around?"

Again, Stratton showed the colors Sam expected, his utter disregard of anyone else's concern. Even if it was well-founded he would not let the younger man believe he had out-thought him. "You more scared of them than you are me? START THAT FIRE!"

"What about the gold?" Burt stammered. "We kill him, we aren't going to find it."

Stratton turned once more with that cold, deadly look narrowing his eyes. Sam's glance flickered from Stratton's face to Burt's, in whose eyes he saw his only hope. "Isn't that right?"

"I said to light that fire, you little bastard."

"But he's … look at him—he's half dead already." Burt was stalling for time. "I sure don't want to lose out on that gold."

Sam hung there staring at this Burt McGrath, seeing him in a whole new light. He wore his fear for Stratton like a hat. Yet he kept standing up to him against the threat of sure death. Young Burt kept bringing up the gold, but deep down Sam guessed that wasn't the issue anymore. He just didn't want to be part of murder.

Stratton's hand came up, slowly, deliberately, and rested on his gun butt. With fingers shaking almost too badly to function, Scrub fumbled a match from his shirt pocket. Casting a furtive glance toward Stratton, he whipped the match across his holster. He leaned down and touched it to the brush pile, making it crackle to life. Even the little trouble maker, as hard a case as Sam knew he was, would not meet his eyes.

A whirring sound, sudden and short, punctuated Sam's near panic. The source of the sound had not registered on him yet when a different sound followed it, a dull *thunk*. With a yelp of pain, Scrub pitched to one side. His horse, tied to a nearby tree, screamed and tried to pull away as the whirring sound came again, the sound Sam now recognized as a bowstring sending an arrow into flight!

Everything was a blur. Sam listened to the fire gain energy. He saw Scrub writhing on the ground and heard him crying, screaming for help. He heard the second arrow strike Burt, and as he twirled at the end of the rope, growing dizzy and nauseous, he saw the young man stumble to the rope where it was tied to the tree. He yanked at it to no avail, tearing the skin of his hand. Then, with one wild, helpless look back at Sam, he scrambled to his horse. Behind Sam rose the thunder of hooves, the sound of Stratton making his getaway. Another time the bowstring twanged, but there was no telltale thud. Sam could hear Burt cursing, fighting his horse, and then, with a groan of pain, he was up into his saddle and galloping away after Stratton. Soon the only sound was that of the crackling flames, and Scrub lay still on the ground.

Frantically, Sam lifted his head, trying to keep out of reach of the rising heat and the growing flames that licked at him. He jerked in surprise as a powerful arm closed around him, a solid body pressed against him. A moccasined foot kicked the flaming brush away, scattering it and making it go almost instantly out. Wisps of smoke snaked upward from the tips of little branches as whoever it was who held him let go, and he swung back on the rope, through the path where the fire had been.

Sam spun in a dizzying circle. The world was a drab array of color—tawny, gray, olive—all melded with the pale blue of the morning sky. Sam felt the renewed urge to throw up. He fought the rope on his hands, grinding it into his skin. Looking up, he could see the tree branch that held him. Looking down, the dead Scrub Ottley. And finally, spinning free on the rope—the form of a silent Indian with his eyes fixed on him.

The Indian suddenly stepped forward, and his outstretched hand stilled the gyrating rope. When he backed up, Sam groaned in disbelief. *The Yaqui!* The one who had beaten him and taken away his gun. The one who had taken away all his hard-earned means of survival!

The Yaqui paced the area as if Sam weren't there. He stopped for a moment to stare at Scrub, the arrow buried so deeply in his back that it protruded five or six inches out his chest, where the gore had dripped into the sand and turned it purple.

The Yaqui bent over and pulled a sheath knife out of Scrub's belt. He studied it for a long time, testing its edge with his thumb. Then he looked over at Sam. Sam, who had tried so hard to survive the desert, who had done things most men could never accomplish. Now here he was at the Yaqui's mercy. And he could foresee one of three things happening. The most horrible: the Yaqui walking away to leave him hanging. No man could survive long with the pressure building in his brain. The Yaqui could cut him down, but that did not fit what he had already seen of him. Or, thirdly, he could kill him. One slice from the knife across his throat would end it all. One arrow through the chest. Or one shot from the rifle Sam had seen the Yaqui brandish earlier.

The Yaqui turned to Sam, and his eyes squared on his face. It was as if he had read his thoughts, and the hint of a smile turned up his wide, thick lips, creasing his face and squinting his eyes. He straightened, staring at Sam's chest, and drew back the knife. Drew it back, and with deadly accuracy threw it.

The knife found its mark as sure as his arrow had found Scrub. It sank deep, making a dull thud.

Chapter Twenty-Six

Sam Coffey had no intention of showing fear. But in spite of himself, the moment the Yaqui let fly with the knife he flinched. He could almost feel the blade sink into him as it made a thud in burying itself almost to the hilt.

But the feeling of the blade was all in Sam's imagination. There was no blade in his chest. The knife was stuck in the ground beneath his head, where the Yaqui had aimed.

The Yaqui gave Sam a long, almost smug look. Sam could not have said if the man was mocking him or challenging him. Whatever it was, he turned on his heel and walked away, stepping off the trail and into the brush.

Sam struggled with the rope on his hands. His head felt ready to explode. The world was starting to blur again with the blood settling behind his eyes, and his ears rang like the clanging of hammer on anvil. He jerked and pulled and twisted on the rope until he felt a warm wet trickle course down the back of one forearm. He didn't care. In fact, he hoped the blood would flow harder, perhaps moisten his skin enough to slide the rope off.

Before he could free his hands, he heard the Yaqui step out of the underbrush leading his horse. The animal was lightly accoutered: a rope for a hackamore and a sparely fashioned Indian saddle. The Yellow Boy Winchester hugged one side.

Leaving his horse, the Yaqui walked to Scrub, crouching. He went through his pockets, extracting matches, tobacco and a jackknife. He looked at his boots and started to pull one off, then stopped and looked at Sam's feet. It was obvious the boots were far too small for Sam, which at the moment seemed to be the only reason the Yaqui decided to leave them. Sam would not have tried the boots anyway, considering his raw feet.

At that moment Sam hated the Yaqui more than ever. Yes, he had saved his life, after a fashion, but that seemed to be only to prolong his suffering. If Sam could have reached a gun he would have shot him dead.

The Yaqui took off Scrub's gun belt and slung it about his own waist. Next, he went to the horse, which rolled its eyes and sidled away. The Yaqui soft-talked to it, soothing it, until the animal held still. He stroked its neck, its sides, down its rump. He ran a hand over its saddle, a worn, dark-stained affair after the Cheyenne style with tapaderos on the stirrups. He opened the near saddlebag and dug down into it for a moment, coming up with a little cotton sack, which he turned over in his hand, studying it. He reached in and pulled out a handful of jerky strips and put one in his mouth, chewing with relish. Walking around the horse to rummage in the other bag, he came back around, pulled the canteen off the saddle horn and took a long swallow from it, popping the cork back in.

The Yaqui, not looking at Sam anymore as he struggled with the rope on his hands, went to his dun. With supple strength, he threw himself sideways with the saddle horn as a handhold and landed in the seat like a gymnast. He rode over and leaned down to untie Scrub's horse, then took its reins and turned. Kneeing his animal, he directed it closer to Sam. With the now-familiar smirk on his face, the Yaqui stared at the white man, who had for the moment stopped struggling against the rope on his wrists. Sam could feel his face deep purple with pooling blood.

The Yaqui nodded his head almost imperceptibly, and he started to turn his horse and Scrub's. Almost as if by accident, the sack of jerky, then the canteen, tumbled to the ground as he started to ride away.

Then he stopped short, his body tensing visibly. Warning bells rang in Sam.

Straining, he struggled to bring his eyes into focus and see beyond the Yaqui. Something was wrong, something that shook even the Yaqui. Just for a moment, Sam's eyes came into sharp focus. He was stunned by the sight of four Indians who had drawn their horses to a halt a hundred yards away toward the canyon of the Yaqui gold. They were not Yaquis. These were the enemy of the Yaquis.

Chiricahua Apaches!

Tom Vanse was awake, but aware? Barely enough to keep guiding Gringo in circles. Fever smoldered deep in his leg—the sun pounded down—his ears rang—sweat ran in rivulets down his neck into his cotton scarf.

Where his leg rode against the saddle, Tom could feel the point of the arrow buried deep. What did a man put on an arrow wound? What did he do with the arrowhead inside? He had tried to pull it out, a monumental task, the pain unbearable. Where was Hermosillo? Where was his own horse? Where was Sam?

Sam!

The only time Tom's mind began to clear was when Sam came floating in on a bloody wind. His friend. Heaven above, what had become of him? *Sam!* Tom's mind reeled, yet he still saw himself as a capable person, able to ride like the wind to Hermosillo and bring back help. He couldn't let Sam die, especially when it had been Tom's idea that they come here in the first place.

But Tom's mind was going under to the shock of the feathered missile in his leg. He had no water. No food. No shelter. And, worst of all, no sense. No sense of where he was, where he was going, even where he had come from. He had somehow outrun his pursuers, if anyone had pursued him at all, but it had gotten him nowhere. Before the shock had set in Tom had decided he must have been waylaid by some chance warrior out hunting, perhaps a Seri or Mayo who had simply seen an opportunity for a good horse and rifle. He had a difficult time believing he would have outrun Yaqui pursuit so easily a second time.

Tom wandered the desert, hoping to stumble back onto the trail to Hermosillo, now that he was lost like a grass sprig in a cowpie. He wanted nothing more than to save his partner, who had offered up his own life for his. He wanted to save Sam more than he wanted to save his own life.

But Tom Vanse was helpless …

Nadia Boultikhine stopped her horse when Abe Varnell did and picked her canteen off the saddle horn, removing the cork and tilting back her head to take a long drink. The water was hot now, but at least it was wet. It felt good on her throat.

Varnell looked back at her, his eyes noncommittal. He took off his bandanna and swabbed his face with it, doffing his hat to sweep the shiny dome of his head with a soiled shirtsleeve. The desert pulsed around them, the voices of an array of birds creating a melodious cacophony in the stillness. Varnell was familiar with the life that thrived here: the fox curled in its insulating den; the hawk perched on some giant cactus; the javelina pawing cool dirt up in the shade of a wash, seeking a new place to lie. This desert had been Varnell's home for many years while prospecting. And now, in spite of the chance of dying at the hands of Yaquis, Apaches or Mexican bandits, he was growing to love it again. It was alive! And so was Abe Varnell.

Most importantly, he had renewed respect for himself. He had overcome his fear of Mexico, overcome it for his friends. And now that he had, he was unconquerable. Nothing could stop Abe Varnell from bringing Sam Coffey and Tom Vanse home, gold or no gold. They were here in peril because of him. They would come home with him or the attempt would kill him.

Nadia was ecstatic with the changes in her companion. He had grown from an old man full of fear to a brave, capable man, one who no longer seemed much past middle age. A man with a heart of iron at times, and of honey at others. Nadia had grown fond of the prospector in their few days together. Even at his age, he was still a handsome man, graceful like an aging buck. He must have cut quite a figure in his youth. Nadia was proud to call him a friend.

Ever since they had met in the saloon barroom the morning before and been approached by the Mexican named Hector things had gone well, at least in one sense. Hector had been able to tell them that Sam and Tom had been through town, and that indeed three men had come looking for them later. He had also told them Sam and Tom had left Hermosillo with good directions to old Paco's homestead.

The bad part was, no one would go with Varnell and Nadia into Yaqui country, not for any amount of gold. But Varnell was determined. And so was Nadia. They had set off for Paco's alone.

The Seri had greeted Varnell with such genuine love and fondness that Nadia could not help the tears that came to her eyes. In spite of living on the border, Nadia did not speak much Spanish, but she listened to the flow of it from the two men and enjoyed watching the mutual love in their eyes. At one point, the Seri became very concerned, and later, when they were riding away, Varnell told her why. The old man had inadvertently helped not three but *six* men on their way toward locating Sam and Tom. Now Nadia and Varnell rode warily, scanning for Indians, bandits, and the six would-be killers who had gone before them ...

*   *   *

"Hold up!" Tracker's voice startled Caps O'Brien and Johnny Riles as his gloved hand shot skyward. Following along in single file, they almost ran their horses into him.

Caps pulled alongside the black man. "What the hell?"

"Somebody comin'."

It took a moment for Johnny's face to show he heard the pound of horse hooves, and Caps several moments longer. His years of dynamiting had been no friend to his ears.

Without a word, Tracker spurred his horse toward the brush line. Caps and Johnny followed. A lone horse exploded over a rise in the trail, galloping toward them with sweat streaming down its sides. The animal had not yet started to lather up, but it was not far from it.

Its rider was Temp Stratton.

Caps and Johnny looked at each other in surprise, then spurred their horses out to meet their partner. Tracker hung back with rifle in hand, scanning the trail behind Stratton.

Recognizing the trio, Stratton sawed his horse to a stop, sending up a cloud of choking dust. "Injuns!" he yelled, coughing at the dust. He spun to check his backtrail.

Tracker caught up. "Injuns? What about the others?"

"I don't know. I think Scrub's dead. McGrath took an arrow, but I thought I heard him behind me, for a while."

"How many Injuns?" Caps barked. "We oughtta be lookin' for cover."

"Couldn't say," Stratton heaved. "Happened too fast. All I know's I left one o' them two partners hangin' by his feet from a tree back there."

"You *what?*" Caps spat. "Where is he?"

"I told you! Dead, by now!" Stratton retorted. "Hell, he was hardly in one piece when we come on him. Them Injuns had tortured him an' turned him loose naked. Wasn't hardly enough left to send home to Gran'ma."

"What about the gold?"

"What do you think?" Stratton snapped. "He was purty near naked. Any pockets he had weren't carryin' no gold!"

Caps ignored Stratton's black humor. "Where is it?"

"How should I know? He didn't have time to tell us 'fore them Injuns showed up an' started flingin' arrows."

Caps spat angrily. "If what Johnny says is accurate, we can't be fifteen miles from where that gold is. I ain't goin' back now—I don't know about you all."

Stratton shot his eyes back and forth at the three of them, disconcerted. Finally, he heaved a huge sigh and sucked in another breath, seeming to settle his nerves. "I hadn't planned on goin' back there. But I'm ever' bit as game as you."

"Just keep one bullet for yourself, that's what I always say." Caps grinned and spat tobacco juice.

Tracker was listening to the talk between the two convicts, and it disgusted him to be with them. What had possessed Burt to fall in with these blackguards? They must have given him a silken line of talk. It was plain they were simple, heartless killers, capable of anything.

His voice broke into their banter. "Dust." He did not point up the trail except with his eyes. The others followed that line to the thin haze of dust and momentarily heard the sound of a horse loping.

"Just one horse," Tracker said when he noticed Johnny getting nervous and searching the brush for a place to hide. Johnny's eyes flickered toward him, and he tried to steady himself.

By the time Burt McGrath's horse came over the rise he was down to a jog, and by the look on Burt's face it was plain he had trouble. Johnny went out to meet him, the others coming a little slower. Tracker was mightily miffed at the kid for bringing him here, but he was glad to see him alive. Burt had his faults, some of them as big as a bloated bull, but Tracker had known him since he was a youngster. Thoughts of finding him dead had saddened him.

Rifle in hand, Tracker rode behind the others, watching the surrounding hills for telltale dust or movement. When at last he caught up they were lifting Burt off his saddle and down to the sand, and Johnny was busily scouting out a good place to make camp. Stratton started grousing about how early in the day it was to be stopping.

When Tracker came to a halt and crouched near Burt's head, Caps looked from the arrow in Burt's side to the black man. "Kid says you know some about doctorin'."

Tracker grunted. "Yeah, an' some about trains, too, like I know they run on steam. But I couldn't build one."

"Howdy, Track." Burt said with a weak smile. "Hey, come on. I've seen you work miracles."

"Damn kid." Tracker had begun trimming Burt's shirt away from the arrow shaft with his knife, avoiding his eyes. The arrow appeared to have struck a rib, for it had started to go in at one angle, then ended up skewing to the side, ripping away a large chunk of superficial flesh. But the rib had kept it from sinking more than a couple of inches. It had no poison on it; Indian poison would have killed Burt by now.

Tracker looked up at Caps. "You plan to camp here? We could ride a long ways after that gold before dark." The statement was an overt challenge: did they intend to let Burt recover any strength?

Caps glanced over at Stratton, whose glittering black glance was trained on him. "We'll camp here if Johnny can find us a good bunch of boulders for cover. If there's Injuns around we best get to cover. Maybe they'll be gone by mornin'. They come this way I'd like to be holed up in the rocks and ready, not standin' out in the sand scratchin' myself."

Stratton's jaw muscles bunched, and his eyes flattened angrily, but he said nothing. He seemed to realize Caps was right—as he always was.

Johnny came back with word that there was a nest of rocks a couple of hundred yards off in the brush, where the flat land gave way to a hundred-yard-wide gully. It was downhill, but the only way to shoot into it would be for someone to stand at the edge of the brush, exposing themselves.

When they carried Burt off, Tracker stayed to cover their spoor, although it was far from foolproof. He could only feasibly go so far back, and any Indian worth his salt could follow tracks that had been disguised as well as ones that had not, once he knew they had been hidden. It was only the accidental passerby who had no reason to be studying the ground for whom Tracker covered the trail. There was no point in leaving road signs for just any dumb white man to stumble onto.

*   *   *

Hanging upside down from the ironwood tree, Sam Coffey's heart leaped into his throat. He stared at the back of the Yaqui and at the Apache warriors who faced him. They were too far to see well, and his vision too blurry, but they must be full of surprise at finding the Yaqui sitting his horse out there in the middle of nowhere.

Fiercely, Sam yanked and twisted and swore at the rope on his wrists. Growling at the pain, with a final surge of strength he yanked free, the blood smearing his hands. He twisted around and found the hilt of the knife the Yaqui had thrown, and reaching down he jerked it from the earth. Then, with all the strength left in him, he strained to rise toward his feet. Failing, he dropped back down, then looked over to see the Yaqui turn his eyes to him, twisting up his mouth with a look that portrayed a strange regret.

The Yaqui turned back and hit his horse hard with his heels. Pulling Scrub Ottley's horse with him, and drawing the Yellow Boy from its sling, he charged the Apaches.

"God, you've gotta help me!" Sam prayed through clenched teeth. He raised up once more, and when he thought he had no strength or endurance left in him he growled and raised up three more inches, slashing with the knife. He cut a nasty gash across his shin but managed to slash the rope halfway through as well. Steeling himself to the pain, he threw the weight of his body hard against the weakened rope. It did not give. He looked over as the Yaqui closed with the startled Apaches.

In one wrenching movement, Sam swung his torso upward, slashing at the rope again. He missed. But under the tremendous stress it unraveled. He felt it give, and with a jarring crunch he landed on the point of his neck. A bright whiteness flashed across his vision. Blood tasted acidic on his tongue. His ears rang harder, and in the back of his consciousness he felt his feet strike the dirt. He strained to roll over, but he couldn't move. The world was black. His whole body ached with pain.

At the last possible moment the Yaqui raised his Yellow Boy and fired into one of the shocked Apaches. The Indian's animal lurched sideways, spilling its rider's limp body. Almost by pure reflex, another

Apache swung his bow at the Yaqui's back as he went by. Instead of running, with his back open to the Apaches, the Yaqui whirled his horse. The two horses, the Yaqui's and Scrub's, got caught for a moment in an eddying mass of horse flesh. Then Scrub's horse broke away, and the Yaqui fired his rifle again, his lip curled. The bow-wielding Apache grabbed at his stomach, and another horse jumped with surprise and slammed into the one next to it, momentarily incapacitating the two remaining warriors in the melee.

Raising a wild yell, the Yaqui turned his horse and fled. The game little mustang went from a standstill to a gallop in mere seconds, a cloud of choking dust funneling up behind him. The two Apaches, still stunned at the sudden turn of the tables, gave their fallen comrades one furtive glance, then struck out on the enemy's trail.

Sam's vision hazed back in, the shots ringing in his head. The color drained into his face when he rolled over and rubbed his eyes. He stared up the slope for several moments and finally focused on two Apaches lying on the trail, one of their horses standing confused nearby and stamping its foot. There was no other living thing in sight, just a trail of dust where galloping horses had disappeared.

Sam sucked in a breath and looked around him for signs of danger. Could he get the Apache horse? Did he dare try? The Apaches, with a Yaqui scalp or not, would be coming back for their tribesmen; no Apache worth his salt would ever leave a comrade's body unclaimed. It was a crawl of a hundred tortuous yards to the horse, and almost astronomical odds against the animal waiting there for a strange smelling white man to crawl up to it, to say nothing of being able to hold it and mount. On the other hand, he had a knife, water and jerky, and whatever he could salvage off of Scrub Ottley's corpse.

He had to move. The only sure things were within yards of Sam, and he went for them. The horse might as well have been a deer for all the good it would do him.

Scrambling to Scrub, he found two matches that must have fallen from his pockets when he lit the fire—or perhaps the Yaqui had purposely left them. The thought of what the Yaqui had done flashed by, but Sam had little time to contemplate the sense of mercy that had come over the brutal warrior. He knew Scrub's pants wouldn't fit him as they were. The legs would be too tight. But then, as much weight as Sam had lost in the past few days, it would be close. Sam's waist and hips were narrow from a lifetime in the saddle, and he had no doubt that part would fit. With that thought burning in his mind he unbuttoned Scrub's pants and wrenched them from him, then with his knife ran a slit up from the bottom of his shirt to the open placket, ripping it and the vest right off of him. Although the thought crossed his mind, he was not hungry enough to take a hunk of the dead man's flesh for sustenance.

He jerked the hat off Scrub's head, tried it for size, then cut a slit in the back of the crown and innermost part of the brim, making it slide down over his hair easily after he cast away his Robinson Crusoe mockery. Leaving Scrub wearing only his long johns, Sam snatched the canteen and the jerky, stuffing one hunk hurriedly in his mouth, and crawled into the brush.

There was no thought of trying to cover his trail. The Apaches, if they had seen him hanging there, would be able to follow him no matter how much time he wasted. He had been with Tarahumaras when they followed a bear over a talus slide, and Apaches were rumored to be the best trackers in the world, so their finding him would be that much more likely. His only hope was to stay out of sight of chance travelers.

Sam tried to stay calm, but it was no surprise that he did not. His first realization of how frantically he had crawled away from the ironwood tree was brought on by the voice of his lifelong worst enemy—the clap of thunder.

Sam could not believe how close the thunder boomed; he had not even seen the storm clouds building. Looking over, he saw half the sky obscured by a nasty dark bulk of cloud frothing so close to the earth it appeared as fog in the mountain canyons.

He cringed, looking around him for refuge. A bolt of lightning tangled down the sky, spider webbing as it broke and whip-tailed along its path. It rolled along the top of the distant mountain with all-consuming power, and two seconds later its stentorian voice rattled the hills. Sam's mouth twitched as the memories flashed across his mind. He saw his father's face—pushed it away. It returned, lying washed with rain, eyes open to the sky, mouth twisted.

Sam could see a clutch of boulders twenty yards away through the brush, and he made for it, crawling faster than he would have thought possible. Somewhere he lost the canteen and Scrub's clothes, but he didn't go back for them. Thunder buckled and detonated twice behind him, as if chasing him, each strike sounding infinitely closer. He scrambled under the thin, sloping shelter of a limestone boulder hanging over the edge of a gravelly wash.

The storm brawled over him with all its fury, assaulting his ears, taunting him. Somewhere close by lightning fried the earth or some hapless tree, and the ground reverberated. Sam buried his head in his hands, not looking up at the violent purple clouds. The roll of drums thrummeled down the draw, shaking the very rocks. But there was no rain, the one thing that might have lessened Sam's hatred of the lightning and thunder. There was no redeeming element to the fury of this storm. It came over him and sent its crackling, broken rays of molten lava to seek him out, stabbing this way and that in the half dark, blinding in their terrible power. The wind drove sand pell-mell, into Sam's hair, down the back of his canvas vest. It whipped at the sunburned flesh of his arms and exposed legs, lashed at his desert-torn hands.

Sam screamed curses at the storm. He closed his eyes, bearing down with all his might to force away the images of his father, mother and brother that kept sneaking in through the walls of his consciousness. Dead. *Dead!* All dead, and the oxen, too. The smell of charred flesh and singed hair everywhere, lingering on the air.

And then all was still. The storm stopped. It was there, horrifying in its power and fury as it boiled unchecked above Sam. And then it was gone. Or perhaps he had managed at last to block out its last grumblings. Whatever the case, after what seemed only several minutes since the last thunder he felt sunrays break over his body. He cast his eyes upward and could see, with irony, the path of the storm and the sheets of rain that it had decided to empty over the desert half a mile beyond him. Those soothing waters might as well have been in Nogales.

Trying to quiet his galloping heart, Sam looked off toward the east. He was still deep in the mountains, so deep within that the playa beyond was obscured by hills and rock. How far did he have to go? How many days had he been here on his hands and knees already? And how long could he continue?

Filling his lungs with dust-shot air, Sam started back along his trail, at least what he remembered of it from the state of panic in which he had made his flight. He found the canteen thirty yards back and drank sparingly of it, wiping his mouth with the back of his hand. It came away with white scum, a mixture of dust and sand and saliva.

He crawled on to where he could see the dark mound that was Scrub's pants, and found his vest and shirt tangled into the side of a catclaw bush. Removing his canvas clothing, he pulled Scrub's trousers over his legs, only having to cut one eight-inch slit in the thighs to make them fit. Scrub was nearly as wide as he was through the hips, in spite of a height difference of six inches, so the pants fit only a little too snugly there. The legs, of course, were far too short, and even after making a cut so that the shirt sleeves fit he could not change the fact that they came three inches up his arms and could not be buttoned. The vest had been loose on Scrub, and it actually fit, as long as he left the buttons undone. It was hard to grasp the vast feeling of comfort the vestments gave him. He had never appreciated clothing so much, in spite of the fact that it was filthy and sweat-caked and had come from a scornful little man.

Sam decided to leave his spear. He had the knife now, which he had guarded jealously as he scrambled away from the dangling rope. He knew it wouldn't be long, considering the amount of cardón cactus in this country, before he found a dead one from which he could take a rib and make a spear far superior to the one he had lost.

Sam stopped on a little knoll to reinforce his knees with canvas and to make himself makeshift mittens. Now, for the first time, he was able to contemplate in depth the seeming acts of mercy by the Yaqui. Here was the same man who days before had made him discard his every instrument of survival, and now he had left him not only clothing, but a canteen with a little water in it, a sack of jerky and even a knife. Was it just that he wanted Sam's suffering to be drawn out, that he did not want him to die yet because watching him struggle was so entertaining? Sam remembered the guarded look in the Yaqui's eyes. He had tried to hide it, but had there not been a certain amount of respect for Sam in that lingering glance?

Despite all his hatred and desire to kill the Yaqui, Sam had a hard time shaking his memory of that last look before the Apaches appeared. He contemplated it long and hard as he started down the knoll, into the swale below, and up the other side. He did not want to think of the Yaqui in anything less than terms of bitter animosity, but the Yaqui, merciful or merely respectful of his strength and nerve, had given him a much-needed edge. And his running right into the Apaches rather than away had most certainly saved Sam's life. That gnawing point stayed with him for many hours, through the next mile of throbbing pain that commandeered his battered body.

Caps O'Brien sipped on weak coffee, the grounds of which were in their third leaching. He strained the pale liquid through his teeth, spat out the granules and looked over at Burt, who lay half asleep on his blankets.

No Indians had come. Here along the rocky edge of the draw they were alone. In the near distance a magnificent storm had passed without affecting them except for a stout wind that swatted sand and seeds around, into their bedding and grub sacks. Now it was dead and silent, the heat pounding down with relentless maleficence. Tracker prowled somewhere higher up in the brush, scanning the country with his field glasses. Johnny slept, and Stratton watched them all in turn and brooded.

As if mere thoughts had called him up, Tracker came weaving down through the paloverde and mesquite trees, his eyes ever watchful although his head did not turn from side to side. He carried himself with admirable grace, that Negro. Grace and a huge respectable knowledge of the ways of this desert. Caps could not help thinking what a good partner he might have made if not for the color of his skin. Of course, he did not know the extent of his honor, either. A man who could not be swayed into a life of crime would certainly have done a fellow of Caps's ambitions little good.

Tracker came and squatted in front of the ashes of their fire. He took the coffee pot with insensitive fingers and filled a cup that was sitting empty on a rock at its edge. The cup happened to be the one Caps had been using, but he looked at it mildly and did not say a word. A year ago he would have killed a Negro brazen enough to drink from his cup. But this one commanded a lot more respect.

"We're going back."

Both Caps and Tracker swung their eyes to Burt, who had spoken. Stratton was watching, too, and he had sat up on his blanket. His face turned hard and even meaner than the normal scowl he wore.

Caps's glance was mild. "Goin' back? What are you sayin', kid? You need to get some rest."

"I don't need rest," Burt said. "My mind's clear enough. It was my money—or at least my father's money," he said with a hint of bitterness, "that got us here. You and Temp ought to be happy with that. But Tracker and Johnny and I, we're going back to Nogales. I already got two friends killed."

"Why the sudden change of heart, Burt?" Caps asked.

Burt frowned. "I didn't come down here to kill anybody. I thought we'd just get the gold and go home."

"But I thought you wanted revenge!" Caps said with a smile. "Hell, Burt! Those two boys beat the tar out of you in front of your entire hometown. That sure didn't do much for your image."

Burt scowled harder and glanced away. "No, but I haven't ever killed a man, and I'm not starting now. Caps, that fellow was near dead already! We just can't go killing men for no reason. He wasn't any threat."

Caps glanced over at Stratton. "Well, I know that, kid. But Temp and that boy had a little run-in there in town, you know. A bit of a set-to. Temp owed him somethin' for it. Geez, kid. You can't expect a man just to turn tail, can you?"

"Turn tail!" Burt's eyes flickered to Stratton. He felt halfway safe because Caps was between him and Stratton, and Caps had always demonstrated a strange power over the bigger gunman. "There wasn't enough left of that man to make a roast out of! But Temp sure did try."

Slowly, his eyes full of silent fury, Stratton came to his feet. His hand was nowhere near his gun, but Burt had no doubt the gun was on his mind. He was amazed at the calm tone of the gunman's voice when he finally spoke. "You an' Johnny can go wherever you please," said Stratton. "But Tracker, he's comin' with me an' Caps. Aren't you …Tracker?" The look in the gunman's eyes allowed for only one answer. Tracker's eyes flickered over at him. He did not give that answer, but at least for the moment he chose not to say no.

"Come on, Burt," Caps said with a calming smile. "You're gettin' delirious. There's a million dollars an' more waitin' for us probably not more than ten miles from here. We got good directions from Johnny how to get there, and a good trackin' man who can prob'ly follow those two fellas' trail right to it. Why would you wanna go back now?"

Putting his hand to his wounded side to sort of shore it up, Burt struggled up to sit against the rock behind him. He grimaced in pain, but under the scrutiny of the two callous men who had dragged him here he refused to whimper.

Tracker's eyes flickered with amazement at Burt's next words as the young man met Caps's eyes squarely. "When we agreed to come down here you said we were going to take the gold from them two boys and humiliate them. Nobody ever said anything about torturing them to death. I don't think I like what's shaping up here. I didn't agree to kill anybody, and I don't think Tracker or Johnny want to either."

Young Johnny had come awake at the sound of the voices, and he sat up groggily and shoved his hat back off his eyes, throwing nervous glances at the others. Listening, Tracker just stared at the ashes of the fire, his eyes hooded.

"Ah, Burt, go to sleep," Caps said. "We'll talk about it in the mornin'. You'll be some stronger then. I'm sure you'll be thinkin' clear." He turned a little, and his eyes flashed a thinly veiled warning at Stratton, who was working up to saying something.

His jaw clenching stubbornly, Burt massaged his ribs around the arrow wound, which Tracker had bound up with a saltwater poultice. "You can talk about it if you want. But we're goin' back. You and Temp can find that gold on your own from here. No reason to worry about sharing it with us."

Caps smiled with seeming good nature. He pulled out a brown twist of tobacco and ripped off a chunk with his teeth. He offered it to Burt, but the younger man did not accept. Then he offered it to Tracker, and the black man, surprised, also refused with a slight shake of his head.

Caps' eyes came back to settle on Burt's, and the younger man met his look squarely. That impressed the dynamiter.

Caps took a deep breath and paused a long time, working the tobacco into one cheek before he spoke. "Well, funny thing is, Burt, you're startin' to sound like you think you're in charge of this party. You're the money of the outfit, my friend. That's all you ever been. I guess I don't need to tell you that Temp an' me, we purty much do like we please." His eyes took on a hard metallic glitter, though his lips were still smiling. He didn't look over at Tracker, knowing he was being watched closely enough by Stratton.

"I'm afraid what Temp says is right, kid. You an' Johnny wanna go back, that's up to you. It's a long walk, but I'm sure you'll make it in a few weeks. But we need Tracker, an' he's comin' with us. He tries to leave here and somebody's gonna wind up dead."

Chapter Twenty-Seven

Some time after the storm, Sam Coffey heard three shots somewhere out on the desert. The rocky hills deflected the sound and spun it all directions, the trees and cactus absorbed it, losing it quickly and completely. He had no doubt the Apaches had found the Yaqui. They had not fared so well the first time, but the Yaqui had been lucky. The odds were pretty good they had taken him this time.

It was not long before Sam discovered the desired dead cardón—the elephant cactus. The silhouette of its many arms reared majestically forty feet above the desert, there on the side of a prickly pear-studded slope. But it was just a skeleton, a collection of columnar ribs, and one of its arms had fallen to the ground. From this arm Sam extracted one fairly straight rib close to six feet long. He had saved some cordage from a yucca, and he put it to use to lash his knife to the end of the rib as a spear.

Sam was moving along the lip of a wide, rocky arroyo not more than an hour later when he saw the hoof. It was a tiny, horse-like hoof, and as he drew nearer he saw that it was attached to the lifeless body of a newborn burro. Had he remained on the main trail he would not have found the burro at all; in this case, that was a point in favor of taking the back road, for this foal looked fresh enough to serve as a meal.

For no obvious reason, Sam's hair suddenly bristled on the back of his neck. He had felt these sensations before, and when he did it had always stood him in good stead not to wait around. But there was little time to react.

Sometimes luck smiled on Sam Coffey, but generally it was the evil grin of *bad* luck—and more in the form of a frown. A twig snapped not twenty feet behind him, and he whirled. This brought him face to face with a beast he had prayed many times to run into on the desert, in hopes of following it to a water hole. Yet on seeing this one, and the insane look in its eyes, he froze, his entire body tensing. Staring him down was a full-grown feral burro, its choppy gray hide matted with burs and mud. It was plain this one was a mother, intent on protecting its newborn baby, even in death. It stood there glaring at him, one front foot poised, its ears laid back flat against its head.

Clenching his jaw, Sam pushed up off his hands. Now on his knees, but keeping his torso low, he brandished the spear in front of him. There would be no wolfen rescue like there had been with the jaguar. This time it was Sam and his makeshift spear against a five hundred pound burro, crazed with grief over the loss of its young.

"Easy, burro," he said. "Easy. I don't mean no harm."

The quietly spoken words were all it took to snap the animal out of its trance. With a squeal of rage, it charged.

Sam had thought he was prepared, but the animal was too fast. So swiftly did it reach him he had no chance to move. Fortunately, the spear was raised, and by sheer chance it jammed the animal in the chest, tearing a bray from its throat. But the force of its haft being slammed against the man's ribs by the five hundred pounds of burro catapulted him backwards. Like a dead log overpowered by the waters of a flashflood he hurled over the edge of the arroyo. He felt himself careening through the air, seeming for a moment to float. Then with a jarring thud he lit in a patch of sand surrounded by rocks. The wind torn from him, he felt his head whirl and through blurry eyes saw the frenzied burro, scrambling for footing on the arroyo's edge.

Breath came back to Sam in a rush, and he rolled over and sat up, gasping, still holding the spear like a lifeline. Cringing, he turned his eyes upward, expecting the animal to come tumbling down on top of him. But at the last possible moment the burro's sure-footedness saw it through, and its hoofs caught on the edge of the rocks, propelling it back up to safety. It turned and looked down at him, giving him one last warning bray. Then it stepped from the rim of the wash and vanished with a switch of its matted tail.

Sam sucked in another breath. "Damn burro. Guess I showed *her* who's boss." He smiled wryly at his own pathetic humor.

Turning, he surveyed the place he had fallen. He was ten feet below the top of the wash, and by the looks of it he hated to imagine how difficult it was going to be to get out of. He could only hope that somewhere ahead it hit a gentle slope, or that at least no more thunderstorms came to fill it full of murderous roiling water.

Watching the sides of the arroyo warily, Sam started crawling, his spear clutched tightly. He had traveled perhaps seventy yards when he turned and looked back the way he had come. There stood the burro atop a rock, watching him. Sight of the man seemed to break something loose in the mourning beast, and it began to bray, over and over and over, until, with a sigh, Sam went back to crawling.

One thing was obvious to Sam now that he found the unharried time to study it. This wash was not just the bed of some ancient creek turned away by a landslide or shifting of the ground. It was a draw down which seasonal flashfloods would crash. This he knew by the thin willows ranked along its edges, and the lack of any stouter trees such as mesquite, ironwood or paloverde, which would not give against the powerful current of onrushing floodwaters. Instead, the grip of their roots would fail, and they would be swept away. Here thrived only the willows that would bend and thus survive such a fury of thundering water.

Undaunted but wary, he crawled down the wash. He still had his canteen, nearly empty now, and half a pound of jerky. He wished he had been granted time to cut off at least a chunk of burro flank, but he would not dare return. Back there was one feisty mother!

It grew dark while Sam was in the arroyo. He wanted desperately back up to the high ground. But just how bad could one man's luck be? A thunderstorm at this point in his trek seemed almighty implausible, considering the misfortune the fates had already heaped on him. Sam looked around until he found two things: a big rounded hunk of sandstone lying out in the sun where it was warm, and a veritable forest of cardón cactus above the wash. The Mexicans referred to such a forest as a *cardonale*.

Behind Sam's searching for these two things was the force of reason. The sandstone he would pull up against himself to keep warm as long as it served the purpose. And the huge cactus might indirectly provide him water. He could not use the cardón itself for moisture, but a cardonale in its vastness draws up a large store of water from the ground during the day which in the cool of night it will partly release, possibly enough to cause the water underground to rise. Armed with that knowledge, Sam found himself a shady spot and dug a hole in the sand with his hands and his spear, down to a depth of about three feet. Then he pulled the hunk of sun-warmed sandstone up close to his chest and lay down to sleep in the sand just under the rocks of the arroyo's steep side. Tomorrow he would find a way out of the big ditch. Tonight he would try to sleep and forget the throbbing pain in his raw knees, feet and hands. Already, the knees of his new pants were worn through, and now his fingers bled from digging the hole. But it was a sacrifice he would make over again. He could live with bloody hands. But he had to have water for them to bleed.

It was just after first light when the rumble came, this time from deep in the southwest.

Thunder!

Sam jerked to a sitting position, wide eyes scanning for rain. All of the sky within view was clear and still sprinkled with the more stubborn of the stars, but again came the deep-bellied rumble, rattling across the desert and making strange reverberations in the naked rock above.

Sam could see no clouds to let him know if the storm was putting down rain. Yet there is a certain tonal quality to thunder that accompanies rain. Sam could not explain it, even to himself, but this thunder sounded wet—menacingly wet. And one look at the steep sides of this arroyo reminded him there was no way out …

Burt McGrath cursed himself for a coward, lying there in the dark camp. He should have never let Caps and Stratton pressure him into this trip. He should have never stolen the money from his father to fund them. He had wanted revenge on Sam Coffey and Tom Vanse for the humiliation heaped on him and his friends, but he had not wanted to kill them, although he guessed he might have mentioned that option once or twice. He had never believed anyone was serious about coming down to Mexico in the first place, so he had figured he was safe talking tough. By the time he realized the trip would be a reality, he had dug himself in too deep.

Burt had reluctantly admitted two things to himself even before Tracker had spoken with him. One, he was not the man in charge here. And two, Caps and Stratton planned to kill Vanse and Coffey once they had the gold. What was to stop them from killing Burt and his friends, too? The thought had plagued him for many miles.

But all this contemplation was for naught. He was in trouble. His father would have been proud of him, he thought with bitter irony.

Tracker had gone off in the direction they left Sam Coffey. He was reconnoitering the trail, looking for possible danger, making sure the trail would be safe to travel in the morning. The black man had not yet come back, but Caps and Stratton felt secure in his return. He wouldn't try to escape as long as Burt was here. He might not talk of his loyalty to his boss's son, but he wore it like a badge of honor.

Burt cursed himself and stared at the fire. His stupid actions had already been the death of Lug and Scrub, and unless something drastic happened it would be the death of Johnny and Tracker and him as well. He no longer had any doubt about Caps and Temp's intentions. They would get the gold, if Tracker could manage to lead them back to it, and then whoever was left to tell the story or to try and share their wealth would die. He would not have been surprised if Caps and Temp tried to kill each other. Gold had been known to drive far better men over the edge.

The outlandish idea of a getaway struck Burt out of the blue. It
hit him the moment Temp stood up to walk out into the brush and
answer the call of nature. He had to run, and now. Once he was
gone into the darkness they would never be able to find him. The
next day he could waylay them if he so chose. He did not want to
kill anyone, but these two men he could. After all, they surely
intended that fate for him. But unfortunately Caps didn't trust him
anymore, and he had taken away his weapons. Not only that, Caps
had told Burt he would not be allowed to touch a gun unless they
were under attack, and that if he did it would be assumed he was
an enemy. But Burt did not have time to worry about such things.
He had only moments to consider this plan. Temp would be coming
back. He could not win against them both.

More than just a killer, Caps must have been one with an
incredible instinct for danger. He was reaching across the fire to
take a piece of rabbit off a spit when Burt moved. Burt had scooted
over closer to Temp's bedding, where his own rifle lay alongside
Temp's, and nonchalantly he reached for it. At that moment Caps
looked up.

Burt froze with his rifle half lifted, and Johnny, somehow sensing
a change in the atmosphere, looked up too. Caps, always on edge,
ducked and rolled to one side. He came up with pistol drawn and
fired. Burt felt the bullet burn along his shoulder. He fell backwards
over his rock seat. Clinging like an animal to his rifle, he threw
himself to the side. Unfeeling to the thorns and rocks that bit his
flesh, he shoved and rolled once, twice, three more times. He knew
the drop-off was nearby, and now it was his only chance.

Another shot blasted from behind just as Burt felt the earth
disappear from under him, and he was crashing down. The branches
of a mesquite tree formed a bittersweet cradle for him as he
plummeted down the slope. He fell past it and slid in the rocks and
gravel. He struck the back of his hand against a large rock, and the
pain of it almost made him let go of the rifle. He was falling
backwards again, then landing, pitching and rolling. He must have
fallen fifty feet before he slammed to a stop at the bottom of the
draw, the world spinning around him.

"Get that kid!" he heard Caps's voice ring from up above.

"Stratton, *get that kid!*"

He could hear Temp's angry voice, and horses fidgeting and whinnying in the dark. Where was Johnny? Had he been smart and fast thinking enough to run too?

Stunned and bleeding, Burt struggled up, and with the rifle cradled tight against him he limped away. He could feel the blood running down his side again, and now down his face, hands and shoulder as well, but he had to distance himself from Caps and Temp. If they found him he would never have another chance. Even if Caps's more merciful side took over, Temp would kill him. He had been wanting to for days.

In the still night Tracker heard the shouts and the shots back toward camp. He was on foot, but his horse was with him. He flipped one of its reins around a branch and dashed through the brush toward camp. Within thirty yards he slowed to a near stop, taking one step every minute or so, searching the dark. He had that advantage of all people of his color, that he could not be seen in the night unless he smiled. He used that fact to full advantage. He had always been proud of his race; tonight he was damn glad of it.

Five minutes had passed as he made his way within sight of the camp. Through the screen of trees he could see Caps and Temp, and after several minutes he made out Johnny, sitting beyond the fire eating a bowl of something with a vengeance, as if to look up from his plate would bring notice to him, and then death. There was no Burt. What had happened? Where was he? They would not have killed him and left Johnny alive, would they?

He crept closer, and when he was within feet he sank back on his haunches to listen. He could smell something foul in the air, the stench of human waste where someone had come out to void himself. It was too close to him, but since he did not know which direction to go he stayed where he was.

"I'm tellin' you," he heard Caps speak, "the kid meant to shoot me. I looked up as he was grabbin' his rifle. He just waited for one of us to leave camp."

That explained the stench in the trees. It was Stratton who had gone out of camp.

"Johnny, what got into 'im?" Caps growled.

Johnny raised his face so Tracker could see the firelight flicker off it. "Uh … I don't know, Caps. I didn't know he was plannin' on anything."

"I'm gonna kill you, too," Stratton's sullen voice carried through the underbrush, although he spoke in a low tone. Tracker heard those words and instinctively started to bring up his rifle.

Johnny's eyes flashed fearfully to Stratton, then to Caps. Caps waved Stratton off. "Leave the kid alone, Temp. He ain't done nothin'."

"Hah! Not yet," Stratton growled. "Neither had Burt, not till he tried to shoot you."

"You gonna try to shoot me, Johnny? After all we been through together?" Caps asked, his voice soft.

"No sir! I'd never try to shoot you two."

Stratton spat. "You ain't got the guts God gave a squirrel, or you woulda gone with 'im and you know it. An' then I'd kill you both like I'm gonna kill him come mornin'."

"There's no reason to kill him. I shot him good, and if he ain't dead at least he's on foot. You can bet this desert will put him under. Stupid kid." Caps suddenly plopped down, shaking his head. "Temp, I just can't believe he'd do that after all we been through." He sat there for a moment, and then Tracker saw him start to smile. He chuckled, then started to laugh. Finally, Caps wiped his eyes. "I'll tell you, Temp, that was somethin'. That kid, he held onto that rifle like a baby holdin' onto a peppermint stick. That was somethin', now. Somethin' else. You can say whatever you like, but that kid's got grit."

Tracker eased his rifle back down to his side and watched as Stratton walked to the edge of camp and looked down the slope that fell away from them. He spat down it and made a long show of scanning the darkness below. He might as well have pointed out the way for Tracker to go. Burt was down there somewhere. He might be dead, if what Caps said was true. But he might also be hurt and needing help. And what else was Tracker good for if it wasn't helping out his boss's son? Especially now that it appeared he had finally come to his senses.

Tracker had only started down into the draw when he heard Stratton's harsh voice. "There's that nigger!"

Instinctively, he turned and threw a bullet toward camp. Without knowing if he hit any mark, he turned and ran down the draw.

Chapter Twenty-Eight

It was morning, and Tom Vanse lay alongside a trail, half afraid to move. The shock of the arrow in his leg had worn off, but the pain was merciless. He was only thankful it kept him alert. Thunder growled heavily across the horizon, and he wondered if it was storming wherever Sam was. That wouldn't make his friend any too happy. It didn't make *Tom* particularly happy, either, but the slightest chance of rain elated him.

Late the afternoon before Tom had observed an odd, sort of melancholy sight, and even as exhausted as he was, he stayed to watch it. It was a burro that stood on the far edge of a steep-sided wash. It wasn't the sight of the burro itself that was so strange, but its actions. Almost as if crying, it stood there on the rocks, braying time and again and looking around like it had lost its mate. Tom had watched it for a long time until it finally hung its head dejectedly, turned, and ambled off into the brush. Shortly after, Tom had collapsed in exhaustion from his horse, falling dangerously near a large clump of sharp-leaved agave. He could not say whether it was something about the jolt itself, or just the close-up sight of the plant, but when he looked at it a distant bell rang in his head.

Now, as the new sun pounded against his eyes and begged him to rise, he sat up and rubbed a hand over his face, listening to another jab of lightning send thunder murmuring along the hills. His mouth and hands were swollen from the agave he had consumed before passing out on the trail, and that frightened him. Had he poisoned himself with the plant? He had been positive it was the one Sam had pointed out to him as a source of life-giving moisture! No, the juice had done his body good, even though his swollen hands and lips did not concur.

He stared down groggily at the end of the arrow shaft protruding from his leg and wondered how long his body could take this pain before succumbing. And what about gangrene? Was he doomed, and so to doom his partner, by failure to bring back help? In all reality, Tom had to admit to himself that Sam was probably gone. But if there was the smallest chance he was still alive Tom had to go on.

Rolling over, he picked up two of the thick agave leaves that had cut his hands while harvesting them in the forenight's gloaming and opened up Sam's saddlebags. There was no room for the plants. The bags were filled with gold and jewels, a sight that made Tom feel guilty. He could not take this booty back to civilization to spend, not knowing Sam had given his life for it. But he could not convince himself to throw it away, either. He would take it back for Nadia.

Gritting his teeth, he held onto the agave and climbed into the saddle, wanting to scream out in pain as his leg contacted leather. He looked out over the landscape. The night before he was certain he had stumbled upon the trail to Hermosillo. One glance at a peculiar flat-topped mountain on his right showed him that was true, for that mountain stuck in his memory. Somehow, by a miracle of God, he was back where he was supposed to be, and even more miraculously the Yaquis had not found him.

Thanks to the instincts of Gringo, Hermosillo now lay due east, and by mid-afternoon they should be there. But then of course there was one more nagging question: when he arrived, could he find anyone to come back with him? The Mexicans he and Sam had spoken with in the village were scared to death of the Yaquis. The more he contemplated what he was doing, the more Tom feared he was on an ill-fated mission. Deep in his heart he knew he was going to have to get some kind of medical care, however poor, then return alone. He stared back in the direction he had come from, praying Sam was back there waiting for him, perhaps hurt but at least alive. Thinking of Sam, who was closer to him than a brother, he could not help ponder the anguish Abe Varnell must have gone through after losing his partner in this same desert.

Tom started to rein Gringo back toward Hermosillo, but at that moment a gust of wind carried to them from across the steep wash, and Gringo pivoted his head and flared his nostrils, letting out a long whinny. Tom stared across the desert, but nothing seemed out of the ordinary. Gringo tried to walk toward the wash, but Tom jerked him back. The horse turned his head again, ears shot hard forward. He nickered loudly.

Tom patted his shoulder, thinking of the burro that probably still lurked not far away. The horse must be smelling it, but why was he interested enough in it to talk to it when they had not interacted the evening before? "Come on, you fool horse. Hermosillo's back this way."

Heaving a sigh, Tom paused before turning toward Hermosillo and glanced back the way they had come. He froze. In lazy little swirls, dust meandered away from the five Mexican caballeros who faced him fifty yards distant.

With the sound of thunder still reverberating down the canyon, Sam Coffey whirled toward the hole he had dug the night before. It was still early, so the cardonale should not yet have reclaimed its massive stores of moisture. Sure enough, in the very bottom of the pit stood an inch or two of water. Feverishly, he leaned in, and with his battered, scabbed hands he flung handfuls of sand out onto the ground. Even as he watched, more dirty water filled the depression. Stripping off Scrub's shirt, he put it over the mouth of his canteen as a filter and laid it in the bottom of the hole. When the bubbles from the canteen stopped rising, he withdrew it and took a long drink, nearly emptying the container. The little well filled more slowly the second time, as he watched the sky, waiting for the thunder and lightning that at any moment might be upon him. Finally, the canteen was filled. Sam capped it and started down the rocky wash at a fast crawl. Within fifty feet he was leaving a fresh trail of blood.

He had only gone sixty yards when a boom of thunder rocked the draw, and the weak flicker of light lit the top of the wash. Sam could not be sure because of the strength of the thunder, but he would have almost sworn he heard the sound of a neighing horse, drowned out by the rumble. Unless it was only some wild horse, that could mean Indians, Mexican bandits or McGrath's bunch. But, with the nearby storm threatening, Sam had more important things on his mind, like getting out of this gully.

Then it came again, this time not a neigh, but a nicker. Sam raised up on his knees, searching the top of the arroyo. Damn, he wished he knew what was up there! But again, odds were it would not be a good thing.

He crawled on, faster, gritting his teeth against the terrible pain. Again the thunder rocketed across the desert, although he still could see no clouds from down where he was. And then he saw it: a possible escape.

The bank was still steep, but scalable? Perhaps, with God's help. Unhurt, climbing out of the arroyo would be a cakewalk. As it was, he would struggle, and his price in pain would be tremendous. But pain was the least of his fears. Using his spear as a crutch, he pushed himself up so that he was standing on his heels. The pain was so horrible he couldn't even cry out. He just bit the insides of his cheeks and pounded hard against his leg, his face contorted like a circus clown. At last, the nerves in his feet settled enough to return sane thought to him, and once more he eyed the steep bank.

Suddenly, sounding mere yards above him, came a crash. It wasn't thunder. Perhaps it was worse. *Rifle fire!*

Sam froze. Four shots, one from much closer than the others. The sound of excited Mexican voices drifted down, then pounding hooves. Sam's eyes flashed back at the cut bank he must take up to safety. But *was* it safe? Mexicans out here this far from a center of civilization did not bode well. But with the increasing thunder and lightning, and the clouds just appearing beyond the wash's edge, he dared not remain in the arroyo.

Heart drumming, he took the slope, walking backwards and pushing into the ground with the spear to propel him upward. He growled away his pain, scrambled and swore and strained, sliding back a time or two, thankful for his canvas moccasins. He looked behind him, knowing he shouldn't. Six more feet up the bank. He felt so weak, nearly overcome by fatigue. The bank steepened. He slipped, and a vision of sliding all the way down careered across his mind. Frantically, he whipped around and flung himself at a clump of brush protruding out the side of the bank. He found as his hands closed on the gray branches that it was a vicious catclaw bush, but he couldn't let go. Nothing could be as bad as sliding back into the gully. Savagely, he grasped the branches, and, with new-found strength in his bleeding hands, he pulled. His toes clawed at the crumbling earth. He slipped and fell hard against the bank, dirt and rocks cascading through the five feet of air that now seemed like a thousand. The curved thorns of the catclaw gouged deep into the flesh of his hands. He growled away the pain again and shoved against the collapsing dirt with his feet. He was able to grip another branch, higher up, and one foot found a solid hold. Even as sharp pebbles burrowed into his feet, he put all his strength into an upward lunge to grasp the roots of an overhanging paloverde.

Sam could not possibly have any remaining strength. Yet over the lip of the arroyo he struggled, and as the first hint of moisture whisked by he found himself rolling onto the rock-studded bank above what might have become his grave.

Staving off pain, Sam spun and looked toward where he had heard the shots and the hoofbeats. Perhaps three hundred yards away—a man galloping recklessly over the desert, five riders pursuing him closely. The fleeing man appeared to be mounted on a buckskin, but he was so far away Sam could not be sure. Sam stared after the disappearing shapes, wishing for his field glasses. And then, in half a minute more, there was left only the hint of drifting dust. Sam was once more alone.

Looking east, he could see the flat plain, the playa that stretched away beyond these tortuous Bacatete Mountains toward Hermosillo. He could not have been a half day's ride from civilization … if he had a horse to ride.

Sam slumped over on the ground, only now beginning to feel the true depths of the damage he had done to his feet and hands, knees and elbows—indeed his entire body. With new moisture in him, he could again feel the wet trickle of blood oozing into his moccasins and on the palms of his hands, thickened by sand and clay. He felt a dribble course down the side of his head into his hair. He must have brushed the catclaw with his face in clearing the bank. It didn't matter. It was good to bleed. Only a man who was alive could bleed.

With a last look of remorse over the crumbly bank at his knife-spear and the agave leaves he had been wearing as a necklace until they tore loose in his struggle, Sam turned back toward the east … and Hermosillo.

The appearance of the Mexican caballeros was to Tom Vanse like a miracle, for suddenly the arrow wound that had started to throb so horribly seemed to disappear.

Tom's mama had taught him enough manners to stop and greet travelers on a lonely road. But he had neither time nor inclination for manners today. Maybe these five Mexicans were friendly. Shoot, maybe one of them was a doctor, one a priest and one the village clown! Tom's leg might be treated and healed as if by magic, and he might be entertained in the process. And then maybe Tom Vanse was Santa Claus!

With a sideways jerk of the reins, he spurred Gringo hard. With the wind whipping in his hair and throwing his hat back on its string, Tom glanced behind him at the Mexicans. Bent low in their saddles, they had whipped their mounts to racing speed. The crackle of rifle shots rose above the sound of pounding hooves. The whistle of passing lead made Gringo run faster still.

Tom jerked his pistol and threw a shot behind him, more to give his pursuers pause than in hopes of hitting them. His only chance was to find shelter and make a stand. Look for the high ground, he told himself. *And save the last bullet for yourself …*

There was a bluff fifty yards off the trail. It rose through an imposing stand of prickly pear, angling upward to terminate in a ragged nest of choppy boulders and cardón cactus only sixty feet higher than the trail itself. It would be enough.

Tom veered off the trail, forcing Gringo to make a valiant leap over a good share of the purple-padded prickly pears before he landed in the middle of another patch, cultivated there by some sadistic god. The pears sprouted in abundance for fifty or sixty yards either direction, predominately on this side of the trail. They scaled the hill another twenty yards in clusters up to five feet tall before surrendering to Spanish bayonet, cardón and the battalions of limestone boulders.

Gringo and Tom ran the gauntlet. The horse, game as a burro, crashed unfeelingly through the cactus, breaking pads away to send them flying. Some of them stuck to his knees and chest. But the blood of frenetic flight pounded rank through the gelding, and he never flagged.

At the crest of the hill, Tom hauled back on the reins. He did not want to stop this far from Hermosillo, but if he had to stop he could not have found a more defensible place. The cluster of boulders, like a man-made castle, crowned the hillock on all borders. They were thick and tall enough for a man Tom's size to lean across them and take aim at anyone trying to ascend the hill with less than friendly intentions.

Flying off the horse, his hurt leg forgotten, Tom dropped against the closest rock with Sam's Marlin in hand. Throwing his hat down on the rock, he leaned the rifle barrel across it and sighted on the nearest Mexican, whose horse was humping fast up through the cactus. These boys were not on some mission of mercy; they had every intention of reaching him before he had time to defend himself.

Too late. Tom's thought was almost idle, although the exclamatory punctuation added by the voice of the Marlin was anything but. In mid-jump over a four-foot patch of purple pear, the bullet took the Mexican high in the chest. He had drawn his pistol, and like a dark splinter it spun off into the cactus as a great invisible hand wrenched him from his horse and tossed him backward, almost jerking one foot right out of the boot as it caught momentarily in the stirrup.

Tom's next shot was aimed at the back of a Mexican whose horse had swapped ends and was making for other parts like his tail was on fire. The horse made it to other parts; the Mexican stayed.

Before Tom could repeat his performance, the other three Mexicans had made shelter in rock clusters and scrub brush, and aside from the grunting and blowing of their horses, which he could hear dimly through the ringing of his ears, the day was still.

Tom was safe … for now. But he had no water, no food, and the arrow was making its presence known more than ever. He was safe from attack, but a long way from Hermosillo, where a doctor's care might be had and where charitable souls might be gathered to ride to Sam's rescue. If the Mexicans only knew, they had but to wait …

*   *   *

The ground above the wash was out of danger of flashfloods, but to Sam an even more heart-rending danger lay in being exposed to the storm. The black clouds loomed low on the horizon, moving toward him and roiling with glowing menace. Having once more to ignore his pain, Sam scanned the terrain and made for the lowest spot he could find, a bowl surrounded by boulders and mesquite. There he snuggled up against a boulder and waited, anticipating the next flash of light and pursuant roar of thunder that he hated even worse than the Yaquis who had put him in this predicament.

He had ceased to think of the man on the buckskin who, fleeing the Mexican horsemen, took refuge on a hill not half a mile distant from him. If Sam had stood and looked up out of his refuge, he could have seen that hill jutting up unobtrusively on the western skyline.

Chapter Twenty-Nine

Burt McGrath would live. Had Tracker Winborn been a boasting man, he might have said it was because of his skill at doctoring, which had mostly been perfected on animals and only incidentally used on humans. But boastful Tracker was not. Burt would live because he was strong and because he was determined. In spite of all his faults, there was good in Burt that Tracker had always recognized even when Sheriff Lightman and others in Nogales had not. Deep in his soul Tracker believed if he could manage to get his boss's son out of this hell alive the people of Nogales would see positive—and permanent—changes in a young man who had been one of the town's most persistent headaches.

Bare-chested, Tracker crouched over Burt. To bandage the youth's wounds he had used his own shirt, and his chocolate-brown skin glistened in the sun, the muscles beneath it long and heavy-veined and ripe with power.

Tracker hadn't made it far from where he first found Burt nursing a wounded shoulder. The boy had lost a lot of blood, and he was weak, so Tracker took him over a shoulder and carried him as far as his vast strength would allow. He sought refuge in a cove of rocks where only one side offered any kind of avenue for pursuit. This alley would reveal their approach within one hundred yards. For Tracker, that was lethal range with a peashooter. Any enemy with the brass to come through that corridor would die ... or wish he had.

Tracker dared not risk a fire, so he was glad when the first gray light filtered over the mountains. After so many hours without a shirt on he awaited that sun with great anticipation.

Then he heard the rifle shots.

Scrambling up onto the boulders that sheltered him and Burt from the bristling winds that were kicking up ahead of the storm, Tracker saw a rider gallop by on a buckskin horse, pursued by five Mexicans. Instinctively, he raised his rifle, and for more than ten seconds he led the front Mexican with the knowledge that a squeeze of his trigger would empty the saddle. But for all he knew the white man could have been some fugitive from justice. The Mexicans may have been a posse. It was that possibility that made Tracker hold his fire as he watched the man on the buckskin ride up and take refuge in a patch of boulders and cardón cactus on a little knoll not five hundred yards distant.

He heard two distant reports of a large caliber rifle, but now he was too far away, and the vegetation too thick to make out the outcome of the shots. After watching for a few more minutes, and feeling troubled by the scene he had just witnessed, Tracker slipped back down through the rocks to Burt.

Burt looked up from where he lay in the sand. His eyes were inquisitive, but Tracker gave him no explanation until he asked, "What was all that ruckus?"

Tracker shrugged, squatting down on his haunches. "Bunch of Mexicans chasin' a white man."

Burt tried to sit up farther. He managed to come almost to a sitting position—and in the process broke his wound open again. He felt it moisten the inside of his bandage, but he ignored the renewed pain. "A *white* man? Out here alone? What did he look like?"

Again Tracker shrugged. "Big man," he said. "Dark hair, light gray hat, red shirt. Buckskin horse. Horse that was brung up with the desert, I'd guess."

Burt grimaced against the pain of trying to work all the way up to a seated position. "That sounds like the horse that Sam Coffey was riding. But the fellow it sounds like you saw on him was the other one—Vanse."

Tracker chewed the insides of his cheeks thoughtfully. "Maybe they had to swap horses. That Vanse, he wear a red shirt?"

Burt shrugged, wincing at a twinge that flashed across his shoulder and side simultaneously. "Matter of fact, he did one day when I saw him. He had a mustache—and a little chin beard."

Tracker looked back up the slope at the tip of the boulders where he had crouched to watch the fleeing rider and the Mexicans pass. "Man of the desert don't waste much space packin' extry shirts around, so I'd be guessin' this'n is him. But I don't know why he'd still be all the way out here."

"He in bad trouble, Tracker?"

" 'Spect so," the black man replied. "Five again' one ain't favorable odds."

"Or against two, either," Burt said meaningfully.

"Less we s'pose that one of the two would be me."

Burt met the mischievous look behind Tracker's hooded eyes. "Unless we suppose."

"Figger you c'n take a six-shooter an' hit a man comin' over that rise yonder?" Tracker asked Burt as he pushed to his feet.

Burt looked past Tracker at the open view of the sand and brush a man would have to travel to reach him. A man with a rifle could kill Burt long before he could shoot him with his pistol, and Burt knew it. But Tracker would need the rifle if he were to do the stranger any good. He looked back up at Tracker, his chest strangely swollen with pride to think the Negro was on his side. "I figure I could."

Tracker almost smiled. He had a pride of his own at the sudden growing his boss's son had done. "I don't figure I hit anyone with that shot I threw last night, boy. That means there could be two comin' 'cross that sand."

"My gun's got six bullets."

Tracker gave his friend a wink, and then he started up through the rocks.

The haphazard shot thrown by Tracker had indeed wounded a man. It had taken Caps O'Brien through the meat between his neck and his left shoulder, and throughout the night Caps had struggled with the pain and shock of the wound. Toward morning he had recovered enough to feel the pain even more intensely, but he could think clearly enough.

With the storm coming, grumbling along the horizon and threatening to crash over them, they decided Stratton should go off on his own and try to track down the black man before he got too far away. Johnny, scared to make a move unless specifically told to, stayed with Caps. Unfortunately, Stratton was not much of a hand at following a trail—the very reason he and Caps wanted Tracker back so badly. Even from the back of his horse he managed to find a line of tracks leading away. But what he did not know was that it was only Tracker's horse, which had pulled its one looped rein free of the tree branch and run. Stratton, finding its spoor out in the trees, followed it toward the southwest, blissfully ignorant to a fact that would have been plain as day to Tracker: these were the shallow prints of an unridden animal. Tracker had headed in the exact opposite direction after tossing his shot up the hill.

The path did not lead Stratton to Tracker. But it did lead to someone …

Sam huddled in his shelter of boulders as the storm picked up fury. The sand eddied around him, and the bushes shuddered and crackled against each other. Sam crouched there and cursed the Yaquis who had put him in this spot. More than ever he wished for just one shot at Cajeme or the lone Yaqui who followed him. Sam had tangled with men in his past whom in his anger he would have thrashed. He had even tangled with one or two he would not have minded seeing dead. But never before had he so strongly tasted the desire to kill. The Yaquis had won an honorable place at the top of a new list. Even though he would never get a chance at one of them, thinking about it took his mind off the lightning that cracked around him and threatened his sanity.

Sam was huddled there waiting out the storm when a light sprinkle of rain skittered over him, fresh and fine. Suddenly, he felt the sensation of being watched, and he whirled. A saddled horse was standing at the edge of the clearing!

The man's sudden movement caused the horse to shy, and it veered to the left and loped across the flat, disappearing into a grove of mesquite before Sam could even begin to formulate a plan of how to catch it, much less give any thought to where it had come from. After it had gone, his first thought was that whoever the man on the buckskin was he had had some luck. The horse must have belonged to one of the Mexicans.

A blast of lightning shook the rocks that hid him and made Sam duck down against the sand, a violent shiver running through him. He sat up, blinking his eyes against the glare of the light that had temporarily blinded him. And then, over the sound of the wind in the rocks, he heard another horse jog up behind him. He spun about.

There, shrouded in the day's new light and aiming a rifle at Sam, sat a big man on a bay horse. A crooked grin—a *mirthless* grin—stretched over the man's bearded face as he shook his head. "Well, I'll be purely damned," said the man. "I thought I left you a Christmas tree ornament."

It was Temp Stratton.

Tom Vanse was doing all he could to remain upright. The Marlin lay across the rocks getting hotter by the minute, so hot he hardly dared touch it. But with his hurt leg he didn't dare put the rifle down in the shade, where he would have to bend down and get it if the Mexicans rushed him.

He had to laugh at his predicament here in the heat and sun, for half a mile away loomed thunderheads, and a veritable squall seemed underway. A fistful of lightning streaks hit ground over fifteen minutes' time, and a rain curtain hung out of one particularly dark patch of cloud. Here he stood, ironically soaked with sweat beneath a sun that only seemed to get hotter against the storm that popped and raged so near. Perspiration dripped out from under his hat into his eyes, making him wryly ponder the meaning of the term "sweatband." Cool little rivulets tickled down his sides and darkened the cotton of his shirt. His head was baking. His face felt raw from the sun glaring back into it from the rocks.

He had seen no movement from the Mexicans below, but he would have seen if they had left. He did not think they were closing on him, either. To do that without his spotting them they would have to be on hands and knees, and the cover of cactus and thorny brush precluded that possibility.

So he waited. And every minute he grew weaker from the loss of moisture, and from the pain wracking his thigh. Waiting was his only choice … but to wait here for very long was to die.

A large jab of lightning drove to the ground not far away from Tom, shaking him. He had no fear of lightning, as Sam did, but the storm had grown frighteningly close in the past several minutes, finally managing to drive the sun off his back.

His leg felt like it was falling off. The hour he had spent leaning up against the boulder might well have been the longest of his life. He could feel the red in his eyes as much as he could feel the grit in his teeth and hair and in his ears. Tom was tougher than most. He had survived conditions that might have killed lesser men, and would surely have left some shaken and deranged. But he was beginning to think if he did not get out of this predicament he would die here.

A shot rang out below, surprising him so badly that he jerked back from the rock, little pieces of grit pattering about him as the bullet whined off the stone. He looked up in time to see the puff of smoke drifting lazily away from a clump of prickly pear.

Lack of cartridges was not one of his problems, with three boxes snuggled alongside the gold in his saddlebags. He started levering the rifle and peppering the cactus with bullets until a Mexican dashed out of the cluster and raced for a more tenable position. Tom could not swear he killed the man with his next bullet, but he put him down hard.

Here he stood, waiting for a desert gully washer to drench him to the skin, shooting at 'Cans—*Mexi*-cans. It was amazing what a man found funny when great pain or weariness came over his body.

He wiped the sweat from his forehead and rubbed his eyes. Where were the other two Mexicans? He pressed cartridge after cartridge through the loading gate of the Marlin until it once again held a full complement, his eyes scanning the cover below. Nothing alive came to view except for a shrike perched atop a cactus.

And then rifle fire again broke the quiet, backed by a rumble of thunder. Four shots, in quick succession, a man screaming out, and one horse loping away downslope through the prickly pear and jagged rocks. Then all was quiet for two minutes.

Suddenly, a man appeared from the brush, one hand over his head, the other arm hanging loose and bloody at his side. It was a Mexican in a white straw hat. To his left another one came from the cover of cactus, his hands also raised. Tom squinted down at them, suspecting some kind of ruse.

Then a third man appeared behind them holding a rifle trained on their backs. He appeared to be a colored man, if Tom's mind wasn't playing tricks on him.

"We're comin' up!" the black man's voice rang out. "Hold your fire."

Tom knew there were colored folk down in this country, slaves who had escaped, some who had joined up with Indian tribes. For all he knew some of them might have joined Mexican bandits as well. So he kept his rifle ready, although if they were indeed setting a trap for him it was fairly elaborate.

The black man brought the two Mexicans within twenty-feet before Tom straightened up, trying to hide the fire in his leg. "I think that'll be far enough."

The trio stopped, and the black man spat into the cactus. "Looks like y'all was in need of help. You got somethin' to say to these boys?"

"I'm still tryin' to figure out who *you* are. Where in tarnation did you come from?"

The black man chuckled. "They call me Tracker. I hail from Nogales, and I figure I'm about your best friend today."

Tom gritted his teeth. In spite of trying to will it away, the pain in his thigh was becoming almost unbearable. "And just how you figure that?"

"You mean besides takin' care o' these two? Because I can doctor you up—looks like yore hurt."

Tom gave the Mexicans a brief look. "So you're Tracker, from

Nogales. That's where I came down from myself."

"I know that," said Tracker. "I been followin' you. You an' yore friend."

Tom's heart jumped, and just for a moment he didn't feel the pain in his leg. Tracker knew about Sam? Of course, if he was with McGrath's bunch he would know. And he might be here after the gold. Lightning lit the skyline, and thunder pealed.

"We're doin' a lot of beatin' the brush, mister, and way too little of findin' out who you are. You say you been followin' me. You with that bunch of roughnecks in town?"

"I was, but I don't think we have a whole lot of time to talk about that. What do you want me to do with these two?"

Tom looked irritably at the Mexicans. "Take away their guns. They can walk home."

The black man stepped closer and shucked the pistols from the Mexicans' belts. When one of them looked at him he waved downhill with his rifle barrel. "Go! Vaya!"

Confused but not stupid, they went, first slowly, then at a stumbling run. Tom and the black man watched them for more than three minutes, and when all they could see was their hats bobbing up and down in the brush now and then Tom turned to this man who appeared to be his ally. He wasn't sure he wanted to know any more answers right now, but he had to ask. "You seen my partner?"

Tracker stared at him for several seconds, his eyes softening. "I ain't personally, but some of the others did."

Tom stopped breathing involuntarily. He did not like the tone of Tracker's voice nor the look on his face. "Where is he?"

"A couple miles back thataway, I think," replied Tracker. "But I don't think he fared good, mister. Fact is, I think he's dead by now. Some Injuns come upon them, and the others took off. I can't imagine much good come of it for him."

Tom tried to hide the sickness that welled up in the pit of his stomach. Before he could speak, Tracker said, "How bad is that leg?"

"It's gonna have to wait till we find my friend."

Tracker waved across the desert face, out where the glowering storm lingered and boiled. "Back there—somewhere."

"How far from Hermosillo are we?" Tom asked.

"Five hours, maybe. Or a hard four."

Tom glanced off in that direction, then looked back at Tracker. He wanted to go to Hermosillo. He *needed* to go, in the worst way. But he couldn't, not till he knew for sure about Sam.

Off to the east he noticed a faint dust cloud, and he turned his full attention that way, half afraid it was either from Tracker's friends come to complete the trap and finish him off or another bunch of Mexicans or Indians. He had never pictured such an endless nightmare when he brought Sam along on this joyride. This place was more crowded than the San Antonio plaza at sundown!

Tracker picked up a pair of field glasses that hung against the bare black skin of his chest. He studied the dust for a long moment before letting the glasses drop.

"I'll be— It's a woman," he said. "A *white* woman. And a man— one packhorse. They been ridin' hard."

Tom stared at the dust. "Can I look through those?"

Tracker pulled the binoculars from around his neck, handing them to Tom while he continued to watch the riders' approach. It only took Tom a moment before he lowered the binoculars and swore softly, admiringly. "That's a woman, all right," he said. "That's the most woman I ever seen."

Tracker grunted. "Didn't look all that big to me."

"No. But she's a lot of woman all the same." With that, Tom limped back to Gringo, where he was lashed to a bush, and with great strain he struggled into the saddle. He jogged back over to where Tracker stood. "I don't know where your horse is, partner, but I hope you don't mind me ridin'. That partner of mine, that's his woman. I'm gonna have to ride down and tell her what happened."

Tracker clucked his tongue. "I understand. If you know them folks, you jus' go on. It won't take me long to catch up."

The black man's last words had barely escaped his lips before Tom was riding down the hill, his leg torturing him at every jostle but not nearly as much as his heart. Nadia Boultikhine was down there. And Abe Varnell. He should have been elated. But he did not know how he was going to tell that woman about Sam.

* * *

Temp Stratton, his duster lit briefly by a flash of lightning, leered at Sam. His rifle was aimed loosely at his midriff, and the hammer was back.

Sam, shocked to silence, couldn't even think to curse his luck. Where were his angels in all this hell? It seemed at every turn they were taunting him. Remembering the unreasonable hatred of this man, Sam found his tongue. "You still want that gold?"

Stratton laughed. "Mister, I got me a nigger that can find that gold. The way you're stove up I don't need the likes of you."

He raised the rifle. The bore was aimed at Sam Coffey's head.

With little thought to the move, Sam dove to one side, and the rifle cracked. The shot missed! But Sam landed hard on a rock, and the blow knocked the wind from him. He couldn't move!

He heard Stratton laugh, a harsh sound with little humor. "You stupid, clumsy—" Even as he spoke, he started to jack another shell into his rifle. The lever made its short downward swoop, but it never came back up to seat the new cartridge.

The flash and the crack, then the pursuant shaking of the earth all seemed to come as one. Above Stratton the black belly of the cloud parted, and from deep within the glowing yellow maw a huge arm of light flashed down the sky, curling, and rolling, zagging, ripping, streaking like a gargantuan whip. It was a mere point of phosphorescent light by the time it made it to earth, but that point drilled through Stratton's hat, straight down through his tensed body into his horse, and from there into the desert ground. As if he had taken it off and thrown it, the hat sailed several feet into the air before twirling back down. The horse, arching its back, leaped straight up, its hooves smoking, and came down dead in a heap of beast and man. Patches of Stratton's beard and his shaggy eyebrows were bare and singed now, and one of his boots lay several feet away. His face stared with ghoulish, empty eye sockets up at the sky as the clouds continued spitting fire and water, knocking the smoke out of his clothes. The storm wandered beyond Sam Coffey.

Sam could hear nothing. His ears roared, and for many seconds, perhaps a minute, he stared unbelieving at the heap of horse and man. Then, numbly, he crawled away from his meager shelter as the rain began to pelt down in earnest. The Winchester rifle was frozen in Temp's grip. Shaking, Sam reached over and pulled the pistol out of the dead man's holster, avoiding looking at his face and the holes where his eyes had been.

Already soaked to the skin, Sam struggled into the shelter of the bushes and rocks and stared out at the scene of death spilled before him in the rocky clearing. He still could not quite fathom what had taken place. Realization came to him only as the rain ebbed and he felt the hard cold wood and metal of the pistol in his fist. The next moment he saw a man walking his horse carefully through the mesquite trees.

It was the Yaqui.

Chapter Thirty

Sam stared long and hard at the lone Yaqui, brave and sure of himself on his horse in the midst of the storm. In the far reaches of his mind Sam wished he could be like that, but was the Yaqui truly brave—or a fool—to be riding so high in the midst of the lightning's fury? Perhaps the Mexicans and all his other enemies had driven this Yaqui far from caring whether he lived or died. No matter. Sam was about to help the Yaqui on his way. He might have escaped the lightning, but he could not escape Sam now that he was armed. Before Sam lay the opportunity he had dreamed of.

Even with this thought overpowering his mind, when the Yaqui rode into the sandy clearing, Sam hesitated. He had never shot anyone from concealment, and the prospect unsettled him. In spite of the cool air, the pistol grips against his palm were growing warm and moist with his sweat. He waited, watching the Yaqui. The Indian was soaked by the rain, his muscular torso glistening, his hair hanging tight to his scalp and sticking to his cheeks. But the rain slowly waned, and judging by the sunshine perking in the sky it would entirely stop in minutes.

The Indian scanned all around, but he seemed far more concerned about the dead rider and horse than about his surroundings. He had obviously heard the rifle shot, which was why he had ridden here. He must have heard and seen the lightning strike as well. But the surprise of seeing the dead man and horse seemed to take all caution from the red man. That surprised Sam, not fitting anything he had seen of the Yaqui.

The Yaqui dropped from his horse, landing on the balls of his feet, and looked at Stratton. He walked over and pried the rifle out of the dead man's hands, studying the open lever curiously. His eyes flicked to the man's holster, saw it was empty, then flitted around for the pistol that had filled it. Of course it was not there. It was primed and waiting in Sam's hand, and its bullet was going to take the Yaqui's life …

Then the Yaqui's eyes dropped to the trail dragging through the wet sand. His face, always noncommittal, stirred, his eyes widening suddenly then just as quickly narrowing as his body tensed. Sam knew what that look meant. It signified that one dreadful moment when a man realizes he has committed some unpardonable, inescapable error, the moment he knows he has blundered greatly enough to cost him his life.

The Yaqui's eyes tore along the remainder of the trail, and in less than a second his and Sam's gazes were locked. Clenching his jaws, Sam cocked the pistol. The Indian's chest looked huge in his sights.

Their eyes held, and Sam's finger tightened.

But then, still, he waited. The Yaqui stared, expression once more noncommittal. *Do what you must,* the look seemed to say. Sam gritted his teeth. *Pull the trigger! Kill him!*

But he couldn't. He could not kill this man, even after the days, the bloody, painful miles, he had wished death upon him.

Then, with an odd expression, the Yaqui cocked his head. His eyes changed slightly yet in a vastly meaningful way. He began to nod his head, and his lips parted.

He began to speak. The sound was so foreign amid the rustling brush and the cool pattering of the after-rain, the chirping of songbirds, that for a moment it seemed unreal to Sam. The Yaqui spoke in his own tongue, his voice soft, full of respect. There was no fear in his eyes or voice. It was as if he never contemplated the thought of his own death, as if he never believed Sam held his life in his hands. He spoke for a full fifteen seconds, ended with a succinct nod, and with a crinkling of his eyes he simply turned back to his horse, took one last glance down at Temp Stratton, and flung into the saddle. Then he turned the horse to ride back into the desert. His voice hovered in the still, rain-washed air.

He was gone for half a minute before Sam lowered the pistol.

Johnny Riles and Caps O'Brien could hear the faint shots and the lightning that cracked all around them. They listened wordlessly to the desert orchestra and the ring of men at war. Sweat poured down Johnny's face. Nearby, rain had fallen and quenched the thirst of the desert and he could smell its vibrant essence, but here it was as dry as ever. Never had he wanted water more. Fresh well water, stream water, river water—anything but the hot metal sort of tea the contents of his canteen had become.

Johnny had let his friend Burt run away, and that left him here friendless, a notion he had pondered for hours. Now, with the sun baking his brain, Johnny stood up suddenly and glanced toward Hermosillo. He returned his eyes to Caps, who sat with legs sprawled and looked up at him. There was a question in Caps's eyes.

Johnny, still not speaking, shuffled toward his horse. He had almost reached it when Caps's voice stopped him. "No-o, Johnny. You'll have to go without the horse. I'll need him to pack gold."

Johnny tensed. He was not surprised Caps had read his mind. The outlaw always had seemed able to think far ahead of the rest of them.

"Oh, Johnny." The boy raised his head a little as a sign that he heard, and Caps smiled at his back. "Always remember, if they catch up to you—leave the last bullet for yourself."

Johnny lowered his head, looking down at his battered boots and the pistol on his hip. For some reason Caps had trusted him enough, or respected his courage so little, that he had not bothered taking his gun like he had Burt's. Bringing his eyes up to survey the desert, Johnny started down the steep embankment.

Less than a mile away, Burt was hurting, but his mind was still strong. Thoughts of his father, Abijah, filled his head. How was he going to pay him back the money he had stolen to finance this journey? It didn't matter. He would pay it, one way or another.

But at the moment these ponderings were secondary to his main concern, watching the horizon for Caps and Stratton. He had no doubt that at any time they would be clearing the rise. And they intended to make sure he could never pay his father back one dime. Burt would die, if not by Caps then most certainly by Stratton, who he believed had always hated him, even while he and Caps were first hatching their scheme to use him and his friends as shields against whatever enemy might fall upon them.

But Burt would not go without a fight. He would kill the first man who came over the rise if it took every bullet in the six-gun. Of course one of them would finish him off, but he would make sure he did not die in vain.

It was as if his raw determination called the man up. At first it was just the crown of a hat, then a face, then a torso. Then an entire man walking straight toward him, following his and Tracker's trail.

Well, you cur, you walked into this. It did not matter to him whether it was Stratton or Caps. Whichever it was, he was about to die.

He raised his pistol, aiming carefully at the approaching man.

Caps O'Brien watched Johnny walk to the edge of the drop-off and then, with no hesitation, disappear over its precipitous edge. He would never see Johnny again. He had no doubt he and Burt would die out there. Tracker might make it out alive, but the two boys never would. A faint stir of pity went through him, but it was quickly gone. Johnny was a stupid boy. He should have stayed.

Caps sighed and looked at the horses, then shrugged his wounded shoulder loosely to test it. It was worse than a crease, but the bullet had touched no bone. And Caps had lived through worse in Yuma. There was no chance he was going to let this stop him from getting his hands on that gold.

After hearing the latest shot, he assumed Temp had found Tracker. But in spite of Temp's prowess with firearms he wondered who of the two had come out on top. Tracker could take Temp down at a distance with that rifle of his, and it had certainly been a rifle shot he heard. But one thing was for sure. Caps was not going to sit listless in the sun any longer. There was way too much shooting around here for his comfort, and the only thing he knew to do was to be on the move. Even if Tracker had killed Temp, that didn't mean Caps couldn't still waylay him and force him to trail the way back to the gold. Deep inside, Caps had the irritating feeling that he was chasing a wisp of smoke, considering whatever had happened to Coffey and Vanse. But how does a poor man abandon dreams of untold wealth?

Struggling to his feet, Caps went to his horse and climbed on, taking the reins of Johnny's and Burt's mounts. He rode up to where he had last seen Stratton, and it was very little time before he located his trail leading away. Now and then he could see the tracks of the horse his partner was following.

It didn't take long before he found his quarry—or so he thought. A hundred yards away, across a shallow depression and through a thicket of mesquite, a shape moved, a shape he knew instinctively as human. He peered closer, and what he discovered set him back hard in the saddle. Leaning over a dead horse that appeared to be Temp's was a shabbily dressed man with scraps of cloth covering his feet. Caps caught a quick breath. This couldn't be! But it was! It was Sam Coffey!

With a good study to pinpoint the man's exact location, Caps climbed off his horse, pulled out his pistol and started to circle around through the brush. For a couple of minutes he couldn't see much ahead of him. But his sense of direction was flawless, and as he saw the clearing of light-colored sand ahead he smiled grimly. He came into the opening with revolver poised.

To greet him was only the heap of a dead horse, a foot sticking up over its side. There was a moment when the world—the wind, the birds, the insects—was still. Caps stared at the horse, at the foot protruding there, and all of a sudden realized, through his surprise, he was looking at Temp Stratton.

And then a voice full of power and hate rang nearby. "Don't turn around."

Sam had felt more than saw the approaching danger. Instinctively, he had scrambled behind a clump of rocks and waited, and soon he heard someone rustling through the brush. The man stepped out, now on foot. It was the second of the two men he had run into in town, Caps O'Brien.

A hush was on the air. Caps was frozen. The sun bore down, and there was no wind.

"I'll be damned …" The words came from O'Brien as if he were talking to an old friend. "I'll be damned, mister! Lightning go and save you?" Sam didn't answer, and Caps went on, his voice quiet, edged with shock. "My ol' pard, Temp Stratton." For many seconds there was silence, as Caps stared down at the remains of his cohort. Finally, he raised his head, his back still turned to Sam. "They always swore he had the luck of the devil. Looks like the devil cashed in."

The man paused for a long silence, and then Sam saw his chest swell with a huge breath. He started to turn around, and Sam growled again, "*Don't—turn—around.*"

Caps turned his head, trying to find Sam through the corner of his eye. "Well, I guess it's best this way. The boy told me what Temp tried to do to you, hangin' you up on that tree and all. I want you to know that was none of my doin'. I never did take to Temp's devilish ways. You remember I was the one saved you there in town."

Sam grunted, unable to resist that bait. "Maybe *you* saved *him*."

It was like Caps to laugh at that. "Whichever. But I stepped between you. I hope you know that thing with the tree and the fire would never have happened if I'd been there. So … what say you an' me partner up and go after that gold?"

Sam gaped at the man's back. He had grit, sure enough. It took a moment for Sam to find the words to respond, but when he did there was no warmth to his voice. It reflected the complete feeling of hatred he bore this man, a feeling that stemmed from a sure knowledge that Caps O'Brien would have gladly killed him like swatting a mosquito if the odds had been in his favor and if he had found him with the gold.

"There's only one place you're goin', boy. That's back to the law. There ain't no gold anyway—not anymore."

Caps's back stiffened, and he shot a look both ways, trying to figure out exactly where Sam was. He took a deep breath. "Ah, come on, pardner. There's no reason for us fightin' each other."

"That's right," said Sam. "Just throw down that pistol."

With no warning, Caps whirled, bringing his gun to bear. Hand steadied across his left forearm, Sam fired. The bullet went low of its intended mark, but Caps buckled as if his legs had been severed. Even on the ground the outlaw was game. He rolled and started shooting toward Sam like a man almost out of chances.

Then his hammer came down with a dull click, then another.

Caps growled out in frustration and anger. He clawed at the sand, trying to worm his way toward Stratton and the dead horse. His legs trailed behind him like dead snakes.

Sam crawled out of the rocks. If he hadn't been in so much pain, full of so much venom at his predicament, he might have laughed. In all of history had there ever been a duel fought by two men on their bellies?

Caps whirled on him like a trapped animal, and they were face to face. Sam had come to his knees and held Stratton's pistol. He could see blood on Caps's left side, above his belt. He was guessing the bullet had lodged in his spine, explaining his useless legs.

"Don't shoot!" Caps blurted. "Don't shoot! I'm done."

Sam glared at Caps. He had failed in getting his gold, so Nadia would lose her boarding house. He had perhaps lost his best friend, not to mention the skin on the soles of his feet, and had not been able to stand like a man for days. He had been set loose in the desert, sunburned, attacked by wild animals and Indians. And he had been hung upside down over a fire to be tortured. Only sheer fortune had provided his ironic rescue by the Yaqui. And here was one of the men who had hounded him for no other reason than to take any gold he found and to kill him. He should pull the trigger on this man, but grasping the broken spine and paralyzed legs he only pitied him.

"Throw me that iron and knife," Sam growled. "The belt, too."

Caps complied. He now had no weapons on his person, at least no obvious ones.

"Where's your partners?" Sam's voice was harsh, made more so by his raw throat.

Caps grimaced and looked over at Stratton and his horse. "All gone."

"Then I guess you stay here by yourself, 'cause mister, there's no way I could lift you into a saddle. I'll leave you the makin's of a fire, but then you're on your own. I'll send somebody back for you when I get to Hermosillo."

Caps stared at him, the lower part of his shirt and the waistband of his pants now soaked with blood and a stench about him that burned the fresh desert air. It seemed he'd been gut-shot too.

If Sam's condition was pitiful, O'Brien's was dire. But Sam would be damned if this man who had hounded him would see him crawl. And there was no need. After the Yaqui had left him Sam had managed to fashion a pair of crutches. He had utilized a hatchet from Stratton's saddlebags to cut up several stalks of cardón cactus, then lashed them together using the dead horse's saddle strings and a bundle of cord also gleaned from the saddlebags. He had not had a chance to try the crutches yet, but with Caps O'Brien watching him, giving him extra impetus, and with agave pads and a spare pair of Stratton's socks protecting his feet, there would be no better time.

Taking the crutches in his hands, he positioned them both just right, and with great effort he stood up, the dark shadows of his eyebrows and his thick beard mercifully hiding the pain that slashed across his face. With slow, shaky steps, he turned toward the trees from which Caps had emerged. His feet cried out at him, unused to this pressure on their wounds, but without showing Caps the level of his pain he started in search of the horses he knew must be tied on the far side of the mesquite grove.

It was perhaps the longest walk of Sam's life. But he made it, with sweat running profusely down his face, brought on by the pain. Thanks to the agave pads and the socks, but mostly thanks to the crutches, he was able to walk the entire distance back through the trees. It was there he found three horses waiting for him.

Almost more painful than the walk was climbing aboard one of the horses, but the horse was patient and let him clamber up. It rolled its eyes and blew out its nostrils, concerned most likely by his strange appearance and stench, but it made no move to escape him.

Feeling like a king on a throne, Sam turned and nudged the animal back through the trees, fighting his way as he led the other two animals along. It seemed so glorious to be once again on the back of a horse. He just wished it could have been Gringo.

As he came out into the clearing a surprising sight greeted him. Caps was leaning up against Stratton's horse, legs stretched out before him. Sam would not have believed he had the strength to slither that far. Strangely, Stratton's rifle still lay untouched.

"I thought long and hard about goin' back with you, mister … what was your name?"

Sam turned his head suspiciously to one side. "Coffey."

"Ah. Coffey. Good soundin' name. Wish I had some to drink," he said with a good-natured laugh. "Coffey, I thought long and hard about waitin' for you to send back help. But I looked longer and harder at my legs. You paralyzed 'em, Coffey. I seen a man like this once, and he never could walk again. That's assumin' any damn Mexican *curandero* could pull me through this bullet you nailed to my backbone. Even if I live, I just don't know what I'd do without my legs. 'Sides, I'm smellin' somethin' that ain't none too healthy. I know I ain't had a bath in a while, but this is my guts." Again, a big grin broke across his face, but it turned quickly to a grimace of pain.

Sam scanned the outlaw. There was something very odd about his demeanor. His words rang hopeless, yet the look on his face, when he wasn't laughing or in pain, seemed to be one of absolute peace with his world. Also, his hands were hidden down along the sides of his legs. That in itself bode no good. Had Caps found another weapon on Stratton? A bad feeling crept along Sam's spine, and he pulled out Stratton's pistol, leaving it dangling along his side as his eyes bored at the crippled man.

"I don't know what you'll do either," said Sam slowly. "But I don't see as you got a choice—unless you're plannin' on usin' whatever you got in them hands."

Caps chuckled. "Coffey, I know you've killed me. So do you. You know, my family lived in Texas, and we was always worried about Comanches. My ol' daddy always used to say they could torture a man worse than you could ever believe—especially those squaws. He'd say, 'You fight 'em long, boy, an' you fight 'em hard. But when you're runnin' low on ca'tridges, always save the last one for yourself.'"

With that, Caps lifted his hands. Under a flick of his right thumb, a match flared to life, and one glance at the other hand revealed a stick of primed dynamite. The hands came up too fast. The match touched the fuse too close to the stick, no more than half an inch away. The fuse sparked and started to burn both ways.

Sam knew he was dead. He was too late even to raise his pistol. Caps had him dead to rights. His last image of Caps was of a man with a big toothy grin, gritting his teeth and squinting against the sparks and smoke.

Jerking the reins, Sam wheeled his horse. The blast was deafening. The horses exploded, too, and in Sam's weak state there was nothing he could do. His mind intended him to stay in the saddle, but two jumps and he felt himself flying through the air. His training only helped him ease the fall, landing on a shoulder and rolling. But he could hear the horses scattering through the trees. Then all was silent. Dropping his arm, Sam sat up and stared after the horses and swore.

Knowing what he would find, he slowly turned his gaze back to where Caps had been. There was no point in looking. Caps's "last bullet" had done exactly what he had intended it to.

Sam looked away distastefully. There was gore scattered here and there on the wet sand, and a few drops of blood on Sam. He wiped at a couple of spots on his torso, looked once more toward the path of the retreating horses, then lay back wearily on the sand, his feet burning as if he were standing in a bed of coals. For many minutes Sam did not move, just gritted his teeth and prayed for the pain to leave him.

Burt McGrath had done many foolish things in his life, but none nearly so bad as almost killing his best friend, Johnny. When he recognized his distinctive walk, he had dropped his pistol and waited with immeasurable gladness for his friend to reach him.

"I almost killed you, Johnny boy," he said when Johnny stopped in front of him.

"I'm glad you didn't. I come to help you get home."

Burt grinned, then laughed. "Well, I hope there's a way. It doesn't look like you have a horse, and neither do I or Tracker."

Johnny looked quickly around. "Where is he?"

"He went off to help one of those men we were following."

Johnny squenched up his face. "Huh?"

"It isn't the one Temp hung up by his feet, it's the other one. At least that's the only thing we could figure. He hung around looking for his partner."

"Well, a good pard don't come along every day," said Johnny with a smile, plopping down in the warm sand next to his friend.

Sam Coffey had no idea how long he lay there, wanting in one way to die but feeling the strength inside him to make it all the way to Hermosillo. It was just that the horse had been so close! And now he was back where he had been an hour earlier—but of course with a mountain more to contemplate. Since his rising that morning, two enemies were dead, one of them by the strangest twist of fate he had ever encountered; lightning, his worst enemy, had ironically for one moment in time become an ally. And after that another enemy, the Yaqui, had come within his pistol sights and gone away without Sam's making good on his vow to kill him. A matter of enormous importance, he had stood up and proven able to walk, although only with crutches, and only for a hundred yards or so—and in great pain; and he had ridden a horse which now was no longer there, and might as well never have been.

Sam drew a deep breath and looked across the flat desert. Hermosillo was not so far away. He had always been strong, and nothing could stop him now. With that determination, he rolled over and crawled toward Caps and Stratton and the horse to see what he could salvage. When he had taken all that would do him any good, including a well-fitting shirt that belonged to Stratton, his gun belt, some matches, a bag of jerky, and a half-full canteen, he crawled back over to where his crutches and pistol had fallen during his spill from the horse. He holstered Stratton's pistol and put Caps's down in the waistband of Scrub's pants. The crutches he glared at with gritted teeth. Pushing away all thoughts of pain he took them in hand and struggled to his feet, ignoring the burning pain throughout his body, concentrated in the soles of his feet. Then he turned with bitter determination and made his way toward Hermosillo. He might not make it far before he had to go back to his hands and knees, but at the moment it felt good to stand so tall.

It was then he saw the dust cloud. Judging by its volume, it was made by at least four or five riders. The dust was close, and he guessed they were already coming through the mesquite stand. He looked at the gun belt and holster girding him and at the pistol in the holster and the one down in his waistband. He couldn't win. He had known since coming into this desert hell that the odds were against his riding out. But he was Sam Coffey, and whoever this was would play hell in putting him down.

At least he would die standing.

Reaching down, he shucked Caps's pistol, which he had reloaded. He let his right crutch fall to the ground. Then, pistol hanging at his side, he waited. Nearer, nearer, nearer still came the horses, blowing out their nostrils, forcing their way through the thorny mesquite. What would emerge this time—Yaquis? Apaches? Mexicans? He hoped their method of murder was effective—and fast …

Chapter Thirty-One

A in't it funny what thinks a man when he is set to die? About the wrongs that he has done, and all the reasons why?

From the back of Sam Coffey's mind came two lines from one of the poems Tom liked to recite. Never before had Sam remembered a thing from any of those poems. *Ain't it funny what thinks a man?* Sam smiled wryly. Funny, all right.

It was also funny how his feet didn't hurt at that moment. How good the desert smelled after all the rain. How odd it was to be standing here while two men who not very long before had meant to kill him were both now dead, neither by his hand.

Funniest of all—how good it was to be alive!

And here he stood, ready to die. His only regret was letting Nadia down.

Sam cocked the pistol hanging at his side. For much of his life he had read signs, and the stories told by clouds of dust were one of the most important. The story told by what he saw on the other side of the mesquite grove was one of insurmountable odds. He had no fancy ideas of a successful showdown. What mattered here was Sam's pride. Foolish pride, but *his*. At least the lightning hadn't got him. It had spared him for another fate.

The horses were fanning out through the mesquites. He keened his ears. There were four of them. Or was it five …? More than he could handle. But not odds that had never been beaten by a single man with God's good will on his side—which unfortunately had never seemed to be Sam Coffey.

He lifted his left hand and looked at its palm. He had to smile sardonically. It looked nothing like the hand of a white man. It was a mass of scab, cracked, still bleeding lightly in places, in others seeping clear liquid. There were thorns scattered around in it, and bits of sand and gravel. Why did he not feel those anymore? Because now, perhaps, other things, like life itself, were more important.

When the first horse broke through the trees on his right, Sam raised the pistol calmly, prepared to empty that rider from his saddle.

But this rider was not a "he." It was a she. Sam Coffey. Immobile. Stunned to silence. For a moment he lived in a dream. The world spun all around him, and for the first time in his life he thought he was going to faint. Then his sight lightened again, and the world held still.

In the far reaches of his mind Sam heard other horses crackling through the brush, then coming to a shuffling standstill in the sandy clearing. Voices gasping. A quiet curse of disbelief. But he could no more remove his eyes from the apparition before him than he could walk on his ears.

The first friendly human voice Sam had heard in days erupted from the most beautiful lips he had seen in all his life.

"Sam!"

In her haste, Nadia Boultikhine almost fell from her horse, leaving the reins dangling. She stumbled toward Sam, walking in her own kind of daze, her face a mixture of horror, sadness and elation.

"You were— But they— I thought you were dead! Sam! What in the world have they done to you?"

Sam thought back over his recent reunion with this woman, and how badly Tom had thought they both needed a bath. That had been nothing compared to his current condition. He grinned a broad grin. "Wanna hug a sour goat?"

Nadia stared at him, dumbfounded. Then her glance shot back and forth between his eyes, and she laughed through her suddenly streaming tears, reaching out to draw him close. She was laughing and trying to talk, and neither sounded like what it was meant to be. She was crying too hard.

Sam's other crutch fell away as he put his arms around Nadia. She became his crutch. But he couldn't bring himself to touch her with his gnarled and bloody hands. "Sorry, woman. I smell like a bear's … belly."

Nadia laughed harder. "Sam! You smell like heaven, to me."

"That's funny, 'cause I been through hell."

While Sam spoke to Nadia, there was a big shadow lying along the ground, part of it going across Sam's legs. Casting it was a man whom at times Sam had *considered* his shadow, and that man was having a tough time holding himself back when Sam turned and looked at him.

"And there's Curly. You son of a gun."

Tom Vanse couldn't help the tears that flooded down his cheeks as he laid his bear hug on Sam. A cough escaped the older partner. "Be careful about squeezing me too hard, old pard. There's too many holes for the blood to squoosh out."

Tom laughed, grabbing Sam by the shoulders and holding him away. "I don't know what kind of hell you been through, Sam, but you look like the devil."

Getting a good look at Tom for the first time, Sam noted the pallor of his face, and he scanned down his length, spotting the broken off shaft of the arrow in his thigh. "Damn, Tom! We gotta get you to a doctor."

Tom laughed again, then laughed harder. "It hurts like hell, old pard. And maybe they'll have to cut my leg off. But you're the only man in the world who could look like you do and tell me *I* need a doctor!"

Sam grunted in answer. He knew they both must look like they had been dragged by horses, down Bloody Creek and over Ugly

Mountain. He looked beyond Tom to see Abe Varnell standing there looking at him uncertainly. "We found your gold, Abe. Just where you said."

"And it looks like you found all the other things I talked about, too," Varnell said sheepishly. "I wish I'd never gotten you into this."

"Hell, old pard, I ain't had this much fun since my grandma got hydrophobie."

Varnell forced a laugh, glancing around uncomfortably. There was a glimmer of tears in his eyes.

Tom noticed Sam looking over at Tracker, and he nodded at him. "Sam, this here is Tracker. He's the one that found you and caught those horses up. He's been through a little hell himself. But he's on our side."

Sam just nodded a cautious greeting. Right now he did not care for an explanation. There would be plenty of time for that. All he cared about was getting on a horse and getting back to Hermosillo as fast as they could. That arrow in Tom's leg had to be taken out right away. His own wounds were painful, but Tom's was the kind that would kill.

Sam looked over at Nadia, who was still watching him as if trying to convince herself he was real. "Now—" she suppressed a sob "—you *really* look like something the cat dragged in," she said, smiling as another two trails of tears rushed down her cheeks.

"Tell the truth, woman," Sam replied gruffly. "I feel like somethin' the cat tried to bury!"

Nadia's brief laugh died away, and she searched his eyes. "Sam, I saw the cereus in bloom."

A chill ran up Sam's spine. His own queen of the night was standing before him. "So did I, Nadia. So did I."

Tracker broke the silence for the first time. "We gotta ride, people. I got a hurt man back in the rocks, an' somewhere wanderin' out here is a stupid kid—unless that feller killed him." He indicated the remains of Caps, which he had been studying for some time as if to make sure it was really who it seemed to be.

Nadia and Tom looked over at Caps, and the woman shuddered. Sam didn't try to explain what had happened. If they made it to Hermosillo they had the rest of their lives to talk about the nightmare that had taken place there.

Sam had never been so glad to see a horse as he was when he laid eyes on old Gringo. When Nadia picked up and handed him his crutches, he hobbled over to the horse and held out his battered hand. "Howdy, old boy. Come to see me, huh?" The horse shook its head emphatically and shoved its nose out at Sam, almost knocking him down. He had to hang onto the headstall with one hand to keep from losing his balance, in the process dropping his right crutch. Leaving it on the ground, he used the horse as support to get around to his side, and he climbed aboard him with the help of Tracker.

Then, with Tom bringing up the rear of the cavalcade they rode a half mile away, stopping when Tracker held up his hand. He rode up over the crest of a hill leading two horses, and a minute later they heard him call out to advance.

Riding over the same crest, Tom and Sam recognized Burt McGrath, then Johnny Riles, crouched down in a cove in the rocks. Sam stared at the pair through hard eyes, particularly McGrath. He would not soon forget his presence when Temp Stratton tried to burn him at the stake. But he also remembered how hard the young man had tried to spare him, and how horrible was his fear—obviously the only reason Burt had let Stratton drag him up the tree limb in the first place.

As if everyone there already knew something horrible had taken place between Sam and Burt, the group fell silent. Burt struggled to stand up, then he and Sam met gazes, and for a long time they stood that way. Finally, Sam gave a sharp nod. "I didn't get any chance to thank you."

Burt swallowed hard. "I don't deserve it."

One side of Sam's mouth rose, cracking that side of his face into wrinkles. "That feller was a hard man, kid. You did all you could without gettin' yourself killed." It was as simple as that. He turned away. The only thing that mattered now was getting Tom to a doctor as fast as they could ride, and getting Nadia out of this desert, where potential death waited at every turn.

But then it was too late.

Sam heard Tom swear. His friend's voice was filled with awe. He turned to follow the line of his eyes, and his gaze came to rest on a dozen mounted Indians on the crest of a hill two hundred yards away. Even as he saw them a dozen more rode up on a knoll to their left, and another half dozen appeared on their right, all mounted, all armed. The day ran on silently, the quiet broken only by the swishing of the horses' tails. A thin sheet of dust drifted away like smoke from the shifting hoofs of the Indian horses.

His heart fallen, Sam looked over at Nadia. She met his eyes bravely, and before he could speak she said, "I know, Sam: save the last bullet."

Sam clenched his teeth. He turned back to the Indians, knowing by now they were Yaquis. Even at that distance he could see the stocky frame of José María Leyva—Cajeme. And beside him sat the big ugly brute who had taken the hide from his feet.

"This won't be pretty, boys," Sam said quietly. "But take it from me: you don't want them to get you alive." Saying this, he pulled his Marlin from the scabbard, looking it over appreciatively. He blew the dust out of it and cracked the lever to check for a shell. He saw the glitter of a cartridge already chambered as he heard Tom's voice to one side.

"It's full, Sam."

Burt McGrath's face had gone white, and he looked around for a place of concealment. Then his whole body stiffened, and Sam saw him take a deep breath. Burt, in that moment, had made up his mind to die like a man. He cocked a pistol that had been hanging at his side.

There were an easy thirty Yaqui warriors within sight. At the distance, Sam couldn't tell which was the one he knew as "the Yaqui." The others were moving now, kicking their horses into motion, flanking them. They came slowly, agonizingly so. One step, then another, advancing as if to draw every ounce of fear to the surface of these intruders' hearts.

Johnny Riles spoke, his voice shaky. "Should we shoot? They're gonna surround us."

"That's a sure way to get us all killed," replied Sam. "You don't shoot unless we shoot first."

The Yaquis and their horses had formed a crescent shape now, fanned out with at least ten feet between each of them. If it came to shooting they would have to pick their targets carefully.

The warriors halted. Sam's heart was pounding, and somewhere across the desert he could hear the raucous calling of a bird. Dust sifted all around them. The Yaquis were close. One hundred and fifty yards? Perhaps. Maybe closer.

Suddenly, five of the warriors broke free from the group and started forward. At one hundred yards, when he could hear the crunching of gravel under the horses' feet, Sam recognized the Yaqui and his dun. They came on, seeming to slow down even more the closer they got, until their walk became a plod, raising almost no dust.

"Shoot now?" Johnny's voice broke the stillness. His hands were white, clenched in fists. They were also empty.

"What with?" Sam asked sardonically. "Hold still, boy. They're not ridin' in this close just to fight us with seven to five odds in our favor."

A minute later the warriors drew to a halt at strategic positions around Sam and the others. The Yaqui was in front of Sam, and he nudged his horse closer. For a long time he and Sam stared at each other, two strong-willed men each measuring the strength of the other. Sam had hated this Yaqui, had wanted only to see him dead. Now he could no longer confirm that hatred. As badly as he wanted to hate him, the only word he could find for what he felt was … respect.

The Yaqui's eyes scanned the group, looking speculatively at Nadia, and at Tom. They stopped longest on Abe Varnell, stirring with recognition. Then, without any other sign that he knew who Varnell was, he moved his dun again, coming to a halt alongside Sam, their legs nearly touching. He looked Sam up and down, and as much as he might try to keep expression from his face, it was filled with the same respect Sam was feeling.

The Yaqui slowly reached over and with deft fingers unfastened the buckles of one of Sam's saddlebags. He raised the flap and nodded succinctly at sight of the enclosed treasure. Without expression, he buckled it back up then untied the saddle strings, and with considerable effort even for his muscular arm he hefted the bags to sit over the withers of his own horse.

He glanced around at the men who had come with him, then jerked his head back toward Cajeme and the others. The Yaquis turned without glancing back and returned to their place on the hill. Sam and the others just watched them go, but even when they were gone the heaviness in the air did not change.

There was no sound among Sam and the others, no sound but Burt's breathing, and for Sam, the beating of his heart in his ears. Nadia, her face strong, betrayed fear only because Sam expected it and sought it out. She looked up at him, begging for reassurance which he could not give.

Tom's voice ended the stillness. "Well, that's all there is left." Sam and the others looked over to see him holding up a gold nugget the size of his big toenail between thumb and forefinger.

Sam grunted. "That's all you can think about," he said wryly.

"Actually, I was thinkin' about Claudus McKnight," Tom said, forcing a grin. "You think they'll find gold like his partner did with him when they're diggin' our graves?"

"Maybe," replied Sam. "That nugget you're holdin'."

The Yaqui had reached Cajeme by now, and Sam studied them and wished he could know what they were discussing. Should they take cover in the rocks? They could hold off this bunch for several hours before they overtook them—maybe more. He knew and trusted in his own marksmanship, and he had seen Tom take down a running deer at a hundred yards and more. Yet for some reason he did not suggest hunting a hole, and neither did any of the others. All were mesmerized, hypnotized by the thought of their own violent deaths. Maybe they were just too tired to care.

Cajeme pointed toward Sam and his companions several times, and each time the entire group of warriors would turn and gaze their way. The Indians must know, too, that some of them were about to die. You could not attack a group of seven armed men with expectation of coming away unscathed.

"They'll be coming down," said Varnell suddenly. "They'll be coming for me."

Sam's eyes flashed to the older man. "For you?"

"Hell yes," Varnell replied, his voice strangely soft, even peaceful. "They told me not to come back. I came back once and escaped them, and now I'm back again. This time I'll die."

Sam clenched his jaw muscles, then turned to watch the Indians. Even as he turned he was surprised to see the Yaqui break free from the group once more. Cajeme and ten more warriors came away with him! They loped toward them, twelve Yaquis riding to face seven guns. Sam couldn't help admire how graceful the lithe, muscular Yaqui looked atop his dun horse of the desert. And Cajeme, well, he would have commanded admiration in any society.

They came thudding to a halt, and their cloud of dust sifted over the group. Cajeme had eyes only for one man: Abe Varnell. Slowly, he rode to him, the feet of his horse raising little puff clouds of dust. Intense black eyes seemed to bore through Varnell's skull, but to the prospector's credit, he did not look away. The rest of the Yaquis, weapons ready, stared on in silence.

There was something deadly in the glare of Cajeme, something … perhaps hate, perhaps anger, perhaps loathing. His right hand gripped a Winchester rifle, and his knuckles had gone pale. He turned his horse sideways, and the rifle bore rested on Varnell's midsection. Cajeme had but to jack the lever of the rifle and pull the trigger to put the prospector down, yet Varnell made no move. And he did not look down.

Suddenly, Cajeme spat on the ground at the feet of Varnell's horse. "So today you have found your courage," he said through twisted lips.

Then with no more attention for the prospector he stepped his horse away and stopped in front of Sam. The noses of his horse and Gringo were not two feet apart.

Cajeme scanned the rest, his gaze pausing appreciatively on Nadia and touching on each of the others—except Varnell—as if immensely enjoying the power of intimidation. Last, his dark, steady eyes settled on Sam, and he nodded.

"So. You have faced and conquered the land of the Yaqui. You are no ordinary man."

Sam watched him but didn't speak.

"This is Tetabiate," Cajeme motioned to the warrior Sam had known only as the Yaqui. "In your language it is spoken, 'Rolling Stone.' Tetabiate has told me how you conquered el tigre. He also speaks of how you could have taken his life. Yet you chose against it."

Still, Sam held his tongue.

"You do not need to speak. It is enough that you listen. We understand each other, you and me. This world is not full of strong men. Because you are strong, and because Tetabiate is strong, you chose another road. You could have killed him with ease. He, too, could have killed you, as I could have.

"Brave men need not always kill one another. This you have shown. You, white man, the spirit-who-moves-in-all things has smiled upon. I am told of the things you have done. I am told how your god sent down your 'light-ning' when your enemy would have killed you. Fire from the sky—strong medicine, white man. *Strong* medicine. A fire from the sky that strikes your enemy down—a token that you are smiled on above any man I have met. Yaqui *or* white man. I cannot know why the spirit-who-moves-in-all-things would smile upon a white man like you. But you, He who decides such things wishes to live."

Then he turned his gaze once more to Varnell, and it darkened. "But that one …"

Sam looked over at Varnell, his eyes hard although there was a big soft spot in his heart for Abe Varnell. "That one is my friend. I would fight you if you tried to bring harm to him."

Cajeme raised his eyebrows. He seemed about to laugh. "*You* would fight *me?*"

Sam met Cajeme's gaze levelly. "Abe Varnell came here lookin' to save my life. He didn't have to come at all."

A half-puzzled look washed across Cajeme's features, and his eyes flickered over Varnell's face once more before returning to Sam. "Then perhaps he truly has found courage," he said, and he punctuated the words with a nod.

Cajeme looked over at Tetabiate and motioned toward Sam. Tetabiate looked at his leader for several seconds, then shifted his eyes to Sam. There was a long pause while Sam's eyes were drawn inexplicably to Tetabiate and they gazed at each other, unblinking. This was no contest to see who would look away first. It was simply two men studying each other calmly, trying to read into the fathomless depths of the other's strength and courage. Sam could not deny it: this Yaqui was in a world apart from his, but he was a man to ride the river with.

And then the drawn-out silence was broken, and the words—the *English* words—that came from the lips of the Yaqui, Tetabiate, made Sam's jaw go slack.

"Inside of you beats the heart of el tigre, white man."

Sam clamped his mouth shut. He wanted to speak, but there were no words on his tongue or in his head.

Tetabiate, eyes smiling, spoke again. He spoke almost perfect, stilted English, probably the only kind he knew. "In the tongue of the People we do not say the words 'thank you' that your people are very fond of. You have spared me, I have spared you. It is enough. I will say this: you should have been born Yaqui. But you were not, white man, and if we met in battle tomorrow we would have to kill each other."

Sam gathered himself. "Most likely. Be a damn shame, wouldn't it?"

The Yaqui's cheeks creased with what almost could have been called a smile, and he scanned the group again. He sat there in his saddle as straight as a rod and as proud of his manhood as man can be.

Suddenly, Tetabiate the Yaqui lifted the saddlebags that lay across his horse's withers and held them out to the side. For all their weight, he held them there until his veins began to bulge, and just at the point when his shoulder started to shake he let the bags drop with a heavy thud.

Cajeme, face tired, smiled at the puzzled expression that came over Sam's face. "No more is there gold in the Yaqui place in the canyon. All is gone, all but this. This is yours, brave one. Now go. The Spirit chooses you to live. Go. Take these others from Yaqui land and do not return." His eyes flickered but briefly to Abe Varnell, then returned to Sam. "No more mercy. Even for warriors."

Sam just stared at Cajeme and Tetabiate. What should he say? What *could* he say?

"I will not forget what Cajeme and Tetabiate have done." Sam heard his own voice as if from far away.

Cajeme nodded, his eyes hooded. He turned his horse and rode back up the slope. Tetabiate hesitated a moment longer, aware of everyone's eyes upon him.

Suddenly, he reached down into a canvas sack that hung alongside his leg and pulled Sam's holstered pistol from it, the belt wrapped around it. He hefted it, then tossed it to Sam. With a cryptic look, he reached in again and drew out another object. It was Sam's jackknife, which they had taken from his pocket when he was captured. The Yaqui looked down at it for a moment, flipped it over once in his palm, then tossed it to Sam. "White man's knife," he said. "For when other white men hang you from trees." He gazed at Sam and Sam gazed back. The Yaqui's face was perfectly serious, but suddenly it broke into a smile, a smile Sam couldn't help matching. With that, Tetabiate wheeled his horse and galloped back up the hill.

All of the Yaquis drew together in a knot, and with Cajeme and Tetabiate closest to Sam they paused, facing downslope. Up came the hand of Tetabiate, palm out in sign of peace toward Sam Coffey. Cajeme's hand followed.

One side of Sam's mouth came up in a weary smile, and he raised his own hand in farewell to the Yaquis.

Then the Yaquis turned their horses and rode away. The spirit-who-moves-in-all-things had chosen Sam Coffey to live. Who was Cajeme to defy the will of gods?

Epilog

In the year that ensued, Mexican federales managed to overcome the Yaqui people still in rebellion in the Sierra Bacatete. Hundreds of Yaquis were destroyed, killed in battle or executed as prisoners of war. In 1887, taken by the treachery of his own people, Cajeme (He-Who-Does-Not-Drink) was put to death by firing squad in the Sonoran town of Cócorit.

Yet the spirit of Cajeme, the greatest leader ever known to the Yaqui people, was not so easy to kill. A Yaqui previously unknown to Mexican authorities rose up in Cajeme's place, a Yaqui known by the Spanish name of Juan Maldonado. In 1901, Maldonado, like Cajeme, was also betrayed and put to death by one of his own lieutenants. The Yaquis buried him under his Indian name: Tetabiate.

Yet even with the death of Cajeme, then Tetabiate, it was not until after 1910, twenty-four years following the surrender of the last hostile tribe in America, the Chiricahua Apache, that the final Yaqui rebels were subjugated at last.

Holey Sock Biscuits

½ cup shortening (butter or bacon grease works great)
2 cups flour
2 tablespoons sugar
3 teaspoons baking powder
1 teaspoon salt
¾ cup cow juice (milk)
(Alternately, extra sugar and/or cinnamon for trail biscuits)

Heat oven to 450°. Cut shortening into flour, sugar, baking powder and salt with fork until mixture resembles fine crumbs. Stir in milk until you have a ball of soft dough.

Knead dough and roll out, best on a lightly floured surface. Roll or pat down to ¼ to ½ inch thick, for Tom's trail biscuits, ½ to ¾ thick for table biscuits. Cut to desired size with biscuit cutter or cup. Place on ungreased cookie sheet, one inch apart. Bake at 450° for 10 to 12 minutes for table biscuits, 400° for 15 to 16 minutes for trail biscuits. Trail biscuits can also be rolled in sugar and cinnamon before baking, in which case the pan should be lightly greased.

See you down the trail. Don't forget to say howdy to Sam and Tom while you're out there!

Acknowledgments

Not many past works of Western fiction have needed a page such as this. Many Western writers have been of the opinion that a novel is, first and foremost, fiction, and that this gives them the irrevocable right to do with history—and even common credibility—as they please. Such has never been my belief, and thank heaven it is changing for many others as well.

Having said that, I present my all-important list of readers, friends and associates who have given me invaluable help with the technical matters that make such a book come to life on the page.

Richard Nelson, whose expertise in the field of desert survival was invaluable. Brian Howell, who always comes through in a pinch when the subject turns to cow horses and roping an ornery bovine. Dee O'Brien, for her unfortunate eye-witness account of how a person can be affected when struck by lightning. David Lundy, who has been instrumental not only as a proofreader and emotional buoy but without whose generous help Howling Wolf Publishing might not be alive even today. My wife, little Debbie, Loui Novak, Ron Ciancutti, Gina Romero, James Drury and my mom, Cherie Jonas, who were lightning fast with their much needed technical advice, besides being a cheering section without which a man could not triumph. And Ryan O'Hearn, for his inspirational suggestion that I add the Holey Sock Biscuit recipe for your enjoyment, the perfect way to end *Yaqui Gold*.

I could try to list the resources, both in book form and on the Internet, which provided me invaluable information, but that could take a chapter in itself. So let me use this blanket praise: to all those who have seen fit to study and to publish historical accounts of Yaqui, Mayo, Tarahumara and Seri ways of life and their tribal histories; to those who have taken your invaluable time to provide the rest of us with scores of volumes on desert survival, and edible and poisonous plants of the Sonoran Desert; and to those who have left their vivid portrayals of 1800's life in the American southwest, I take my hat off to you all.

About the Authors

Clint Walker, born in Hartford, Illinois, is best known for his 1950's and '60's Western series, *Cheyenne*, where he potrayed wandering gunman Cheyenne Bodie. During the filming of *Cheyenne*, Walker also made Westerns for the big screen, with such memorable tales as *Yellowstone Kelly*, *Fort Dobbs*, and *Gold of Seven Saints*. Probably his best known films are *Night of the Grizzly*, which still gets regular air play, and *The Dirty Dozen*, with Lee Marvin and Charles Bronson. Clint, standing six feet six inches tall, weighing two hundred fifty-five pounds, with a chest measurement of forty-eight inches and a waist of thirty-eight in his prime, dwarfed his fans and co-actors alike, in more ways than one. Forty years after production, to his hundreds of thousands of fans Clint Walker is still known as "Cheyenne."

Kirby Jonas, of Bozeman, Montana, now makes his home in Pocatello, Idaho, with his wife Debbie and four children, Cheyenne, Jacob, Clay and Matthew. Jonas has eight books in print, including the number one best seller *Death of an Eagle*. Growing up, Jonas's heroes were James Drury, on NBC television's *The Virginian*, Peter Breck (Nick Barkley), on ABC's *The Big Valley*, and, of course, Clint Walker, who inspired the main character in three of Jonas's published novels. It seemed a natural progression of things when Walker approached Jonas with the idea of writing *Yaqui Gold* together, but Jonas's head remains firmly planted in the clouds. Jonas, a former police officer, now makes his living as a fulltime firefighter for the city of Pocatello.